A Spent Bullet

LOUISIANA 1941

D1606069

Curt Iles

WestBow
PRESS
A DIVISION OF THOMAS NELSON

Other books by Curt Iles

Deep Roots
A Good Place
The Wayfaring Stranger
The Mockingbird's Song
Hearts Across the Water
Wind in the Pines
The Old House
Stories from the Creekbank

Copyright © 2011 Curt Iles

www.creekbank.com

All rights reserved. No part of this book may be used or reproduced by any means, graphic, electronic, or mechanical, including photocopying, recording, taping or by any information storage retrieval system without the written permission of the publisher except in the case of brief quotations embodied in critical articles and reviews.

WestBow Press books may be ordered through booksellers or by contacting:

WestBow Press
A Division of Thomas Nelson
1663 Liberty Drive
Bloomington, IN 47403
www.westbowpress.com
1-(866) 928-1240

Because of the dynamic nature of the Internet, any web addresses or links contained in this book may have changed since publication and may no longer be valid. The views expressed in this work are solely those of the author and do not necessarily reflect the views of the publisher, and the publisher hereby disclaims any responsibility for them.

This novel is a work of fiction.

Cover design by Chad Smith, The Touch Studios
www.thetouchstudio.com
Map by Debra Tyler TylerBird Media, LLC

ISBN: 978-1-4497-2232-6 (e)
ISBN: 978-1-4497-2233-3 (sc)
ISBN: 978-1-4497-2234-0 (hc)

Library of Congress Control Number: 2011915528

Printed in the United States of America

WestBow Press rev. date: 8/26/2011

In memory of my uncle,
Clint Iles.
I often wonder what your life would have been like.

1941 Louisiana Army Maneuvers

Part I

The Battle for the Bullet

"I want the mistakes made down in Louisiana, not over in Europe.
If it doesn't work, find out what we need to make it work."

– General George C. Marshall
Chief of Staff, U.S. Army
Spring 1941

"Monday I go to Louisiana. . . . The old-timers say we are going to a God-
awful spot complete with mud, malaria, mosquitoes, and misery."

– Colonel Dwight D. Eisenhower
August 5, 1941

Chapter 1

The Bullet

"How unhappy is he who cannot forgive himself." – Publilius Syrus

Wednesday, August 13, 1941
DeRidder, Louisiana

Elizabeth Reed had only met one soldier she liked, and he had wounded her deeply. So when the blond G.I. tossed the bullet, she didn't flinch even as it landed at her feet.

The soldier leaned out of a crowded Army truck. "You're beautiful. Write me." He pointed at her feet. "*The bullet*—write me." The empty cartridge had a note folded inside. The bullet-tossing practice was called "yoo-hooing" and was an attempt to get the attention—and addresses—of local girls.

A loud wolf whistle from the truck grated on her like fingernails across the slate board in her classroom. The same soldier called out, "I'd love a kiss from a pretty Southern girl like you."

Elizabeth coolly nodded at a large matronly woman near her. "Are you talking to me or *her*?" The troop truck exploded in laughter. She fanned away the dust. "Soldiers. They're all the same." Traffic began moving and the smoking truck rattled across the railroad tracks. Her ten-year-old brother Ben, behind her, had missed the tossed bullet. He spied it just as Elizabeth drew her foot back to kick it. "What's that?"

"A soldier threw it. It's a note stuck in an empty cartridge." As he knelt, she pulled him away. "Leave it alone. It might *blow up*."

"Lizzie, you're playing with me." He bounced on his toes at the three-o'clock train's whistle. "They're here."

Yelling from the convoy's last truck replaced the whistle. Elizabeth clamped her hands over Ben's ears. "Sometimes what they say isn't for fresh ears."

He twisted loose. "My ears ain't fresh."

"Benjamin Franklin Reed, you're impossible. It's *aren't*—not *ain't*."

"Well, either way, my ears *ain't* fresh."

A soldier yelled from the truck, "Is this Detroit?"

"Nope, this is DeRidder, Louisian*er*." Ben had always been allergic to silence.

Elizabeth bent down. "We live in Louisian*a*, not Louisian*er*."

"Ain't that what I said?" His face was pinched. "Is this how you'll be treating me in your classroom?"

Grabbing him in a playful headlock, she goosed him until he said, "Uncle." Elizabeth looked up at a tall grinning soldier. "I'll wrassle you next if you're through with him," he said in a rich west-Texas drawl.

She felt her face flushing. "I believe I could whip you too." She grabbed Ben's hand. "Come on. Our train's here."

"Where are y'all going?" Texas said.

She cringed when Ben said, "We're here to pick up some chicks."

The soldier laughed. "Well, count me in."

Elizabeth pulled on Ben's shirtsleeve. "Let's go before the train leaves."

He knelt on the sidewalk. "But what about the bullet?"

"Leave it." He was slowly rolling the cuff of his overalls. "*Come on Ben.* A dollar's waiting on a dime."

He scampered forward. "Poppa says that there are three things a soldier likes best: dogs, kids, and pretty girls."

"In that order?"

"Probably not."

"Well Ben, which one are you?"

"I'm not a dog or a pretty girl, so I guess I fit in as a 'kid'." He squeezed her hand. "And if I eyed those soldiers right, you definitely fit the 'pretty girl' part."

"You think so?" She hurried on ahead.

Ben stepped in front of her. "Lizzie, are you mad at *me?*"

She froze. "Why would I be mad at you? I love you like a son." She licked her fingers, trying to tame the unruly cowlick in his dark hair.

"But I'm your *brother,* not your son."

"You're ten years younger than me, so I guess you're kind of both."

"You seem mad at *someone.* Is it those soldiers?"

She drew in a long breath. "I'm not mad at them . . . just *tired* of them."

"Is it 'cause they're men?"

"Who's been talking to you?"

"Well, Peg said . . . some soldier hurt you."

"Is that so?"

"She claimed being your twin lets her see into your heart—says you got *wounded* by a soldier—said you were eligible for a *Purple Heart.*"

Her jaw tightened. "Maybe a broken heart, but not a purple one." She looked around. "Peg said she'd meet us here before the train arrived." As they neared the depot, she rubbed Ben's ear. "Watch for those army trucks." He was digging in his pocket, so she repeated, "*Watch* for those trucks."

"I will."

Her twin sister Peg's words hung like the dust in the air. *Hurt by a soldier. Wounded.* Elizabeth heard her own voice bouncing in her soul. *It's your own fault. You don't have anyone to blame but yourself.*

She bit her lip. It *would not* happen again.

Chapter 2

Bad News

CLOSE VOTE EXTENDS SERVICE TERM FOR THOUSANDS OF SOLDIERS

(Washington) By a vote of 203-202 yesterday, Congress removed restrictions pertaining to federalized National Guard units. This close vote means National Guard soldiers will have their terms extended and may be moved to locations outside the United States.

Private Harry Miller had never hated a place like he hated Louisiana. As his National Guard convoy reached the end of the paved road outside DeRidder's city limits, he braced himself for the teeth-jarring washboard road. Through the chalky red dust covering them, Harry scanned the bleak cutover landscape. His tent mate, Shorty, leaned over. "Cheer up, Louisiana's not really the end of the world—but you *can* see it from here."

Harry wiped his face with a grimy bandana. "The only thing worse than your Louisiana mud is your Louisiana dust."

Shorty—Private Lester Johnson—grinned. "And the only thing that can trump either one is this Louisiana August humidity."

"At least it's consistent," Harry said.

"Yep, consistently *miserable*."

Harry spat. "We don't call it 'Lousy-anna' for nothing."

"How many more days before you leave Louisiana?"

"In seventy-two days . . . "—Harry glanced at his watch— ". . . twelve hours and about thirty-seven minutes." The truck turned off into a bone-shaking side road. He stood and scanned the stump-covered field filled with hundreds of tents. "Reminds me of one of those military graveyards with row after row of headstones."

Shorty nodded. "Looks like they already had a war here, and the trees lost."

Harry wiped his face with his slouch hat. "This place even *feels* like a graveyard."

"That's why we call this part of Louisiana, 'No Man's Land'."

"Why's that?"

"It was a neutral strip between Spanish and French territories. It became a hideout for outlaws and anyone else that didn't want to be told what to do."

"Folks like your family?"

"Exactly. My family got run out of Alabama, and have been here ever since."

"You sound proud of it."

"I'm proud of my No-Man's-Land-Outlaw-Strip roots."

Harry surveyed the barren stump-covered fields. "Looks to me like it's still 'No Man's Land'."

"You hate the Army, don't you?"

"Probably more than any of the half-million soldiers playing war out here. The only thing that keeps me going is that if I wasn't here, I'd be in a Wisconsin prison." The truck jerked to an abrupt halt and a dusty cloud settled over them as the convoy turned east. An enterprising boy was selling newspapers, and one of the soldiers bought a copy of the day's *Lake Charles American Press*. Harry's unit, Company K, comprised of mostly National Guard soldiers from Michigan and Wisconsin, kept a constant betting pool going about whether the Detroit Tigers or Cubs would finish lower in their respective leagues. As the soldiers tore into the sports page, the front section fell to the floor. A soldier retrieved it and began reading out the headlines. The word "extension" caught Harry's attention.

The reader cursed. "It says here our time is being extended." Harry tore the paper from the soldier's hand. There it was in bold headlines: CLOSE VOTE EXTENDS SERVICE TERM FOR THOUSANDS. . . . The convoy began moving as nausea swept over Harry. His worst fears were being confirmed—he was stuck in the Army, and that meant being stuck in Louisiana. This was its own prison sentence. His Army service had gone from days to maybe years. Another soldier, who'd also been counting the days, sarcastically called out their National Guard unit's motto, "We'll be back in a year."

The cussing and bellyaching continued until the trucks pulled into a cutover area that appeared to be their field camp. A soldier whispered, "Here comes trouble," as Company Sergeant Kickland came around a tent.

A.L. "Red" Kickland, known simply as "Sarge," loved showing off his stripes. His favorite whipping boy was Harry, who provided plenty of opportunities to serve as a target.

Sarge was short with cropped red hair and a ruddy complexion from which he got his nickname. When he was mad—which seemed most of the time—his face turned crimson. The hot Louisiana sun had further deepened his cooked lobster look. A veteran of the Great War, he prided himself on riding the young soldier whom he considered "soft." He was loathed by most of the men in Company K.

He stepped to the truck's tailgate and barked in his raspy voice, "All right, boys, let's unload." A blue bandana was pulled over his face for the dust. He lowered his mask. "Welcome to your new home—downtown Fulton, Louisiana."

Harry grimaced as he jumped down, causing Shorty to say, "That leg still bothering you?"

"Three straight days of twenty-mile marches will do it." Harry grunted as he hefted his pack. "Especially with sixty extra pounds."

A new Company K soldier said, "Where're the hot showers, Sarge?" Harry immediately recognized the accent as from one of New York City's boroughs.

"Do I look—or smell—like there are any showers around here? This ain't your Waldorf-Astoria. This is bivouacking at its best." Sarge's face flushed.

"Or worst," Shorty muttered.

The New York private, a skinny Jew named Cohen, jumped to the ground.

"Chiggers, we *have* arrived." The other soldiers laughed—most had already experienced Louisiana chiggers firsthand.

"Soldier, they call chiggers 'redbugs' down here," Sarge said, "and when they set up housekeeping in your drawers you'll understand why."

A veteran of nearly a year in Louisiana added, "New York, you wait 'til those ticks and mosquitoes start *maneuvers* on you. You'll be wishing they were redbugs."

Harry didn't see Sarge coming up behind him until Shorty whispered, "Harry, get rid of your gum." He spit it out before snapping to attention. Sarge hated gum chewing while on duty and could spot a wad from fifty paces. "Miller, what'd you just spit out?"

"Nothing, Sir."

Sarge walked to the offending wad in a sawdust pile at the base of a climbing wall. "Get down there and pick it up."

Harry stood over the spot.

"Pick it up with your mouth. That's where it came from." Harry glanced at Sarge who stood, arms crossed, feet apart. "You heard me." Harry scanned the small cluster of Company K men but everyone avoided eye contact. He started to argue, but knew better. He knelt down, put his face in the gritty sawdust, feeling his face redden as he blinked back tears. Being humiliated like this was more than he could take. "Go over in the bushes and spit it out and don't be spitting gum where we're walking." Harry walked slowly over and spit it out and cleaned the sawdust from his mouth.

All the men had left except for Shorty. "Sorry. That was pretty bad."

Harry glared at the back of the retreating sergeant. "One of these days I'm going to get even with him. I'm going to kill the sorry. . . ." A honking jeep approached from which a driver threw out two sacks of mail. "Mail for Company K." As soldiers came running, Harry walked away.

"Wait around," Shorty said. "You might get some mail."

"None's coming for me." Harry had only received two pieces of mail in the past three months, and neither had been pleasant. The first was a letter, which he could still quote word for word:

Harry,

I've thought long and hard of how to do this, and there's no easy way. I'm breaking off our engagement. The truth of the matter is that I've fallen in love with John—John Talbert.

I don't know how this happened, but it did. I hope you'll understand.
Helen.

Even now, three months later, he couldn't believe he'd lost his fiancée to the man who'd *been* his best friend. A month after the Dear John letter, Harry had received a second piece of mail—a small box containing the ring he'd given Helen. No note. No apology. Just the ring.

Still spitting dirt, he sat under a scraggly oak reliving those two painful pieces of mail. The bitterness in his mouth was from more than just sawdust. Shorty walked by. "I got blanked today on mail." He pulled an object out of his pocket and tossed it to him. "Speaking of blanks, did you know what the guys in the truck behind us were doing earlier?"

Harry held up the .30 caliber cartridge thrown to him. Shorty hesitated. "They were 'yoo-hooing. Throwing out spent casings with notes inside."

"That's against regulations."

"They were doing it anyway."

"That's a good way to get their tail in a crack."

"You're right—if the shells contained *their* names."

"What do you mean?"

"They were doing it as a joke with other soldier's names—mainly yours."

He felt his eye twitching. "What?"

"Yep. Shep threw out a bunch with your name."

"I *am* going to knock that blond-headed rascal's head off!"

Shorty slapped at a cloud of swarming mosquitoes. "Looks like rain."

"Then it'll be hot, miserable, and muddy, instead of dusty."

"Pick your poison, partner."

Harry spat. "My only comfort was that in seventy-two days, my time was up. Now it's extended. Just my luck. Extended." Harry walked to a nearby pile of dried cow manure. As he kicked it, pieces of dried manure flew. The inside was soft and a disgusting green glob stuck to the end of his combat boot. Shorty smirked. "Clean that off before you come into our tent."

"I hate this God-forsaken place," Harry said. Deep down inside, he knew something: it wasn't this place—or even the Army—that made him unhappy. Neither was to blame for his being stuck in the Louisiana Maneuvers.

That responsibility rested on Harry Miller. He had no one to blame but himself.

Chapter 3

A Bird Nest

Elizabeth pulled Ben toward the train depot as he protested. "Lizzie, don't pull on me like a goat at the sale barn." She had him by the overall strap. "You're gonna smothercate me."

She rolled her eyes, trying not to laugh. "Ben, that's not a real word."

"*Smothercate*? Ma uses it."

"Well, just because . . . " They passed a wall of soldiers crowded around the depot entrance. Safely out of earshot, Ben tapped her arm. "Sister, what's a 'real hooker'?"

"*Ben Reed.* Where'd you hear that?"

"One of those soldiers pointed at you. 'There's a real hooker.'"

"Is that what he said?"

"It sounded like it."

"Could it have been . . . uh . . . 'a real *looker*'?"

"I thought he said 'hooker'."

Elizabeth tousled his hair. "Ben, a 'real looker' is, uh, a good-looking woman."

"Like you?"

She laughed. "I don't know about that. But a *hooker*? It's a *bad* name for a *bad* girl. It's not what you want your sister called."

"You want me to go back and whup him?"

"No, we'll let him go this time, but thanks anyway." She hugged him. The little rascal was her favorite person in the world.

Ben stopped in front of the uniformed men piling off the train. "Where are they coming from?"

"From furloughs up north or arriving for new assignments here."

A skinny soldier bumped into her. "I'm *so* sorry, Miss." He removed his cap, but his smirk remained. "Where are you going?"

"As far away from you as possible."

The soldier turned to Ben. "Here to meet someone, little man"?

"Nope, we're here to get some*thing.*"

Elizabeth coughed. "Let's get to the freight landing."

"Do you see our crate, Sister?"

"Not yet."

Ben dug into the middle of the stacked boxes. "I hear them but can't see them." Elizabeth moved to the chirping crate. He pulled on her dress. "Are they still alive?"

She peered through the slats. "Looks like they are." Suddenly, someone grabbed her from behind, loudly crowing in her ear. It couldn't be anyone but her sister, Peg.

"We about gave up on you." Elizabeth eyed her carefully. "I figured you were flirting with some soldier."

"What do you mean *soldier*? I was flirting with an entire platoon. You ought to try it sometimes."

Ben interrupted them, holding up the crate. "Did they really come all the way from Arkansas?"

Elizabeth peered through the slats at the chirping baby chicks. "All the way from DeQueen, Arkansas."

Ben stooped to see. "From DeQueen to DeRidder."

The chirping biddies attracted plenty of attention in the depot, causing her to walk faster. The same tall soldier blocked her path. "So you're a chicken farmer?"

"Well, if I am, you're not my kind of rooster. Goodbye and *good day.*"

The soldier raised his hands in mock horror as Ben, fists balled, stepped between them. "Fellow, I believe you could wart the horns off a brass billy goat. Leave my sister be."

The soldier turned toward Peg. "And who's this pretty country girl with you?"

Ben stood his ground. "She's her twin sister and you can leave *both of them* alone."

"They sure don't look like twins."

"They're that other kind of twin." He scratched his head. "Ma—that's my grandma—says those kind of twins come from—" Both sisters grabbed at him as Peg said, "Ben Reed, Momma said she was going to beat you into next week if she heard you say that again."

Elizabeth hurried her little brother out of the depot back to their street corner, set the crate down, and pulled out two nickels. "Would you like a Coke and snack?"

He punched the air with a fist. "Can I get something *now?*"

"We'll watch the biddies until you get back."

Peg watched him run off. "I love people's faces when they find out we're twins." She touched Elizabeth's arm. "You and your dark hair and skin and me with enough freckles to cover the moon."

"You're just fine like you are." Elizabeth mushed her sister's strawberry blonde hair. "Even if you do look like you just got off the boat from Dublin."

"I'm not the one the guys look at—you are," Peg said. "It's those dark mysterious eyes and your olive complexion, *Squaw.*"

Elizabeth shot back. "Mick."

"Redbone Woman."

"Colleen Blarney."

"Injun."

The war of words continued until a jeep driver honked his horn and yelled, "Hey, kid, get out of the road." Elizabeth spun to see the jeep stopped in front of Ben, who was contentedly holding his Coca-Cola and bag of shelled peanuts. The driver motioned him to the sidewalk. "Son, you're gonna get run over." He turned to Elizabeth. "Ma'am, you'd better watch your—"

"He's my brother."

"Well, you'd better watch your brother." He winked at Peg and peered at the crate. "Got some new biddies?"

Ben walked to the jeep, which had 1931 painted boldly on its hood. "How'd you know we had biddies?"

"First of all, I can read. 'Baby Chicks. Handle with Care.' Besides, I was raised on a farm in Moline, Illinois."

Ben clapped his hands. "Moline? John Deere country."

"Home of the world's best tractors."

"Hey, your jeep number—1931—is the year I was born."

"No joke. I guess that makes you, uh, about ten years old."

Another jeep honked. "Come on, Lawrence. Get moving."

The driver saluted Ben. "Gotta go. Stay off the road and take care of your biddies." He looked past Elizabeth at Peg. "I hope to see you around."

Ben waved. "See you later."

"You might if you stay off the road." The driver winked. "You'd better keep an eye on him." He expertly gunned Jeep 1931 between two large trucks in the convoy and sped off.

Elizabeth turned to her sister. "*You* were the one he noticed, not me. Did you know him?"

"I haven't the slightest."

"The slightest what? You can't end a sentence with an adjective."

"I can if I want to." Peg pursed her lips. "Slightest, slightest, slightest."

Elizabeth nodded at the disappearing jeep. "He noticed you."

"Well, even a blind hog will find an acorn every blue moon or so," Peg called over her shoulder. "I'm going to do some shopping at Morgan and Lindsey."

Ben, washing the peanuts down with a big swig of Coke, said to Elizabeth, "You know, you're my hero."

"Because I bought you a Coke and peanuts?"

"No, 'cause you take good care of me."

She hugged him. "Ben, promise me that you'll watch for traffic."

"I will."

"You stay here and guard the chicks while I'm at the post office." She hurried to the postal building where she'd recently opened a box for her private correspondence. Slipping her key into the box, she pulled out two letters, scanning their return addresses. The first one was in a small envelope with no forwarding address. She ripped it open and read in Dora's familiar script.

August 10, 1941
Shreveport, La

Elizabeth,
*   As promised, I'm reporting to you on Bradley. I saw him last week at church, and he looks truly happy.*
*   Also, I've told no one. You can trust me.*

Sincerely,
Dora

Her hand trembled as she re-read it. *Bradley. Happy.* She glanced around the post office hoping no one saw her tears. She wiped her eyes and read the legal-size envelope, stopping at the typed return address:

Caddo Parish School Board
Shreveport, La.

Ripping open the envelope, she read the first paragraph:

Miss Reed,
We are pleased to offer you a job as an elementary teacher at Byrd Elementary School for the coming year of 1941–42. A contract is enclosed for your signature.

She dropped both letters and clutched her stomach. *What I've dreamed of is in reach. A new life one hundred fifty miles north . . . but why do I feel like . . . like it's a poor decision? What's wrong with me? I always have to make everything so complicated.*

"Miss, Miss—you dropped your letter." An older woman handed her the letters. "Are you all right? Bad news?"

"No, Ma'am. It's great news." She gathered the letters. "Great news." Elizabeth hurried out of the post office. *A great pay raise, in the city where she'd always longed to be. Where her heart was. Bradley. Why did such good news sadden her?*

She hurried to the Beauregard Parish School Board Office. School was slated to begin in two weeks. A rumor had been circulating that opening might be delayed due to the Army Maneuvers. She entered the building and found a secretary. "I'm checking about the start of school."

"You haven't heard? The Board met last night and postponed school until the first Monday in October."

"That's official?" Elizabeth felt her heart quicken. The Caddo Parish letter in her pocket seemed to be calling her name.

The secretary nodded. "It sure is. Soldiers are camped on school grounds, and it'd be dangerous running buses among the military traffic."

"First Monday in October?"

She glanced at her desk calendar. "Looks like October 6 to me."

"Will we still get paid?"

"Teachers will, but support personnel won't."

Elizabeth frowned. Her father's school bus route supplemented his work at the sawmill. A month without bus pay would knock their family for a loop. She hurried out in a daze, quickly forgetting about Poppa's bus salary. She had a difficult decision to make. *Lord, help me know what to do.*

She hurried to the street corner, slipping behind Ben who was counting a column of passing cavalrymen. "Thirty, thirty-one—I'm gonna ride one of those horses even if it harelips the pope."

"Ben, don't talk like that."

He spun around in surprise. "I about gave up on you." He hooked his thumbs in his overalls. "A dollar waiting on a dime."

As the last mounted soldier saluted, Ben jerked his hand out of his pocket to return the salute. As he did, his harmonica clattered to the sidewalk, but that wasn't what caught Elizabeth's attention. It was the five-dollar bill that fluttered beside it. She scooped up the bill, waving it in front of his face. "*Benjamin Franklin Reed*, where'd you get this?"

"I found a bird nest on the ground."

"You what?" She knelt in front of him. "Is there more?"

"Not a five, but I got a whole pocket full of ones."

"Show me." He emptied both pockets plus the snap on his bib overalls, piling the crumpled-up dollars and coins on the sidewalk. She stammered, "Who'd you take that from?"

"I didn't *take* it. It came from selling them cokes."

"What *cokes*?"

"I sold the coke you bought me to a thirsty soldier for a whole dollar. Then I bought some more and sold them to the convoys." He pointed at the small mountain of wadded bills. "That's how I got it."

"You sold *nickel* cokes for a *dollar* each?"

"Yep, and they were as happy to get 'em as I was to sell 'em." He stepped back as if he knew what was coming. "Uh-oh. Looks like something's rotten in Denmark."

"Now, listen here, Shakespeare—selling a coke for a dollar. That's—why, that's highway *robbery*."

Ben looked back toward the street corner. "Lizzie, it wasn't highway robbery. It was right here on First Street." He stood proudly. "Yep, I found me a bird nest on the ground. Right here in D'Ridder, Louisianer."

Elizabeth wasn't sure if she should spank him now or wait until they got home. "How'd you get a five-dollar bill?"

"A truckload of soldiers gave it for a whole case of Cokes." He shuffled his feet. "When I got back, they were gone, so I sold them to the next truck." He watched her scoop up the money. "It's enough money to burn a wet dog, ain't it?"

"That's more money than your daddy makes in a week at the sawmill." She gritted her teeth. "Momma's going to burn *your* wet dog when we get home."

He shrugged. "Sounds like something's rotten in . . . DeRidder." Elizabeth groaned. Sometimes he was more than she could handle. It was going to be a long school year . . . if she stayed. Elizabeth stuffed the money into her purse, feeling for the two letters. It would be a difficult decision, but Shreveport was *her* "bird nest on the ground." This was what she'd dreamed of—living in a city away from the difficulties of rural life. She'd prayed for this opportunity.

Why then did she feel so reluctant about going?

Chapter 4
A Broken Record

As Elizabeth got out of the car at her family's rural home, she pushed the two letters deeper into her purse. She hadn't told Peg about the letters. That could wait.

Ben ran toward their family farm dog, Blue. "Hey boy, didja miss me?" Elizabeth watched him freeze at the sounds from inside the house. He hung his head. "They're fighting again."

Elizabeth handed him the crate of biddies. "Go put these in the brooder." Peg, who avoided conflict like the Bubonic Plague followed him toward the barn. They left Elizabeth alone as she cringed at the loud arguing coming from her brother Jimmy Earl and Poppa. It was clear the root of this ruckus: the war in Europe had come home to Bundick Community again.

The Victrola played in the background. She knew *it* was the source of the trouble. It was "Lindbergh: Eagle of the USA," a song her father and brother had been skirmishing over for weeks. Poppa, whose hearing had been damaged in the Great War, played the Victrola at full volume. Elizabeth listened to the scratchy recording:

Lindbergh, what a flying fool was he.
Lindbergh, your name will live in history.

There was a lull in the arguing.

Over the ocean, he flew on alone,
Daring and danger, he faced all alone.

She listened carefully as the argument quieted and the song continued:

Others may make that trip across the sea
Upon some future day, but take your hats off to lucky, lucky Lindbergh
The Eagle of the USA.

Jimmy Earl said, "I'm tired of that song." This was followed by the sickening scratch of a needle ripping across a phonograph record. She hurried into the house where her father and Jimmy Earl stood toe to toe.

"You've ruined my favorite record." Poppa put the needle back on the record as the *clack-clack-clack* of the needle revolved over the scratch. He took "Lindbergh" off the turntable and flung it against the wall where it shattered into a dozen pieces. Elizabeth felt her own heart splintering.

"Son, you know how much that record meant to me." There was more hurt in her father's husky voice than anger.

"Poppa, Lindbergh's a traitor. He ought to move to Germany since he says we can't beat them."

"Son, there's a lot about it you don't understand."

Jimmy Earl glared. "Lindbergh—and his isolationist friends—are wrong. We can't stick our head in the sand.

"Most of them opposing the war fought in the Great War. They know what it's like." Poppa's voice cracked. "I know what it's like—I was there."

Jimmy Earl braced his feet. "We're going to have to take our stand sooner or later."

"Then let it be later. Too many Americans died fighting a European War. We don't need to do it again twenty-something years later."

"The President says we have no choice but to take a stand."

"Well, Roosevelt is wrong. *Wrong, wrong, wrong.*"

Elizabeth saw the anger ratcheted up in her brother's face. "Poppa, you taught me to always respect the President."

"Saying the President is wrong ain't disrespect. It's simply a matter of opinion—my opinion, in fact."

Jimmy Earl stiffened. "And my opinion is that *your* hero Lindbergh and his 'America First' crowd are traitors. Especially him."

"You don't have to agree with him, but don't call him a traitor. He's a great American."

"No, he's a traitor."

Elizabeth put her hand on her brother's chest. "Jimmy Earl, you've said enough."

He turned on her. "No, Sister. I ain't said *enough.*" Facing Poppa, he lowered his voice. "I feel so strongly about it that I'm joining up."

"What'd you say?"

Jimmy Earl's voice was clear and strong. "I said I'm joining up."

"Joining up?"

"Yes Sir, I'm joining the Army."

"J.E., you can't. You're only seventeen." Poppa was the only one who called Jimmy Earl by his initials. It was his term of endearment for his oldest son. He lamely repeated, "J.E., you can't."

"No, Poppa, you're wrong. I *can* and I *will.*" Elizabeth lowered her head. If her brother had wanted the last word on this argument, he'd just gotten it.

No one had noticed Ben standing in the door. "Jimmy Earl, you can't leave us. What would I do without you here?" The three Reed family members turned toward Ben. Poppa, shoulders sagging, walked out of the house and toward the barn. It was as if his rigid anger had been wrung out, and Elizabeth could only form one word watching him: *sadness.*

Jimmy Earl stormed into his room, slamming the door behind him. Elizabeth put her arm around Ben as he sobbed, "It's always about that dang war, ain't it?"

She stroked his hair. "It seems like everything is tied to that war. Soldiers, maneuvers, the news, the radio, everything."

"Jimmy Earl can't really join the army, can he?"

"He's seventeen. He could probably get in with a parent's signature."

They walked hand in hand to the porch, where Elizabeth sank into the swing and put her arm around her little brother. "Bradley, we never know from day to day what's going to happen."

"Why'd you call me *Bradley*?"

"I didn't call you Bradley."

"Yes, you did. Who's Bradley?"

"I'm sorry Ben. Bradley was . . . someone I knew in Shreveport." She glanced down. "He reminded me of you."

"Then he must be a fine fellow."

"He is."

Ben leapt off the porch, hitting the tire swing in full stride. Elizabeth sat in the swing, the only sounds being the distant drone of an overhead plane, the creaking of the swing chains, and her little brother's whistling as he swung.

There was no doubt. He was whistling "Lindbergh, The Eagle of the USA."

Chapter 5

Melted Ice Cream

WEATHER ADVISORY
CAMP POLK, LOUISIANA
13 AUGUST 1941

EXTREME HEAT AND HUMIDITY WILL BE IN EFFECT FOR BLUE
ARMY AREAS. ALL PERSONNEL SHOULD MAKE MAXIMUM USE
OF SALT TABLETS AND WATER.

Harry looked at Shorty Johnson in the light of dawn. "Why in the world would anyone *volunteer* for this Army?" Their pine-knot fire blazed up when Shorty piled bitterweeds on it, causing Harry to ask, "Does that really keep mosquitoes away?"

Shorty held both palms up. "See any?"

"No, I don't. You actually enjoy being in the field, don't you?"

Shorty shrugged. "It ain't much different from a Louisiana logging camp, 'cept the pay's better and the army's a lot safer. Figured it'd extend my life expectancy."

"If lumbering is worse than this, remind me never to sign up."

"Don't worry buddy, you wouldn't last two days. You got too many citified ways."

Shorty was proud to be a third generation woodsman. This seemed strange since both a brother and grandfather had died in logging accidents.

As a pot of coffee brewed over the fire, a bugle blew "chow call." Shorty stood. "The ice cream boys are back." He brushed past Harry. "Come on, how 'bout an ice cream sandwich for breakfast?" Dozens of soldiers grappled around an old car from which two teenagers busily exchanged ice cream for coins and bills. The feeding frenzy was soon over, and Shorty came out of the pile holding up two sandwiches, tossing one to Harry. Grasping his treat, Harry strolled to the teens. "It looks like the *Great* Depression isn't as *great* as it used to be for you boys."

The taller of the two, folding a wad of money into his wallet, answered. "The Army has sure helped us."

Harry took a bite of his sandwich. "Where'd you get the ice cream?"

"Borden's in Lake Charles."

Suddenly, the circle of happy ice cream eaters parted as a jeep skidded to a halt and a second lieutenant scampered out. "Who blew that bugle?" The younger teen tried to hide the bugle behind his back, which only further infuriated the officer. "No one blows a bugle around here without my official clearance. If I see you again, I'll have the MPs impound your vehicle."

The boys climbed into the car and, as soon as it sputtered to life, roared off in a cloud of dust. Harry walked over to the jeep where a corporal sat in the driver's seat. Harry held out his ice cream. "Want a bite?"

The driver laughed. "No thanks." Harry quickly finished his dust-covered, melting ice cream sandwich, scanning the cloudless sky. As cool ice cream ran down his arm, he shook his head. "Any place hot enough at daylight to melt ice cream isn't fit for human habitation."

The driver laughed. "It's sure different than Illinois. Where're you from?"

"Milwaukee." Harry nodded toward the still-fuming officer. "You carry around idiots like him?"

"I see it all in my job." He held out his hand. "My name's Lawrence."

"Harry Miller." He studied the jeep. "You like driving this thing?"

"It sure beats marching."

The Lieutenant climbed in. "Let's go, Corporal."

Lawrence winked at Harry. "Hi-Yo, Silver, away!"

The jeep spun out coating Harry with more dust as the driver called over his shoulder, "See you later, Kemo-Sabe."

Another bugle call sounded, and it *was* chow call. Another day began for Company K in their temporary home at Fulton, Louisiana. Harry walked toward the mess tent as soldiers were jostling for the few shady spots. Carrying his meal toward their tent, he was followed by the three Company K soldiers who loved tormenting him as much as any biting insect. To his dismay, these three—Halverson, Nickels, and Shep—sat beside him.

Company K was primarily comprised of National Guard soldiers from the central Wisconsin town of Monitowoc. All of them, as well as Sarge and their officers, had grown up together and formed a tight-knit clan that excluded outsiders like Shorty, Cohen, and Harry. Especially Harry.

"Well, how's old lover boy doing this morning?" Shep said.

When Harry didn't answer, Shep continued, "Listen. You're going to have to give up this sad-sack business and get on with life. There's plenty of beautiful women in these Louisiana woods prettier than that gal Harriet."

Harry winced. "Her name's *Helen*."

"Well, either way, the best way of getting over her is finding you a Louisiana woman, hey?"

Harry scoffed, "The last thing I'd *ever* want is a Louisiana woman."

"Well, we have been working on getting you a Louisiana broad."

"Thanks, but no tha—"

Shep cut him off. "It may be a little late for you to say no. We've been working hard to help you, haven't we, Hal?"

Halverson pulled out an empty M-1 cartridge. "On our way down here, we threw out a bunch of these."

Harry shot back quickly. "I already heard about it. Tossing bullets—yoo-hooing—is prohibited. Captain read the new regulation to us last week—something about an MP being hit in the eye by a tossed rock."

Halverson rubbed his head. "Ouch, did the MP write that soldier back?" Everyone but Harry found this hilarious.

Sarge passed by and stopped, putting his hands on his hips. "Miller, the front of your tent is leaning. Get it straight before roll call."

Harry nodded. "Yes Sir."

Once Sarge was out of earshot, Shep said, "He hates you even worse than me, and that's saying a lot." He lowered his voice. "On our ride down here from Camp Livingston, we tossed out a bunch of those bullets. Miller, *your* name was on a bunch of them."

"If I get in trouble because of you guys. . . ."

"It'll be worth it, if you get a woman, hey?"

"How many had my name?"

"Oh, I don't remember—five, maybe six." Shep made a throwing motion. "I threw three of them myself. First one was to a bucktoothed-bowlegged farm-girl outside Leesville. The second one was near Rosepine, but she wasn't buck-toothed; as far as I could see, she didn't have *any* teeth at all."

Nickels corrected him. "No, the second girl was the one with the moustache."

Shep slapped his forehead. "How could I ever forget her?" He put his hand by his mouth. "Now, the *last* bullet I threw was to a real beaut—a fine-looking long-legged gal near the tracks in DeRidder. I don't think she picked it up, but *if* she writes, send her *my* way."

"Fat chance."

"Fat chance of what—you not turning her over to a real man?"

"No, fat chance of her writing. I'm sure you scared her off."

"Well, I did yell that she was beautiful, and every woman loves hearing that. She was a dark-haired looker. If she writes, I want her address."

Harry glanced away. "The way my luck's been, it'll be the bucktooth or the toothless one."

These tormenters, who called themselves "The Three Musketeers," snickered as Shep said, "Oh, I forgot about the fat, old-maid schoolteacher I saw in front of the DeRidder Schoolhouse. I threw one to her, too."

Harry'd heard enough. "Well, thanks a lot, guys. I *really* do appreciate your help."

"No problem. We'd do *anything* for a friend and fellow soldier." Shep patted Harry on the shoulder. "One day you'll probably thank me for this." He handed him an empty cartridge. "This souvenir is for you."

Harry bit his tongue. I doubt if I'll ever thank you for *anything*, Shep. With that, he flung the cartridge into the weeds. He visualized the old-maid schoolteacher and wasn't sure if she was buck-toothed or toothless—but she definitely had a moustache.

He nearly gagged on his next bite of scrambled eggs. It would be just his luck.

Chapter 6

In Cahoots

Ben heard the approaching footsteps and shoved the bullet under his pillow and began innocently singing:

"Do your ears hang low, do they flop, do they flop.
Can you tie 'em in a bow, can you tie 'em in a knot?"

He sat on the edge of the bed as the doorknob turned.

"Can you throw them o'er your shoulder,
Like a regimental soldier . . ."

His mother and twin sisters marched into the room as he slowly finished, *"Do your . . . ears hang . . . low."*

His mother solemnly spread the money on the bed. "Thirty-eight dollars and twenty cents. Ben Reed, I *cannot* believe it."

He shrugged. "It's not like I robbed a bank." Peg winked at Ben, rubbing her hands together as if she was counting money.

Their mother raked a pile of the contraband to one side. "Twenty dollars of this is going to the Lottie Moon offering at church."

"Twenty dollars! Leave me *some*."

"Oh, I'm just getting started." She held up the five-dollar bill. "You're taking this to Widow Young after supper." She stuffed three dollars in her apron pocket. "And that's mine for washing your clothes this month." She raked the rest of the money into a manila envelope. "You'll be getting three dollars and eighty cents later. That's ten percent—and it's all yours."

Ben put his hands on his forehead. "Momma, that's not how they figured it in the Bible. I believe that tithe was the other way around."

"Not in your Momma's math, and in this house, Momma's math is the only kind that matters. Besides, all but fifty cents of *that* is going into a savings account at the bank."

Ben's shoulders sagged. "I've been robbed."

"No. You *robbed,* making those poor soldiers pay a dollar for a coke."

"Please, let me keep a little more." He turned to his sisters. "Y'all are in cahoots with her."

His mother's fist slammed down like a gavel. "Case closed." She kissed him on the forehead. "Appeal denied." Satisfied that justice had been served, she turned on her heel. His sisters, still snickering behind their hands, followed in her wake.

Ben counted to five-Mississippi, listening for returning footsteps. Pulling the brass cartridge from under his pillow, he removed the folded note from the shell, re-reading the four lines of numbers and words slowly. He inhaled the faint smell of gunpowder in the cartridge and slid it into his pocket. He now had a plan and headed into the kitchen. "Momma, can I go over to Ma's house?"

She eyed him carefully. "If you promise not to ruin your supper, and be back 'fore dusk-dark."

"Yes Ma'am." He sprinted out the door as her parting words echoed, "And watch for rattlesnake pilots in those leaves." Blue joined him at the gate, loping along as they crossed the creek bottom. It was a quarter-mile through the woods to the home of his grandmother, Doshie Reed. Her family called her "Ma" and Ben loved her more than anybody in the whole world.

Arriving, he slammed the screen door to announce his arrival. "Got anything for a country boy to eat?" She was working in the kitchen, dressed in the only way he'd ever seen her: long, flowing dress, gray hair up in a bun, skinny arms working hard. In her sing-songey voice, she said, "Well, we don't *usually* feed hoboes, but today I'll make an exception."

He began their ritual. "Ain't your name *Ma?* What kind of name is that?"

"Oh, it's an old Attakapa Indian word." She gave him a big hug. "For the person who spoils you and pours a big dose of love all over you."

Ben had gotten one of her flour hugs. "Ma, you're making that Indian stuff up, ain't you?"

She rubbed his head. "It sounds like *me*, don't it?"

"Sure does." As she hugged him again, he inhaled the smells that marked his grandmother: lye soap, talcum powder, and the faint odor of Garrett's Sweet Snuff. These were mixed with the kitchen aromas of frying bacon and baking bread. He'd timed his arrival right.

"You're just in time for a snack. Would you like Ma to get you a hot peach tart?"

"Momma told me not to ruin my supper."

"Well, what your momma don't know won't hurt her, will it?"

"Not one bit."

She took out a pan of hot tarts from the cook stove. "While they're cooling, you use the fly-swap to keep the flies off." After about a minute, she winked. "All right, a hot tart deserves a cold glass of milk. Go out to the well and bring in the milk." As he raced outside, she warned, "Be careful and don't break the jug." He pulled the rope up from the well and untied the burlap sack that held the gallon of fresh milk, holding the cold jug against his face.

She poured him a pint jelly jar full of creamy milk and set it beside two steaming peach tarts. Between bites and gulps, he said, "How's PawPaw today?"

She nodded toward the bedroom. "He's been in there jabbering all morning."

Ben chuckled. "Ma, he ain't said a word since his stroke."

"Honey, there's lots of ways of talking that don't take words."

"What do you talk to him about all day?"

"Everything and nothing. He's a captive audience, and I try to take advantage of it." She lifted a pan of sizzling bacon. "Run in there and tell him hello."

Ben eased into the room where his grandfather was sleeping. He'd never gotten used to seeing how this strong man—his hero—had withered down to what he was now. "Morning, PawPaw."

His grandfather's eyes opened and were joined by a crooked smile. He tried to form words, but what came out was gibberish, followed by a tear rolling down his left cheek. Ben kissed the tear and pulled up a chair bedside. "It's good seeing you, Pa." Ben rubbed his grandfather's hand, filling him in about recent events in his life. When he saw Ma in the doorway, he said, "How do you and him talk?"

"We tell each other all day how much we love each other."

"How's that?"

"With our eyes, and with gestures, and our hearts."

"Show me."

Ma walked over and sat on the edge of the bed. She placed her flour-covered hand on his cheek, tenderly stroking his face and turned to Ben. "See what I mean?"

"Yes Ma'am, I do."

She turned to Pa. "Spencer, do you wish you'd married Deborah Granger instead of me?"

He vigorously shook his head, a scowl spreading over his long face. She winked at him, "If you had it to do all over, would you marry me again?"

He dipped his head up and down, a lop-sided grin evicting the frown. Ma said, "He's bobbing that head like a woodpecker on a wormy willow oak tree."

"Ma, what'd he try to say?"

"It was 'I love you'."

"How do you know"?

She walked Ben to the kitchen. "I just know." Dusting the flour off her apron, she said, "I hear-tell they're dropping flour-sack bombs from them Army planes. Sounds like a real waste to me. Flour's for making biscuits and tarts."

"Especially tarts." He finished his second tart, then pulled the bullet from his pocket and tossed it on the counter where it rattled against a pot. "Look at that."

"What's that?" She walked to the counter.

"It's a bullet a soldier tossed at me and Elizabeth in town."

She picked it up and removed the note. "Baby, go get Ma's bifocals off the settee."

He returned with the glasses. "Lizzie said he hollered, 'You're beautiful. Write me.' I'm not sure if he was yelling at me or Lizzie."

"I'm *pretty* sure it *wasn't* you," She adjusted the glasses on her nose.

"What's that note mean, Ma?"

She unfolded it and read slowly,

Write me!
Private Harold M. Miller
36630862
Company K, 127th Infantry 32nd Division
Ragley, Louisiana

Ben looked over her shoulder. "What is it?"

"Looks like a soldier's address."

He stood on his tiptoes. "So that's why the soldier threw the bullet at us?"

"Not at *us*, but at your sister. You know she is *one* good-looking woman." She held the bullet in her long fingers. "Did Elizabeth pick this up?"

"Not that I saw. She told me to leave it alone." He finished the milk with a big swig. "But you can see I didn't."

"I can see that." Her eyes narrowed. "Who else knows about this?"

"Not a soul—nobody but me, you, and the Lord above."

"Not even Peg?"

"She was gone when it happened."

"Why'd you bring it to me?"

"'Cause you're the smartest person I know."

"I am?"

"Yes'm, and you make the best peach tarts in the whole world."

"So that's *why* you came."

"Well, that *and* the bullet."

She held the cartridge up to the light from the kitchen window. Ben studied her wrinkled hand and how the purple veins stood out on her hand. In the light from the window, he could nearly see through her thin fingers.

She addressed the bullet as if it was in cahoots with them. "Mr. Bullet, I've been worried about my granddaughter and her boring life." She winked at Ben. "You might just be the answer I been praying for."

"Ma, are you talking to me or the bullet?"

She said, "Both. This bullet might help *us* help *her*." She carefully placed it in a pastel stationery box. "Every tub sits on its own bottom."

"Ma, why do you always say that?"

"Because I like the way it sounds. I'm gonna keep this bullet. The three of us might just go into cahoots together and help Lizzie get some romance in her life."

"But what about Peg?"

"Son, I'm most concerned with keeping her *out of* romance. That girl likes anything wearing pants. But your sister Elizabeth, she's just too serious. We're gonna try to help her."

She peered out the window. "What time'd your momma tell you to be home by?"

"By dusk-dark."

Framing his face with her hands, she kissed his forehead. "You best be going." As he trotted off, she hollered, "And watch for snakes—especially those ground rattlers in the leaves."

Ben was running as fast as he could. He turned to his faithful companion, Blue. "It'd take a mighty quick snake to bite us." The dog barked twice and they picked up speed as they entered the swamp, seeing the lights of home through the trees.

Chapter 7
Words and Letters

Elizabeth was startled awake by the creaking of her bedroom door. Bare feet padded across the floor and covers were pulled back. She waited before saying, "Kind of late, huh?" There was no answer. "What time is it?"

"After midnight." Peg answered wearily.

"How much after midnight?"

Peg yawned. "Oh, about…two or three hours. Were you asleep?"

"Sure." Elizabeth walked to her sister's bed. "But it was a fitful sleep."

"Worried about something?"

"You."

There was a pregnant pause, finally broken by Elizabeth. "When you come in this late, it worries me."

"Well, don't."

"I can't help it."

Peg shifted on the mattress. "I can take care of myself."

"Are you doing anything that could . . . get you into trouble?"

"What do you mean?"

"Were you with a soldier tonight?"

No answer. Elizabeth tried again. "Are you involved with one of them?"

"What do you mean *involved*?"

"You know what I mean."

"Sure I do." Peg turned her back to the wall. "Listen, you're the last person I need any love advice from."

"What's that supposed to mean?"

"You know exactly what I mean."

"I'm afraid I do." She put her hand on Peg's shoulder. "But I need *your* advice."

"Advice on what?"

Elizabeth lit the lantern and pulled out the teacher letter. "On this."

Peg sat up and scooted into the light. "Caddo Parish School Board." She squinted at her sister. "You're not . . ."

"Just read it."

She watched her twin read the letter. It always irritated her how Peg mouthed words when reading. Peg stopped her oral recitation and looked up. "You applied for a job in Shreveport?"

Elizabeth was startled at what she saw in her sister's face: was it fear . . . or sadness?

"You're gonna take it?"

"I am."

Peg laid the letter in her lap. "Then why are you asking for *my* advice?"

"Because I want to know what you think."

"Does that really matter?"

Elizabeth felt tears welling. "It matters a great deal. We're twins. Few people can understand the bond we have. We were womb mates."

Peg winked. "And now we're roommates."

Elizabeth stammered, "I'm serious. I need your advice."

"I don't have the slightest." Peg held the letter up. "Why would you want to go up there and teach?"

"Because I'm dying on the vine here."

"That's the way you feel?"

"Look at me. I'm twenty years old and still sharing a room with my sister. Twenty years from now, I'll be an old maid schoolteacher living in this bedroom, making muscadine jelly, and leading the WMU at church."

Peg shook her head. "That does sound pretty bleak. But why Shreveport?"

"I like it up there."

"Didn't you stay there two years ago when you were . . . um . . . sick?"

"I did."

"Is there a man up there?" Peg knitted her brow. "Lizzie, your hand's shaking."

"It's because I'm worried about you."

"Sounds like you've got enough to worry about without licking over my calf."

"I'm worried that you're going to . . ." Her voice trembled. "I'm scared. *Scared* that you're going to mess up your life." Peg looked away, but Elizabeth moved into her view. "I'm worried that you're going to get pregnant. I'm not sure Momma and Daddy would ever get over it."

"I'm a big girl and can take care of myself."

Elizabeth pulled out the second letter. "That's exactly what *I said*."

"What do you mean?"

"That's what I said when I got involved with. . ." Her body quivered. "When I got involved with him."

"Him?"

"Him. The soldier that broke my heart up there."

"In Shreveport?"

"No, in Natchitoches."

"You never told me."

"It all happened so quick." She handed her the other letter.

Peg slid closer as she read it. "The soldier's name was Bradley?"

"No, that was the baby's name. Bradley."

"Oh, my goodness. Elizabeth. I never knew." Tears streamed down Peg's cheeks. "I always suspected something happened to you up there, but I never dreamed . . . ."

A series of loud booms shook the house, setting off the dogs and chickens. Peg went to the window. "They're shooting the big guns again." She squinted. "Doggone, I see the first light of morning. We done talked the night away."

Another loud explosion rattled the windows. Elizabeth trembled. *The ground's shaking beneath my feet, both literally and figuratively. I wonder what's next.*

Harry sat with the other two outsiders in their platoon—Shorty and Cohen—They'd been up since dawn.

An artillery barrage to the north had started before dawn, awakening everyone. The three G.I.s sat outside picking out ticks acquired during last night's long march.

Cohen had rolled up his sleeves and was scratching his right arm. "This itch is driving me crazy."

Shorty examined his arm. "When'd you get poison ivy?"

Cohen had scratched his arm raw. "It started yesterday. So that's what it is?"

Shorty disappeared into the tent and came out with a cake of soap. "Rub this on it."

"What is it?"

"Lye soap. I borrowed it from a farmhouse last week. Knew it'd come in handy."

"Does it work?"

"Try it."

Cohen lowered his voice. "I've also got it on my rear end."

"How'd you get poison ivy on your behind?"

"Shh, I don't want everyone to know."

Shorty tossed him the bar of lye soap. "I'm not sure I'd use it there. It's pretty strong."

Harry, sitting in his underwear, stuck a hot match head to a tick. "Shorty, why don't you ever get ticks or chiggers?"

"Because I go out prepared." He lifted his pants leg. Green leaves were stuffed in his socks and boots.

"What's that?" Harry said.

"Merkle bushes. The leaves are coated with a wax that insects don't like."

"It works?"

"Do you see me scratching and picking out ticks?"

A whistle blew, followed by a voice, "Mail call. Everyone up."

Shorty stood. "Let's go, Harry."

"Nope. I don't get mail."

"You never know."

"Not me."

Cohen put on his shirt. "Your family never writes? Do you have a mother or father?"

"I've got both. My father broke things off after a, uh, *little problem I had.*" There was a familiar tightness in his chest. "My mother—she just does what she's told—so she doesn't write either."

Cohen and Shorty trotted to the gathering circle of men at mail call. Harry eased back into quiet sanctuary of the tent, determined to ignore the jostling men and mail clerk's loud voice. "Snider. Schwartz. Johnson."

"Shepherd. Cohen. Nickels. James. Krakow. Watson."

Harry closed his eyes and lay back on his cot.

"Knuckles. Newsom. Miller. Jagodinsky. Bridenhagen."

After a pause, the clerk yelled, *"Miller.* Pvt. Harold Miller."

Harry stuck his head out of the tent.

"Miller—Harold. Private *Harold M. Miller."*

Shorty waved. "Harry, you've got mail."

Harry pushed through the crowd, forgetting he was clad in his boxers until Nickels said, "Sure like your outfit, Miller."

Shep slapped him on the back. "I can't believe it—somebody wrote you. Maybe it's Shelly, wanting to make up."

"Her name's Helen." Harry thought about slugging him.

He grasped the envelope and caught the faint scent of perfume. *I can't remember the last time I smelled anything feminine.* The address, written on the floral-patterned envelope, had a slanted handwriting. It didn't bear a Wisconsin postmark, but a smudged Louisiana town. It was dated August 16, 1941—just two days ago. It was clearly addressed to him with his correct serial number and APO address. Letter in hand, he tried to pass nonchalantly through the crowd. Once past, he glanced at the return address.

E.B.R.
General Delivery
Bundick, Louisiana

He sliced open the envelope. What's a *Bundick,* Louisiana? The letter featured the same slanted handwriting:

Pvt. Miller,
Recently, your convoy passed through DeRidder,
you tossed a bulett with your name on it.
You through it and said, "Write me."
After much thought, I've writen you.
I'm a schoolteacher living near DeRidder.
I'm an old-fashioned girl who enjoys making friends.
If you'd like, I'll gladly be your pen pal.
Send a photo, and I'll send one of me.

Sincerely,
Elizabeth Reed.

Harry held the letter up to the sunlight as if there might be some hidden message in it. Glancing past the mess tent, he saw The Three Musketeers—Shep, Halverson, and Nickels—watching him like three hungry buzzards.

Shep cupped his hands. "Is it the bow-legged one or the old maid teacher?" Harry walked behind a tent, re-reading the letter, wincing at the various misspellings and shaky penmanship. *I sure thought a schoolteacher would write better than this.* He tried to envision what 'Elizabeth Reed' might look like, but could only see Miss Crump, an old maid schoolteacher who'd spent a long career torturing second graders like himself back in Milwaukee. She was just the kind of person who'd happily write a young soldier, and *she* was just the type no red-blooded soldier would want to write back. Harry closed his eyes. It'd be like being pen pals with *your own grandma.*

He glanced again at the handwriting. It looked as if someone's grandmother *had* written it. Stuffing the letter in his pocket, he tried to shake the image of an old schoolteacher contentedly passing her evenings writing lonely soldiers.

This image faded and was replaced by Shep's vivid description of the leggy good-looking girl on the DeRidder street. One image nearly nauseated him; the other made his heart beat just a little bit faster. Which—if either—of these images most resembled the *real* Elizabeth Reed?

Harry wasn't sure, but he intended to find out.

Chapter 8

I'll Fly Away

Nearing the soldiers' camp, Ben hefted the hamper of army fatigues to his other shoulder. Twenty steps ahead, Jimmy Earl toted a cardboard box of soldiers' underwear. The brothers were delivery boys for their mother's washing and ironing business. Jimmy Earl covered his hamper with a towel as an approaching convoy stirred up a choking cloud of dust.

Ben trotted to catch up. "How much does Momma get for taking in their washing?"

"Nickel an item."

Ben watched the crate-laden transport trucks pass. "Look how there's a chocolate soldier driving every one of them."

"Yep, that's basically what they have Colored soldiers doing." Jimmy Earl fanned the dust. "Driving trucks and slinging slop."

"Why's that"?

"Some folks think that's all they can do. Word is that they won't let them fly planes either."

Ben knew that flying was his brother's dream. "Will they let a Louisiana farm boy like you or me fly?"

"I hope to find out." Jimmy Earl froze. "Listen."

"To what?"

"A plane—coming in low."

"I don't hear nothing but trucks."

Jimmy Earl saw it first. "It's an A-24. Banshee dive bomber." He jerked Ben into the ditch. "It's coming for the trucks." The staccato burst of machine gun fire erupted from the enemy plane, identifiable by red markings on its wings and fuselage. It was screaming out of the sky at an impossible angle and speed that could only end in a crash.

Just as it pulled out of its dive, the plane dropped a large object. Evidently, the lead truck saw it and veered into the ditch, nearly hitting the boys. Ben watched, slack-jawed, as the hurtling projectile tumbled toward the second truck. The flour bomb hit square on the hood, exploding into a cloud of white powder. *Dead hit.* Jimmy Earl yelled.

The driver, blinded by the flour, careened wildly into the ditch, crashing through a clump of scrub oaks. Shouting and cursing soldiers poured from the trucks, firing their weapons wildly at the disappearing plane. Ben turned to Jimmy Earl. "I've never heard that bad word used like that before."

"Don't repeat it to Momma or you'll be belching soap for a week." Jimmy Earl pointed at a scout car driving into the chaotic scene. "Look, it's an umpire vehicle." An officer climbed out of the car and began taking notes.

"What's an umpire?"

"It's a control officer—an umpire—they decide who wins the skirmishes."

Ben searched the sky. "How'd you know the plane was a Banshee?"

"I know my planes. One of the soldiers gave me an identification book and I've studied it."

The umpire rapped the truck hood with his clipboard. "This vehicle is out for the day."

A corporal stepped forward. "Sir, it's our mess kitchen truck."

"Doesn't matter. It's out of action." The umpire walked to the truck and removed its blue flag.

"But it's got our food . . . and cooks."

The umpire's mouth was tight. "All are out of action for the remainder of the day."

"But what will we eat?"

"That's what they make K-rations for." He motioned to a soldier in the scout car. "Franklin, I'm assigning you to guard this mess truck. It's not to be moved or used."

The unhappy soldiers loaded into the trucks leaving behind their mess kitchen and cooks. Ben whistled. "Something's rotten in . . . uh, DeQuincy. They're not one bit happy." He watched the vehicles driving off. "That was something to see."

Jimmy Earl lifted the box of underwear. "It wasn't real. Only a flour bomb and the soldiers were shooting blanks."

"It seemed real, didn't it?"

Jimmy Earl was staring off into the horizon. "Little brother, I done made up my mind—I'm *joining*—"

"*Joining* the army?"

"Yep, I'm not waiting until they draft me."

"But you're too young."

"I'll find a way."

"What about Poppa and Momma?"

"I'm joining the Army Air Corps. I'm gonna fly."

"*Fly?* You ain't never even been in a plane."

"Nope, but I will." He put the box on his shoulder. "I promise you I will, and I'm gonna be up there dropping flour bombs instead of being on the business end of them here on the ground."

Ben knelt at the large flour outline on Tram Road, picking up the shredded sack. "But you can't leave. What will I do without you?"

"You'll do fine."

They delivered the clothes to the camp, collected their money and began the long walk home. As they passed the mess kitchen truck, three of the cooks and the guard were playing cards in the shade and another was cooking on a portable stove.

"Looks like they're gonna make a good day of it," Jimmy Earl said.

Ben wafted the aroma with his hand. "I love the smell of bacon frying in the morning."

"There's an unhappy group of soldiers that won't have any bacon tonight." Jimmy Earl stopped at the crossroads. "You run on home. I'm gonna stop by the airfield."

Ben scowled. "Why can't I go?"

"This is pers'nal."

"What is it?"

"You said that I'd never flown in a plane. I'm fixin' to do something about it." He turned to Ben. "Scout's honor, you won't say a word?"

"It'll cost you."

Jimmy Earl nodded toward home. "There's a Milky Way candy bar hidden in my sock drawer."

"And I want a cold chocolate soldier from the store."

His big brother flipped him a nickel. "You sure drive a hard bargain."

"My lips are sealed." Ben continued down the road, singing,

"I may never zoom o'er the enemy,
Shoot the artillery, march in the infantry.
I may never ride in the cavalry,
But I'm in the Lord's Army."

That afternoon Ben was still singing when he came out of the henhouse, carrying a basket of yard eggs. He peered through the chicken wire at the biddies they'd picked up last week, singing,

"I'm in the Lord's Army. Yes Sir!
I'm in the Lord's Army. Yes Sir!"

Hearing voices, he sat his basket down and crept to the barn.

"Poppa, you just don't understand." It was Jimmy Earl. Ben crawled where he could see. His father was grooming Dolly, their dun mare, while his brother sat milking Flo. Because their backs were turned, Ben scampered unseen up the loft ladder. Being barefoot was a real asset for creeping, a skill at which he excelled. He crawled to a crack in the loft and looked down just as Poppa held up his currying brush.

"J.E., if you'd listen to me, it could sure make life easier for you."

"I *am* listening, but I've got to live my own life."

Poppa moved down Dolly's flank. "I've been in the army and know what it's like. I don't want you to be no part of that."

Jimmy Earl carried the milk stool and pail from Flo to Pet, sitting with his back to Poppa. The only sound for the next minute was the rhythmic squirt-squirt-squirt of milk splashing in the metal pail. This brooding silence made Ben's skin crawl. Finally, his father softly said, "Its name was Precious."

"What's Precious?"

"Its name was Precious. It was a horse and the sound of it screaming still tortures me." He continued currying Dolly. "I've never got it out of my mind, and it's been a bit over twenty-year-ago."

Jimmy Earl moved the milk pail and walked to the other side of Dolly and began stroking the mare. "Poppa, you're talking about the Great War?"

Poppa stopped his brushing. "I've always been bothered by the fact that a horse dying disturbed me more than men being blown to pieces. Yep, they called it 'the war to end all wars.' What a joke." Poppa knelt to examine Dolly's foreleg. "It was 1917. I was so excited to get out of these woods, go across the Big Pond, and serve my country. I wasn't even that scared, but when we marched to the front lines and I heard that screaming, I knew it was a bad place. I'd never heard such terror-filled sounds and wasn't even sure what it was at first."

Jimmy Earl leaned over Dolly's withers. "What happened?"

"The horse was pulling an ammunition cart when a shell struck nearby. The explosion knocked it to the ground and shrapnel cut it up. It lay there thrashing and screaming, but we couldn't get to it due to the artillery barrage. The cart driver had dove into the trench with us and was crying out, 'Precious, Precious.' Finally, a veteran in the trench sighted his Springfield on the twisting head and put the horse out of her misery.

Poppa stood up. "J.E. I can still hear it in my mind. That war showed me about the cruelty of men against men, and how we'll take animals God made and expose them to that same cruelty." He patted Dolly's back. "I've heard that tanks, trucks, and that thing called the 'jeep' are gonna make Army horses obsolete. I hope it's true. They don't deserve to be put in the middle of men killing each other."

"Did you see many men die, Poppa?"

"Every day—and *every day* I expected to be the next one." He resumed working on Dolly's leg. This was the most Ben had ever heard his father talk about the war. "Jimmy, I'm still bothered by how I remember the horse's name—*Precious*—and I've forgotten names and faces of the men who died next to me."

"It's because of how you—how we—love horses, Poppa."

"Yeah, but I should love people a lot more."

"You do. It's just, uh, different." There was hesitancy, even an uncertainty, in Jimmy Earl's voice.

Poppa reached across Dolly, placing his hand on his son's shoulder. "Can't you understand why I don't want you to be part of no war?"

"I can, but—"

He cut him off. "Can't you understand why folks like me agree with Lindbergh? We've been to Europe and *seen* what war is like. It's to be avoided whenever possible."

Jimmy Earl leaned across Dolly. "But what if that war *can't* be avoided?"

"Right now it can be, so let's do what we can to keep it that way."

"Poppa, I've just about made up my mind to join the army. They're gonna draft me sooner or later anyway."

"Your mind's *nearly* made up?"

"No sir, it's *made* up."

Poppa looked away. "That's not what I wanted to hear."

"I won't be eighteen until the spring. I could lie about my age and get in now, but that's not how you brought me up. I'm asking for your permission to join up."

"When?"

"Now."

His father's shoulders sagged like a deflating balloon. "I won't stop you, J.E.—I *can't* stop you, but I would like to suggest something." Poppa stepped around the horse. "I'll call it a 'compromise'."

"What is it?"

Poppa scanned the barn area, settling on the loft. "Let's take a walk. I don't want any rats in this barn to hear." Ben drew his face back from the crack. Did he know who was up there?

Jimmy Earl touched Dolly as they passed. "Poppa, it's true about the outside of a horse being good for the inside of a man, ain't it?"

"It's the truth." Ben loved how his father and brother had an unbreakable bond in their love of horses. They both had what Ma called "a gentle touch." It was as if Dolly had been part of the melting of hard hearts he'd just seen.

He scooted to the loft door, carefully peering around the opening as his father and brother walked from the barn, with only a milk bucket bumping between them. His father, a man of few physical emotions, put his arm around Jimmy Earl's shoulder. His brother changed hands with the bucket and draped his arm across Poppa's shoulder.

Getting up from his perch, Ben Reed inhaled the barn's strong smells of horse sweat, hay, and fresh manure. From below in the now-empty stalls, a new odor wafted up. Ben wasn't quite sure what it was, but he believed it smelled like love. Whatever it was, he liked it. He'd prayed hard during the last week for Poppa and Jimmy Earl. Through the slats in a barn loft, he'd watched that prayer be answered. He ran out of the barn as fast as he could, not slowing down until he leapt onto the porch. Good news like this had to be shared.

Chapter 9
Best Laid Plans

I've made up my mind. I'm going to take that job.

Elizabeth stood at the bedroom window watching Ben come out of the barn. The late evening sun cast long shadows behind him as he ran toward the house.

She stepped away. *How will my leaving affect him? I can't worry about that—it's time to finally do something for myself. It will be easier for everyone if I'm not teaching him this year.*

Elizabeth slept great that night, waking up with this clear determination: today is the day. The day she was going to accept the job in Shreveport. She'd tell her family the news this afternoon after she'd made it official. Besides, she didn't need their permission to do this. It was her life.

She walked to the post office, signed contract in an envelope. Each step released another pound of the massive weight she'd been carrying. This was the *right* decision at the *right* time. After mailing the contract, she'd go to DeRidder and hand in her resignation. While in town, she'd call the Shreveport office to confirm her acceptance. Calling from DeRidder would ensure privacy on her call. She wouldn't chance using the local phone because Aunt Maudie and her "eavesdropper club" would be spreading the news before she hung up.

Nearing the post office, Elizabeth made a detour—one last visit to her classroom. She hesitated at the door before easing into the unlocked building, her footsteps echoing in the empty hallway. This building, normally filled with the sounds of students, was eerie when empty. She stopped—was someone else in here? She stood stock still, finally convincing herself she was alone.

Holding onto the wall for support, she slipped into her room. Everything was how she'd left it two weeks before. Each of the thirteen desks was arranged in rows with the nametags she'd made. She walked down the first row touching each nametag. Jack Bailey. Sarah Harper. Addie Young. Jessie Cooley. She continued up row two. Bunk Bailey. Myrtle Weeks.

She stopped at the third desk and lifted the nametag. "Ben Reed." Holding it, she fully realized how she'd dreaded teaching her younger brother, knowing it would've been a yearlong wrestling match between two strong-willed siblings.

That problem would be solved today. He would be in this classroom, but she wouldn't. Her classroom would be in Shreveport. Not having to teach her baby brother was another good reason to leave. But if this decision was so cut and dry, why was there a clinging sadness as she held his nametag?

She studied the walls. Who would be the new teacher in her classroom? She corrected herself. This is not *my* classroom. At least not any more. She flipped Ben's nametag back on the desk and hurried out, each step on the creaky wooden floor faster as she put distance between that desk, the school, and her life in Bundick. She was going to Shreveport, and *everyone* would be better off for it.

She hoped the postmistress, Gertie Spears, might be taking a coffee break. Like the telephone party line, Mrs. Gertie was a source of constant local information. She was Elizabeth's second-cousin-twice-removed as well as the community's worst gossip. Getting this letter mailed without Cousin Gertie's knowing would be like slipping the sunrise past a rooster. The letter had a pre-addressed return so she could simply slip it in the mail slot and scamper off. At the steps, she dug in her purse for the letter and someone plowed into her from behind.

"Hey, watch where you're going." She was in the hug clutch of her grandmother. "Ma, I'm sorry." She tried to put the letter behind her back. "My mind was a thousand miles away."

"Evidently." Ma squeezed Elizabeth's shoulder. "And why would your mind be a hundred miles away?"

"I said 'a *thousand* miles.'"

"Either way. A hundred or a thousand's about the same once you're away from your nest."

"I've got a lot on my mind." Elizabeth avoided her grandmother's eyes.

"Evidently." She smiled. "Your PawPaw was asking for you this morning."

"Really?"

"I bet he said your name five times. Why don't you walk home with me and see him?"

"Sure. I just need…"

Ma patted her shoulder. "To mail your letter? Go ahead." Elizabeth turned to see Mrs. Gertie, wearing a curious vulture-like grin, standing at the window. Elizabeth whispered, "That old-goat-twice-removed heard every word." She stuffed the envelope back in her purse. "I'll mail it on the way back."

She always had mixed emotions about seeing her PawPaw. Before his stroke, he called her "the cat's meow" and she reveled in being his favorite. Since last year's stroke and his subsequent bed-ridden state, this once-robust man had become a shell of what he'd been. The pain of seeing him this way always resulted in a cold stone in the pit of her stomach and she always had to force herself to visit him.

As she eased into his room, the stone grew into a sharp-edged boulder. At the sight of her, his lips quivered and a tear rolled down his left cheek. Before the stroke, he'd hidden his emotions, but now it seemed as if a lifetime of withheld tears was leaking out his good-side eye.

He mouthed her name, "Liz-zi," holding out his left hand. Elizabeth leaned down and kissed him on the cheek, smelling the strong odor of Cotton Boll tobacco. Pulling a straight chair beside his bed, she began softly stroking his arm. He could hardly speak and she couldn't speak without breaking down, so their visits were mainly silent.

His eyes still showed the deep love he had for her. It was an unbreakable connection that no stroke or illness could shake. She whispered, "I love you, PawPaw." They both began crying quietly. The only difference was that her tears flowed from both eyes; his big cow tears poured down one cheek. He pulled her close with his good arm. "Don-go." Elizabeth was astounded at how strong his grip was, even after a year in bed.

"Don-go."

"Pa, I'm in no hurry to go."

He waved his hand, gesturing wildly toward the wall. "Don-go."

Ma came to the door. "You're mighty talkative today, Spencer Reed."

"He's insisting I not go."

Once again, "Don-go."

"See?"

Ma wiped his drooling mouth with her apron "He loves company, especially yours." She kissed him. "What are you trying to say, Honey?"

His voice was hoarse but it was the same two words—"Don-go" accompanied by frantic gesturing at the wall.

Ma followed his arm. "Spencer, what are you pointing at?" He babbled on. She shrugged. "It's definitely a direction or place he's pointing toward."

Ma turned to him. "That's the north wall. Are you pointing north?" He nodded and his eyes brightened. She shrugged. "Lizzie, I don't understand."

"I think I do, Ma." Elizabeth stepped to the bed. "Let me talk with him alone."

"Alone? I'm the only one who can understand him."

Elizabeth walked her grandmother to the door. "I need to be alone with him."

Ma waved her hands in disgust. "All right, every tub sits on its own bottom."

Elizabeth wearily sat in the bedside chair. "PawPaw, I know you're pointing north for some reason." He smiled. She was on the right track. "Your sense of direction has always been perfect. You taught me how moss always grows thickest on the north side of trees."

She stroked his face, bringing a wink and then a tear from his eye.

"Are you trying to tell me something? Are you telling me not to . . ." She rubbed her throbbing temples. " . . . not to take that job in Shreveport?"

He kicked the bed sheets with his good leg. Elizabeth's voice cracked. "How did . . . you know?"

"Don-go, Lizzi." He resumed waving his arm toward the north wall, doing it so vigorously that he nearly rolled himself out of bed.

"You're telling me *not* to go to *Shreveport*?" He shook his head as tears poured from his good eye. She had to know for sure. "Are *you*—telling *me*—I *should* go?"

"Nooo. No."

"So—*you're* telling *me not to go*?" She leaned in close. "Nod your head three times if that's it. Nod if you're telling me not to take the job in Shreveport."

He slowly moved his chin up and down three times before grunting. "Don-go." He lay back, exhausted at getting his message past the silent cage surrounding him.

Elizabeth's heart felt like a punctured balloon. The confidence she'd possessed early that morning had poured out, leaving only emptiness and uncertainty. It also felt as if all of the oxygen had been sucked out of the room. She was choking and had to get out of here. She also felt a rising anger toward the man in this bed. He was puncturing her dream.

She pecked his cheek. "I love you, PawPaw. I'll see you later." She didn't look back. At the door, she heard his raspy voice. "Don-go." She angrily slammed the door, brushing past Ma.

"Lizzie, what's wrong?" Elizabeth didn't stop even as Ma grabbed for her. "You're upset. What happened?"

"I'll be fine." She turned at the porch. "I just need to clear my head."

"You can talk to me."

"I will . . . but not right now."

Ma wiped her hands on her dress. "It's your call. Every tub sits . . ."

Elizabeth cut her off. "I don't want to hear that." She felt for the letter in her pocket and waved. "I've got to get to the post office before Mrs. Gertie closes it."

Three hours later Elizabeth stood behind four soldiers in a DeRidder pay phone line. As each G.I. left, she glanced at the lobby clock. Did the Shreveport school board office close at four or five? It was now nearly four and only one soldier was ahead of her. Finally, he ran out of change before he ran out of steam. He winked, brushing up against her as he went by.

She wiped the receiver with her kerchief. It was still warm from the soldier's breath. She looked at the clock. 3:57 PM. Her hand shook as she dialed 0. "Operator, would you connect me to ME5-6579?" She deposited the coins into the slot, each one clinking metallically into the phone.

"Caddo Parish School Board. May I help you?"

"Yes Ma'am. I need to speak with Mr. John Doughty, please." She scanned the lobby glad to see it empty. When a voice came on the line, she cleared her throat. "Mr. Doughty, I'm calling about your job offer at Byrd Elementary. Until today, I planned on accepting your generous job offer, but things have happened and . . ." Once again, she was in a room with no oxygen. Struggling for breath, she croaked, "Regretfully, I'm going to decline it."

It didn't even seem that it was her voice. She glanced at the contract beside the phone. "No sir, my mind is made up."

He curtly said, "You do realize this opportunity may not come again?"

She leaned her forehead against the wall. "Yes Sir. I do." She softly placed the receiver in its cradle. *I will not cry, and I will not be bitter.*

She walked to a nearby restroom and washed her face. Staring into the cracked mirror. "I'm not going anywhere. I'll be right here."

An accusing voice seemed to taunt, *but what about Bradley?*

She walked away before returning to the mirror for one last self-statement. "I was looking for a reason to stay. Pawpaw gave it to me. I never belonged up there anyway. I'm staying."

But a word from the telephone call rang in her heart. *Regretfully.*

It was a word she knew well.

Chapter 10

The Hayfield

Ben Reed was playing marbles with his best friend, Mal Cooley, when he heard a vehicle coming up the Cooley driveway. "It sounds like a jeep."

Mal pocketed his marbles. "Pa said if that soldier came back, he was gonna shoot him." He ran toward the house. "Let's go see it."

The two boys stood in the driveway where the jeep, carrying two soldiers and a civilian, stopped. As one of the soldiers walked to them, Mal whispered, "He's the captain that Pa ran off last time."

The officer wiped his hands on his fatigues. "Is your father home?"

Mal gestured toward the porch. "Yes Sir. He should be coming out that door with his shotgun any moment."

On cue, Mr. Cooley appeared, shotgun cradled in the crook of his arm. The Captain retreated toward the jeep as Mr. Cooley advanced. "I thought I told you not to come back."

The middle-aged civilian, dressed in a white shirt with suspenders, stepped out of the jeep. "Mornin' Mr. Cooley. How are y'all today?" Ben knew he was a local from his mannerisms and speech.

"Fair to middlin'. And you?"

"Doing fine." He calmly walked toward the house as Mr. Cooley left his shotgun on the porch and met him at the gate.

The civilian offered his hand. "Mr. Cooley, I'm Marvin Beavers." Mal's father stood with his hands on his hips. Beavers seemed unfazed. "I know you've turned us down about the Army using your hayfield—"

Mr. Cooley spat a stream of tobacco juice. "You done come to a goat's house looking for wool. I ain't changed my mind." He pointed to the east. "I want those planes *gone*."

Beavers, sporting a serene smile, said, "I respect that, but—"

Mr. Cooley jabbed a finger toward the jeep. "And I told your buddy not to come back."

Mr. Beavers raised his hand. "Mr. Cooley, I *made* the Captain come with me. Told him he'd have to come or lose his job. You wouldn't want that, would you?"

Mr. Cooley shrugged. "I guess I can't blame him for followin' orders."

Beavers took out a folder. "We've got a new offer that might change your mind."

"Doubt it."

Ben and Mal climbed a nearby mimosa tree, watching as Beavers spread the papers on the hood of the jeep. "Come take a look."

Mr. Cooley followed him to the jeep. "I got a complaint on those aeroplanes landing at my hayfield. They're scaring all of my chickens. My hens ain't laid since the first plane flew over."

Beavers looked up from his papers. "Is that so?"

"It is, and one of my cows done had a miscarriage 'cause of them." The veins on Mr. Cooley's neck bulged. "I own the sky above this place—at least as high as my gun will shoot. I don't want *no* more planes flying over my barn."

Beavers scanned the sky. "Mr. Cooley, I can't promise you that. I've come prepared to offer other things, but that's not—"

"Well, if I shoot one down, it'll be no fault of mine."

Captain Blaze stepped from the jeep. "I wouldn't recommend shooting at our planes."

The civilian flashed a stop sign at the captain. "Let me handle this." He calmly turned back to Mr. Cooley, "Now about your hayfield lease—"

The farmer snorted. "By the way, Mister. This ain't a hayfield—it's my lespedeza field."

"*What?*"

"*Lespedeza.* Japanese clover. It's *my* pride and joy. I ain't interested in your money— my cows can't eat dollar bills. They need lespedeza." He jabbed a bony finger toward the airfield. "And your rubber-band planes are tromping it down." As he spoke, an observation plane from the airfield roared over the barn. Geese, chickens, and guineas scattered noisily, as Mr. Cooley sadly shook his head. "See what I mean?"

The papers fluttered to the ground and Beavers said, "Mr. Cooley, could we go inside?"

"Well, I guess so." He hesitated. "It was right rude of me not to invite you in." As he led them to the house, he sneered at the captain. "Normally, I wouldn't offer Captain-Whistlebreeches a cup of cold coffee, but since he's with you, I'll tolerate him."

The Captain said, "If you don't mind, first I'd like to use your bathroom."

Cooley called to Mal. "Son, take this man out to see Aunt Sally." Ben could see the Captain's confusion as well as Mr. Beavers' amused smile.

"Who's Aunt Sally?" the Captain said.

"It's where my boy's taking you—to our outhouse."

"Outhouse?" The captain was hopping on one foot.

"Yep, see it over there?" He pointed to a dilapidated leaning structure. Even Ben, a rugged country boy, avoided the Cooley outhouse, a haven infamous for black widows, wasps, and chicken snakes.

The Captain weakly said, "I believe I can wait."

As the men went inside, the two boys hurried over to inspect the jeep. The driver, standing beside it, said, "You call your outhouse 'Aunt Sally'?"

"Poppa always says that he's going to see Aunt Sally when he heads out there." Mal proudly said. "Do you need to go see Aunt Sally?"

"Ain't no way." The driver removed his helmet.

Ben recognized him. "Hey, you're Jeep 1931."

"Do I know you?"

"You don't remember me? I'm Ben. We met on the street corner in D'Ritter."

"DeRidder?"

"Yep, D'Ritter. I had a crate full of biddies."

The driver slapped his forehead. "I just about ran over you, didn't I? If I remember right, you had a fine-looking sister."

Ben proudly tapped his chest. "That's me, and what's your name?"

"I'm Corporal Clyde Lawrence."

"And you're from Moline, Illinois, ain't you?"

"You've got a good memory." The soldier reached out his hand. "Tell me your name again."

"I'm Ben. Ben Reed."

Driver Lawrence strolled to the shade, sat, and unfolded a newspaper. "If the Red army sneaks up, come wake me."

Mal slipped to the base of the tree and whispered to Ben, "Follow me." There was a stack of firewood between the resting jeep driver and the boys, allowing them to crawl directly behind him where Mal said, "Surrender or die." The soldier jerked upright, grabbing for his pistol, as he hit his head on a low limb. Mal held a pine knot gun in the soldier's face. "We caught you off guard."

"You boys ought to be in a patrol unit." The soldier was grinning.

"Maybe we *are*." Mal leaned on the jeep. "Mister, you're kind of jumpy, ain't you?"

The driver patted his sidearm. "It's not good to slip up on an armed man."

Mal fired back. "And it's not good for an armed man to let two boys get the jump on him." He flashed his pine knot gun. "Besides, we *are* armed, ain't we, Ben?"

Ben pulled his own wooden gun and cocked it with a click of his tongue. "Stand and deliver, Stranger."

The soldier touched Ben's gun. "What is that?"

"You ain't never seen a pine knot gun?" Mal scoffed.

The soldier held the pistol-shaped pine knot. "It does resemble a gun." He asked Mal, "What's your name?"

"Mal Cooley."

"I guess Mal stands for Malvin?"

"Nope, it stands for Mallard. *Mallard* Cooley."

"And he's got a brother named Teal," Ben said.

"Is that so?" The soldier suddenly pounded the hood. "Duck." Both boys shrunk back. "Got you back, didn't I?"

Mal returned to his jeep inspection, fiddling with the air valve on the front tire.

Corporal Lawrence followed him over. "Watch out. There's only one *lever* on it—and that's 'leave her alone.'" He winked. "That's what my daddy always said when I was fooling with something I shouldn't."

Mal pointed at the hood. "Why's US 1931 painted on it?"

"It's the jeep's ID number."

"Mind if we take a look under the hood?"

"No problem." Corporal Lawrence raised the jeep's hood.

Mal leaned in. "That's a mighty small engine."

"Small but powerful. It's a four-cylinder but can really carry the mail. It'll climb anything and is light enough to easily get out of a ditch. Only weighs a little over a half-ton." He tapped the five-gallon gas can attached to the rear. "The army that moves fastest will win the war."

"What war?" Ben said.

"The next war."

"Can you take us for a ride?"

"I'd love to but Captain wouldn't take kindly to it."

The porch screen door creaked open and the captain called out, "Corporal, what's that hood up for?"

He slammed the hood and jerked to attention. "Just recruiting two future drivers, Sir."

The three men—the Captain, the civilian Beavers, and Mal's father walked from the porch. Beavers patted Cooley's shoulder. "The Army really needs your hayfield for these maneuvers. I have permission to sweeten this deal."

"I'm listening." Ben noticed a different attitude in Mr. Cooley.

"First, the Army'll come in and fix your cattle guards." Beavers pointed down the rough drive. "Replace them outright. That'll take care of your cattle and horses getting loose." He paused. "Next, they'll have a bulldozer dig you a cow pond when we're finished with the airstrip."

Mr. Cooley squinted. "What will this cost me?"

Beavers waved the papers. "Nothing but signing these."

The country man rubbed his chin. "If the Army's willing to do that just for using my land, I guess I'm okay." . . . but there's one more thing I'll need 'fore I sign."

Beavers wrinkled his brow. "And what is it?"

"When they bring the bulldoozer out here, I wanna drive it."

"*Bulldoozer?*"

"Yep, the bulldoozer they'll use to dig my pond. I want to drive it a little."

"We can arrange for that." Beavers looked up. "If you'd like to drive the bulldoozer—I mean bulldozer." Ben saw the smile trying to break loose from the corners of Mr. Beavers' mouth.

The two men stepped to the jeep's hood where Mr. Cooley said, "Show me those papers." He studied each page, occasionally saying, "Hmmm" or "I see."

Ben leaned in Mal's ear. "Can your daddy read?"

"Not one word."

Finally, Mr. Cooley said, "Give me a pen." He x'ed his name on each spot Beavers pointed to.

Beavers placed the signed papers in a folder. "You've got my word on the cattle guards and cow pond."

"Your word's good enough for me, Mr. Beavers." He nodded toward the porch where his wife stood. "The missus and I appreciate it." He hollered back to the house, "Momma, we're gonna have us a fine cow pond."

The two men shook hands as Ben whispered, "Looks like the Battle of Cooley's Hill is over." He and Mal eased behind the jeep where he heard the Captain say, "Let's get out of here before the old coot changes his mind."

Beavers looked offended. "He won't. His word is his bond."

"Do you really believe that?"

"Sure I do. Captain, I've been around these parts a lot longer than you have. It's different out here in the sticks. Just because the Cooley family seems poor and backwards, doesn't mean they're not honorable."

The Captain grimaced. "I'm not sure who won."

"We *both* did. He got what he wanted, and so did we."

"I guess it'll work out as long as he doesn't shoot down any low-flying plane." The Captain scanned the sky. "Heaven forbid."

Beavers called over to Mr. Cooley. "Ride over with us to see the airstrip." The two soldiers and two civilians crowded in. They couldn't see Ben and Mal crawl up behind, waiting for the right moment. From this eavesdropping position, Ben heard Mr. Cooley say, "Captain, I want you to know I still don't like your government's *enema-domain.*"

"What?" the Captain stammered.

"You heard me. You and your government's *enema domain*—the right to take a fellow's land to build your army camps, and roads, and whatever."

"You mean *eminent* domain."

"Whatever you call it, I don't like it."

When the jeep cranked, the two kneeling boys latched on to the rear bumper with their feet and hands for a rough but wonderful ride to the airstrip. The jeep stopped at a grass strip where three planes were parked. As Lawrence stepped out of his jeep, he saw the two boys. "How'd you get here so fast?"

Ben hiked his thumbs in his overalls. "We're fast runners."

The two civilians, Beavers and Cooley, ambled over to where the future pond would go. A Sergeant approached the jeep and asked Lawrence. "Corporal, are you driving that crazy man?"

"What crazy man?"

The sergeant pointed at Mr. Cooley. "The nut that owns this hayfield."

The driver pointed at the civilians. "They've just finished working out the details for use of his hayfield."

"What about the calves?"

Lawrence turned. "What calves?"

Ben hadn't noticed the half-dozen calves bawling non-stop in a nearby field. In another pasture past the strip, a clump of momma cows was mournfully mooing. The sergeant stifled a yawn. "We haven't slept a wink the last two nights."

Ben pulled on Lawrence's sleeve. "Mr. Cooley's weaning his calves."

The sergeant turned toward Ben. "Yep, he's weaning them as revenge against us invading his hayfield. It's like psychological warfare we heard about at boot camp." The sergeant spat. "Two days ago the old rascal walked by the tents, leading a calf by the rope, smiling as he said, 'Evening, boys.' He led those six calves over here, and they've not stopped ten seconds in two days."

One by one, the calves started a new round of distressed lowing. The cows, equally pained, answered from their field.

Corporal Lawrence turned to Mal. "Son, do you think your old man did that on purpose?"

Mal dug both hands into his overalls pockets. "I ain't no mind reader."

Past the calf pen, Ben saw Jimmy Earl and Peg walking by. He whistled like a bobwhite quail and waved. Jimmy Earl walked to them while Peg stood at a distance.

"Corporal Lawrence, this here's my brother, Jimmy Earl."

The driver said, "Who's the pretty girl over there?"

"That's my sister, Peggy Sue." Ben said.

Jimmy Earl, always curious about machinery, circled the jeep. "Why's the year 1931 painted on it?"

"It's not a year. It's my ID number."

"1931 is the year I nearly died," Jimmy Earl said.

"What happened?"

"My appendix ruptured. I was six years old and just about didn't make it." Jimmy Earl moved around the jeep. "Mind if I take a look under the hood?"

"Not a bit." The corporal turned to Ben. "I'd like to meet your sister."

Ben, ever the matchmaker, walked to her. "Peg, come meet Corporal Lawrence." When she hesitated, he took her hand. "Come on, he won't bite."

Ben introduced her. "Corporal Lawrence, this is my sister Peggy Sue Reed."

Lawrence said, "Are you the same sister who brought him to DeRidder to get those biddies?"

"No, that was my twin sister, Elizabeth."

Ben, helping the conversation along, said, "They're not regular twins. They're confernal twins."

Lawrence said, "Did you say *confernal* twins?"

"He means 'fraternal twins.'" Peggy Sue grabbed for Ben's overall strap, but missed as Ben continued. "Ma—she's our grandma—says those kind of twins come from when folks have relations twice in one night."

Peg gasped and picked up a dirt clod, flinging it at Ben as he scampered for cover. "I'm gonna beat you to death with a crooked pine knot when we get home."

Lawrence laughed. "Be careful. He's armed."

Peg quickly changed the conversation. "Corporal, tell me about these little planes."

"They call them Grasshoppers. It's an L-4 Piper. They use it for scouting and observation. It's small enough to land just about anywhere."

Ben stepped closer. "Tell her—"

Peg shot him a frost-killing gaze. "Motor-Mouth Ben Reed, why don't you go play in those planes or something." He moved out of clod-range but not past earshot. Corporal Lawrence and Peg engaged in the silly small talk that people their age loved. His ears pricked up when he heard the soldier say, "Look, I . . . don't mean to be forward, but I'd like to keep in touch. Would you be interested in writing me?"

Peg's face relaxed into a wide smile. "You're not being forward, Corporal. I'd love to write."

"You can call me Clyde."

"Thank you, *Clyde*. By the way, no one calls me Peggy Sue. I'm just plain old Peg."

"It's nice meeting you, *Plain-Old-Peg*." They both laughed as Lawrence scribbled out his address. Ben noticed how the soldier's hands were shaking.

One of the planes taxied down the grass runway before gunning its engine and climbing into the sky. Ben hurried over to Jimmy Earl, who watched raptly until it disappeared over the horizon. He turned to Ben. "I talked that pilot into taking me up."

"You better ask Momma."

"What Momma don't know won't hurt her." He grinned. "I'm gonna fly in one of those planes if it's the last thing I ever do."

Ben, as usual, got in the last word. "Even if it harelips Charles Augustus Lindbergh?"

"Yep, even if it harelips both Charles Augustus Lindbergh *and* Franklin Delano Roosevelt."

Chapter 11
Grasshopper

Elizabeth stepped away from the clothesline as the sputtering plane came over the tree line. It was clearly in trouble—losing both speed and altitude—and heading right toward their garden. She turned to where Jimmy Earl was cutting okra and Ben was hoeing half-heartedly behind him. At the other end of the garden, Poppa was in the pea patch.

"That Grasshopper's coming in." Jimmy Earl dropped his bucket. The plane, trailing a thin ribbon of smoke, had chosen their field for a crash landing. Elizabeth tried to scream at Poppa, but the words stuck in her throat.

Ben yelled, "Poppa," but his back was to the plane. Jimmy Earl and Ben dropped their implements, and scampered out of the plane's path. The plane's momentum carried it through a barbed-wire fence, its tight strands snapping with a twang. It bounced in the air and came back down on the first row of okra. The landing gear began shearing off the tops of the plants, making a rhythmic "Pfft, pfft, pfft." When the fuselage touched down, torn okra plants flew in every direction as it fishtailed across the garden. It now entered the pea patch where Poppa was bent over. He turned just as the plane hit the second time. Trying to run, he tripped over the bucket and fell. As the skidding plane plowed through where he lay, the bucket flew into the air. The plane's wheels dug into the plowed ground, tossing up clods of dirt, dust, and blue engine smoke, skidding past the garden and through a second barbed-wire fence.

It was a chaotic scene: bellowing cows scattering in the second field, the garden obscured by a haze of dust and smoke. The plane sputtered to a stop in the cow pasture, its nose dug into the ground, tail sticking up vertically. Elizabeth sprinted to where her father had fallen, fanning the dust to find him. She tripped over his body. He lay straddled across a row, peas still in his hand. She knelt beside him, leaning down to see if he was breathing.

"Poppa . . . are you alright?"

There was no answer or movement. Jimmy Earl, standing behind her, said shakily, "I tried to warn him."

She turned and saw Ben, his mouth twitching. "Is he dead?"

She leaned closer. "No, he's breathing." Elizabeth ran her hands up and down his body, searching for any wounds or broken bones.

He weakly opened his eyes. "I . . . I'm—"

She touched his face. "Relax Poppa. We're all here."

He kept pointing, struggling to speak.

"Poppa, it's all right. Jimmy Earl and Ben are fine." She pulled them into view. "See?"

Struggling to breathe, he put his hand to his throat as Ben cried. "Poppa, say something."

He gasped, trying to form words. Jimmy Earl put his hand on his father's shoulder. "Poppa, are you alright?"

"Wind." He rose up on one elbow, gasping. "The fall . . . knocked . . . the wind . . . out."

"Did the plane hit you?" Jimmy Earl said.

"Heck, no. I fell."

"Are you OK?"

He sat up on both elbows, taking a deep breath. "I'm fine. . . ." He looked into the faces of his children. ". . . other than wetting my britches."

Jimmy Earl shook his head. "I thought for a moment you were a goner."

"What about that pilot and his plane?"

Jimmy Earl pointed across the field. "That Grasshopper ate our okra, but it looks in fair shape."

Poppa, his color and humor returning, studied the rows of flattened okra. "Ben, you said you were tired of cutting okra. Looks like the U.S. Army heard your *prayer* and sent a bombing raid."

Elizabeth watched the pilot climbing out of the small cockpit. "That pilot looks as if he's fine, but I bet *he's* the one that wet his britches." When the pilot removed his helmet, he didn't look old enough to drive a car, much less fly a plane. He looked even younger up close, and his wide grin reminded Elizabeth of an older Huck Finn.

He and Jimmy Earl seemed to know each other, talking as they moved where Poppa sat. The pilot took a knee. "Looks like I kind of messed things up."

"We'll get over it," Poppa said. "What about your plane?"

"Other than a bent propeller and its nose being buried in the ground, it's fine."

Jimmy Earl stepped in. "Poppa, this is Hiram Platt. I met him a few days ago at the airstrip. He's from Minnesota—the same town as your hero, Lindbergh. Little Falls, Minnesota.

Poppa shakily stood to his feet, limping toward the plane. "How much does that thing weigh?"

"A tad over eight hundred pounds."

"I've got a plow horse that weighs more than that."

The pilot, obviously proud of his plane, nodded. "That's why it's called the 'Grasshopper.' It's light and can land on a postage stamp."

Poppa glanced back over the okra patch. "I can see that. Sounded like your Grasshopper had a little cough."

"I don't know what happened. It started sputtering right after takeoff." The pilot pushed on the plane's fuselage. "It won't budge."

Poppa stepped back. "Son, it's stuck tighter than Bill's wet hatband, but we're going to git it out. He turned to the boys, "J.E., you and Ben go get our plow team." In about ten minutes, Jimmy Earl returned with the plow team. Poppa took charge, looping the lead ropes over the plane's tail. "Haw, Dolly. Let's pull it loose. Come on, Pete." The horses strained and the plane's nose broke free of the ground and was pulled out of the garden. Mr. Reed tipped his hat triumphantly. "All of that new equipment's good, but when it comes down to it, real *horsepower* still gets the job done."

The pilot saluted and brushed the dirt off the bent propeller. "But there's more than one kind of horsepower."

Poppa wiped his face. "I reckon there is, but I still trust my kind better than yours." He peered into the sky. "What are ya'll looking for up there?"

"We're tracking armor movements. Seeing how the tanks are holding up on the roads and trails. One of the main purposes of these maneuvers is proving tanks and jeeps can do better than horse cavalry."

Poppa kicked at the dust. "I wouldn't be too sure of that. When this dust turns to Louisiana gumbo mud, y'all's vehicles will be useless, but I've never seen a horse bogged down yet."

"Sir, cavalry horses didn't help Poland against the Germans."

"Well, this ain't Europe." Poppa pointed at the ground. "It's the home of mud that'll suck a vehicle under. I bet y'all will leave tanks buried in the mud before this is over."

The pilot pulled a map out of the cockpit. "The best way to cross Louisiana swamps is from the air."

Poppa put his hand to his ear. "Did you say riding a *mare*?"

"No, Sir. From *the air.*"

Poppa stared up into the sky before nodding at the grounded plane. "If you can *stay* in the air, that is."

Ben, standing behind Elizabeth, began singing in a falsetto voice,

Lindbergh, o what a flying fool was he.
Lindbergh, your name will live in his-tor-eeeee.

She playfully slapped at him. "Some people are always stirring up trouble."

He scooted away. "You can't run me off. I'm here to stay."

Elizabeth took a deep breath. I'm here to stay too. Staying here was the right thing to do, *wasn't it?*

A faraway voice accusingly whispered, *You've messed up.* The thick Louisiana mud seemed to be steadily sucking at her feet. She was here to stay. Only time would reveal if this had been the right decision.

Chapter 12

The Blues

Tuesday, August 19, 1941

"Where's your redbug line tonight?"

In answer to Shorty's question, Harry moved the letter he was writing, pulled up his pants leg and began scratching. "Up to my knees now."

Shorty sat on the tent floor. "Yep, redbugs love joints."

"Why's that?"

"It's always hotter there. Kind of like your underarms. Why aren't you trying my merkle bushes?"

"I tried it and the limbs scratched me worse than redbugs."

"You wait until they get to your waist, you'll wish you had." Shorty snatched up a photo of a smiling Harry in dress uniform. "You know you clean up pretty good." He flipped the photo on the floor. "Who are you writing?"

Harry held up the letter. "You think I'm crazy to be writing that girl?"

"What girl?"

"Elizabeth Reed."

"Who?"

"The schoolteacher who picked up the bullet and wrote me."

"Oh yeah—the one that you're not sure if she's old, fat, and ugly or," he coughed, "young, fat, and ugly."

"I know it's nuts, but I'm going for it." Harry squinted at the photo. "It does make me look like a smart-butt soldier."

"Maybe that's who you are."

"Thanks a lot. We'll see how it goes when she writes back."

"*If* she writes back." Shorty crossed his arms. "And *if* the photo is really of *her*."

Harry looked up. "*What?*"

"Have you ever thought about how Shep and his buddies might be behind that letter?"

Harry threw down his pencil. "You're making me sick."

"Mind if I read your letter?"

"Help yourself." Harry laid his Springfield rifle on a towel, removed the bolt action, took out the firing mechanism, and began carefully cleaning and oiling it, as his partner cleared his throat.

Shorty adjusted the lantern before clearing his throat.

"Dear Elizabeth,

I . . . received your letter and was . . . pleased at your reply.
I would love to start a . . . writing corr . . . corres."

Shorty's reading was like roll call, with each word painfully pronounced. Harry grimaced. "It's *correspondence*. Man, didn't you ever go to school?"

"No more than I had to."

He began again,

"I would love to start a writing correspondence with you. As you requested, I've en…closed a recent photo. I'm from Milwaukee, Wisconsin, and have been in Louisiana since . . . February. I look . . . forward to your reply.

Sincerely,
Harold Miller"

Shorty folded the letter and tossed it across the tent. Harry stuffed it in his pocket, changing the conversation: "So those redbugs—those chiggers—they like joints?"

"Better than a fat man likes cathead biscuits and sawmill gravy."

"Where'd you get all of these sayings?"

"It's just part of how we talk down here."

"You people are *strange*."

"You're the *crazy* one: writing a girl when you don't even know how she looks."

"You've got a good point. I'm not sending this letter." He laid his rifle down and stepped outside into the darkness. He took in the sights and sounds of the night. In the distance, hundreds of lightning bugs blinked on and off. Evidently they hadn't gotten the order that tonight was a blackout night. The two choruses—crickets and frogs—competed for top billing in a deafening musical duet he'd come to enjoy. It was as if the insects were in harmony with one another. In spite of being a city boy, Harry was entranced by the sounds and sights of the natural world in Louisiana.

Mixed in with these night sounds, he detected something else. It was music—the human kind. He walked further into the darkness, straining to hear. "Hey, Shorty, speaking of joints, come listen."

Shorty put his head through the flap. "Man, you're gonna step on a copperhead out here."

"Shh. Listen." Harry pointed to the southeast. "It sounds like music from a beer joint."

Shorty put his hand to his ear. "It's music from a Colored beer joint."

"Let's go check it out."

Shorty looked at his watch. "Curfew's in thirty minutes."

"Come with me."

"No way. I ain't getting mixed up in no trouble across that road. If they stay on their side, I'll stay on mine."

"I'll see you later, then."

Harry walked into the darkness as Shorty said, "Man, you're crazy. Remember, it's different across that road. You ain't no more welcome over there than they are over here."

"Oh, don't be ridiculous."

"Harry, this is Louisiana, not Wisconsin."

"They're both the land of the free and brave."

"There are different levels of freedom down here."

He waved him off. "I'll be fine." Nearing the road, he stopped at a garbage can. Pulling the letter out of his pocket, he removed his photo before crumpling the letter. Writing Elizabeth Reed had been a bad idea from the start. Anyway, it was probably a joke the guys were playing on him. He tossed the wadded paper in and replaced the lid. "Good riddance."

Harry slipped to the edge of the road, using the tall grass to hide from the passing sentry. When the guard was about fifty yards away, he sneaked across.

He followed the sound of the music and laughter, which led him to a wooded area near a row of tents. His heart beat loudly at the thrill of being somewhere he wasn't supposed to be. This was not his usual behavior, but the music drew him like a moth to a lantern. Creeping past a row of transport trucks, he entered the Quartermaster's Camp. To get caught in this area would mean trouble.

He knelt, watching the campfire from where the music was coming. He picked out a guitar, a banjo, a harmonica, and a bass drum keeping rhythm. There were several men singing, but one deep bass voice dominated the vocals. He counted eight black men huddled around the fire. Harry decided to listen from the cover of the trucks.

He hated the Army's segregation regulations. Everyone wearing the same uniform but never mixing. Training separately, traveling separately. It was stupid that he couldn't freely walk up and enjoy the music around the fire. Being from urban Milwaukee, he'd always been comfortable around Negroes. It was hard to understand why they weren't considered fit for anything but cooking or driving trucks. He figured a Colored soldier was as capable as a White one.

He picked out the deep voice singing,
"Harlem may not be heaven,
But it seems mighty close."

Several of the men howled and clapped as the singer continued,
"Yeah, Harlem may not be heaven,
But the Lord put lots of brown-skinned angels there."

The bass drummer smacked his washtub in a quickening beat. A tall soldier standing beside him played a washtub bass. Sitting amongst the three guitar players was the player that captivated Harry's ear. He was blowing on a harmonica. The soldier caressed it in his hands like a lover and produced a wailing sound and tone that stunned Harry. It was hard to describe. It was sad, then sassy and saucy, and it seemed to be calling his name.

"Don't move, or I'll shoot." The order didn't come from the harmonica but came from behind Harry as the cold steel of a gun pressed against his back.

He raised his hands. "No problem. I'm not trying to cause trouble."

As he turned, the gun dug deeper into his ribs. "I said, *don't* move." He should've listened to Shorty's advice and been back on his side of the road.

"Keep walking slow and steady over to the campfire. Hands on your head." As Harry and his captor walked into the light of the campfire, the music stopped as if directed by a bandleader's baton. They were all staring in disbelief. One of the guitar players laughed out loud. "Reuben, is that thing loaded?"

The gun dug into Harry's ribs. "*He* thinks it is."

Harry turned to see that he was being held at gunpoint by the end of a fiddle stick. The large soldier, a sergeant, grinned. "You shouldn't be sneaking around where you don't belong."

"Reuben caught him a poacher," The guitar player said.

Harry felt a mix of both embarrassment and relief. "How'd you ambush me?"

The big sergeant poked Harry with the bow. "I was out there taking a leak when you came by tromping like an elephant. I wasn't sure what you were up to, so I followed you." His eyes narrowed. "What *are* you doing over here?"

"I heard the music from across the road and just came to listen."

"You sure be a brave man slipping up here in the dark."

"Or a mighty foolish one," one of the others said coolly.

Harry walked toward the fire. "Look fellows, I'm not looking for trouble. I came over because I heard good music." He shrugged. "Following good music has got me in lots of trouble over the years."

One of the guitar players strummed a chord. "Same thing's true for me. It's kept me in trouble most of my live-long life." The circle of men hooted in agreement. The guitar player slapped Harry on the shoulder. "Come over here, and we'll all get in trouble together."

He played a chord and asked Harry. "What was that?"

"Key of G."

The player winked. "Gee what?" He strummed another chord.

"E minor, I think." Harry said.

"Pretty good ear. Come sit by me." Harry, hands in his pockets, took a seat on the log. The guitar player slid over. "My name's Willie. Do you play?"

"Not anymore. I used to play the violin—I mean the fiddle—but it's been a long time."

Reuben, the soldier who'd captured Harry, walked to the fire, dumping several limbs and pine knots on the fire. "Listen, Cracker. There's a price if you wanna hang with us." There was an uneasy silence. Harry scanned each man in the circle. Neither their faces nor the firelight revealed what this price might be.

"What is it?"

"You'll have to wait and find out. If you're not man enough to pay it, you can go back the way you came."

Harry sat still on the log. "I'm staying."

The guitar player sitting by Harry said, "Come on Reuben, cut him some slack."

The harmonica player broke the impasse by launching into a long bended blues run, then launching into a soulful solo that Harry knew came from the deep sorrow these men must have endured living in a White man's world—and an army tilted toward the White man. The other players began whooping and hollering as they joined in. It was simply wonderful. Harry didn't know the song; he didn't know if it was even a song, but he knew one thing: it was the blues.

After a few instrumental runs, the vocalist began,

> *"Got up this up this morning, looking fo' my shoes.*
> *You know about that: I had those old walkin' blues."*

He sang it like he'd lived it. Like he meant it, as the others moaned and swayed along. The song went on for probably fifteen minutes as each player took the lead. Everything about it was vibrant and real. It was different from the way Harry had learned music. No music sheets, no conductor, just raw feeling and emotion.

It was music from the heart. Music for the soul. The men passed around a bottle of whiskey. When it was offered to Harry, he said, "I better pass. That's what put me in the army in the first place."

Willie the guitar player snatched the bottle. "Well, I'll take yours and mine too." He held up the bottle. "This may've got you in the army, but it's what keeps me sane in this crazy army."

Several bottles and several hours of non-stop music later, Willie said, "Why don't you play Reuben's fiddle?"

Harry shook his head. "Not tonight. I don't want to break the spell. Maybe next time." He had no idea what time it was, nor did he care. The music was all that mattered. Even though it was completely different from his classical training, it transported him back home to his life before the Army. To his life before the accident—the accident that had ended more than a life. The accident that had ended Harry's dream of a musical career. He'd not played a violin since that night, and planned never to play again. It'd been so long since he'd been wrapped in the loving embrace of music, and tonight he realized how much he'd missed its loving caress.

This trance was broken when one of the soldiers stretched his arms. "I believe I see the first trace of light in the east." Willie strummed and sang, "Mmmm, everything's gonna be all right in the morning."

Reuben stood. "It's time for the benediction. Let's do it in a minor key." The players launched into a touching slow mournful song. Harry didn't recognize it, but was touched by its deep feeling:

> *"I am just going over Jordan,*
> *I am just going over home."*

When it ended, only the crickets were singing. Several of the men wiped away tears.

Harry stood. "That was beautiful. What was it?"

"It's called 'Wayfaring Stranger,'" Willie said. "It was my father's favorite song."

"I'd best slip back into my camp before things start stirring across the road."

Reuben spat. "Across the road." He walked up to Harry. "Now, it's time for you to pay your admission. I got a song for you." He cleared his throat.

"Airplanes flying cross the land and sea
Everybody flying but a Negro like me.
Uncle Sam says, Your place is on the ground,
When I fly my airplanes, don't want no Negro around."

There were about five verses, all reflecting the same theme. Reuben never took his eyes off Harry. "Now tell me, white boy, what key was that in?"

"The *wrong* key."

"What do you mean?"

"What you sang about isn't right."

"But that's the way it is."

"But that doesn't make it right."

Reuben moved closer. "Who'd you pull for when Joe Louis fought that German, Schmeling"?

"I was for Louis. He's an American."

"What about last month when Louis fought that white boy Conn."

Harry stood to his full height. "I pulled for Billy Conn. I'm half Irish."

Reuben grabbed Harry's arm. "You think when this war starts they'll let Joe Louis fight as a regular soldier? Hell, they'll have him loading trucks or slinging slop just like the rest of us."

"I just know I'd share a foxhole with Louis any day."

The harmonica player held up his instrument. "Listen brother, while *you're* getting shot by the Germans on the front lines, *I'll* be sitting in my truck playing this harp."

This broke the tension for everyone except Reuben. "Even if it means being on the front lines, I want to be thought of as good as any soldier. I was brought up to believe I ain't no better than any man." He put his meaty fist in Harry's face. "And there ain't no man better than me."

Reuben turned and strode toward the trucks. Harry surprised even himself when he said, "Wait, I've got a question for you." The sergeant stiffened. "What is the blues?"

Reuben turned to the tall bass fiddle player. "Ira Lee, you like talking so much. You tell him." Ira Lee hadn't spoken all night, and his voice was soft, slow, and relaxed. "The blues ain't nothing but a man feeling bad about a woman he once had."

Harry smiled. "That's the best definition I've heard."

"Ira Lee don't say much, but when he does, it's worth listening to," Reuben said.

Ira Lee kicked his washtub bass. "I just play my music and drive my truck. I was taught that actions speak louder than words."

Reuben walked to Harry. "Cracker, I got one more question." He pointed at one of the singers. "Hezekiah and me been having a running argument and need an outside source to settle it."

Harry looked at Hezekiah, then Reuben. "Shoot."

"Is the kind of music you been listening to all night—the blues—is it a good man feeling bad?" He pointed at Hezekiah. "Or a *bad* man feeling *good*?" Reuben, arms crossed and feet apart, stoically waited for an answer while his friend Hezekiah sported a half-grin. Was this a serious question or not?

Harry opened his arms. "All I know is that this bad man—me—came over here feeling bad, and now I'm leaving feeling better. Thanks."

"Blessed are the pure in heart, for they've had the blues." Hezekiah sang it.

Harry saluted. "I'd just about lost my song." He nodded at Reuben. "But tonight you men helped me start getting it back." He backed away into the dark and slipped along, watching closely for guards. He eased across the road toward his tent. It would be a short night but he had one more chore before turning in.

He reached into the garbage can, feeling around for the crumpled piece of paper. He held up his letter to Elizabeth Reed in the dim light of the morning and took a deep breath. "You'll never know if you can fly until you're willing to jump off the cliff."

Harry Miller slipped into his tent, whistling softly under his breath. He was getting his song back, and it sure felt good.

Chapter 13

School's Out

Three Days Later

Elizabeth crossed the low water bridge on her way to the Dry Creek post office. In spite of the late summer heat, she was glad to be in her beloved swamp. Birds were singing in the oaks, but she couldn't stop for long. The mosquitoes and horseflies would carry her off and she had two letters to mail before closing time. One was a Sears order for her mother and the other was Elizabeth's weekly letter to Dora in Shreveport.

She squeezed into the small area that served as their post office. "Morning, Mrs. Gertie. I need to purchase two three-cent stamps. Do we have any mail?"

"Looks like you've got a letter." Elizabeth took it outside, studying the strange envelope. It was definitely addressed to her. The postmark was two days ago and came from APO Ragley, Louisiana. Army Post Office? She scanned the return address. Private Harold Miller. *Who is Harold Miller and how did he get my address?*

Using her fingernail, she opened the envelope and a photo fell to the porch. Picking it up, she studied the smiling face of a young soldier. On second glance, she knew it wasn't a smile—it was a smirk. The jaunty angle of his cap matched the curling lips and confident eyes. *I don't know who he is, but I'll bet he thinks he's God's gift to women. Well, he won't get close to this woman.*

On second glance, she had to admit he was somewhat good-looking with a strong chin and piercing eyes. She unfolded the single-page letter, impressed with its neat penmanship.

Dear Elizabeth,

I received your letter and was pleased at your reply and would love to start a writing correspondence. As you requested, I've enclosed a recent photo. I'm from Milwaukee, Wisconsin, and have been in Louisiana since February.

I look forward to your reply.

Sincerely,
Harold Miller

She re-read the letter.

"I received your letter." *What letter? I didn't write a letter.*

" . . . start a writing correspondence." *I don't even know who you are.*

"Photo as requested . . ." *I didn't request any photo of you.*

She glanced up to see Mrs. Gertie in the doorway. "Elizabeth, that must be a powerful letter." The same smirk was on the postmistress's face as on the soldier's photo. In a syrupy voice, the woman said, "I like the way you read it aloud."

"Did I really read it aloud?"

"Yep, the second time."

"Mrs. Gert, I believe you're just as nosey as my grandma."

"I'll admit I'm pretty nosey, but I can't touch your grandma with a ten-foot pole."

Elizabeth held up the letter as a lawyer would a key piece of evidence. "I promise you one thing, Mrs. Gert. I'll be back before closing time." She waved the letter. "We're nipping this in the bud. I don't *know* who sent this, and what's more, I don't *plan* to.

Mrs. Gertie Spears leaned on the windowsill. "Well, if I'm closed or gone when you get back, just slide it under the door." Elizabeth waved the letter as her sign of goodbye and began the two-mile walk back home. Going through the swamp would give her a good chance to formulate her reply. It wouldn't take long to write. She would get right to the point.

Reaching the neck of the woods, she detoured to check on her grandparents. Coming up to their house, she heard Ben talking loudly in the kitchen. Entering the room, Elizabeth said, "Well, what are you two plotting today"?

"The retaking of Vicksburg from those Yam-Dankees."

"Ben, I'm going to wash out your mouth with coal oil."

Ma wiped her hands on her apron and led him toward the door. "General Beauregard, you'd best be going. I need to have a little talk with your sister." Walking past Elizabeth, he began whistling "The Battle Hymn of the Republic."

Ma threw up her hands. "Don't be whistling that yam dankee song!"

"Ma, you're the whole reason he uses that word!"

Ben stood poised at the screen door. "It's Elizabeth's favorite song. She especially likes my schoolteacher version of it." He cleared his throat.

"My eyes have seen the glory of the burning of the school.
We have tortured all the teachers and have broken all the rules.
We have smashed all the windows and broke down all the doors,
And it ain't my school anymore."

Elizabeth clenched her jaw. "Little brother, if I hear you singing that at school, or even whistling it, I'm going to whip you, then let Mr. Miller finish up. I promise."

He slammed the screen door behind him.

"Glory glory hallelujah, hit my teacher with a ruler.
Met her at the bank with a loaded army tank,
And she ain't my teacher anymore."

Elizabeth grabbed a handful of wet, purple-hull peas from the table and tossed them at the screen door as Ben sprinted for safe haven in the woods.

Ma rubbed her purpled fingers on her temples. "Lord, that boy can give me a my-grain-brain-aching-headache."

"Ma, it's *migraine*."

Well, whatever it is, he gives me one." She tossed a handful of hulls in the bucket. "But I do love the little rascal." She pulled out a chair. "Got time to help shell peas?"

"Yes, Ma'am."

"Where have you been?"

"Post Office."

"Any mail?"

"One letter." Elizabeth rubbed the envelope in her pocket.

"Who for?"

"It was to me."

"Is that so?" Ma's stare was unflinching. "Who was it from?"

"I'm not sure." Her grandmother seemed too interested, so Elizabeth moved the conversation. "Did you know they're not starting school until the first week in October?"

"That's official?"

"It is."

Well, it'll mean you'll have plenty of time in September," she gestured at the envelope sticking out of Elizabeth's pocket, "for writing letters."

"Ma, Is your middle name 'Nosey'?"

"No, you know it's Theodosia. Doshie for short."

"I'm going to call you "Nosey Doshie" from now on. You're as bad as Mrs. Gert."

"I admit I'm nosey, but I'm not *that* nosey."

Elizabeth set her pan on the table with a clang. "I'm tired of having all of this time on my hands."

Ma grasped Elizabeth's left hand. "Looks to me like you got purple on your hands, not time."

Elizabeth stood. "I've got to be going. There's a quick letter I need to write and mail."

"You could write it here. It'll save you making that long walk back."

Elizabeth washed her hands, closely watching Ma. "I believe I will stay and write it here. If you promise not to bother me about my business."

Ma slid a box of pastel stationary across the table. "My lips are sealed."

Chapter 14

The Same Creek

After mailing her terse reply to the mystery soldier, Elizabeth walked home satisfied that she wouldn't be bothered again. She'd made it perfectly clear.

Poppa was sitting with four soldiers on the porch. Most days after supper, a group from the nearby medical tent visited the Reed home, often bringing their laundry for washing and ironing, hanging around until Momma offered them some fresh biscuits and muscadine jelly. The soldiers enjoyed the good food, friendship, and flirting with Peg and Elizabeth—especially Peg.

Nearing the porch, she was surprised that one of the soldiers was a woman, dressed in a military nurse's uniform. She recognized the three men, who'd been frequent guests. "You fellows remember Lizzie-Beth?"

He turned toward the nurse. "Now, tell me your name again?"

"I'm Emily. Emily Larsen."

Elizabeth reached out her hand. "Welcome to our home. Where are you from?"

"Arizona. Yuma, Arizona."

The nurse was petite with short blonde hair and a winning drop-dead smile. Elizabeth knew she'd be busy fending off every soldier within twenty miles. "How long have you been here?"

"I arrived today from North Louisiana. I was stationed at Smith and before that, I was in Ruston."

"Smith? I never heard of that town?" Poppa said. "What's it near?"

The nurse blushed. "It's what we call… Natch… It's what you call 'Natcha—touch-us." She tried again. "Natch-tock-is."

Elizabeth stepped in. "Natchitoches. It's where I went to school. It's 'Nack-uh-tish'."

The nurse shrugged. "None of us can say the word right, so we call it 'Smith'."

Poppa laughed. "You call Natchitoches 'Smith'?"

Elizabeth felt that sickness in her stomach. She remembered how he—the soldier in Natchitoches—couldn't say the name either.

"You're from Arizona, so you're used to summer heat?" Poppa said.

She wiped her face. "Our heat's the dry kind. This heat sticks to you."

Elizabeth went inside and helped bring out coffee and water for the soldiers. On her second trip out, one of the medics was carefully inspecting Poppa's hand. He touched the raw wound and traced the red-streak that extended up his arm. "How'd this happen?"

"A shoat tusked me."

"A what?"

"A young hog cut me after we trapped it."

He gravely studied the cut. "This cut is badly infected. How long ago did this happen?"

"Four or five days ago."

"You've got to get it treated. You could lose your hand." He crossed his arms. "Come with me to our camp."

"Son, I can't come ri't now."

"Can you come in the morning?"

"I guess so."

"OK, be there at nine tomorrow and ask for me. My name is Crawford. We've got a new kind of medicine for infected wounds. It's a wonder drug." He stood. "It's really important to get it treated."

"He'll be there." Elizabeth said. Poppa glared at her, but she didn't flinch. She'd been pestering him about getting it looked at.

Momma came out, placing a large package of biscuits in Crawford's hands. "This is for your midnight snack."

Poppa leaned his good hand against the porch post. "How much will that medicine cost me?"

Crawford stopped at the gate. "Another batch of biscuits and some more jelly."

Poppa looked puzzled. "Did he say a hatch of eggs and some pork belly?"

Elizabeth rubbed her father's head. "We're going to buy you one of those tin ear horns so you can hear. It was a batch of *biscuits* and some more *jelly*." Poppa scratched his ear, and winked. Elizabeth was never sure what he didn't hear versus what he didn't *want to* hear.

"Poppa, I'm walking with the nurse part of the way home."

"Did you say you're walking to Rome?"

She tossed a dirt clod at him. "Sometimes I don't know what to do with you." He sat back in his rocker and waved her off. Elizabeth hurried down the lane to catch up with the group. She and Nurse Larsen fell back as they compared notes about their lives. Elizabeth stopped at the crossroads. "It's nice meeting you, Emily. I hope we meet again."

"I'm sure we will."

Elizabeth didn't sleep well that night, worried about her father's hand. At breakfast the next morning, she examined the wound. "Poppa, it's worse. That red streak's moving up your arm."

He clenched his fist. "I was thinking it was better."

"You *are* going to have it looked at."

"I've never liked hospitals. It's where people go to die."

"It's not a *hospital*—it's a medical headquarters."

"I'm afraid ol' Sawbones is waiting on me."

"You heard the medic say you could lose your hand. You're going, and I'm taking you."

He left the room mumbling. Momma sat down by her. "You can get him to do things no one else can—not even me, his wife of twenty-four years."

"It's just that I won't take no for an answer."

Peg, arms crossed, stood at the kitchen door. "It might be 'cause you two are just alike."

Elizabeth winked at her twin. "You think so?"

"Honey, I *know* so."

Poppa returned with his hat and boots. "Well, if we're going, let's get it over with."

They walked along the road in the early morning sunshine. He wiped his brow. "I'll be glad when the first cool spell blows through." He put his good arm around her shoulder. "Honey, I'm sorry for being ornery."

"Poppa, you are ornery, but I'm worried about you."

"And I appreciate it, Lizzie." As they approached the creek crossing, Elizabeth held up her hand. "I hear horses coming." She glanced at Poppa but he showed no recognition—his hearing was that bad. Just as they rounded the bend at the crossing, a squad of mounted cavalrymen loudly splashed into the creek. Their leader, a lean sergeant, rode over when Poppa said, "Where are you boys headed?"

"Scouting ahead looking for Patton's tanks." The sergeant, much older than the others, had a calm demeanor and polite smile.

Poppa stepped to the horse's side. "That's a fine mount."

The trooper proudly petted the tall chestnut. "This is Uncle Sam—been my partner for seven years—best horse I've ever had." He leaned down, removed his riding gloves, and extended his hand. "I'm Ed Regan. First Cavalry out of Ft. Bliss, Texas."

"Levon Reed, formerly of the 45th Division."

"I figured you for a Great War man. "

"Y'all didn't ride all the way from El Paso, did you?"

"No sir. We came by train."

"Mind if I pet him?" Poppa stepped to the horse, stroking its wet chestnut flank. "I hear tell this may be the end for horse cavalry."

The sergeant shifted, his cavalry saddle creaking underneath him. "That's what we keep hearing."

"What will they do with y'all?"

"The grapevine says we'll be transferred to the tank corps." The sergeant spat. "Word is the horses will be sold off, and you know what that means."

Poppa untangled several cockleburs from the horse's mane. "That makes me sick."

The sergeant turned back toward the column. "But Uncle Sam will never see a glue factory—or slaughterhouse—if I have anything to do with it."

Before she or Poppa could ask more, the cavalryman rejoined the ranks moving northward. Poppa pensively rubbed his chin. "This world's changing so fast it's hard to know if the changes are good or bad."

Elizabeth put her arm around him as they watched the cavalry squad trot up the trail. "Poppa, is it good or bad about the horses?"

"Both. Horses shouldn't be in the middle of fighting and killing." He slowly waded into the creek. "But our way of life—which has always been tied to animals—is fading away."

Elizabeth knew from his face, the subject needed changing. "They say you can't stand by the same creek twice. Do you really think so?"

He scooped up a handful of creek water, letting it pour between his fingers. "I know so. You can return to this creek, but it will have changed and so will you. I came back from France and expected everything to be the same as when I left in 1917, but it wasn't. Most of all, I'd changed. Everybody noticed it. It was like they expected me to cross an ocean, fight a war, and come back home and just pick up where I'd left off."

A lone plane was crossing the horizon, and he studied it a long time. "They had no idea what I'd seen." He sadly shook his head. "They had no idea what I'd done." He led her across the narrow footbridge and up the far bank. "You came back from Natchitoches changed."

"Poppa, I was in Smith, not Natchitoches."

He laughed. "Well, wherever you went, you came back different."

"You can't stand by the same river twice."

"Ain't it a fact?"

They walked up White Onion Hill to the medical camp. A large sign read: 53rd Battalion Medical HQ. Behind it were three large tents. She noticed how her father's hands were shaking. "What's wrong, Poppa?"

"I can't go in there."

"This isn't a hos…"

He cut her off, jerking away, "I can't go in there."

"You've got to."

"No, I don't."

Elizabeth felt the panic in her father's voice. She knew her power to get him to give in to her will, but this same sense let her know when she couldn't, or shouldn't, push him. He sat on a stump and pulled out a tin of Prince Albert, shakily pouring tobacco onto the cigarette paper. He spilled most of it on the ground. She knelt beside him, seeing the tears welling in his eyes. Taking the tobacco and paper from him, she began rolling his cigarette for him. "Poppa, why can't you go in that tent? What happened over there?"

She handed him the cigarette and held his hand to light it. He took a deep draw that seemed to settle his nerves. "One day four of us got caught out in No Man's Land. That was the crater-filled area between our trenches and the Germans.

"The Hun—the Germans—pinned us down with machine gun fire, so we just lay there in the mud hoping to stay alive until dark. Then they dropped mustard gas on us. Three of us put our gas masks on, but the fourth guy, a brand new soldier, had left his mask in the trench. He didn't want to carry the extra weight."

Poppa was staring at something that Elizabeth knew she couldn't see and frankly she was glad she couldn't.

"It's a horrible thing to be in the mud with a man dying slowly from poison gas. Darkness finally came and we scampered back to our trench, carrying the fellow with us. They hauled all four of us to the medical HQ." He pointed at the tents. "It looked exactly like those.'

He coughed and took another drag. "Gas doesn't kill a man at once, it chokes him slowly. I can still hear him dying."

Elizabeth pulled her father closer. "I'm sorry."

"But I can still hear him coughing up his lungs in that tent." He bowed his head. "And that's why I can't go in there."

Elizabeth kissed him on the cheek. "You don't have to go in there. Wait here and I'll get the medic." She hurried to the tent and soon returned with Corporal Crawford, who knelt beside her father. "Hey, Mr. Reed. I figure I'd better pay you back for those biscuits with some good medicine." He pulled out a packet and tore it open. "This white powder is supposed to be a wonder drug. It'll clear up that infection in no time flat."

"What's it called?"

"Sulfa powder. Does the trick and does it quick." Holding the swollen hand, he dusted the powder on the cut and used a dampened swab to work it into the wound. He stood. "Don't mean to rush off, but we're pulling out in a minute. If it's not better by tomorrow, come back by. If I'm not here, someone'll help you." He squeezed Elizabeth's arm. "I predict his wing will be good as new in a few days."

They walked home quietly. Both father and daughter knew how to enjoy being together without words. Poppa stopped at the creek crossing, standing for a long time watching the southward flow of Bundick Creek. "You know that water will eventually run into the Gulf of Mexico down at Cameron." He put the toe of his boot in the water. "Bundick will run into the Ouiska Chitto down below Doodlefork. There it meets the Calcasieu and winds its way to Lake Charles and on to the Gulf."

He sat on a log, rolled another cigarette and smoked it leisurely as she sat beside him, rubbing his shoulder. "You know this is where I was baptized."

"I didn't know that, Poppa."

"There were fifteen of us baptized by old Brother Miers right there. It was after a big brush arbor meeting in 1922."

He tossed the butt into the creek, and it was pulled into an eddy, soon disappearing beneath the dark water. "Yep, you can't stand by the same river twice." He stood facing toward home. "I reckon sometimes that's a good thing. You only get one chance, and when it's gone, it won't be back again."

Chapter 15

Paperwork

Two days after the crash landing in their okra patch, a jeep approached the Reed home. A Captain, his clipboard papers fluttering in the breeze, stepped out of the jeep. Elizabeth watched from a window as Peg said, "What's up?"

"Soldiers."

Peg motioned toward the jeep. "That driver is good-looking."

"You've never met a man wearing pants you didn't think looked good."

"I believe I know that driver." Peg sashayed out the door. "I met him the other day at the airstrip." She waved at him, not seeing the faucet pipe in front of her. She tripped over it and sprawled to the ground. The jeep driver leapt out and trotted to her rescue. Peg sat up, dusting herself off as the soldier held the broken pipe. "It broke clean off." He peered into the ground, as if expecting a gusher to spurt forth.

He helped Peg to her feet and she took the pipe. "Don't worry about that. Poppa had already, uh, turned off the water to it. I'm glad he did, or we'd have a mess right now."

Elizabeth, from her window view, smirked. "The only mess out there is you, Peg." The pipe was one of Poppa's jokes. He'd jobbed the faucet and two-foot length of pipe into the ground. No one had running water within twenty miles of Bundick. More than once, soldiers had requested water from their front yard faucet and Poppa always answered, "Our water well is out right now, but I'll draw a bucket from our waterhole for you."

The jeep driver pushed the faucet back into the ground. "There you go, Peggy Sue. Good as new." Elizabeth moved where she could hear better. How did he know Peg's name?

"It's good to see you again, Corporal Lawrence," Peg said. "I didn't recognize you without Jeep 1931."

"She's taking a break today. Getting a wheel bearing changed."

"You're not here by accident, are you?"

"Not at all. I wouldn't pass up the chance to go on this dangerous mission with the Captain, or see a pretty girl like you."

Peg scowled toward the window. "Corporal Lawrence, let's go over here by your jeep. There's an old maid that lives with us who's a terrible gossip." Robbed of her eavesdropping post, Elizabeth moved to the back porch where the Captain and Poppa sat rocking.

"Captain Blaze, this is my daughter Elizabeth. She's a schoolteacher. If it's OK with you, I'd like for her to sit in on this. I don't always hear too good."

The Captain stood, removing his hat. "It's nice to meet you, Ma'am." He cleared his throat. "Mr. Reed, as I was saying, the Army wants to make it right from the plane crash in your field."

"It really didn't do much damage."

"Nevertheless, the United States Army wants to make full restitution for the crop loss, fence damage, and your trouble."

"It weren't no trouble. We patched up the fence right easily. The only damage was to our okra crop and it wouldn't have made much more with winter coming on."

"Regardless, we want to reimburse you."

"No Sir, you don't need to do one thing."

The Captain was as determined to make it up as Poppa was not to let him. "Let me explain, Mr. Reed—to you and your daughter." He nodded at Elizabeth, and she detected a coy smile trying to break loose. "We are trying to show the good folks of Louisiana that we respect and honor their rights. If there is damage to property, livestock, or crops, we want to correct it. You would be doing us a favor to allow us to."

"How's that?"

"Word will spread of the Army's fairness in dealing with your situation. It will ease some of the tension between the military and landowners." He pulled a sheet off his clipboard. "This is paperwork absolving us of further damage and paying you a fair price for the damage."

"What's *absolving* mean?"

Elizabeth interrupted, "It just means we won't blame them for what happened, and won't sue them."

"Sue them? I ain't never sued nobody in my life." Poppa huffed. "Mister, that's not how we do things around here."

Elizabeth touched her father's arm. "He's not doubting you. It's just the way things are done."

"My word's always been my bond—and it's good enough...."

"Mr. Reed, I understand and trust you completely." The Captain offered his hand. "Your handshake is all I need." Poppa extended his hand, and the two men clasped in a jaw-clenching test of strength on who had the strongest grip as well as the most integrity. The Captain let go first. "Thank you, Mr. Reed. It's settled. Now just so they won't hassle me back at headquarters, will you or your daughter sign this sheet?"

Now that his honesty wasn't being tested, Poppa relaxed. "I'll let my daughter sign for our family. Elizabeth gripped the pen, but stopped as Poppa said, "Captain, this is my other daughter, Peggy Sue."

The Captain looked at Peg, Elizabeth, and finally Poppa. "You're raising some fine-looking daughters." He turned to Elizabeth. "If you sign, you'll need to come to Camp Polk to pick up the money."

Elizabeth lifted the pen from the paper. "Poppa, why don't you sign?"

"I'm carrying a load of soldiers to town on my bus tomorrow morning."

Peg stepped up on the porch. "I'll be glad to take care of it." Elizabeth handed her the pen, and her twin quickly scribbled her name. This had something to do with the jeep driver out front.

The Captain cleared his throat. "Now there's one more thing. The government will be paying you fifty dollars."

Poppa's mouth gaped. "*Fifty* dollars?" He pointed toward the garden, "Fifty dollars for that?"

"You're not satisfied?"

"Satisfied? That's way too much. Heck, all I did was take a little baling wire to fix the fence. And that okra? I was so tired of cutting it, I was glad to see it go." He blinked at the Captain. "I'd eaten so much boiled okra, I kept sliding off the bed sheets at night—ending up right on the floor."

The Captain's jaw gaped, so Elizabeth said, "He just means he was sick of eating okra."

"I see. It'll be fifty dollars." He waved the signed paperwork. "The only catch is that you'll have to come to Camp Polk to pick up the check."

"But we don't have a vehicle that's running." Poppa said.

The Captain was nonplussed. "No problem. I'll send my driver tomorrow." He turned to Peg. "Ma'am, since you signed it, you'll need to come. It's okay if anyone else wants to come." He winked at Elizabeth and placed his hand on her lower back as he said to Poppa, "Sir, is that all right?" While saying this, Elizabeth felt his hand dropping back to her behind.

Poppa waved him off. "Sure, Peg is my daughter and one of the *executioners* of my estate, so she'll do fine."

The Captain winked at Elizabeth, and she gave him her best Mona-Lisa-tight-lipped smile. "If you put your hand there again, the execution is going to *be yours*."

He coughed and turned to Peg. "Miss Reed, the driver will be here at 1300 tomorrow to pick you up."

"Thirteen hundred?"

The captain chuckled. "That's tomorrow at 1:00 PM."

"Will the driver out front be taking me?" There was total innocence in her question.

"Most probably. Is that a problem?"

"Not a'tall, Captain. In fact, I'd like to request him."

"No problem then, 1300 it is."

The family walked with the Captain to the jeep where Peg introduced her father and Elizabeth to Corporal Lawrence. He shook Elizabeth's hand. "I met you in DeRidder."

"Really?"

"Yep, you were with your little brother and you had a crate of biddies. I nearly ran over him in the street.

"Yes, I remember that."

"Where's your brother?"

"He's fishing on the creek today." Elizabeth pointed toward the chicken yard. "And the biddies are over there."

Lawrence peered around the jeep. "They're growing well."

The Captain put on his cap. "Well, on to the next battle . . . I mean assignment." He made one last leer at Elizabeth as he climbed into the jeep.

Peg put her arm around her. "Lizzie, I believe he likes you. Maybe we can go on a double date."

"No way. The Captain's married."

"He didn't have a ring on."

"No, but he had a tan line on that left ring finger where one usually is . . . or should be." She put her hands to her throat. "I'd rather drink muddy water and sleep in a hollow log."

Poppa danced an Irish jig as he finished the lines of the song, *"than to be here in Atlanta, get treated like a dirty dog. T for Texas, T for Tennessee."*

He put his hands on his hips and did a stomping-boot beat on the porch. *"We're getting fifty dollars . . . that I never expected I'd see. Oh lady—oh a laydee, oh—a laydee.*

Elizabeth glanced over his shoulder. "Poppa, look behind you." A stunning double rainbow stretched across the sky, framed by dark storm clouds.

He grinned. "That rainbow's got a pot of gold at the end of it." He went an octave higher on his yodel. "Oh, a lady-oh—fifty dollars—oh a lady-oh."

Chapter 16

Two Letters

WEATHER BULLETIN
25 AUGUST 1941
DERIDDER ARMY AIR BASE

SCATTERED THUNDERSTORMS WILL PREVAIL IN EASTERN
MANEUVERS AREAS. ALL AIR TRAFFIC SHOULD BE AWARE OF
POSSIBLE LIGHTNING AND SHEAR WINDS. NEXT BULLETIN AT 1800

Harry carefully laid the two letters out on his cot. He'd read both of them a dozen times and was still befuddled. Shorty stepped inside the tent, and Harry held the letters out. "Hey, Buddy, look at these."

"What is it?"

"It's two letters I got from Elizabeth Reed."

"Who?"

"Elizabeth Reed, the schoolteacher."

"Oh, yeah." Shorty held the letters, closely studying each one. "They're on the same girlie-looking stationary, but can't both be from the same person. The handwriting's completely different."

He handed one to Harry. "Isn't this the same handwriting as the first one? It sounds promising, sorta like an invitation to meet her."

Shorty gripped the second letter as if it might be poisonous. "This one's definitely not an invitation. Whoever wrote it used a poison pen." Laboriously he read,

Private Miller,

I appreciate your recent letter and photo. However, I am not presently interested in carrying on any correspondence. I'm not sure how you got my name and address, but request that you do not write again.

Please do not take this personally. I simply feel that it is not a good time for either of us.

Sincerely,
Elizabeth Reed

Shorty shrugged. "She didn't beat around the bush, did she?" He reached out. "Hand me the first one—the nice letter."

He read,

Pvt. Miller,

I received your letter and photo and am very interested in meeting you.

I'd like to invite you to our church, Bundick Baptist, this Sunday. We start services at ten a.m.

Hope to meet you soon,
Elizabeth Reed

Shorty studied it, re-reading each word, before looking up. "What do you make of it?"

Harry held up a photo, which Shorty snatched away. "Whoa." He turned to Harry. "Is that Elizabeth Reed?"

"That's what it says on the back."

He flipped it over before returning to the photo. "She's a looker." Shorty read, "Bundick Faculty 1940–41." He whistled. "I never had a teacher that looked like that."

Harry took the photo from him. "I like her confident smile."

Shorty leaned over. "I like her dark hair and eyes. Wonder what color they are?" He grabbed the photo. "I'd like to see the rest of her."

"Give me back my photo."

"Which letter did the photo come in?"

"Which one do you think?" Harry held up the first letter.

"What do you make of it?"

Harry laid the photo between the two letters on his sleeping bag. "I don't know what to think."

Shorty's head pivoted as if he was watching a tennis match. "Which letter is *really* from Elizabeth Reed?"

"I have no idea. It might not be either of them."

Shorty squinted. "That's a troubling thought. What's your plan?"

Flinging both letters onto the floor, Harry said, "I'm not sure I'm going to do anything." He picked up the photo, shaking his head. "Then again, you never know."

Shorty stepped outside and said, "Harry, come see this." He joined his tent mate as they stared at a wondrous double rainbow in the eastern sky. "It's gotta be an omen," Shorty said.

"Of what?"

"An omen that you're meant to meet that girl." Within a minute, the rainbows faded leaving only dark clouds moving across the sky. In its place, Harry saw the image of the photo. The photograph of the girl he hoped was the real Elizabeth Reed.

Chapter 17

Airborne

Elizabeth saw the red streak across Jimmy Earl's forehead. "What happened to you?"

"I got clothes-lined." He brushed his hair down his brow just as Momma set down a glass of cold milk for him. "Jimmy Earl, I heard you up during the night."

He choked on the mouthful of grits he was wolfing down. "Uh, yes Ma'am. I heard a commotion out in the henhouse and figured it was that red fox."

From the kitchen, Momma said, "Did'ja find the fox?"

"No Ma'am."

Elizabeth grabbed Jimmy Earl's arm. "The only fox in that henhouse last night was *you.*"

"Lower your voice." He deftly changed the subject. "Where's Peg and Ben?"

"They left early for Camp Polk."

He slurped his coffee. "They've gone with the Corporal to get the plane crash money?"

"Fifty dollars." Elizabeth lifted up his bangs. "What happened?"

He leaned closer. "I snuck out last night . . . and took a plane ride."

"Get out of here!" Elizabeth leaned back in surprise.

"I was running back and *clean* forgot about the *clothesline.*"

She traced her hand over the crimson welt. "You must have been flying pretty low."

"I was flying pretty fast." His face glowed. "It was *wonderful.*"

"Were you scared?"

"Heck no. I've never felt more alive. To see the world—these same woods and roads I've seen from eye level all my life—to see it from up above—I can't describe it."

His eyes narrowed. "Elizabeth, I know what I'm going to do with my life. I'm gonna fly."

"Get out of here."

"I'm gonna do it even if it harelips Orville Wright *and* his brother Wilber." He pounded the table. "I'm gonna do it if it harelips the *whole world.*"

She put down her coffee cup. "Get out of here!"

Jimmy Earl leaned closer to where she could smell the coffee on his breath. "That's just what I plan to do—get out of here."

It was about just before dark when Elizabeth heard the whining jeep coming up the driveway. Poppa was drinking coffee at the kitchen table and walked to the window. "I hear them coming. Peg, Ben, and that soldier made a day out of it."

Momma looked up from peeling potatoes. "Does that surprise you?"

He brushed sawdust off his overalls. "Pearline, nothing that wild daughter of yours does surprises me."

She held up a peeled potato. "You know, she does remind me of you."

"I was never *that* wild."

"Yes, you were, and that's what attracted me to you."

Elizabeth watched her father ease up behind her mother. "Do you still think I'm wild?"

"Levon, I've tried taming you, but I'm not sure I've succeeded."

He pointed as the jeep careened up the path, accompanied by whooping from two of his children. "You better use your taming on settling *them* down."

He turned to Elizabeth. "Why can't they be calm and sensible like you?"

"Poppa, do you mean boring and vanilla like me?"

"But they're not bad traits." He downed the rest of the coffee in one gulp.

The dust from the jeep boiled into the kitchen, causing Momma to huff, "They don't have a lick of sense." Peg triumphantly pulled a bill out of an envelope. "Fifty dollars, Poppa. A fifty-dollar bill with a picture of Ulysses S. Grant."

When Peg placed the crisp new bill in his hand, he whistled. "Everyone gather around." He motioned to Corporal Lawrence. "Son, come join us." With the six of them gathered in a circle on the porch, Poppa said, "Let's join hands." The Corporal hesitated as Poppa bowed his head. "Lord, these recent years had just about put us under, but these soldiers have been a godsend. I believe we're gonna make it now, and we just want to thank you for this gift and all of your blessings."

He stopped for a moment and Elizabeth peeked. Poppa was wiping his eyes with a red bandana. "Lord, we thank ye. We really do. In Jesus name. Amen."

Even the soldier said, "Amen." He stared at the family as if he'd just landed his jeep on the planet Mars, but quickly regained his composure. "All right, Mr. Reed, it's time for your jeep ride."

Poppa waved him off. "I believe I'll pass."

"No Sir. Captain Blaze's orders were to take you on a ride. I can't go back without that." The corners of his mouth turned up. "I guess I'd have to *stay the night* with you folks if I don't give you a ride."

Poppa cleared his throat. "Well, if that's what it'll take to get rid of you, let's go."

Ben pulled on Poppa's sleeve. "Can I go, too?"

"No, Son. Your legs ain't long enough yet."

Peg stepped forward. "Let him go, Poppa. I'll help Momma with supper. Corporal Lawrence is staying for supper."

Poppa stepped back. "He is?" He dropped his arms in resignation. "Who's in charge around here?"

Peg smiled sweetly. "You are, Poppa."

He strode toward the jeep. "Well, since *I'm* in charge, I'll let Ben go." He turned toward his family. "And don't any of you give me no Missouri-smiles."

"Whoo-eeee." Ben began his victory dance.

Elizabeth stepped off the porch. "I believe I'm going too."

"What?" Peg said it, but all four family members stood slack-jawed.

Elizabeth climbed in the jeep. "Yes, poor-old-boring-and-vanilla-Elizabeth is going on a wild ride."

Peg whispered, "Now don't you go and steal my man."

"Don't worry about that, sister."

Poppa took the front seat and Ben slid in beside Elizabeth in the back, punching her, "It's gonna be better than the tilt-a-whirl at the parish fair."

They spun out, and with the engine and wind noise, Elizabeth strained to hear Lawrence's words to Poppa. "Tram . . . Ben . . . said it'd be . . . challenge . . . this jeep."

Poppa, a look of terror spreading over his wizened face, said, "We ain't going to the tram, are we?"

Ben sat up. "Corporal Lawrence has been bragging about how this jeep can climb. I bet him a coke it couldn't climb the tram."

"Y'all let me out right here." Poppa leaned a foot out of the jeep, but Lawrence only sped up as he turned onto the gravel road leading toward Bundick Swamp.

"Hang on, fellows." Elizabeth, eyes closed, needed no encouragement on this, her hands clenched in a death grip on the back of the seat.

Ben kept yelling, "Better than the fair. Way better." Ahead of them lumbered a slow stump truck, taking up the middle of the narrow gravel road. Lawrence sped up, setting down on the horn. The big truck eased to the right as the jeep, half on the road and half in the steep ditch, sped by.

When the tram came in sight, Poppa hollered, "Stop this thing and let me out."

Ben leaned against her, and she felt him trembling. She closed her eyes. *I'd jump out, but this jeep's going too fast and he's holding my hand too tight.* Elizabeth had never liked crossing the tram even in a wagon. A mile long, it had once carried the timber railroad over Bundick Swamp. It consisted of earthen levees on each end and a narrow long trestle over the creek. After the sawmill at New Hoy shut down, the railroad abandoned the line and the trestle was planked and used as a roadway.

Lawrence, gearing down, left the elevated roadway and swept down into the ditch. Elizabeth looked up at the steep embankment as it whizzed by. Nodding up, Lawrence shouted, "So this is the *hill* ya'll think I can't climb?"

"This is it." Ben tightened his grip on Elizabeth's hand. Lawrence jerked the wheel sharply and the jeep clambered at an impossible angle up the incline. Elizabeth expected the vehicle to overturn at any moment, killing them all. They were still ascending, engine whining and tires spinning, as Lawrence said, "Come on baby, show them what you got."

When the jeep reached the top of the level roadway, it became airborne and she stared at the drop-off on the other side. Corporal Lawrence slammed on the brakes, twisting the wheel expertly, causing the light vehicle to fishtail on the road. They sped along on the level roadway, but Elizabeth knew they were nearing the part of the tram she feared most: the roughly planked ten-foot-wide trestle. It was so shaky that her father's school bus could not cross it loaded. Each morning, the principal met the bus at the far end and escorted the children across on foot, while Poppa drove the empty bus across the rickety bridge.

Her stomach churned at the increasing thump-thump-thump of the planks beneath the jeep. They were going way too fast. In places, it was twenty feet down to the swamp. She closed her eyes and hung on tightly. She only opened them when Ben said, "Watch out for that wagon." A hundred yards ahead, a wagon was creeping across the bridge. It was the Barrett family wagon—easily recognizable by the mismatched pair pulling it: an old run-down horse teamed with one of the last oxen left in the area.

For the first time, Corporal Lawrence showed a little restraint. He geared the jeep down and came to an abrupt stop that threw all four of them forward. They were over the actual creek, and Ben leaned over and spat, watching as it splattered in the dark water below. Poppa, his voice shaking, said, "Corporal, about halfway between us and that wagon is a pullover where two vehicles can meet and pass. See it there?"

Lawrence revved the engine. "We'll let them pull aside." He turned to Ben. "Bet you can't pull a tail hair off that horse as we pass by."

"Betcha I can." Ben leaned out of the jeep. As they spun out, Ben said, "Something's bad rotten– in Doodlefork—if he don't get that wagon out of the way."

Old Mr. Barrett leisurely guided his wagon to the pullover as Lawrence gunned the jeep. Poppa, who'd taken his hat off at the beginning of the ride, now placed it over his face. Elizabeth, holding tightly to Ben, ducked her head as they flew by, hearing a man's voice, "Crazy bunch of...."

At last they neared the end of the bridge. She made up her mind if they got across it alive, she'd get out and walk the low road back to Bundick. Ben waved his hand in pain. "I hit my hand on that mare's flank." They left the planked trestle and were back on the embanked roadway.

Suddenly, Lawrence gunned the engine. "Here comes the *fun part*." He jerked the wheel to the right and they went flying down the embankment. Once again, the jeep fishtailed, seemingly near an out-of-control spin before hitting solid ground at the bottom. Elizabeth blanched. She knew exactly where they were headed: the gap. It was a ten-foot-wide opening where an old bridge had been removed. The dirt was heaped on both ends of the gap, making for a perfect ramp.

Elizabeth could only think of one word: *abyss*. Her stomach dropped as the jeep went airborne. Clearing the open span, it hit with a jarring thud that rattled every bone in Elizabeth's body. Even Ben was stunned speechless . . . for a few seconds, before squealing, "Let's do it again."

Corporal Lawrence blew out. "I about overdid it, didn't I?"

Ben leaned up, "Better than the parish fair, huh, Poppa?"

Poppa didn't say a word—he was leaning out of the jeep, retching.

"Poppa's done lost his lunch."

Elizabeth picked up the crescent wrench that had slid under her feet during the wild ride. Would it be manslaughter or murder if she hit Corporal Lawrence?

Poppa pointed back. "My teeth. My teeth."

Ben climbed up between the front passengers. "Poppa done lost his teeth when he was throwing up." Lawrence jammed on the brakes and began backing up.

Poppa struck him on the shoulder. "Stop it. You'll run over them—just let me *git out*." Poppa climbed out, his voice trembling as he jabbed a finger at Lawrence. "Leadfoot, you'll never get me back in that thing again."

"Maybe not, Sir, but it *was* fun, wasn't it?"

"Fun? It was crazy. You're crazy." He cast a damning look at all three of them. "You're all crazy."

Ben said, "Better than the Parish Fair, huh, Poppa?"

Poppa turned to Elizabeth. "Well, what are you gonna do?"

"What do you mean?"

"Are you gonna walk home with me?" Elizabeth climbed out of the jeep, following her father as he picked up his teeth and went over to a water-filled rut and washed them off. He put them in his pocket and began walking the low road back through Bundick Swamp. Looking back over his shoulder, he threw his head at Lawrence and Ben. "You're crazy. You're all crazy." He looked at her. "Why'd you ride with that lunatic?"

"That's just what we *boring* and *vanilla* schoolteachers do when we get a wild hair."

He muttered toothlessly, "Lizzie-Beth, you ain't never had a wild hair in your life."

She grabbed his hand as they walked around the ruts of the low swamp road. "Poppa, a person doesn't know if he can fly until he jumps off the cliff."

He studied the tram road looming above them. "Sometimes it's a narrow line between *flying* and *dying*." All Elizabeth knew was this: she'd never felt *more* alive than right now. She liked the empowering feeling of setting people on their ear by doing something unexpected.

She might just get used to this.

Chapter 18

Stranger in a Strange Land

SUNDAY, AUGUST 31, 1941
6:00 AM WEATHER
NATIONAL WEATHER SERVICE LAKE CHARLES, LOUISIANA

QUIET WEATHER IS FORECAST FOR THE REMAINDER OF THE
LABOR DAY WEEKEND. HEAT AND HUMIDITY WILL CONTINUE
WITH AFTERNOON HIGHS IN THE UPPER 90'S. BEGINNING
TUESDAY INCREASED CHANCE OF RAIN IS FORECAST.

What in the heck am I doing here? The car sped off, leaving Harry stranded in his own No Man's Land. He looked at his watch—fifteen minutes till ten. Across the road, clumps of country folks, dressed in their Sunday best, were filing into a white wood-frame church. Harry pulled out the photo of Elizabeth Reed, blew out a breath and crossed the road. It's too late to turn back—I've crossed my Rubicon.

He placed the photo in his pocket between the two letters, one of which was from Elizabeth Reed. In the next hour or so, he'd know which one. He never saw the ambush coming. The barking dog, hackles raised and growling, blocked his path. Every person outside the church stopped and stared. What a way to make a good impression.

A boy in overalls raced to his rescue. "Rev, you settle down, *now.*" The dog, its tail tucked between its legs, whimpered away and crawled under the church. The boy turned to Harry. "Rev don't like soldiers."

"Is his name "Reb?"

"No Sir. I said 'Rev' as in Reverend. He's our church dog."

"Church dog?"

"Yep, most faithful member of our church; never misses a meeting."

Harry knew he'd made at least one friend—not the dog, but the boy. "Does Rev belong to you?"

"No, my dog Tripod only has three legs. It's too far for him to hop to church." The boy stuck out his hand. "I'm Mal Cooley."

Another boy trotted up, a little older and dressed better in pressed jeans and a clean t-shirt. Mal said, "Morning Ben. We got a soldier visitor this morning." The freckled boy grinned shyly and saluted.

Harry snapped to attention. "Private Harry Miller reporting for duty, *Sir.*"

The boy's eyes widened as he sprinted to an older lady where he began gesturing toward them. Harry said, "What's wrong with him?"

"His name's Ben Reed," Mal said. "He's just one of those Reeds—Daddy says that they're 'bout a bubble off.'"

"What?"

"You know, their bread didn't get quite done in the oven."

"Who is he talking to over there?"

"That's Ma. His grandma. Look, they're coming over here."

Ben Reed was marching with the older woman in tow. It clicked: Ben *Reed*. Elizabeth *Reed*. The boy must be kin to Elizabeth Reed. Who was this woman coming toward him? The jokes about the old maid schoolteacher swirled in his mind. Could this be the real Elizabeth Reed? Harry considered running.

The woman broke into a wide smile. "Good morning, Private Miller. We are glad you're here to worship with us. I'm Elizabeth Reed's Ma, and this here's my grandson Ben, and we're glad. . . ." The ringing church bell drowned her out. A man walked up and patted his shoulder. "Welcome soldier, you're just in time for Sunday School."

The old woman smiled sweetly. "When the worship service begins, you come sit with us. Ben'll find you. You're our guest today."

Ben escorted him to a nearby building. "Your class is in there. I'll be waiting outside for you."

Harry grabbed the boy's arm. "Do you know Elizabeth Reed?"

"Sure I do—she's my sister." He pushed Harry toward the door. "Hurry or you'll be late."

Six men in wooden chairs were sitting around a rickety table. One was a corporal with a medical patch. He stood and extended his hand. "I'm DeWayne Crawford from the 503rd Medical down the road from here. Glad to see you in the Lord's House."

"Harry Miller. Milwaukee, Wisconsin. 32nd Red Arrow."

"32nd? You're a long ways from your camp. What brings you here?"

"I'm not really sure what I'm doing here." At least Harry was being honest.

When the soldier narrowed his eyes, Harry quickly added, "But I'm sure glad to be here today."

The teacher, clad in new overalls and a white shirt, cleared his throat. "If you've got your Bibles, turn to Philemon 1." He turned to the other soldier. "Corporal Crawford, would you open us in prayer?" The soldier prayed a long, flowery prayer that seemed to never end. Harry was sure he'd prayed for everything but the price of tea in China.

When he finally said, "Amen," the teacher led a discussion that had something to do with the Apostle Paul and his intervention on behalf of an escaped slave named Onesimus, or something like that. Philemon was the slave's owner and evidently also a friend of Paul's. During the discussion, the teacher got his pocketknife out and cleaned his nails. He definitely had the calloused dirty hands of a working man. He stopped, pointed the knife at Harry and said, "Soldier, you ain't said nothing. What do you think about ol' Paul and Philemon?"

Harry nearly fell off his chair. "I'm just here to listen today." Mercifully, a bell rang outside the door and the men shut their Bibles and stood. The teacher said, "Next week's lesson is from Hebrews 11. Harry's mind wasn't on Hebrews, but on Elizabeth Reed. The photo in his pocket was burning a hole.

"Private. . . ." Harry didn't hear the teacher the first time. "Private . . . Private Miller, will you lead us in a closing word of prayer?" Harry's mouth went dry—he'd been found out. The wolf in sheep's clothing had been unmasked. Panic set in as he tried to think of a way out. Finally, a memory flickered in his mind, and he reverently bowed his head. "God is great. God is good. Let us thank Him for our food. Amen."

All of the men said, "Amen." The teacher clapped a beefy hand around Harry. "Good prayer, Private. Nobody's ever complained about a short prayer or a short sermon. You'll be staying for dinner on the grounds, won't you?"

"Uh, what's that?"

"Y'all don't have dinner on the grounds in Mill-walk-key-misconsin?"

"I guess not."

"It's where we stay after church and eat. You picked a good day to come."

Harry followed the men as they filed out of the classroom into the bright sunlight toward the nearby auditorium. Ben Reed was waiting for him. "Follow me."

At the door, they met the minister. He was a well-dressed man and greeted Harry, "Glad you're here, soldier." His eyes were kind and his handshake firm. "Private, we always give military visitors a chance to say a word. Would you like to pray or give a testimony?"

"Uh, no Sir. I think I'll pass."

"Fine. Welcome to Bundick Baptist Church." Ben led Harry into the stifling hot auditorium, which held about fifty people, split evenly between men, women, and children. They went to the third pew from the back, where the boy motioned for him to slide in next to the grandmother. Harry discreetly slipped Elizabeth's photo out of his pocket, scanning the church. Ben leaned over. "She ain't out here yet. She'll be in the choir."

"She's pretty, ain't she?" The grandma smiled. A suspicion washed over Harry. The two people sitting on either side of him were the source of one of the letters. Looking down at the photo, he knew which one, and felt sick. The choir members entered from a side room, singing about "The Promised Land." Ben leaned over. "Elizabeth's the third one from the left. Front row."

Harry wouldn't have immediately recognized her. Her hair was longer and she was even prettier than the photo. Harry looked her up and down—she was good-looking from head to toe. No wonder Shep remembered her as "a real looker."

She was focused on her hymnal and showed no awareness of Harry's presence. He uneasily realized she probably knew nothing about this visit. Evidently Elizabeth Reed hadn't invited him. Elizabeth Reed's little brother and grandma were the culprits. He'd been ambushed. Glancing toward the back door, he began plotting his escape. He stared at her in the choir. Why would a woman that beautiful need someone to fix her up?

The song leader called out, "Page 276—'Leaning on the Everlasting Arms.' We'll sing the first, second, and fourth stanzas." Ben placed the opened hymnal in Harry's hands. He tried to concentrate on the song, taking his mind off his predicament. He liked the song—especially the chorus—where the choir sang their parts,

Leaning, Leaning,
Safe and secure from all alarms.
Leaning, Leaning,
Leaning on the everlasting arms.

As the song ended, the choir director wiped his face with a red bandana before sneezing loudly into it. Ben leaned over. "Watch him. He'll look in it." Sure enough, the song leader carefully examined the contents of his bandana before stuffing it back in his pocket. Ben continued, "Daddy says Brother Aaron sneezes so loud, he's looking to see if he lost his false teeth."

Harry snickered into his hand. The grandmother leaned over. "It ain't his false teeth he's looking for, he's a'feared he sneezed that little brain of his right out his nostrils." Harry was sitting between two people who commented on every part of the singing service.

During a break, the pastor gave a rousing welcome. He had a young man stand. "All of you know that Jimmy Earl's leaving tomorrow for basic training. We're gonna miss him but wish him Godspeed. At the end of the service, he'll be up front for you to speak to him."

"That's my brother," Ben said. "He leaves on the train tomorrow for boot camp in Missouri."

Next, the pastor recognized the soldiers present in the service. There were about a half dozen in attendance and each stood and told their name. Four of the others, including a fine-looking nurse, were from the nearby medical headquarters. A tall corporal in the back stood next. He was obviously nervous as revealed by his squeaky voice. "I'm Corporal Arnold *Snow* from *Idaho*." Amused scattered laughter filtered through the congregation, leading the pastor to say, "Corporal Snow, you may have a future in poetry." He let the crowd quiet down before adding, "We sure won't forget your name."

It was Harry's turn. "I'm Harry Miller. 32nd Division by way of Milwaukee, Wisconsin." As he sat down, he closely watched Elizabeth Reed. She put her hand over her mouth, and seemed to glare, arms crossed, at him. During the remainder of the announcements, she stonily stared out a side window.

The corporal he'd met earlier in Sunday School walked to the pulpit. "Turn to the Gospel of Luke, chapter 15, beginning with verse 4. Today's message by Reverend Bowden will be entitled, 'The Value of a Lost Sheep'."

He began, "What man of you, having an hundred sheep, if he lose one of them, doth not leave the ninety and nine in the wilderness, and go after that which is lost, until he find it? And when he hath found it, he layeth it on his shoulders, rejoicing. And when he cometh home, he calleth together his friends and neighbors, saying unto them, Rejoice with me; for I have found my sheep which was lost. I say unto you, that likewise joy shall be in heaven over one sinner that repenteth, more than over ninety and nine just persons, which need no repentance."

He shut his Bible. "This is God's word. Let it speak to your heart."

Ben elbowed him. "Are you a lost sheep, Private Miller?"

Harry looked around the strange church and nodded. "I believe I am." He winked at Ben. "I'm a lost sheep a long ways from home."

"Really?"

"Yep, I'm a stranger in a strange land."

Four offering bearers came forward and passed offering plates among the congregation. To reach his billfold, Harry removed the two letters, and Ben said, "What's that?"

"Why don't *you* tell *me?*" Harry whispered as he removed two crisp dollar bills from the wallet.

Ben shrugged. "I don't know nothin' 'bout nothin'."

"Where I come from, lying in church is a sin." Harry said.

The boy never flinched. "And where I come from, showing up at church to see a girl ain't a reason for attending."

"Who said I . . ." Harry narrowed his eyes. "Did you send one of those letters?"

The boy glanced at the letters. "I can't write that good. Ask her." He winked at Grandma who raised her eyebrows while dropping a handful of coins in the plate.

The choir members began coming down, and Harry said, "Why are they leaving?"

"They're not leaving. They're coming down to sit with us."

He watched Elizabeth Reed walking toward their pew. She never made eye contact, slipping into the pew in front of him. Quick as a cat, Grandma leaned up. "Elizabeth, this is Private Miller."

She cut her eyes his way. "Nice to meet you."

Grandma patted her shoulder. "Private Miller, this is my granddaughter Elizabeth."

He tried to smile, echoing her weak greeting. "Nice to meet you, Elizabeth." She stiffly turned back to the front, as Harry felt beads of sweat bursting out on his forehead. He'd just grit his teeth and tough it out. It'd be over sooner or later.

Ben elbowed him. "That's my daddy."

A man with a guitar sat in a folding chair near the pulpit. He motioned to the pianist. "Margaret, let's do this in A flat." He launched into a song with an Irish feel, one that Harry wasn't familiar with.

There were ninety and nine that safely lay
in the shelter of the fold.

It was a ballad about the scripture they'd just read—the story of a lost sheep and the kind shepherd's passionate search for it. The man had a simple baritone voice. There was no microphone and none was needed as the small auditorium had great acoustics. The singer, slouched in a chair, strumming a beat-up guitar and backed up with chording on the piano, sang in a spare but fetching style. The man simply sang from his heart.

Harry noticed the man was missing a finger on his fret hand, and leaned over to Ben. "What happened to your father's finger?"

"Sawmill finger. It's pretty common around here."

It didn't affect his playing one bit. The voice and guitar style were both natural and fresh. So fresh that when the song ended, Harry blurted, "Beautiful." Elizabeth Reed stiffened, but he saw a slight smile at the corner of her mouth.

"It was beautiful." Ben said. "And so is she." The two country people on either side of Harry—a grandmother and her grandson—had him under a full-court press.

The preacher stepped to the pulpit, carefully adjusting his reading glasses, opened his Bible and removed his wristwatch. Ben continued his commentary. "When he takes his watch off, it don't mean one thing." Grandma reached around Harry and thumped the boy's ear, causing him to react with a loud, "Ummph." The pastor began sharing Jesus' story about the lost sheep. A sheep far from the fold. Far away from the safe place. Harry understood it well. Being a musician, he related to the Lost Sheep song. It was a link for him to the sermon. After telling and retelling the story for nearly an hour and examining the parable from every possible angle, the pastor's tone changed. Ben lowered his voice. "He's gearing it down for the end."

The pastor prayed and the congregation stood while the choir director led in a song he'd announced as "Softly and Tenderly." As they sang, "Softly and tenderly Jesus is calling; calling for you and for me," several folks, mostly women and children, came down front, praying at the altar or talking with the pastor. It seemed like some type of confession time. Harry liked the refrain, "Come home . . . Come home . . . Ye who are weary come home."

After about eight or nine verses and the final "come home," the service came to an end. The pastor held his hands up. "We're gonna ask Uncle Cricket to ask the blessing on our meal. Don't anybody leave—there's plenty for everyone."

An older man hobbled to the front. Harry asked Ben, "Is his name really *Cricket?*"

"That's all I've ever heard him called. He's got a brother named Beetle and an older sister called June-Bug."

Ben squinted reverently as Uncle Cricket prayed fervently, and Harry made his escape. There was no reason to stay and further embarrass himself or Elizabeth Reed. This had all been a mistake. A terrible misunderstanding.

Slipping out the church door, he steeled himself not to look back. *I will not stop. I will not look back.*

Chapter 19

Have a Great Life

Harry was nearly to the road when a male voice called out, "Hey boy, where you going?"

He sped up. Don't stop.

"Halt, soldier. *Halt now.*"

Harry stopped and turned back toward the church. The guitar player—Elizabeth's father—was walking toward him. "What's the big hurry, Soldier?" Mr. Reed put a hand-rolled cigarette to his lips, took a deep drag, and blew out a blue fog. "I had to come out for a smoke. Sitting in there too long gives me the dang willies."

Harry studied the man's relaxed manner. *He has no idea who I am or why I'm here.*

"My name's Levon." He put out his meaty hand.

"Harry. Harry Miller."

"You're a Red Arrow soldier, huh?"

"Yes Sir."

"You don't have to "sir" me. I fought beside your division in France. They were tough—the French called them '*Les Terribles.*'"

"What division were you in, Mr. Reed?" Harry felt relaxed with Elizabeth's father.

"I was in the 45th." He stepped back. "How'd you know my name?"

"What?'

"I didn't tell you my name."

"Uh, I was sitting by your son Ben. He told me."

He laughed. "I can believe that. That boy's never met a stranger."

"Isn't that your other son who's leaving for the Army?"

Mr. Reed rubbed his forehead. "He joined up against my wishes." He threw down the cigarette. "Did you join or were you drafted?"

Be careful with your words. "I joined. My Uncle Sam made me an offer I couldn't refuse."

Mr. Reed laughed. "Been there—done that." He waved his hand. "Come eat with us."

"I really need—"

"No, you've got to stay for a meal. Our victuals are way better than what you'll have back at camp." He blocked Harry's path. "Come eat with my family. I know what it's like to be away from home. We'd be honored for you to be our guest."

Ben sauntered up. "I thought I'd lost you, Private Miller."

"I just needed some fresh air."

"Ben, take this soldier over to meet our family," Mr. Reed said. "He's our guest."

"What do you like to eat?" Ben said as they neared the tables of food.

"Anything that doesn't eat me first." He scanned under a grove of oaks where women were busily putting pots and dishes on long tables of plywood and sawhorses.

"That's dinner on the grounds." Ben rubbed his belly. "The women are loading them up."

Elizabeth was slicing a pie, chatting with another young woman. "Your sister's beautiful."

"She don't think she is."

"She doesn't seem too happy that I'm here."

"It surprised her. She'll warm up."

Mr. Reed walked up to her and pointed toward Harry.

"Ben, does your daddy know anything about the letters?"

He shrugged. "I don't think so."

Elizabeth placed the knife on the table and walked toward Harry. From the look on her face, he was glad she'd left the knife behind. She coolly extended her hand. "Private Miller, I'm, uh, glad you're staying." Her hand was soft and delicate, and it was shaking so that she used her other hand to steady it.

"Elizabeth, Private Miller here," Ben said.

She cut him off. "I believe I heard Momma calling you." He sagged his arms before walking away, leaving an uncomfortable silence in his wake. Finally, she broke the impasse. "So you got my letter?"

"I did."

"And you came anyway?"

"I got *two* letters from you."

"Two?"

He pulled them from his pocket. "Here."

Elizabeth took one of the envelopes. "That's the one I wrote. Let me see the other one." She quickly scanned the envelope and letter. Her face clouded before she looked up. "I cannot believe this."

She searched the crowd. "My own Grandma. Ma—Theodosia Reed." She pointed at the smiling old lady, stirring a pot, standing where she could watch their every move. She gave a cat-that-ate-the-canary smile and waved. To Harry's surprise, Elizabeth burst out laughing. "She is one of a kind. They broke the clay mold when they made her."

"Your *own* grandmother wrote the letter inviting me?"

"She did. That's her handwriting." For the first time, she looked directly at Harry. "Ma thinks I'll never get a man—I mean a boyfriend—or get married—without her help." He noticed her eyes—they were a deep and passionate brown. He wondered what was behind them. Being from a land of blue and green-eyed people, her dark eyes were exotic. And her syrupy slow Southern accent was mesmerizing. Compared to everyone else he'd met today, her grammar was impeccable. It was probably tough to develop *that* in the land of "ain't" and double negatives lurking behind every bush and tree. But she hadn't surrendered her accent one bit. Just refined it and made it beautiful.

She waved the letter. "She wrote this one inviting you." She held up the other letter. "I wrote this one—telling you not to bother me . . ." She stopped. "I'm sorry if I seem rude. It's nothing to do with you—it's all these folks of mine that treat me like a da—like a ten-year-old. They think I'm gonna dry up on the vine and be an old-maid schoolteacher."

Harry winked. "That wouldn't be good."

Her eyes hardened. "I don't need anyone to ride in on a white horse and rescue me."

"Oh, don't worry. I'm infantry, not cavalry." He backed away. "I was leaving anyway."

"No, no. Don't leave. Now that you're already here." She rubbed her head. "Oh, I don't even know how to talk."

"Let's go eat so we won't have to talk," Harry said.

Elizabeth laughed. "And so we won't both keep putting our feet in our mouths." She nodded at the crowd standing with Ma. "Besides, we'll give them something to talk about." They went to a long table where rows of pots stretched in a seemingly endless buffet line. They were arranged by meats, breads, desserts, vegetables, and casseroles. As they moved along the table, Elizabeth explained about many of the dishes. "That's Aunt Emmer's peach cobbler. Get some now, or it'll be gone."

Coming to a large pot of snap beans, she whispered, "Pass that one up. It's from the Brown's. Momma says they don't wash their hands after changing a diaper or delivering a calf."

"Thanks for the warning." Soon, his plate was heaped. "I can't handle any more."

"Just one more thing. That's Ma's chicken pie. If you don't get some, her feelings will be hurt." She leaned over and spooned a generous helping on his plate, accidently bumping up against him. He liked how fresh she smelled.

"Your grandma's good at cooking up lots of things."

"What?"

"She cooked up getting me here."

Elizabeth pointed toward Ben. "And she was in cahoots with that little rascal over there."

"How do you know?"

"Because he's the one that picked up the bullet you threw out in DeRidder."

"I didn't throw out a bullet."

"That's how he got your name."

"But I didn't throw it. Some so-called buddies of mine did it as a joke."

She had a wonderful laugh that flowed up from within and spread over her face. "So here we are . . . and neither of us meant to be here. Someone else threw the bullet . . . someone else picked it up . . . and here we are eating chicken pie together."

"Maybe it's just fate."

Her face tightened. "I don't believe in fate."

"Maybe it's luck."

"I don't believe in that either."

"What do you believe in?"

"Chicken pie and God's guiding hand." She turned back to the table. "Now, you must try Aunt Betty's sweet tea." She handed him an icy glass. "Take a sip."

Harry took a large swig, and coughed most of the tea out his nose. "That's so sweet it hurt my teeth."

She laughed. "Let's sit over here by ourselves."

Harry balanced the plate on his knees as Elizabeth sighed. "This is crazy, isn't it?"

"Everything's crazy in my life. It's the Army way."

"You don't act like a normal soldier."

"Is that a compliment?"

"Definitely. You don't seem like most soldiers I've met."

"I'm not. I didn't plan on being one." He took a small sip of tea. "It was something I couldn't pass up."

"Were you drafted?"

"Not exactly. I joined the National Guard after my parents booted me out."

"Booted you out?"

"I got in some trouble and my parents—well, really my father—had had enough. Joining the Army was the best solution for all of us."

"Have you reconciled?"

"No." Suddenly the chicken pie didn't taste as good. "And I don't see that changing."

They ate the rest of their meal in uneventful small talk until Ben walked over. "Private Miller, come meet my brother Jimmy Earl."

Elizabeth stood. "I need to help clean up. Go meet Jimmy—you can give him some advice on the Army."

"The only advice I have is: stay out."

"I believe it's a little late for that." As she hurried off, Harry studied the long hair flowing down her back and the willowy way she walked. He liked everything about her.

Ben tugged on his arm. "I'm supposed to watch you until she gets back."

"Thanks. Can I ask you a question?"

"Sure."

"Did you have anything to do with this letter?" He waved the letter in the boy's face.

"That's not my handwriting."

"That wasn't my question."

"Maybe so, maybe not. You sure ask a lot of questions."

"And you sure do lots of scheming." Harry stuffed the letter in his pocket.

"It's what I do well."

"I've noticed that."

A long line of well-wishers crowded around Jimmy Earl Reed. Ben pushed through. "J.E., this is Private Harold Miller, Elizabeth's *boyfriend*."

He grinned. "All I can say is that you have my condolences."

"I'm not her boyfriend . . . I just showed up. . . ."

An older woman kissed Jimmy Earl on the cheek. "We're so proud of you."

He turned to Harry. "She works pretty hard at *not* having a boyfriend."

"And I've worked equally hard at *not* getting a Louisiana woman."

"Sounds like you two are going to make a fine pair." He had the most deliberate slow Southern drawl Harry'd ever encountered.

"Where'd you get that slow drawl?"

"I been working on refining it for nearly eighteen years."

Harry shook his hand. "Good luck in basic training. You'll love the drill sergeants."

"I've heard that."

"And the drill sergeants will love your drawl."

"I bet they will." Jimmy Earl squeezed his hand. "And good luck to you, Private." He nodded toward Elizabeth. "If you break that filly, you'll be the first one."

Ben led him away, and Harry glanced at his watch. "Look, it's time to catch a ride back to camp. I'm going over to say goodbye to your sister."

She was wearing an apron and was elbow deep washing dishes in a washtub. She dried her hands off. "Are you leaving?" Harry wasn't sure if he detected relief or regret.

"It's time for me to get back to camp." He stepped toward her. "Elizabeth, I want to thank you for making me, uh, feel welcome. I know this was a complete surprise to you."

"I don't believe your visit was a surprise to *everyone* here." He detected a slight slice of a smile at the corners of her mouth. "I hope I haven't seemed rude."

"Not at all. Surprised, yes. Rude, no."

"It's nothing personal, Private Miller. It's just the timing. There'd be no future. No time."

Her manner irritated Harry. "It's not like I asked you to marry me or anything. I just enjoyed spending the day with you . . . and your family."

She blushed. "It's just that I'm not interested . . . not ready for a relationship. I'm just getting over being hurt and not ready to put my heart on the line again."

"I understand that."

She smiled. "I will give you this: you're not near as cocky-acting as your photo."

"How's that?"

"It was the jaunty angle of your cap and that smirk. I figured you thought you were God's gift to women." Her voice lightened. "You seem pretty down to earth."

"I'd like to see you again."

Her jaw tightened. "Let's leave this good day where it is and move on." She turned to walk away.

He couldn't believe she was brushing him off. "Well then, have a great life!"

"What'd you say?" She whirled around.

Harry waved. "Have a great life!"

Her jaw dropped and she hoarsely said, "Well . . . uh, you too." She hurried away, leaving Harry kicking at the sand beneath his boots.

He put his hands on his hips, staring at the country church, grassless yard and dusty road. "Harry Miller, what in the world are you doing here?"

The answer came from behind him. "Why, you came to meet a fine Southern woman." It was Elizabeth's grandmother. "I could tell she liked you."

"I'd hate to see her when she didn't like someone."

"Oh, that's just Elizabeth playing hard to get. She liked you. Come back again and you'll see."

"You expect me to come back and put up with *that*?"

She squared her feet. "I heard that you men from up North were tough and wouldn't quit. That's what my grandpa, who fi't them up in the Virginia Wilderness, said about your people."

"Fit them?"

"Fi't them—Fought them in the War for Southern Independence."

"You mean *The Civil War*?"

The old woman scoffed. "My grandpa said there weren't nothing *civil* about it . . . but he also said that you Yankees were worthy opponents." She walked around him, seemingly sizing him up. "You're not going to give up on that girl this easy, are you?"

"I'm not giving up on anything. Who said I was even interested in her?"

"Your eyes, your face, *and* your heart."

"Well, maybe you're wrong, Ma."

"Ma might be wrong about some things, but not this one. Did you call me 'Ma'?"

"I did."

"Good. Ma'll see you next time."

"Next time? Don't hold your breath." Harry smirked as he walked to the roadside and put his thumb out for a passing jeep. It slid to a stop and Harry climbed in.

Ma walked over and crossed her arms. "See you next time, Private Miller." He waved as the jeep tore out, throwing gravel toward the old woman. She didn't flinch. As the jeep sped off, he knew that Elizabeth's grandma was still standing her ground. Evidently, it was a family trait.

The only sound was the wind and it seemed to say, *Have a great life*.

Chapter 20
Labor Day

Monday, September 1

It was the day Elizabeth had come to dread. September 1st. What made it even worse was that she couldn't tell anyone why. Last year—1940—the first of September had fallen on Sunday. She'd skipped church and spent the day in bed, saying that she had a stomach virus. But that wasn't the truth. It wasn't a virus—it was a broken heart. She carried the pain inside everyday, but it seemed to erupt anew when September rolled around.

After today, she'd have an additional reason to cringe: Jimmy Earl was catching the train to Shreveport and to boot camp at Ft. Leonard Wood, Missouri. He'd been accepted into the Air Corps and couldn't wait to get away. Elizabeth fully understood. She'd had her own chance just two weeks ago.

She'd intended to be on this same train for Shreveport, but when it came time to grab the opportunity, she'd hesitated, and now it was out of reach. She reminded herself: I did the right thing in staying. But this morning, it didn't feel as if she had. She sat on the edge of the bed, looking out the window at a flock of noisy crows hopping around in the yard. Suddenly one flew off and she thought of the words of David in one of the Psalms, "If only I had wings like a bird, I'd fly away."

If only they drafted women. It would be her no-choice way out of Bundick. But she knew better. No matter where she was today, it would still be September 1st and she would still be lugging her broken heart.

It had been broken two years ago today: Sept. 1, 1939. The anniversary—or more accurately, the birthday—was something she'd deal with the rest of her life. Ironically this year's September 1st would fall on Labor Day.

She'd gone *into labor* on this day two years ago. Once her pregnancy began to show toward the end of the spring semester of 1939, she'd moved to Shreveport to live with her best friend at college, Dora Jo Cook. Her own family in Bundick believed she was working a summer job in Shreveport. When the fall semester began, she told her family she had scarlet fever and needed to stay in Shreveport.

The labor pains began on the morning of September 1st. During her long day of labor at Charity Hospital, the first news arrived about Germany's invasion of Poland. A nurse moved a radio into the hall as they listened to sobering updates of a new European war.

She'd signed all of the papers weeks before so she wouldn't change her mind. After they returned her to the hospital room after the baby's delivery, the nurse said, "Would you like to hold the baby before . . .?" She'd planned not to, but at that moment said, "Yes."

She held him for about ten minutes, amazed that what she'd carried inside her body for nine months was in her arms. He was a part of her as she was of him. His tiny hand grasped her finger. Elizabeth knew life would never be the same after today, but it had to be done. She reminded herself that her decision wasn't a selfish one, but the best for the baby. The door opened and the stone-faced nurse came to the bed. Elizabeth kissed him before carefully handing him to her and turning her face to the wall.

The door opened again, it closed, and he was gone. The walls closed in on her like a vise and she'd never been so lonely in her life.

Two years later, she still wasn't convinced she'd done the right thing. On this new September morning, the old self-accusations flew about in her mind just like the cawing crows in the yard. She rubbed her eyes. *You're going to drive yourself crazy if you don't let it go.*

Her mother knocked lightly at her door. "Baby, are you all right?"

"Yes, Momma. I'm just not feeling too fresh this morning."

"Well, if you're going with us to the train, you'll need to get moving."

"Yes Ma'am. I'll be right out."

After a quick breakfast, the Reed family loaded up in Rob Lindsey's Model A for the trip to DeRidder. Elizabeth, sitting in the back, watched Jimmy Earl slowly circling the yard as if it might be a long time before he stood there again. *Jimmy Earl, you can't stand by the same river twice.*

Ben leaned out the window. "You're not bringing a suitcase?"

"Nope. I won't need it where I'm going." As he climbed into the car, quietness settled over the family; even Ben didn't say a word. The silence said it all: nothing would be the same after today. It wasn't just a change for Jimmy Earl; it would affect everyone in this car.

The DeRidder train depot was a mass of activity. Soldiers were milling about, waiting for the northbound train's arrival. Jimmy entered the depot to finalize his ticket. Momma, stifling tears, scanned the crowd of soldiers. "Lord, don't they all look young."

The soldiers parted as a black car backed up to the depot landing. A hush fell and Elizabeth saw why. It was a hearse. Four soldiers unloaded a flag-draped wooden coffin. Soldiers and civilians alike removed their hats as the coffin was carried from the vehicle to the train.

Elizabeth grabbed Ben's hand as he said, "What is it, sister?"

"Shh."

As the coffin was deposited into the baggage car, a civilian approached the funeral director. "Mr. Roberts, what happened?"

"It's a soldier. He drowned in the Sabine River over the weekend. He's on his way back home."

"And where's that?"

"South Dakota." He glanced at the paper in his hand. "Sturgis, South Dakota."

"Never heard of it."

"It's in the Black Hills."

Jimmy Earl, ticket in hand, walked up. "What's going on?"

"A soldier drowned in the Sabine," Elizabeth said.

Jimmy Earl shook his head. "That's a wicked river."

"He's going home to South Dakota."

Elizabeth's parents were on the other side of the hearse. Poppa stood bareheaded, his arm around Momma, who was dabbing at her eyes. They looked much older. Older and sadder.

The conductor leaned from the train car. "All aboard." The travelers formed a line and began loading. The soldiers among them seemed delighted to be boarding a train leaving Louisiana. Jimmy Earl hugged each family member one by one. He knelt, putting his hands on his younger brother's shoulders. "Now, you're going to have to take good care of things while I'm gone."

"When will I see you again, Jim?"

"I don't rightly know . . . but I'll be back." The whistle blew and the engine began powering up. Jimmy Earl turned at the top step and waved before stepping into the first journey of his new life. Elizabeth put her arm around Peg. "You can't stand at the same river twice."

Her twin looked away. "Ain't it so?"

Ben ran up and down the platform until he found where Jimmy Earl was seated. He ran alongside as the train inched northward. Elizabeth's last view was of Jimmy Earl's face and palm pressed against the glass.

The few well-wishers scattered, leaving only the Reed family—Poppa and Momma, Ben, Peg, and her—alone on the platform. They seemed frozen in time, afraid or unable to move. She knew where the icy tightness in her stomach came from. It was September first. Labor Day, 1941. Now that date would mean something else: the date she lost another family member. A nurse didn't take him away—he left on a northbound train.

It was the same train taking a Northern soldier on his final ride home. Elizabeth didn't believe in omens and wasn't superstitious, but shuddered as the train's whistle echoed at the North Street crossing.

Part II

The Battle of Red River

September 11– 22, 1941

"You seem like a soldier
Who's lost his composure,
You're wounded and playing a waiting game
In no-man's land no-one's to blame."

−From the song "See the World" by Gomez

Chapter 21

Rattlesnake

Ten days later . . . Thursday, September 11th

Associated Press

(Washington) President Roosevelt will address the nation tonight at 9:00 p.m. Eastern. He is expected to address continued German U-boat attacks on American shipping, including the recent "USS Greer" incident. Sources within the White House say that the President will present his strongest case to date against the Nazis.

Just after sunset, Elizabeth saw a soldier hurrying up the drive. He held a long stick from which a dead snake dangled. There were already about a dozen soldiers on the Reed porch, and they scattered when they saw the snake. Poppa was fiddling with the family farm radio that he'd moved on the porch for the President's fireside chat. He looked up. "That's a ground rattler."

The soldier dropped it off the stick. "Is it poisonous?"

"Definitely. It's a pygmy rattlesnake. Around here we call them ground rattlers." He put his boot on the head before lifting its tail. "See those small rattles?"

The soldier hopped back. "I nearly stepped on it coming over here."

In the dusk-light more soldiers arrived, gathering around the porch. Speculation was that Roosevelt's speech would put America on a solid war footing in response to recent German aggression on the high seas. Most of the soldiers were from the medical unit up the road. In the midst of them, Poppa sat huddled over the radio, fine-tuning it as 8:00 neared. An approaching thunderstorm contributed to the static from the radio.

One of the medics knelt by him. "Mr. Reed, they're predicting a tropical storm to move in off the Gulf. Is that the same as a hurricane?"

Poppa was glued to the radio. "No, it's mainly rain—more like a hurricane without the wind. It can rain for days if the storm bogs down."

"Have you been through a hurricane?"

"Several small ones. The last big one here was in 1918. I was still in France, but I believe it was in August." Poppa nervously wiped his hands on his overalls. "I want everything perfect for this broadcast and the reception is bad because of the weather." Elizabeth cringed when he called to Ben, "Son, go and move the antenna a hair toward the east." Poppa had rigged up an old metal box spring in a tree and connected it to the radio. He believed it improved reception, while the women of the house viewed it as the tackiest-looking thing they'd ever seen.

Peg came out with a pan of their mother's hot biscuits, fresh butter, and muscadine jelly. She bumped Elizabeth as she squeezed by. "I see Mary's listening while poor ol' Martha is slaving away."

Poppa cleared his throat. "You boys come get one of the wife's fresh cathead biscuits. I've got the radio tuned to WWL in New Orleans. It's our best clear channel." The clock in the house chimed eight and a grave announcer's tinny voice set the stage for the President. The soldiers—normally joking, flirting, and wolfing down food and drink—all quietly leaned in as the familiar voice came across the airwaves. *"My fellow Americans, the Navy Department of the United Sates has reported to me that on the morning of September fourth the United States destroyer 'Greer', proceeding in full daylight toward Iceland…"*

Static obscured the transmission and the frantic tuning from Poppa until he found the signal again. *"She was then and there attacked by a submarine. Germany admits it was a German submarine…."* As the signal faded in and out, Elizabeth studied the serious faces of the men around the radio.

About three minutes into his speech, Roosevelt soberly said, *"When you see a rattlesnake poised to strike, you do not wait until it strikes before you crush it…"* The signal faded out as every soldier on the porch looked up in amazement. One spoke for all, "We're going to war."

Roosevelt's voice filtered through the interference. *"There will be no shooting unless Germany continues to seek it."*

Elizabeth watched her father's faraway gaze she knew so well. He was the only person on that porch who'd actually been battle-tested, and the President's words seemed to melt him. He took his hand off the radio and walked to the porch edge, where Elizabeth joined him. He said, "I wonder if Jimmy Earl's listening to this up in Missouri?" Poppa sat on the steps, his head in his hands.

She put her arm around his shoulder. "Poppa, I suspect nearly everyone in America is listening to this, including Jimmy Earl."

"I just feel like the whole world's crumbling around us and there ain't nothing we can do."

She rubbed his grizzled chin. "It's going to be all right." Elizabeth glanced at the radio where a soldier had taken over the dial and lost the signal. It didn't really matter—they'd all heard enough. The speech ended in a garble of words, static and electrical popping from the nearby storm. One by one, the soldiers thanked the Reed family for their hospitality and began leaving in small groups. Poppa stood in the yard shaking each soldier's hand. As they faded into the dark, it was as if they'd never been on the porch.

Poppa leaned on a post. "I'm sure worried about those boys."

Elizabeth put her head on his chest. "So am I—I wish Jimmy Earl was here."

The loud chorus of crickets, frogs, and locusts filled the airwaves of Bundick. Poppa sighed. "I wonder if the night insects sing like this up in Missouri?"

Fireflies flashed all through the edge of the woods in a duel with the lightning in the distance. Poppa scanned the sky, "It's coming."

"The storm?"

He blinked as if he'd forgotten she was beside him. "It's coming whether we want it or not."

She knew what he meant. The war.

Chapter 22

Sugar

Loud pounding on the front door startled Elizabeth. She opened it to find a tall soldier silhouetted against the late evening sun. "Sorry to bother you, Ma'am. I don't know if you remember, but I met you at your church a few weeks ago. I'm Corporal Snow."

Peg had slipped up beside Elizabeth, and she said, "Of course we remember you. You're 'Corporal Snow from *I-dee-ho.*'" Peg laughed in spite of the elbow Elizabeth planted firmly in her ribs.

He smiled weakly. "It does rhyme, doesn't it?"

Peg nodded. "You'll always be known here as 'Corporal Snow from the great state of Idaho.' Come on in. Would you like some coffee?"

"I don't have time. We're pulling out in thirty minutes."

He glanced out the window. "I'm not supposed to tell you this . . . "

Peg leaned forward expectantly. "Go ahead."

"Miss Reed, there's lots of waste in the Army. . . ."

"You can call me Peg."

"Yes Ma'am."

"And you don't have to call me Ma'am."

"Yes Ma'am, Miss Reed, I mean yes." He shook his head. "Uh, what's wrong with me and my tongue?"

Peg's mother stuck her head into the room. "Hello, Son."

"Howdy, Mrs. Weed, I mean Reed."

The three Reeds tried, but failed, to contain their laughter. Peg said, "Momma, the corporal has some secret information."

"I'm all ears."

He lowered his voice. "We're headed north for the big battle and just buried all of our extra food over by the Tram Road. We're under orders not to tell, but I can't stand wasting things. It's how I was brought up."

"Waste not. Want not," Momma said.

"You've been kind to our unit, and I figured this information would be a way of saying thanks."

"Won't ya'll be coming back to get the food?"

"Probably not. Besides, lots of it's perishable."

"What kind?"

"Some canned goods—and bags of russet potatoes." He wiped his brow. "Being an Idaho farm boy, it made me sick to put them back in the ground." He grimaced. "We also buried six twenty-five-pound bags of sugar."

"Sugar!" Momma turned to her daughters. "They're throwing away things that people've been kilt over."

He pointed out the window. "There's a tropical storm blowing in from the Gulf tonight. That sugar won't last in the ground."

"If the piss ants don't get it first."

Elizabeth cringed. "Momma, don't talk like that."

"It's the truth. Corporal, because of rationing we can't get any sugar."

He nodded. "If you'll get me a pencil and paper, I'll sketch a map of where it's buried." He drew on a paper bag. "You'd best go after dark. There'll be guards posted until we leave, and by the way, there's twenty-five pounds of coffee buried too."

He fidgeted at the door. "There's one more thing I'd like." He smiled at Peg. "If, uh, if I gave you my address, would you write me?"

"I'd be happy to write you, Corporal." Peg and Elizabeth walked him to the front gate. As he trotted off, Peg held the two slips of paper in her hand.

"Which one are you working on first?" Elizabeth said.

"I believe I'll start with the sugar map."

Momma waited on the porch, hands on her hips. "There ain't no way we're letting that sugar ruin." She turned to Peg. "Are you going to write that soldier?"

"I sure am."

"How many soldiers have you promised to write?"

Peg studied for a moment. "I believe he'll make seven. Maybe eight."

"Think you're spreading yourself a little thin?"

"It's not like I'm engaged to any of them. And besides, it's the patriotic thing to do."

"Horsefeathers!" With that benediction, Momma huffed back in the house. Elizabeth saw another figure coming up the trail. Poppa was home from the sawmill.

He stopped at the gate, studied the sky, and rubbed his leg. "It's fixing to set in raining."

"You think so?" Elizabeth said.

"Yep, my knee's aching; rain's coming."

"The soldier who just left said a tropical storm is coming."

"What soldier?" Poppa glanced as if a soldier might be hiding in the chinaberry tree."

"Corporal Snow came by with some important news."

"Who?"

"Remember at church: Corporal Snow from Idaho?"

Poppa rubbed his chin. "Oh yeah, I remember him."

"His unit is leaving for the big battle."

"Good."

"Poppa, he left Peg a little going-away present—he gave her some sugar."

"Sugar?"

"He said that they buried all kinds of food over by the tram, including some bags of sugar."

"Real sugar? And we can't even get a dipperful with ration cards."

"And a twenty-five-pound bag of coffee."

The first pattering of rain pelted the roof and caused Poppa to glance up. "So I guess y'all went and got it?"

"No sir, we didn't. We thought. . . ." Elizabeth could see her father's dander getting up.

"And why not?" Poppa's voice had raised an octave and sped up to three-quarter time.

"I've always known how strongly you felt about taking free stuff from the government, so we decided to wait."

"I do feel strongly—but *sugar* is different—it'll ruin out in the rain, unless the woods hogs get to it first. There's only one thing I hate worse than taking something from the gov'ment—seeing the gov'ment waste stuff." He put his hat back on. "What are we waiting on? Let's go."

Two hours later, the five Reed family members tromped back to the house in the pouring rain. Three of them—Poppa, Elizabeth, and Peg—carried a bag of precious sugar on their shoulders. They'd covered it with their raincoats. Behind them, Ben pushed a wheelbarrow full of canned items. Momma carefully protected the sack of coffee under her raincoat. Poppa was in an expansive mood. "Pearline, go ahead and get some water boiling. We're going to drink coffee until we're sick. Make it stout—strong enough to walk—thick enough to cut with a knife."

All night long, Elizabeth heard the vehicles passing northward and the hard rain pelting the tin roof. She woke to singing from the back porch. Slipping on her robe, she went to the window. Ben was sitting cross-legged, playing with a car he'd made out of a block of wood. He sang in a falsetto voice,

> *Zacchaeus was a weeing man*
> *And a weeing man was he.*
> *He climbed up in a sycamore tree*
> *Just to take a pee.*

Elizabeth rapped on the pane. "Momma said if she heard you singing that, she was going to bust your hide." She poured a cup of the fresh coffee and went to the front porch where Poppa sat watching lines of soldiers tromp by in the thickening mud. He drained his cup, flinging the grounds into the yard. "At least they won't be complaining about that swirling dust no more. It's turned into tire-grabbing, boot-sucking mud. Look at those deep ruts."

"How much did it rain during the night?" Elizabeth said.

"Nearly two inches." He pointed toward the crossroads where lines of trucks, horses, and infantrymen tangled in a confused bottleneck. "Fog and bog; the two greatest enemies of an army on the move. Yep, we've got the bog. I figure by tomorrow morning, the fog'll be here too."

"They'll find out those tanks and trucks are useless in Louisiana gumbo." He stood up to spit. "It'll take horses and mules to move on these roads."

"Poppa, I thought you wanted to see horses taken out of the army?"

"I do, but deep in my heart, I want their worthiness proven to these new-thinking folks."

"You can't have it both ways."

He nodded toward a passing column of soaked soldiers. "This ain't a real war. I can have it anyway I want."

Chapter 23

Footsloggers

At 5:30 a.m. on Monday, September 15, the first battle phase of the Louisiana Maneuvers began during a tropical storm. Harry and Company K were south of the Red River village of Boyce when they heard the first sounds of battle. Trudging north in a two-abreast column, they were no longer cursing the red dust. They were cursing red mud.

"It's just like maple syrup," said a new soldier fresh from New England.

Shorty pried his boot out of a rutted track. "No, it's gumbo. Louisiana gumbo."

Regardless of what regional description they used, the soldiers prefaced it with a string of cuss words. It was a boot-sucking, jeep-sticking, tank-bogging, miserable mess. During a break, Harry and Shorty sat under the edge of an oak. Rain dripped down Harry's hat as the wind intensified with every gust. "I've never been this wet in my life."

"And I've never been this tired." Shorty stretched out. "I've got a bad blister on my right foot." He removed his legging and brogan shoe. "How'd we end up out here?"

Harry shifted where gusting rain wouldn't sting his face. "I guess it was our lot in life."

Shorty pulled a C-ration can from underneath his poncho. "How about some lunch?" He held up the unlabeled can. "Let the buyer beware."

Harry examined it carefully. "I say it's stew and beans."

"Naw, it's got to be the stew and hash."

"If it is, you can have it." He quoted the official Company K meal motto, "The last gets the hash, unless it's smashed."

"Just one way to find out." Shorty pulled out his can opener.

Harry groaned. "Stew and beans."

Shorty moved the can underneath his poncho to keep off the pelting rain. "I'll split them with you."

Harry waved him off. "No thanks, I'll just stick to the crackers." He opened the B-unit and removed the crackers and raisins. "Tell me again what we're doing out here?"

Shorty spooned up a dose of the beans. "Being footsloggers."

"Footsloggers in a Louisiana hurricane?"

Cohen walked over. "Is this really a hurricane?"

"Nah, it's just a tropical storm," Shorty said.

Sarge called out. "Everybody up. Let's move." As they moved steadily northward on foot, the first sounds of battle reached them. It sounded as if a huge thunderstorm was occurring over the next hill. Moving carefully, the platoon spread out in battle position. Reaching another open field, Sarge stopped. "Looks like a perfect place for hidden snipers or machine guns. Let's study this area before moving on."

As they took prone positions, Harry inhaled. *This is only a war game, it's make believe.* He checked the safety on his rifle before wiping his palms on his pants. Sarge lay beside him, studying every bush and tree. To their left, another Blue Army platoon had also stopped at the edge of the field.

"A perfect place for an ambush." Sarge lowered his binoculars. "I know they've got to be close. I can nearly smell them." On the other side of Harry, Halverson lit a cigarette. Sarge reached across, knocking it out of his mouth. "Get down, you fool!"

"Ah, come on. It's just a game."

Sarge collared Halverson. "Take this seriously. It may just be maneuvers, but we're all being judged, so get serious." He shook him roughly. "What you learn here may save your life in the future. You may not care about your life, but I don't plan on getting killed because of your stupidity. *Get down.*" They silently watched for ten more minutes before Sarge nodded. *"Springer, Miller, Johnson.* I want you to scout ahead." He pointed north. "They're out there somewhere. Move carefully, make visual contact if possible, and report back. Any questions?"

"How far do you want us to go?" Shorty said.

"Keep moving until you make contact, then fall back and report to me."

Their training had been that the best way to cross open ground in hostile territory was to spread out, hunker down, and run like heck. That's exactly what Harry did as Springer and Shorty followed. They stopped at a small rise where they squatted and caught their breath. Shorty pointed to the left. "Look at that other platoon, they're strolling like they're at the county fair." He stiffened. "Listen. I hear planes."

Harry heard it too and scanned the low clouds. "Where are they?"

They were fifty yards from the next tree line, so they sprinted toward its safety, diving into the undergrowth as the planes cleared the treetops and began strafing the open field. The strolling platoon was standing in a wad in the open field, gawking as the planes roared over. "Look at those idiots, " Shorty said.

The platoon didn't see a Red Army dive-bomber roaring in from another direction, but Harry did. "My God, look at that." A perfectly timed bomb was hurtling down toward the field.

Shorty whistled. "If it hits one of them, it'll kill him." A few seconds before impact the soldiers saw the falling bomb and scattered like a covey of quail. It exploded on impact, throwing a white cloud high into the air, obscuring any view of the soldiers. Harry was sure the bag must have hit one or more soldiers. However, as the white powder settled, they were all covered in various shades of white, but were still standing.

"They've been dusted," Shorty dryly said.

"No, they've been *floured,*" Springer said. "And if that bag had hit them, they'd been *floored.*

"If we had some grease and a hot fire, we could fry them all for supper."

"In a war, they'd all be dead," Harry said.

Shorty picked up his rifle, cleaning the mud out of the barrel. "Yeah, but in a *real* war, they'd all been running to beat Sunday."

"Look at that jeep with the white flag," Harry said. Two men with binoculars were standing beside the jeep. "I don't know if they're umpires or officers, but somebody's going to answer for that platoon standing around twiddling their thumbs."

"Look at those idiots," Shorty said. "This is just about stupid."

"It may be, but it's our job. Let's get it done."

Springer stared at him. "When did *you* decide to become a soldier, Miller?"

"About the time those planes were cutting loose with machine gun fire."

"It seemed real, didn't it?"

Harry stood and brushed himself off. "Let's go find the Red Army."

In stark contrast to the open field, the next part of their reconnaissance was thickly wooded with numerous briar patches, as well as several creek crossings. Every step brought them closer to rifle fire, the jackhammer-like sounds of machine guns, and boom of artillery. Taut with tension, the three soldiers hunkered down, moving from tree to tree. Mixed in with the battle sounds were the distinct sounds of men's voices. Harry knew their baptism in battle, albeit a mock one, was just ahead.

A road and clearing loomed ahead. They eased to the road where they could lay unseen in the underbrush. Harry detected movement on their left flank. "There they are." Several jeeps, a staff car, and three large trucks crept along the road. "I can't tell if they're marked Red or not. I'm going to check it out." He crawled toward the vehicles and the battle noise just beyond them, then glanced back after covering about fifty feet.

Shorty cupped his hands. "What do you see?"

Harry shrugged in reply and continued on in the mud and wet leaves. The convoy of vehicles stopped and soldiers climbed out stretching and lighting cigarettes as if this was the end of a parade instead of battle. Suddenly, the battle noise ceased, so Harry slid forward for a closer view. The soldiers and vehicles were not marked as Red or Blue Army, and they didn't wear white umpire armbands either.

What kind of trick was this? An officer called out. "Shirley, why'd you turn it off? Get it going again." A soldier threw down his smoke and ran to the truck. Harry now knew it was a trick but wasn't sure against whom. He crawled back toward his partners, motioning them forward.

"What gives?" Shorty said.

"Come see for yourself." They made their way toward the road, where Harry pointed out the large speakers mounted on the truck. "It's a sound truck."

"Well, I'll be . . . " Shorty stood but Harry pulled him back down.

"All of that battle noise was a recording. There's nothing real about any of this."

"If I had a live grenade, I'd go blow that puppy up," Shorty said.

Springer cussed. "I think we ought to shoot them just for the general principle of it."

Shorty Johnson, always ready for a fight, reached in his pack. "I do have a smoke grenade. Let's throw it in amongst them."

Harry shook his head. "But they're not marked as enemy."

"I know, but it'd sure make me feel better about these briar scratches we got crawling over here."

The momentary silence was broken by booming artillery from the first sound truck, and it was joined by rapid machine gun fire and rifle fire from the second truck.

Springer laughed. "Better than Hollywood."

"Let's go back and report on what we found," Harry said. "I wonder if they'll believe us?"

Before returning to the thicket, Shorty said, "Those sure are fine speakers. I'd sure like to hear 'Mule Skinner Blues' yodeled over them."

Springer eased beside Harry. "You know why Sarge sent you on this mission?"

"I have no idea."

"He was bragging that he was going to either make you into a soldier or kill you trying."

Harry drew in a deep breath, thinking about how he hated the man. He muttered, "*He* may be the one that dies trying."

Chapter 24
Coals of Fire

"Baby, wake up. I got a job for you." Ben awoke to his mother standing over him. He heard the pounding rain on their tin roof. "Rain's been steady all night." She caressed his hair. "I need you to go with Peg back to where the food was buried. The Corporal said they left two barrels of hog slop."

An hour later he and Peg returned soaking wet, with the two barrels on a slip pulled by Dolly. Both barrels brimmed over with food waste. As they pulled up beside the barn, the pigs smelled the food and went to squealing and fighting each other. "There are lots of sayings about hogs and eating. Like 'I waited on you like one hog waits on another'."

Ben shoveled the slop over the fence into the trough. "How about 'as hungry as a hog'?"

Peg pulled her scarf over her nose. "Whew, you stirred up that smell and it's rank! I'm going to the house."

He didn't mind one bit. Normally, he'd be at school stuck at a desk, wrestling with his multiplication facts. Shoveling hog slop—even in a downpour—beat that any day. About a foot deep into the second barrel, the shovel struck something. It was a pasteboard lid. He pried his fingernails under the edge and lifted it away.

"My Lord, lookee there." No one heard him but the chomping pigs and they ignored him. He ran to the house. "Momma, you gotta see this for yourself." When she hesitated, he grabbed her arm and led her to the barn. "Look in that barrel."

She waved away the slop and pig odor. "That'd gag a grown maggot." She stood over the lip of the barrel. "It's full of baked hams."

"Do you think they're still good?" Ben said.

She picked one up and sniffed it. "Smells fine to me. They're baked and should be eatable."

"Why'd they throw good meat away?"

"Probably the soldiers got sent out before they could serve the hams. They'll be gone for a week."

"What are we gonna do?"

She glanced off down the hollow. "We're going to make a whole lot of folks happy." She shooed him toward the house. "Go get the wheelbarrow and line it with some fresh feed sacks. I'll fetch the girls and we'll start drawing water to clean them off."

For the next hour on the porch, they washed, cleaned, and excitedly developed their distribution plan. "I also want to send some of the sugar and coffee," Momma said.

Elizabeth drew a map of their neighbors, dividing it into four parts. Peg carefully laid the clean hams on a sheet as Momma said, "There's fourteen hams."

"How many are *we* going to keep?" Ben said.

" Just one."

"*One?* We found them. We ought to keep more than one."

She lifted his chin. "We didn't find them—that soldier told us about them." She patted his head. "Besides, if we keep two someone won't get one, and a second one'd ruin before we finished the first."

Elizabeth circled the names of four neighbors and handed it to Ben. "You'll enjoy handing out hams even more than eating them."

Ben licked his lips. "I'm not sure I'd enjoy anything more than eating fresh ham."

Momma filled his tote sack with four hams, small bags of sugar, and a tin of coffee. She inspected his list. "Now head out to Aunt Emma's, the Spurlocks, the Ortegos, and swing back by the Tates."

He set the sack down. "I don't want to go by the Tates. Those boys are always mean to me."

"Well, I bet they won't be after tonight." She popped him playfully on the behind. "Now get a move on."

The hams were heavy and only became heavier as he walked the half-mile to Aunt Emma's. The rain soaked him and soon he was shivering. It was nearly dark and the barking dogs and chattering guineas brought the old woman to the door. "Who goes out there?"

Hiding behind a live oak, he lowered his voice. "It's Sainty Claus." Getting no response, he said, "Ho Ho Ho."

She closed and latched the door. "Who is it?"

Ben set down his sack, cupped his hands and gave his best quail whistle, followed by, "My name's 'Bob White' and I've got somethin' for you."

She opened out the door. "Ben Reed, you're gonna get shot coming up to a widow woman's house this late." He hefted this sack onto the porch, putting his hand under it and shaking it. Aunt Emma drew back, nearly dropping her lantern. "It's not a snake or nothin' live, is it?"

He lifted the ham out, holding it aloft with both hands. She set her lantern down and knelt. "My goodness. *It is* Christmas." Her eyes glistened in the lamplight. "Where'd you get that?"

"It's a gift—a gift from our uncle."

"Your uncle. Which one?"

"Uncle Sam."

She glanced up. "Is this from the soldiers?"

"There's more." He pulled out the sugar and the coffee. The old woman clasped the ham to her breast like a newborn. "Son, tell your momma how much I appreciate this."

"Aunt Emmer, I've got to be going on my other rounds."

Before he could make his getaway, she pulled him close, leaving an overpowering whiff of sweet snuff, stale coffee, and ham grease on him. "I don't want you to never forget this night, and what your momma did. It truly is more blessed to give than to receive."

He couldn't escape her grasp or words. "Pearline and Levon Reed done given you a good name with good deeds like this." Finally, she loosened her grip. "It's your job not to mess it up."

"Yes Ma'am." Lifting his sack, which was now one-quarter lighter, he hopped off the porch. "I'm on my way to the Spurlock place."

"God bless you, child."

He looked back at her. She embraced the ham in one arm and held the lantern with the other as tears coursed down her face. "God bless you."

"He already has." Ben had to agree—this giving away stuff felt pretty good. Maybe not as delicious as a slice of baked ham, but tasty in a different way.

The next two visits were just as fun as Aunt Emma's. The families were delighted with the ham, sugar, and coffee. By the time Ben left these homesteads, he'd been hugged, squeezed, and nearly kissed to death. However, a cold chill of dread came over him as he neared the Tate home. He didn't expect a warm welcome from the dogs nor the humans. The three older Tate boys loved tormenting younger kids, especially Ben. He normally didn't go remotely near to their place. As he passed a stump hole, he thought how convenient it'd be to toss the last ham in and kick dirt on it. Some varmint would eventually eat the evidence, and he could hurry home.

He recalled the infectious joy on his momma's face and continued on to the Tate home. The first chore would be getting past the dogs, which had a deservedly mean reputation for biting strangers and neighbors alike. He reached in the bag, pulling loose a strip of hide from the ham, before breaking off a stout sweet gum limb. He'd use the carrot-and-stick approach. Maybe one would work.

The dogs began cutting up as he neared the gate. He hollered "Hallo" and they stopped.

The barking was replaced by low growls moving toward him. Tossing the meat strip in their direction, he sprinted for the safety of the porch.

He heard a muffled voice from in the house. "What's going on out there?"

"It's your neighbor, Ben Reed. I've got a gift for you."

"Who?"

"Ben. Levon Reed's boy. Your boys know me." Ben whispered, "They ought to know me as many times as they've whupped me upside the head."

"Come up on the porch and show me what you've got." Ben had never met Mr. Tate, but knew it must be his voice. The door cracked open, and a bare-chested bear of a man stood looking down on Ben. Behind Mr. Tate, he made out the shadowy silhouettes of several children.

He flashed the lantern in Ben's face. "Boy, what you got in that tote sack?" As Ben reached into his sack, Mr. Tate put his hand out. "Stop." He never took his eyes off Ben, speaking over his shoulder. "Frog, you and Cooter come in here. Do y'all know this little pip squeak?"

"Know him well, Daddy." It was Cooter, the oldest of the Tate bullies.

The man nodded at Ben, who reached into the sack—and with the flair of a magician pulling a rabbit out of a hat—held up the ham. "My momma sent this over for you."

Mr. Tate stepped back and squared his shoulders. "You tell your mother we don't need no charity."

"It ain't charity. You done paid for it."

"What?"

"It's government ham. Army waste." Ben handed him the ham. Mr. Tate took it and sniffed it as if it might be poisoned with strychnine.

"It's a gift from my family to yours."

"Why?"

"Because that's what neighbors do for each other."

Mr. Tate squinted. "How'd y'all git it?"

"We found it and a bunch more that the Army threw out."

"What about the others?" Ben didn't like the look in the man's face. It reminded him of how a dog looks when another dog has more in its bowl.

"We gave them to our other neighbors. Folks like y'all."

"You gave them *all* away?"

"All but one."

The man's face softened. "Your momma only kept one and gave us one."

"Yes Sir." He pulled out the sugar and coffee. "This is yours, too."

Mr. Tate opened the coffee tin, sucking in a deep whiff. "We ain't had coffee since my wife died last year." His voice broke. "I really appre—"

"Mr. Tate, if you or one of your boys will hold those dogs, I'd best be going."

"You dogs git under that porch and stay," Mr. Tate thundered and the dogs whimpered and slunk under the house. Mr. Tate put his huge hairy hand on Ben's shoulder. "Son, you tell your momma something for me. I ain't never had anyone give me something this nice. It means the world to me and my family."

Ben heard the catch in the man's voice. "If there's anything you and your folks need, me and my boys will help." He nodded his head. "Won't we, boys?"

The boys, now arrayed in the doorway, echoed, "Yes Sir."

As Ben trotted away in the rain, he knew he was safe. Safe from the Tate biting dogs as well as the Tate brothers. He knew his days of being tormented were over, and it was due to a fresh ham.

He couldn't get out of his mind the look on the man's face as he held the ham. It all reminded Ben of a Bible verse. It was something that Jesus said about heaping coals of fire on your enemies' head by being kind.

He wasn't sure *where* the verse was, but he'd *seen* it back in the Tate family yard.

He hurried home, light on his feet as he crossed the swamp. He couldn't wait to get home and get a thick ham sandwich with a cold glass of milk. His stomach growled. Hang on, there's a sandwich waiting on us.

He wasn't sure which would feel best: a juicy baked ham sandwich, giving away coffee and hams, or heaping coals of fire.

Today he'd done all three. That made it a good day. A really good day.

Chapter 25
Air Raid

Sarge was skeptical about the story of the sound trucks, but soon saw it for himself. After listening to "the battle" for a few minutes, he led them as they slipped unseen around the road and continued north. Companies on each flank, all moving toward Red Army territory, joined them. Once again, the sounds of battle reached them and they realized it was real. A scout squad, returning from the forward area, reported. "There's a big battle at a bridgehead about five miles from here. Word is that Patton's Red tanks are massed on the other side. Our forces are trying to blow the bridge."

A few minutes later, Company K stumbled onto a well-hidden anti-tank position. On each side of the road, howitzers and half-tracks were arrayed under camouflage netting. The perimeter of the gun placements was the edge of a swampy area called a bay gall. It was a strong position impossible to spot from the air.

Harry and Springer were on lead again and were the ones who "discovered" the position. An M-1-wielding corporal stepped out of the bushes. Breathing a sigh of relief at the soldier's Blue markings, Springer said, "You fellows are covered up."

"Thanks, Buddy." The corporal motioned them inside. "Get under here so you don't give away our position." He offered each of them a cigarette. "Listen to that." It was the drone of a plane. "They're hunting for gun placements like ours."

"I don't believe they'll find it," Harry said.

"Hope not. By the way, my name's Slack." He nudged Harry. "Watch this air raid." Three crouching Company K soldiers hurried down the narrow road. The first was Sarge, followed by Shep. Nickels, carrying the platoon's heavy Browning Automatic Rifle, brought up the rear. Just as Sarge came around an open spot, a gray object swooped down, hitting him on the shoulder, eliciting a loud, "What the—?" The aggressive bird took aim at Nickels, brushing a wing by his face.

Corporal Slack said, "I believe ol' King wing-whipped that second one. Do y'all know them?"

"Better than we care to admit," Harry said.

The soldiers retreated from the attacking bird, which repeatedly swooped down on Shep's back. Slack laughed. "We've had lots of fun out of King. He's pretty serious about protecting his territory."

"What kind of bird is that?" Springer said,

"A mockingbird."

"I've never seen one."

"Where are you from, man?"

"Wisconsin."

"Y'all don't have mockingbirds up there?"

"Not that I know of."

"We got lots of them where I'm from. It's my favorite bird. Nothing else sings quite like it. It'll pick up other bird songs, even human sounds, like dinner bells and whistles." He pointed to where the long-tailed bird sat on a limb. "Listen." On cue, the bird began a string of sounds that were repeated in bursts of five or six songs over and over.

Corporal Slack offered Harry a canteen. "I like its song, but I mainly like its attitude. It guards its territory against all invaders, birds, humans, and animals—especially animals. We had one back home that tormented our cat from daylight till dark."

Harry said, "Where's 'back home' for you?"

"Texas—Fort Worth, Texas."

"Did I hear you call the bird by name?"

"Oh, yeah. Its name is 'King.'" The soldier nodded at the bird, which was happily singing on a nearby limb. "It's king of this area and you don't go through here without tipping your hat—or helmet."

"Is King with the Blue or Red Army?"

"Neither, King's an equal-opportunity harasser."

Springer called out. "Sarge, we're over here." The other soldiers, joined by others, detoured around the mockingbird and slipped into the anti-tank placement. Nickels cussed at the bird from the safety of the shelter. "I'm going to shoot that bird with my BAR."

Corporal Slack kicked the Browning. "You don't have nothing but blanks in that thing, and besides, 'King' won't obey if an umpire tells him he's dead."

"I'll get it with a stick or a rock."

"You bother King and you'll answer to every man in this unit. He's our mascot."

"Well, mascot or not . . . ." Nickels stopped when the corporal raised his hand.

"I hear planes."

He motioned to the soldiers. "Everyone under here." They crowded under the camo, crouching as if that would hide them better as a formation of planes came over. "They're Red Army all right. Look at those red patches on their wings." The planes fired their machine guns at a nearby grove of trees. Harry, under the safety of the shelter, saw a group of bombers flying behind smaller escort flyers. A string of bombs tumbled down as the Texan pointed. "They're after the bridge."

When the drone of the planes faded, Sarge said, "Do you think they got it?"

The corporal shrugged. "It's hard to say. Earlier today, our planes were bombing the bridge to keep the Red tanks from crossing. The fact that the enemy is bombing it probably means we repelled their assault.

"What will you do?" Sarge said.

"Our orders are to wait here and guard this road. What about yours?"

"Ours are to advance until we engage the enemy." Sarge motioned the platoon forward. "Let's keep moving. We're headed to that bridge."

Chapter 26

Dreams

When Elizabeth awoke, her mind's accelerator was jammed to the floor. She lay in the dark with her heart racing. She kicked loose the tangled sheets and realized her bedding was sweat-soaked. Rain peppered the house. Had it rained all night or had she just dreamed it?

She'd had another one of those dreams. She reminded herself: this is not real. It's just a dream. Yet her panicked breathing and rushing heart told a different story. It seemed real. She even examined her arms in the faint light for scratch marks and scanned about the dark room for any sign of the bird. She sniffed for smoke. There was none.

Across the room, Peg slept soundly, oblivious to the bed-tearing, heart-thumping, dry-mouthed terror her twin had awakened from. Elizabeth was thankful *she* was the one who endured these bad dreams, and not her sister. *Lord, if it has to be one of us, I'm glad it's me.* It ran in their family. Poppa had them. Many mornings, he'd sat forlornly over a cup of coffee. She knew there'd been another bad dream.

Bradley. As usual, he'd been part of the dream. He always showed up on these troubled nights. Sitting on the bed, holding her head, she tried to recreate the crazy, disjointed, and disheartening dream.

Had it been one dream or three? She recalled waking up in the middle of the night. But had that been before, during, or after the dream? Or dreams?

She slipped on her housecoat and went to the kitchen just as the clock chimed five. Building up the cookstove fire, she put a drip pot of coffee on. Caffeine always helped her recover from a bad night of dreams. She slipped inside Ben's room. He was snoring lightly, feet hanging off his bed. She crept over and kissed him. "I love you, Ben." He'd been part of the dream.

She returned to the kitchen, sitting at the table in the dark as the coffee pot dripped and the warm aroma of fresh coffee filled the room. She smiled at Poppa's saying that if a man could bottle the smell of coffee and sell it, he'd be a millionaire.

Filling her cup, she walked barefoot to a porch rocker. Even the crickets and frogs had settled down for the night. Only one brave dog howled in the distance. She began to emerge from the dream, but emerging and forgetting were two different things. This nightmare had taken place in her classroom. They most always did. In the past, she'd gone to school dressed in her slip, got in a fistfight with a smart-mouthed parent, and successfully fought off a pack of orange wolves . . . all from her classroom at Bundick School.

In hindsight, her real life was pretty boring and those dreams seemed comical after the fact. But last night's dream—or dreams—was troubling. She'd been asleep in her classroom when a bird fluttering about had awakened her. Bundick School was on fire. Elizabeth's worst fear was dying in a fire. Ever since one of her best childhood friends had tragically died in a house fire, she'd lived with that deeply buried fear. In the midst of the burning school, she searched for her students. She'd found all of them and herded them out of the building. Calling roll outside, to her horror, she realized Ben was missing.

She rushed back into the inferno, screaming. But she wasn't calling for Ben. It was Bradley. She was searching for Bradley. He was the one missing. *Elizabeth sipped on the hot coffee, burning her lip. At least the burn reminded her that this was reality. The other was just a dream.*

As the flaming building fell around her, she called for them both: "Ben . . . Bradley . . . Ben . . . Bradley . . . At least she would die with them.

Suddenly, a uniformed soldier backed out of the flames carrying someone. At first glance, she thought the soldier was him: Bradley's father. She turned toward the flames—knowing she'd rather burn than face him. The soldier grabbed at her and she fought him off until she realized it wasn't *him*. It was Jimmy Earl. "Sister, I've come to rescue you."

She pushed him away. "Don't rescue me. Rescue Ben and Bradley."

"I must rescue you first so you can rescue them."

"There's not time."

Jimmy Earl reassured her. "From where I come from, there's always time." He grasped her hand and led her through the flames. "If we just follow that bird, we'll be safe."

They emerged in front of the school as it collapsed, imploding in a hiss of flames and smoke. In the midst of this, another soldier ran out of the building. He had a boy under each arm. Ben and Bradley . . . they were safe.

She ran to the soldier, realizing it was that Private. The one from Wisconsin who'd visited her at church. Harry Miller. He grinned and saluted. "I told you that you could depend on me." Then he walked back into the inferno, and that's when Elizabeth woke up, sweat-soaked as if she'd actually escaped from a fire. Heart pounding as if she'd dashed from a burning building.

But it was only a dream. Another jolt of coffee confirmed that truth. This was reality. That had only been in her mind. But what did it mean? Did dreams mean things? Did God still speak in dreams?

She emptied the cup and went back for another round. Daylight was peeking over the eastern horizon. A damp fog lingered over the woods. In spite of the rain, a lone mockingbird began singing his repetitive song from the Red Maple by her window.

Another day was beginning in Bundick Community.

Chapter 27

The Bridge

As Harry's platoon approached the bridge, they found a chaotic scene. The bridge itself was intact. Flour bombs don't actually destroy bridges, but the white-powder mushrooms on the bridge decking told the story: One of the armies had succeeded in knocking it out. Control officers and M.P.s guarded each end. Everyone present was either a white-banded umpire or a Blue Army soldier.

To the side of the creek, a group of about twenty Red Army soldiers sat on the ground, guarded by a ring of Blues. Shorty saw them too. "Prisoners. Our first sighting of Reds and they've already been captured."

Sarge moved toward the bridge. "Don't worry. From what I've heard, there are plenty more ahead and lots of them are in tanks."

An engineering team was working on constructing a pontoon bridge over the creek. The problem was that the rain-swollen creek was out of its banks, and there wasn't a good location to anchor the ends of the bridge. Nearby, a half-track had unsuccessfully tried fording the creek. Its rear tracks and bumper were the only parts sticking out of the water.

A cavalry scouting squad had just crossed the creek on their horses. They were on the far bank, their wet horses glistening in the sun as the riders watched.

"Shep, you come with me," Sarge said. "The rest of you take a break."

As they tried to find spots out of the rain and mud, Cohen sat down beside Harry and Shorty. "Have you guys heard the story about the platoon crossing the blown-out bridge?"

Shorty threw a pinecone at Cohen. "Yeah, you've told it a dozen times."

That didn't deter Cohen. "A Louisiana bridge was taken out of action by a bomb and marked as off-limits. An MP guarding the approach was surprised to see a platoon hot-footing it across the bridge. He pointed to the ford where other soldiers had swum across. 'Hey, you can't cross that bridge. It's out of action. You've got to pretend it's not here.'

The platoon leader said. 'We know it's out. We're pretending we're swimming.' Before they could be stopped, they were across and gone."

"They ought to have given the platoon leader a medal for Yankee ingenuity," Harry said.

Sarge and Shep trudged back up the hill. "Everybody up. There's an infantry crossing where we can cross downstream."

The unit slipped along the muddy bank to two intersected trees that had fallen across the creek. A rope handhold had been tied from one side to the other. The raging creek was at the level of the trees. In fact, to reach the first tree they would need to wade out into the current. It was not a sight that built confidence.

Cohen whistled. "Sarge, do you think it's doable?"

He pointed to mud and boot prints on the logs. "Looks like they've been doing it all day. If someone else did it, we can too."

Two soldiers walked out of the woods on the other side. Sarge motioned to them. "Did you cross here?"

One waved. "Barely, and we don't plan on going back."

"What's the key?"

"Keep a grip on the rope. Watch the second log. It's rotten."

"OK, Shorty, you're our smallest man," Sarge said. "You and Miller are going first." That was fine with Harry. The sooner he was across the better. He didn't want to stand there behind twenty other men.

Harry turned to Sarge. "How deep is the water before we get to the first log?"

He smirked, "You're fixin' to find out." Shorty waded off into the muddy creek. He'd earned his nickname honestly and couldn't reach the rope above him. Soon the water was chest deep and he struggled as he held his rifle above him.

Harry waded in. "Wait for me." He could grasp the rope and soon caught up. Shorty was fighting the current, so Harry grabbed the back of his pack. "Just stay close until we reach the log." It was about waist deep where the log came out of the water. Burdened by their soaked packs, they struggled to get up onto its slick surface. Finally by helping each other, they succeeded, holding tightly to the rope for support.

Sarge cupped his hands. "Shorty, you stay there and help the others up. Miller, go across and do the same on the other end." Harry gritted his teeth. He was fearful of crossing the log but going back wasn't an option. Gripping the rope with both hands, he carefully took baby steps. Where the two logs met was the trickiest part. The second tree was a pine and his initial step onto it caused the bark to slip loose, nearly sending him into the creek. He could feel the log vibrating underneath him from the strong current. The soldier's description of the decayed pine log had not been an exaggeration. Harry wondered if it would hold the weight of many soldiers. He quickly stepped along, gripping the rope and nearing dry ground. Hopping on to the safety of the far bank, he called back. "Be careful. That second log is rotten."

Shep, Springer, and Cohen came next, spreading out and making a quick crossing. Springer said, "I believe I wet my britches when that rotten log kept shaking."

"It won't matter. You're wet from head to toe." Harry nodded as Sarge, Nickels, and Halverson crossed together. He watched as they bunched up at the second log. "Spread out when you get to the second log."

Sarge shot him a glance. "You let me take care of this."

Harry shrugged as Cohen whispered. "Hal can't swim and he's deathly afraid of water."

The three of them climbed onto the second log and slowly made progress toward the bank. Harry scanned the other bank. There were eight more of their men to cross and another infantry unit was lined up behind them.

Suddenly, he heard the sickening crack of the second log. It gave way, leaving the three soldiers hanging onto the rope. Halverson, panicking, grabbed Sarge, causing him to lose his grip on the rope. The second crack was even more chilling: Sarge's feet went in the air and his head smacked the log and he slumped facedown into the fast current.

Halverson still had his grip on the rope, screaming as he dangled waist deep in the water. Nickels, leading the trio, lunged for a tree limb extending from the bank. All eyes were on Sarge as he floated unconscious in the swirling current. Harry looked at the soldiers standing beside him. Most were card-playing buddies of Sarge. They'd all grown up together in Monitowoc, but none of them moved as Sergeant Kickland—*their* Sergeant Kickland—was swept downstream.

Harry never remembered how he made his decision. He just did it, running downstream before diving in. Luckily, he'd removed his pack and extra gear after crossing, but he quickly found that trying to swim in a soaked uniform and boots is difficult. In spite of this, he began to close the distance.

Just as he neared him, Sarge sank. Harry lunged for his pack, got a handhold, and was pulled under with him. But he didn't let go . . . at least not yet. He was blinded in the muddy water and not sure which way was up. He bumped against a large limb and grasped it with his free hand. His lungs bursting, Harry clawed for the surface.

As his head burst out of the water, he felt Sarge's pack come loose. The big man's limp body was buoyant enough to rise long enough for Harry to get a death grip on his sleeve. They were both caught in the fork of the limb, but their heads were above water.

A small trickle of blood oozed from Sarge's ear and his breathing was shallow. Harry hoped he hadn't swallowed too much water. There was nothing to do but hold on. Their heads bobbing in the water, he whispered in his tormentor's ear. "You sorry buzzard. I'd been planning ways to knock you off, and now I've went and saved your butt."

Soldiers on both sides of the creek were running and yelling. Harry lifted his head enough to see they were stranded in the middle of the creek. He heard horse hooves on the sandbar and shouting. He only knew one thing: He was glad to be alive. In fact, he was even glad to be alive in Louisiana.

Chapter 28
Hanging On

Every second was a strain for Harry as he held Sarge against the strong current with one hand and gripped the slick limb with the other. He was dizzy and still coughing from the copious amount of creek water he'd swallowed. The limb was slipping from Harry's grasp, pulled by the strong current. He couldn't hold on much longer. Behind him he heard a shout. "Come on, Sam. Let's go."

The loud splashing had to be a horse and rider. Sure enough, a horse's head appeared beside him and he felt Sarge pulled from his grasp. A soldier yelled, "I've got him." Harry turned to see the cavalryman dragging Sarge as the horse struggled toward the far bank.

The limb slipped from Harry's hand and he was jerked under. He bobbed up and flailed toward the near bank. The weight of his boots and soaked uniform kept pulling him under. Finally, he felt solid ground under him and struggled onto the creek bank. A medic from the pontoon group helped him up and led him to the road where an ambulance was waiting. Sarge lay on a stretcher on the roadway, still unconscious and pale.

Harry directed the medic toward Sarge. "I'm fine. Take care of him." Company K soldiers began arriving and gathered in a worried circle. Cohen knelt by Harry. "Man, are you okay?"

Harry retched up a fair amount of creek water. "I guess I swallowed more than I thought."

"Speaking of thinking . . . what made you jump in?"

Harry felt light-headed. "I didn't jump . . . somebody pushed . . ." That was the last thing he remembered. He awoke later on a stretcher as a medic straddled him. "How are you feeling, big boy?"

"I'll be better if you get off me."

"Sure, Miller. You're quite the hero."

Harry sat up and saw Sarge on a nearby stretcher. "Is he going to be okay?"

The medic nodded. "He's got a bad knot on his head, probably a concussion, but he'll be fine."

Harry threw up more creek water and wiped his mouth. "I should've let the sorry rascal drown."

"Private Miller, that's not the way a church-going man ought to talk."

"I'm not. . . ." He looked at the medic. "I know you. . . ."

"Sure you do. We met at church a few weeks ago." He stuck out his hand. "I'm Crawford with the 503rd Medical. We were in Sunday School together."

"Yeah, I remember you."

Crawford grinned. "What was a 32nd man doing at a church that far from camp?"

"I was there to meet a girl."

"That's what I figured. How'd it go?"

Harry's head throbbed. "Worse than terrible."

In spite of his protestations, Harry was loaded into the ambulance beside Sarge. Crawford said, "We just want to look you over for a few hours." He glanced at Kickland who was moaning. "Your partner may be staying with us a little longer."

The platoon members were gathered at the ambulance doors. Shep stepped forward. "We've got all of your gear, Miller. We'll see you later." There was a strange look on Shep's face, completely different from the past. It even showed in the tenor of his words. It was a tone of respect.

Harry sat up in the ambulance. "Where's that cavalryman who saved us?"

Another trooper called out. "Sergeant Ed, this soldier wants to see you."

The sergeant, leading his horse, walked forward.

"Sergeant, I want to thank you for what you did. My name's Harry Miller."

"I'm Ed Regan and the real hero is my horse, Uncle Sam."

Harry couldn't see the horse from his ambulance. "Please thank Uncle Sam for helping save us."

Harry got a hot shower and a real meal at the field hospital. They even brought him dry clothes. It would have been a nice place to stay, but he was antsy. He stopped a passing medic. "I need to get back to my men."

The doctor glanced up from his chart. "Your men? Aren't you a private?"

"Yes Sir, but I need to be with them."

The doctor nodded at the drumming rain on the canvas tent. "I figured a fellow would be happy to hang around here."

"I would, but this is not where I belong."

He flipped the chart closed. "Then, we'll get you back there real soon." Scribbling on the chart, he said, "Orderly, get the papers ready to release this soldier." Before leaving, Harry slipped to Sarge's bed, finding him sleeping soundly. He had a terrible knot on his head, but his color was good.

A nurse grabbed Harry's arm. "You're the one who saved him?"

"Yeah, I had to do it. The joker owed me twenty dollars. It was the only way I was going to get it."

The cute nurse pursed her lips. "I'm sure you'll get your money."

And that's how Harry found himself arriving at Company K's bivouac after dark. They were camped on the edge of a cotton field between Boyce and Flatwoods. Shorty looked up from a poker game. "Well, look who's back, the great hero!"

Everyone greeted him and wanted to know about Sarge. After giving a report, Harry said, "Guys, I'm beat. I'm turning in." Shorty directed him to their tent and Harry crawled into his sleeping bag. He began to drift off, put to sleep by the steady patter of rain on the tent. His life had changed today. He wondered if it would still be different tomorrow.

The next morning dawned cloudy but the rain had slackened. The platoon got an early start, marching for about three hours before hearing the first faint sounds of battle. A string of dive-bombers came over and they dove into cover. It was difficult to distinguish if the planes were friendly or enemy, so they took no chances. A scouting party from Company C trotted by. "Enemy light tanks followed by infantry are about a mile north moving this way." A second lieutenant began arranging the platoon in a semi-circular pattern across an open field, bisected by an old logging road. The officer said, "If they come through here, we'll ambush them."

"Ambush *tanks?*" Cohen said.

The lieutenant pointed to foxholes and mounds of dirt left from an earlier position. "We don't even have to dig, just get concealed. Let the tanks pass us, if we can get an anti-tank unit up, they'll take them out. We'll finish the infantry off with rifle crossfire."

Shep raised his hand. "With the drier weather, we've seen the tanks fanning out across open areas like this instead of sticking to the road. What if they do this?"

"Good question. We simply stay in our holes and let them roll past before firing. The element of surprise will still be on our side."

A new soldier said, "What if a tank comes toward our fox hole?"

"Stay low. They'll most probably go around you."

"Most probably?"

"They've got no reason to run over a foxhole. You stay put."

The soldier said, "I'm not gonna be no tank pancake."

"If it gets too close, get up and run."

"How close is *too* close?"

"You'll have to make that decision. Just don't panic and give away our position." As the men deployed, the lieutenant stopped Harry. "You take that new guy with you and keep him calm."

The officer pointed toward an umpire vehicle south of the roadway. "I'm going to tell them to conceal themselves better. I'll radio back for an anti-tank unit to move up." He turned to Nickels. "Get your BAR set up. "

Harry, Shorty, and the new soldier found a foxhole big enough for the three of them. It was knee deep in water and they used their hats to bail it out.

The new soldier punched Shorty. "I ain't getting run over by no tank."

"Well, neither am I. Just stay calm."

"What's your name?" Harry said.

"Brick. C.J. Brick."

He grabbed his shoulder. "Listen, Brick, it's going to be fine. This isn't real. It's make believe."

"If a tank runs over us, it won't be make believe."

Shorty laughed. "You've got a point. Just stay close to me."

"But I ain't staying if it means getting run over by a tank."

"*Stay with me.*" Shorty put a finger in Brick's face. "Don't run unless I run. If I shoot, you shoot."

They kept moving around in the foxhole to keep from miring deeper in the mud. Suddenly, Shorty lifted his hand. "I hear tanks." The clackety-clank of the tanks came nearer by the minute. Harry was the first to see the line of tanks approaching. "Six tanks in single file with an infantry platoon scouting ahead."

Within minutes the foot soldiers neared the foxholes. Two of them passed within fifty feet and one said, "This is stupid. The Blue Army's probably twenty miles away by now."

Hunkered down, Shorty whispered, "We got a surprise for them." As the tanks reached the field, they deployed across the open field. "They're fanning out and coming our way."

Four of the tanks veered diagonally away from the road, but two continued toward their foxhole. Brick elbowed Harry. "They're coming our way."

"I can see that. Stay calm."

The tank drivers were communicating by hand signals. Behind them a company of soldiers fanned out. The haphazard way they carried their weapons made it clear they had no idea they were walking into a trap.

Harry watched the tanks. "One of them's turning away." One of the tanks slowed to a crawl before taking a perpendicular turn to the west. "But that one there is coming straight our way." The tank was now less than a football field away, climbing over stumps and fallen trees. As wood splintered, Harry wondered how much a tank weighed.

Brick grabbed his arm. "It's coming our way."

"Stay calm." Nevertheless, Harry's heart pounded as the tank continued in a straight line for their foxhole. Shorty, who'd stepped up on a stump to see, pulled out a smoke grenade.

Thirty yards in front of their foxhole spot was a pile of empty gasoline jerry cans. Harry tightened his jaw at the sickening sound of crushing metal as the tank rode over the cans. Brick, sinking in the mud, tried to wiggle loose. "I'm outta here."

Harry shoved him down. "Not yet. Stay still." He peered over the mound. The tank was bearing down on their position.

"I ain't staying here—" Before he could finish, Shorty shook him. "If you run, I'm gonna throw this live grenade at you."

"That's not a real grenade."

Shorty pulled the pin. "Don't try me." The tank was now within twenty yards and the ground was shaking beneath its weight. Shorty nudged Harry. "Don't you think…?"

"It's going to turn." Harry peered over the rim and saw the underside of its carriage and clods of dirt flying off its massive tracks. Suddenly, the gears shifted and the tank made a clattering turn away from them. As the three soldiers crouched, the tank lumbered by within a few feet and the edge of their foxhole collapsed, covering them in dirt to their knees. Four Red Army infantrymen, hugging close behind the tank, trotted by. Harry hunkered down, clicking off the safety on his rifle.

A sudden barrage of artillery burst forth from the woods. The tank destroyer unit unloaded on the unsuspecting tanks. Blue machine gunfire erupted from both sides of the roadway. The tanks and their foot soldiers were caught in a deadly crossfire.

The four Red soldiers sprinted for Harry's foxhole. Remembering that rules prevented rifle fire within twenty feet, he shoved Brick's rifle down just as the soldiers tumbled into the foxhole. Harry held up his fingers as if he was shooting them. One of the Red arrivals was a First Lieutenant. Shorty handed him the grenade. "Pop. Pop. You're dead."

The officer was stunned into silence while his three partners seemed happy to be anywhere out of the line of fire. Brick climbed up on the foxhole's ledge and quickly emptied his clip at sprinting Red soldiers. Harry and Shorty joined him in the fun. The open field echoed with the popping of small arms fire and men yelling, but the main noise was the jackhammer rattling of four or five machine guns, as they laid down a field of fire on the surprised invaders. It was exhilarating. Harry felt a sense of purpose that slowed down the action and allowed him to grasp exactly what was happening.

An umpire's shrill whistle and the waving of the white truce flag signaled the end of this skirmish. A Red Army umpire vehicle screeched to a halt near Harry's foxhole and was soon joined by a group of Blue umpires. Shorty climbed out of his foxhole. "Let's go listen."

The umpires spread their map and charts on the hood of the jeep as soldiers from both armies mixed together, sharing cigarettes and stories. Harry and Shorty walked to a barbed wire fence to eavesdrop on the umpire's conversation. The four Red soldiers who'd shared their foxhole walked past. "We fried your goose," Shorty said.

The cocky young officer stopped. "You did not. We had more concentrated fire and won the battle."

Shorty scoffed. "Won the battle, my behind. Y'all never knew what hit you."

The Red Lieutenant said, "If you did, it's because you didn't follow control officer guideline 248-b1." He held up a tattered umpire's manual. "It's right here."

Shorty scoffed. "Bull. *My* manual says that 'all's fair in love and war'." Three strands of rusty barbed wire separated the two men. Shorty stepped to the fence, rising to his full height as he faced the officer, who was a full head taller.

The officer chuckled. "We licked you good." He nodded at the umpires. "You'll see in a minute."

"No way."

Reaching across the top strand of wire, he jabbed a finger in Shorty's chest. "You can shut your mouth, you little runt."

Much to Harry's surprise, Shorty didn't strike. This only encouraged the officer who was revealing himself as a practiced bully. "We whipped you real good, pipsqueak." Saying this, the officer shoved Shorty with both hands, causing him to tumble backwards.

A Red soldier walked to the Lieutenant. "Sir, calm down." Harry noticed how the umpires had stopped deliberations and their full attention was on the altercation at the fence. The officer reached across the fence, grabbing Shorty's shirt. "I don't need any sorry buck private telling me who won or—"

He never finished. Like a rattlesnake striking, Shorty Johnson's right fist connected with the officer's chin, and he slowly slid down in a heap at the foot of the fence.

Cohen walked up. "Knock out. Third round. Winner and still *champion of the worlllllld*, Joe Louis aka Shorty Johnson."

Nickels, grinning proudly, said, "The taller the tree, the harder it falls."

But it wasn't a KO—the officer wobbly rose before the count of ten—but all of the fight was out of him. Pointing at Shorty—but safely out of reach—he spit blood. "You'll answer for striking an officer."

"And *you'll* answer for provoking him." It was a hard-faced umpire—a major who'd watched the entire fracas. He pulled out a pad. "Come over here, Lieutenant." He pointed at Shorty. "*You* wait here for me."

He led the brash officer away from the crowd as the young lieutenant gestured wildly. On each rant, the major's response boomed, "But you asked for it."

Back at the fence, Shorty Johnson held a post-fight press conference. Even one of the Red soldiers reached out in congratulations. "It made my day to see him go down. You really dough-popped him."

A fellow soldier added, "It made my year. He's been asking for it, and you gave it to him."

Another soldier, with a Southern accent, said, "You clay-rooted him."

Shorty shrugged. "If he'd kept his flytrap shut, I wouldn't have hit him."

The umpire's whistle pierced the air and officers from both armies gathered around the jeep. The lieutenant had returned, still rubbing his jaw.

The umpires' ruling was completely in favor of the Blue Army. The hotheaded Lieutenant threw down his manual and stormed off. The chief umpire crossed his arms. "It's final. Five of the six tanks out. Thirty-two Red-soldier casualties."

The Lieutenant stopped in mid-stride. "There's no way you can judge it that way. No way."

Cohen nudged Harry. "I believe he's gonna kick dirt on home plate."

"It reminds me of newsreels of that Dodgers manager, with his hat turned around, in an umpire's face," Harry said. "What's his name?"

Cohen and Nickels answered in unison. "Leo Durocher."

"Yeah, that's him."

Watching the Lieutenant finish his fit, Cohen said, "I'm glad we're not under his command. In a real war, an idiot like that'll get a lot of soldiers killed."

"If one of them don't kill him first," Nickels said.

"I believe Shorty'd do it within a week."

"I'd give him three days. Four at most."

The Major stepped beside the Lieutenant. "Groves, go over by that tree and wait for me."

"He's done put him in the corner," Harry said.

"Private, front and center." The Major motioned to Shorty.

Shorty snapped to attention.

"What's your name?"

"Johnson, Sir. Lester Johnson."

"Where are you from?"

"Right here, Sir."

"You like fighting?"

"I don't seek it, but don't run from it either."

The Major smiled coyly. "I have a feeling that you'll get to do plenty of fighting soon. You'd better save it for the Germans … or Japs." He was about Shorty's height and got toe to toe with him. "I'd better not hear your name again unless I'm pinning a medal on you. We can't have soldiers hitting officers." He nodded toward the time-out tree. "Even if they are acting like a jerk. Understood?"

Shorty stared ahead. "Sir, Yes Sir.

The Major walked to Harry. "Yep, they said the purpose of these maneuvers wasn't just trying out equipment. It was also trying out men." He shook his head at the sulking lieutenant. "To find out who *can't* lead." He stopped, studying Harry closely, "and who *can*." He didn't try to disguise his disgust. "It's idiots like that officer who get good men killed in real combat." The major motioned to Harry. "Son, I watched through my binoculars when that tank nearly ran over your foxhole. You and your two partners were cool under pressure. Good job." Harry saluted as the officer returned to his jeep.

Shorty playfully put a fist in Harry's face. "Miller, I believe we're going to make a fighting soldier out of you, yet."

Chapter 29
Crossroads

Four days later . . . Saturday, September 20

Harry, Shep, and Shorty were drying out around a campfire. The rain had finally tapered off, but every stitch of clothing they wore was damp and soured. Harry was attempting to dry his socks over the fire without burning a hole in them.

"Word is that Sarge will be back with us by the second battle," Shep said.

"First of all we've got to end this one." Shorty moved one of his drying boots away from the fire. "Any word on the ending?"

Shep stirred the coals with a stick. "The scuttlebutt is that they'll pull the plug today or tomorrow." He turned to Harry. "You know why he hates you so much?"

"Who?"

"Sarge."

"I have no idea why."

"It's because of your father."

Harry dropped a sock and quickly kicked it out of the embers. "What's my father got to do with Sarge?"

"Isn't your father a high-powered lawyer in Milwaukee?"

"He is."

"Your father represented some big corporation that put the Kickland family out of their fishing business on Lake Michigan, and he carries a king-size grudge. When he connected you to your father, it put a big red bull's-eye on your back.

Harry stared into the fire. He couldn't—or wouldn't—look at Shep. Shorty said, "Do you think Sarge's attitude about Harry will change 'cause of him saving his life?"

Shep nodded. "I know mine changed." He stood. "Every one of us knew what needed to be done, but you're the only one that had the guts to do it. The fact that he hated your guts made your act even more impressive." He poked Harry with the stick. "Why *did* you do it?"

"I'm not sure. I don't even remember making a conscious decision."

Shep bit his lip. "My family has a long military history. An uncle of mine told a story from the last war."

"Why do they always call it 'the last war'?" Short put on his boots.

"'Cause there's always another one coming. Anyway, my uncle told about a German grenade—he called it a 'potato masher'—landing in their trench. A soldier from Oregon named Sager jumped on it. The grenade was a dud and didn't go off, but that didn't detract from how the men viewed Sager as their hero. My uncle stayed in touch with him for the rest of his life. He said that Sager stood at a crossroads that day in the trench and made a split-second decision."

"Kind of like Harry's decision to save Sarge?" Shorty said.

"Exactly." Shep said, "What would you do?"

"What . . . do you mean?"

"About a hand grenade."

"I'm not sure. I hope never to find out. How about you?"

"I'm not sure either."

Shorty kicked an ember back in the fire. "I wonder if it's something a fellow decides ahead of time or if it's a split-second decision."

Harry watched the firelight dance on the serious faces of his two fellow soldiers. "I guess everyone comes to a crossroads in their lives. And what a man does determines everything about his future, maybe even life and death."

Shep grinned. "Miller, you're a real philosopher. So the creek *crossing* was your *crossroads?*"

"It was one, but I have others to face."

Loud banging on pots broke the quiet of the camp as cheering floated over from across the road. A soldier ran up. "The battle's over. They called a truce."

Shep stood. "It's time to get pig-eyed blind drunk."

Harry watched him run off to find his drinking buddies. "I guess that's his crossroads."

"And what's your next crossroads?" Shorty said.

"I'm going back to Bundick. I'm going to see Elizabeth Reed."

"The schoolteacher? From what you told me, that's pretty brave."

"Brave . . . or maybe foolish, but I won't know if I don't go back."

Chapter 30
Second Helping

Sunday, Sept. 21

"Crossroads." Harry drew in a deep breath. "Crossroads. I'm here." He strode toward the front doors of Bundick Church. He couldn't believe he was back, and sure couldn't explain why. He only knew this: he'd made up his mind to fight *for* Elizabeth Reed. The only problem was that he wasn't fighting off an army. His battle was *with* Elizabeth Reed. She might brush him off again, but it wouldn't be because he didn't try.

Because of the unit's late night arrival back at their assembly area, Harry'd gotten a belated morning start and had a difficult time hitching rides. As he slipped in the church's back door, the choir was singing a special. He glanced at his sweaty palms, one on which he'd written with a pen, "Cowards die many times before their deaths." He muttered the rest of the Shakespearean quote, "...but the valiant never taste of death but once."

He quietly slipped into a back pew. "I might be a *fool*, but I'm not going to be a *coward*."

As the song ended, the pastor stood. "We've got five candidates today for baptism."

He scanned the choir and where her family was sitting: no sign of Elizabeth Reed. He felt a strange mix of relief and disappointment. Maybe this wasn't such a great idea after all.

A Colored man slid over and stuck out his hand. "I'm Riley."

Harry nodded. "Good to meet you."

Ben Reed spied him and hurried back. "Everybody said you wouldn't come back, but I told them you would." He leaned across. "Morning, Mr. Riley. Have you met Private Miller?"

"Just did."

"He's gonna marry my sister Elizabeth."

Mr. Riley broke into an open-faced grin. "Really?" He turned to Harry. "Congratulations."

Harry turned to Ben. "Really?"

"Yep, I had a dream about it."

Riley whispered, "Mr. Ben, you better lower your voice or Miz Pearline'll come back here and take a switch to all three of us."

Harry spotted Elizabeth, who was sitting on the other side of the church among other young people. She glanced back, saw Harry and set her gaze forward. This didn't stop the two girls on either side of her from giggling as they stared at him.

The song leader called out the next song. "It's page 54 in the maroon book. 'On Jordan's Stormy Banks.'"

Ben elbowed Harry. "Watch this." He held up what was meant to be an imaginary rod and reel as the choir launched into "On Jordan's stormy banks I stand and cast..." At that precise moment, Ben "cast" his rod, set the hook, and reeled in his catch as the choir sang, "...a wishful eye to Canaan's fair and happy land...."

The pastor followed with a sermon on the baptism of Jesus. After what he called a "time of invitation" he stood, arms outstretched. "We're going to dismiss after a word of prayer and go straight to the creek. This will be our last baptism until late spring, so we want everyone to join us." Just as on Harry's earlier visit, the pastor called on Uncle Cricket to dismiss in prayer, after which the congregation sauntered toward the nearby creek.

Harry was following Ben when someone tapped him on the shoulder. It was Elizabeth Reed. "Have a great life."

"And you, too."

"I didn't expect *you* back."

"I came because I liked the preaching."

"Really?"

"Nah, it was the dinner on the grounds."

"We're not having that today."

"Well, I guess that only leaves one reason: I came to see you."

She blushed. "I was afraid of that."

"Well, here I am."

"I can see that."

"I know I'm kind of being pushy."

She put her hand up. "Let's just enjoy being together." Her smile was warmer, making Harry curious. They stopped on a bluff overlooking the creek, where she said, "Have you ever been to a creek baptism?"

"I haven't." He'd never been to a baptism of *any* kind.

Ben wormed his way in between them, nodding toward the creek. "Poppa said so much sin's been washed off in this hole that the creek's plugged up downstream tighter than a beaver dam." He tugged on Harry's arm. "Pvt. Miller, have you been baptized?"

"Not that I remember."

"Ben Reed, it's rude to ask personal questions." Elizabeth's irritation erased her earlier smile.

Harry waved her off. "It's okay."

"I was baptized last year," Ben said.

"In this creek?"

"Yes Sir."

"Why do you baptize outdoors?"

"Is there any other place?"

"Churches up north have an inside baptistry."

"We do it out here 'cause that's the way Jesus did it." Ben said, "Why haven't you been baptized?"

"I guess I've never thought much about it. Why do you folks baptize—I mean, do you believe it washes your sins away?"

"Heck, no." Ben laughed. "Poppa says you come out of Bundick Creek dirtier than when you went in. Baptism is an *outside* act about something that's happened *inside*—in your heart."

Harry turned to Elizabeth. "I guess you've been baptized?"

"Right here at age eight." When she said this, she moved closer to Harry and he smelled her perfume. He liked the way things were going. On the sand bar below, the congregation sang, "Shall We Gather at the River," as their voices blended in the natural amphitheater of the trees and creek. Harry smiled. "Listen to the a cappella singing echoing off the woods and water."

"What's ah-cap-fellow singing?" Ben said.

Elizabeth put her arm around him. "It's music without instruments." She steered him toward the crowd on the sand bar. "It also means without *you*." As he sulked off, she turned to Harry. "I can tell you like music."

"Better than I like to breathe." He closed his eyes as the singing wafted over him.

"Music tames the savage beast."

"It's always tamed this one." He smiled. "I also like creeks—I had sort of a religious experience at one last week."

"Really?' She laughed nervously. "Private Miller, you're different from last visit. What happened?"

"I'll answer your question if you'll call me 'Harry'."

"All right . . . *Harry*. What's different?"

"I was at a crossroads and made some decisions."

"Did that have anything to do with you coming back?"

He nodded. "You're different too."

Her eyes brimmed. "I had a dream."

"Was it a good dream or a nightmare?"

"A little of both."

The pastor prayed as four converts waded out into the dark greenish creek. Harry peeked and saw several of the new converts cringe as they reached the deeper water. Elizabeth whispered. "The creek gets colder as the days shorten."

Harry smiled. "I could tell from that woman's face."

In spite of the chattering teeth of those in the water, the pastor gave a stirring review of Jesus' baptism before turning to the song leader, who was safely on dry land. "Let's sing that first verse of 'On Jordan's Stormy Banks' again."

As the song leader waved his arm and the crowd sang, Harry looked for Ben and his fishing rod. "Where's Ben?"

"No telling." The song ended and the actual baptism began. One by one, each was baptized in the name of the Father, Son, and Holy Ghost. As the third person came forward, Harry caught a glimpse of movement around the creek bend, and nudged Elizabeth. "Look at that."

"Oh my goodness," Elizabeth said as a flotilla of empty beer bottles and C-ration cans floated into view near the baptism area. They floated silently right through the midst as the pastor tried to maintain a semblance of dignity. The snickering started at the edge of the crowd where the younger folks stood, and spread like a flood until it broke out in uninhibited laughter among everyone, including the converts. One of them—an adult man—plucked a beer bottle from the water and tossed it onto the far bank as a woman in the crowd shouted, "Praise the Lord."

The only person not laughing was the red-faced pastor. As a final insult, the last beer bottle floated against him and he angrily slapped it away like you would a horsefly.

Elizabeth nudged Harry. "Look there." Ben and a boy in overalls were coming around the bend. At that moment, Mrs. Reed burst out of the crowd, collaring Ben as she broke off a pine limb, and began wearing him out.

As they disappeared around the bend, Harry shrugged. "He should've run while he could." Elizabeth, red-faced, elbowed him as Harry added, "He could've run off and joined the navy." He pointed toward the last of the bottles floating out of sight. "He's already an admiral with his own fleet."

"Harry, this isn't funny. It's embarrassing." He tried to stifle his laughter, but failed miserably. Elizabeth began giggling and they leaned on each other. It'd been a long time since Harry had touched a woman. Even in the middle of a laughing fit, her soft body felt great. From the way she didn't pull away, he wondered how long it'd been for her.

As the final convert was baptized, the faithful scattered, leaving them alone up on the bluff. She touched his hand. "So you like music?"

"I do."

"Why don't you come by our house? We're having a porch singing later this afternoon."

"I'd love to." He pointed toward the creek. "Besides, I'd hate to leave and miss out on seeing what happens next around here."

Chapter 31

For a Song

It was a long walk to the Reed house, but not long enough for Harry. He would gladly walk to Wisconsin beside Elizabeth Reed. As they neared her home, she became uncomfortable. "That's our house. It's simple—not much to look at."

It *was* simple: rough, log siding; spacious front porch; open hallway down the middle; rusted tin roof. But it had character and appeal, and Harry immediately fell in love with its homey look. "Why's the hallway down the middle?"

"It's a dogtrot home—the middle porch is where the dogs pad back and forth," Elizabeth said. "Do you have porches up North?"

"Not many. It's too cold much of the year."

"Do you have lots of snow?"

"Piles of it. Have you ever seen snow?"

"Not much. We have a dusting every few years . . . but no piles."

Harry liked the way she peered into his eyes and for the first time noticed how dark and inviting hers were. From inside the house, a guitar was being tuned. The screen door creaked open and Elizabeth's mother stepped onto the porch.

"Harry, this is my mother, Pearline Reed," Elizabeth said. The way she studied him revealed that she was the key person guarding the gate into Elizabeth's heart.

"We're glad you're joining us for dinner, Private Miller."

These Southerners and their meal names drove him crazy. Lunch was dinner and dinner was what they called supper. He wasn't sure he'd ever get used to it.

He removed his hat. "It's good to meet you, Mrs. Reed. I saw you at the creek."

She reddened and Harry stuttered, "I mean, Elizabeth *pointed* you out."

She brushed flour off her dress. "Hard to miss, wasn't I?"

He gave a half-salute. "You've got a strong right arm. That limb broke long before you did."

She leaned on the porch railing. "If it hadn't broke, I'd still be wearing Ben Franklin Reed out." She blew out a breath. "That boy ruint the baptism."

"Well, it's one that won't ever be forgotten."

"That ain't necessarily a good thing."

"Where is the little admiral? Admiral Ben."

"He's been confined to his room and will be taking his meal there." Everyone else gathered around for a tableful of country food. Harry couldn't remember when he'd ever enjoyed a meal and visiting this much.

The women cleared the table and Elizabeth's father, guitar in hand, motioned to the front porch. "Take a chair and join us." They were soon joined by Ma, who cradled a violin, tuning its A string, and Elizabeth. "Your grandmother plays the violin?" Harry said.

"No. Ma plays the *fiddle*." She placed her hand on his, and as their eyes met, Harry saw something: it was a mixture of joy and fear. One of those emotions was going to

---

win. His job was to make sure the spark of joy burst into flame. Just like that A-string, a note was plucked in his soul: *Put your heart in it and win her.*

Mr. Reed introduced the other players, including a younger man in overalls. "This is Mr. Aubrey from Cole Central Community.

"Aubrey will be the next parish fiddle champion," Ma said.

The younger man rosined his bow. "Ma's won the contest seven years in a row. The Beauregard Parish title will be hers until she retires."

"Why do you call it a parish?" Harry said.

"It's part of our French history." Elizabeth said. "Beauregard Parish is named after that general who started the Civil War."

"How do you say his name?"

"Boor-gard."

Harry tried saying it but each attempt brought good-natured laughter. He heard a squeaky voice behind him. "It's *'Boar-Hog.'* We live in Boar Hog Parish."

Harry, turning to see Ben, said, "The Admiral's back in action. How was your time in the brig?"

He rubbed the seat of his overalls. "I'm still on fire."

"Next time, Admiral, before launching your fleet, get *downstream.*"

"You know, you've got a good point." Ben winked at Elizabeth. Straight chairs scraped across the rough porch planks as the music started. Mr. Reed led the rhythm and direction of each song. If he was the conductor, there was no doubt his mother—Ma—was first-chair violinist. Harry couldn't take his eyes off the tall, thin woman as she held the fiddle like a mother holding a newborn.

On the third song, Ma took over. It was a rolling song that began in 4/4 time before shifting to cut time. Mr. Reed strummed his guitar, sweat beading on his forehead as he tried to keep up. Elizabeth whispered, "It's 'Eighth of January.' It's the song she always wins the fiddle contest with."

She played, eyes closed, softly swaying as the notes flowed from the fiddle. She'd claimed a worn section of the porch as her kingdom. Harry wondered how many times she'd played this song in that spot. Her instrument was old and cheap-looking, but her playing made it come alive. It seemed an extension of her hands. "It's a song about Andrew Jackson's victory at the Battle of New Orleans," Elizabeth said.

Harry recalled his mother's words after a Milwaukee performance by a visiting Russian classical violinist. She'd whispered, "He makes everything in the room beautiful by his playing." This was true whether in an ornate concert hall or a dogtrot porch in the woods. When Ma ended her song, he blurted, "She makes everything . . . beautiful."

The old woman curtsied and Elizabeth squeezed his hand. Harry wasn't sure which of the two ladies he was falling in love with. Without taking a break, Mr. Reed called out, "Let's do 'Life's Railway to Heaven,' key of D." Tapping his foot like a size-ten metronome, he led the players through the song with key changes, nodding and gesturing at who'd lead the next verse. After that song, the players carefully re-tuned their instruments with Mr. Reed's ear being the final judge on perfection. Satisfied, he said, "Two Little Girls in Blue."

"This song has been in our family for generations," Elizabeth whispered.

"Where did this music come from?"

"From the heart."

"No, I mean *where* . . . how'd it get here?"

"Most are mountain songs from the Appalachians, where our ancestors migrated from. They didn't bring the *mountains,* but they brought the *songs.*" As her father sang of lovers drifting apart, she added, "They're songs of sadness and hard times—something mountain people and Southerners know about."

"They do have an Irish feel to them."

"Most of us in the Piney Woods have Scotch-Irish roots. What are your roots?"

"My father's German and my mother is Irish."

"*Miller* doesn't sound German?"

"That's because my father's family changed it from Mueller in 1914. Regardless, my roots aren't deep like yours." They turned their attention back to the musicians who alternated between sad songs, upbeat jigs, and slow waltzes, often jumping directly from one genre to another. Harry especially liked a fast hymn called, "When We All Get to Heaven." Mr. Reed had an especially rich bass voice, and dipped his head to get lower as he echoed, "...and *sing and shout* the victory."

As the hymn ended, Mr. Reed took out a red bandana, wiping off his face. "Let's keep it lively with 'Roving Gambler.'" This song had the same rhythm of the previous hymn but was more concerned with the *here and now* than Heaven, causing Harry to whisper, "Your father's got quite a diverse repertoire."

"It is eclectic."

"That's a big word for a country girl."

The hurt in her eyes was confirmed as she said, "We're not stupid down here."

"I didn't mean it that way."

As "Roving Gambler" ended, her father walked over. "Lizzie, play *just* one for us."

A dark cloud crept over her face. "I'll pass."

"What do you play?" Harry said.

"The fiddle."

"I'd love to hear you."

"I haven't played in a long time. I'm out of practice."

Ben broke the impasse. "I'd like to sing a solo. It's a new song I've just learned." He bowed, cleared his throat and began,

"I know a song ... that gits on everybody's nerves.

I know a song that gits on everybody's nerves."

He grinned. *"I know ... a song that gits on everybody's nerves,*

And this is how it goes."

He took a breath. "I know a song...."

Mrs. Reed, trying not to laugh, said, "Enough. That is enough. I *will* send you back to your room."

Ben's natural protector, Ma, launched into an Irish lament in the same key as Ben's song. After she finished, Mr. Reed motioned for Elizabeth to take his fiddle. Again, she waved him off.

As the sun set in the swamp, insects began buzzing around the kerosene lanterns on the porch. Mr. Reed said, "Let's move this show inside away from the skeeters." They carried their chairs, coffee cups, and instruments into the living room. As soon as the chairs were circled, the music started again.

Peg, who'd been playing a mandolin, said, "Poppa, will you sing 'Angel Band'?"

He nodded at Elizabeth. "Not until she plays."

"But Poppa . . ." Elizabeth said. She didn't budge, in spite of her father's pleading. Six songs later, Elizabeth's grandmother walked over and placed her fiddle in Elizabeth's lap. "Honey, you know you can't tell Ma no."

"No..."

"Your answer should be yes. God gave you a gift."

Harry saw a cloudy mixture of tears and anger in her eyes. Elizabeth rose and walked slowly to the center of the room. Her hands came up and she tucked the fiddle gently under her chin. The music that resonated off the strings was as beautiful as the woman playing. It had the sound of an old Irish air. Harry felt as if he were watching the grandmother forty years ago. The same swaying, the closed eyes, the same soulful style.

Harry looked at the rough-log walls, flickering lanterns, and the inky darkness outside the windows as a woman named Elizabeth—who hadn't held a fiddle in a long time—played with skill, passion and feeling. She played the mournful song deliberately but with confidence. Her playing featured an understated passion, and the result was beautiful.

On the second verse, her father joined in,

"I am a poor wayfaring stranger,
Wandering through this world of woe."

Mr. Reed sang the refrain,

I am just going over Jordan,
I am just going over home."

Harry knew where he'd heard it: it was Reuben's benediction from the Blues night. It was the same song being played now by a girl he was falling in love with. He recalled Elizabeth's words at the baptism, "Music tames the savage beast." It was true.

As she drew the bow across the fiddle for the last note of this haunting song, Ma sighed. "I believe that girl's getting her song back."

Elizabeth set the fiddle down, hurrying from the room. "Please excuse me."

Ma took Harry by the arm. "That girl's got her song back—and it might be because of you."

"You think so?"

The old woman winked. "I really do, but it's her decision to make. Every tub sits on its own bottom."

"What?"

"Every tub . . . it means we're responsible for what we do." Suddenly, Harry clearly realized what he must do to win Elizabeth's heart. Mr. Reed cleared his throat. "It's been a long time since we heard from Lizzie. I guess I'll have to keep my promise." He turned to Harry, "This song was sung by my grandpa just afore he died." He pointed to a corner of the room. "He was in a bed right there. Some folk call it, 'Angel Band,' but we call it 'My Latest Sun.'"

In a deep whiskey-soaked voice, Mr. Reed began,

My latest sun is sinking fast,
And my race is nearly run.
My strongest trials, they now have passed.
My triumph has begun.

His guitar sat in his lap. It was as if this song needed no accompaniment.

O Come Angel Band
To my immortal home

On the second verse, everyone sang as they reached the chorus. "*Oh come angel band.*"

On the third verse, Elizabeth eased back into the room, smoothing her dress as she sat beside him. She'd been crying.

"Elizabeth, that was beautiful."

"Thanks." She patted his hand.

He now knew what he must do when the song ended. He walked to Ma, and held out his hands. "Do you mind?" She handed him the fiddle and bow. He remembered the last time he'd played: the day of the accident. He'd tried a couple of times but couldn't find his fingers or heart.

Holding this instrument in a rural home, he knew how odd he looked in his uniform, military haircut, and strange accent. But when he drew the bow across the strings, he knew he would no longer be a stranger. He could become one of them. He placed the violin under his chin in the precise manner he'd been taught as a child. He recalled how elegantly Elizabeth Reed had played it a few minutes ago. What should he play? His repertoire was classical. He remembered a song his mother had taught him—one she always requested he play. "This is called 'Shenandoah.' It was—I guess it still is—my mother's favorite."

He closed his eyes. This was so familiar, yet so new. Drawing the bow, he retreated into that wonderful place where he'd always felt most at home—playing music. He played one verse, and another, not daring to open his eyes. This was his addiction, and it grabbed him like never before. He heard the soft strum of a guitar, followed by a few melodic lines on another violin . . . or rather, fiddle. He'd always made a key change on the last verse. Eyes still closed, he called out, "Key of G" and his accompanists didn't miss a beat.

Playing the last note, he opened his eyes to everyone staring at him. Ma was dabbing a hankie at her eyes. "Son, you made the fireflies sing on that one."

Mr. Reed shook his head dreamily. "I heard the wind whisper in the longleaf pines." Elizabeth stood, hand over her mouth, as tears dripped onto the floor. Her father broke the spell. "The fiddle dances while the violin plays. You turned that old fiddle into a violin right before our eyes."

"It's all the same." Harry shrugged.

"Same instrument, but a different song." He slapped Harry on the back. "Yep, the fiddle dances while the violin plays."

Ben grabbed the violin, peering through the *f-holes* as if some magic had turned his grandmother's fiddle into a classical violin. "Why'd you close your eyes while you played?"

He looked around the room. "I didn't want this dream to end."

Ben tugged on his sleeve. "I didn't know you could play *and* sing."

"I just play."

"You were singing."

"Nah."

Ma sang softly, "Shenandoah, I love your daughter." She winked, cutting her eyes toward Elizabeth. "You kept singing it… like you meant it."

Harry glanced around at the log walls, dirt chimney, and cheap linoleum rug on the uneven floor. He'd been in concert halls and mansions, but this room possessed something they lacked, and it was much more than the music. It was something else. It was family. Something he'd missed out on.

At this moment, it was what he wanted more than anything else in the world.

He was homesick. Not homesick for Milwaukee or even his parents. He was homesick for a *home*. He ached for what these people had. He looked up into the crosshairs of Elizabeth's grandmother's eyes. Harry remembered his mother's tales of Old-Country-Irish women who could cast a spell on strangers. Maybe she'd done that to him. If it was a spell, it was a good one.

Ben nudged him. "Private Miller. You think there'll be fiddles up in Heaven?"

"Never thought much about it."

He pointed at his grandmother. "Ma says there'd better be, or she ain't staying."

"The way she plays, there'll be fiddles when she arrives. I think even the good Lord would want to hear her."

"What about violins?"

"I'm not sure about that."

Ben was on a roll. "We had a preacher in revival last year that called the fiddle 'the devil's instrument.'"

"No joke?"

"You ought to have seen his face the next night when Ma pulled out her fiddle and played 'The Old Rugged Cross.'"

Harry glanced at his watch and frowned. "It's about time for me to go."

Ma turned to her son. "Levon, you'd best show this boy how to play the saw before he leaves." Mr. Reed took down a handsaw from a nail on the wall. Sitting in his chair, he placed the saw handle between his knees and gripped the top of the blade with his left hand. Holding the bow with his right, he drew the bow across the smooth side of the blade while bending the saw. It was a strange rendition of "Amazing Grace," reminding Harry of a Hawaiian guitar. It was strange *and* beautiful. Glancing around the room at this circle of family and friends who'd taken him in for this evening as their own, he repeated softly, "Strange and beautiful."

As Mr. Reed hung the saw on its nail, Harry rose. "I hate to leave this fine music, but I can't be late back to camp."

Mr. Reed held up his hands. "One more song. We always end with my favorite. Let's do it in A flat." He sang,

"*Come ye sinners, poor and needy,*
Weak and wounded, sick and sore."

It was in a haunting minor key and the refrain gripped Harry on all five verses.

"*I will arise and go to Jesus,*
He will embrace me in his arms.
In the arms of my dear Savior,
Oh there are ten thousand charms."

When it ended, Harry said, "You'll never know how much it's meant to me to be here." There was a catch in his voice. "Thank you."

Elizabeth walked with him to the door followed by Ben. Harry held the door as Elizabeth squeezed by. Ma collared Ben. "Son, you stay in here. You'll catch cold out there."

The two young people stood on the porch as the night sounds of the crickets and nearby frogs filled the air. Harry's heart pounded in rhythm to their chirps. "Your family sang that last song like you meant it."

"We do." Elizabeth stepped closer. "Harry, where'd you learn to play like that?"

"I started playing at a young age but hadn't played in a long time. I'd kind of lost my song."

"Sounds like you've got it back."

"I believe I'm starting to." He put his hand on her arm. "What about you?"

She glanced down. "I'd kind of misplaced mine, too."

"Are you getting it back?"

Her dark eyes brimmed. "I sure hope so."

Harry wasn't sure if a kiss would seal this moment or doom it. There was only one way to find out. He pulled her close and pressed his lips to hers. It wasn't an extremely long kiss, but it was a kiss that Harry knew came from two hearts, not just one.

Before pulling away, he nudged her ear. "Thanks for helping me find my song."

"You're welcome." They both turned to see two watching faces, pressed to the window. She tapped the pane. "Ma, you and Ben are the two nosiest people in the whole world." She grimaced. "I apologize for my family being crazy."

Before stepping off the porch, Harry hugged her and kissed her lightly on the cheek. "Elizabeth Reed, you haven't seen the last of Harry Miller."

She didn't answer until they reached the gate. "Well, have a great life."

He pulled her close and this time the kiss was long, passionate, and made him weak in the knees. He stepped away and waved. "Have a great life, Elizabeth Reed."

Harry wasn't sure he'd ever get this night or the last song out of his mind. He recalled only part of the refrain, and sang it all the way until the crossroads.

"I will arise and go to Jesus;
He will embrace me in his arms."

Part III

The Battle for Shreveport

September 23–28, 1941

You've got a chance to put things right
So how's it going to be?
Lay down your arms now
And put us beyond doubt
So reach out—it's not too far away
Don't mess around now, don't delay

-"See the World"
Gomez

Chapter 32

Push Comes to Shove

TUESDAY, SEPTEMBER 23
BATTLE ORDER TO THIRD ARMY (BLUE) FORCES

PHASE TWO OF MANEUVERS WILL BEGIN TOMORROW (09/24/41)
AT HOUR 1200. BLUE ARMY OBJECTIVE WILL BE THE CAPTURE
AND OCCUPATION OF SHREVEPORT, LA. DIVISION AND CORPS
WILL RECEIVE PLANS RELATING TO SPECIFIC DIRECTIVES.

Harry, sitting on a pine stump, listened to the argument. It began when Nickels knelt beside Cohen, who was asleep under a tree. ".400." Cohen didn't move, so Nickels repeated, ".400."

The sleeping soldier didn't open his eyes, but replied, "56 beats .400 any day."

Nickels poked him. "I say .400 trumps 56. It's a bigger number."

Cohen sat up. "You're full of it. Ted Williams can't tie DiMaggio's shoes."

Nickels, the world's greatest Red Sox fan, was sensitive to any slight of his team, especially from a Yankees fan. ".406 . . . 37 home runs…120 runs batted in. Williams should be MVP."

Their tempers were rising as Nickels said, "How many games are left in the season?"

Cohen, who came from the Bronx, said, "Six games before the Yankees begin the World Series." He smirked at Nickels. "One more Ted Williams stat: Red Sox 17 games out of first place." He dusted his hands off. "Your team is a bunch of losers."

Nickels charged Cohen, wrapping him up and taking him down. The Yankee fan hit the ground hard where he lay kicking, gasping for breath.

Shorty Johnson knelt by Cohen, fanning his face. "Nick gets a TKO in the fourth round. We'll pin a purple heart on Cohen at a later ceremony."

Harry walked up to Nickels. "It's not fair how you bull-rushed him. If you're going to fight, fight fair."

"He shouldn't have run down Ted Williams."

"Man, if you're going to fight, at least fight about something important. Like a girl or someone insulting your mother."

"The Sox are pretty important to me," Nickels said.

Cohen, sitting up and regaining some semblance of breathing, said, "Nick . . . that was dirty . . . you never gave me. . . ." He jabbed a finger. "You better watch . . . your back every minute. I'll get you back. . . ."

Nickels spat in the dirt. "I'm not scared of you."

"You'd better be."

Harry helped Cohen up. "Take a walk, man, and cool off."

Cohen roughly pushed him away. "I'll get him for that. . . ." Suddenly, his face drained. When Harry turned, he saw why. Sergeant Kickland stood, arms crossed.

"I'm gone for six days and this platoon goes to hell in a hand basket."

"How long have you been standing there?" Nickels said.

"Long enough to see you making a fool out of yourself." Other than a bruise on his forehead, Sarge looked fine. "You two come over here with me." The circle of onlookers scattered. Sarge was back and business as usual was over.

"You saved his life and he didn't even look at you," Shorty said.

Harry shrugged. "I'll be fine if he just leaves me alone."

When Sarge finished dressing down the two fighters, he motioned to Harry. "Miller, I want a word with you." They walked about twenty yards before Sarge stopped and broke into an uncomfortable smile. "Thanks." He extended his hand. "Thanks for saving my life. I'm indebted."

"You're welcome."

"Miller, as hard as I've been on you, why in the world did you dive in?"

"It's just what one Red Arrow man does for another." Sarge's Adam's apple bobbed as if words were stuck in his throat. Harry stepped closer to Sarge. "You rode me due to my father?"

Sarge took a deep breath. "When I first learned who you were, it gave me a good reason to take out all of my anger on you." He grimaced. "But after a while, it became personal against you."

"Personal?"

"My dislike toward you wasn't about your father. It was the *waste* I saw in you. I saw the potential of what you *could* be: a soldier and a leader of men. Instead, I saw a lazy boy with no direction and drive. It . . . it . . . *you* made me sick."

This was the type of spiel Harry's father loved to spew, but it was different now. He nodded at Sarge. "Go ahead. I'm listening."

"When you came to my unit at Camp Beauregard, I made up my mind to *make* you into a soldier or kill you trying."

"I'm still here."

"Yes, you are. And I believe these maneuvers are making you into a soldier."

"We'll see." Harry slowly extended his hand. "Look, I'm sorry for whatever my father did to your family's business."

"It wasn't your fault. Bygones are bygones." Sarge grabbed Harry's hand. "I want to say it again—thanks for saving my life." He squeezed painfully hard. "But don't think I'm going to let up on you one second."

Harry winced and rubbed his hand. "Fair enough."

Shorty waited until he was out of sight before walking over. "Well, how was it?"

Harry grimaced. "Same ol' horse's behind as before—but I'm glad he's back."

Chapter 33
Birthing Babies

Two days later . . . Thursday Night, Sept. 25

In spite of the pounding rain, the dog's hoarse barking woke Elizabeth. She peered out the window and saw a lantern bouncing down the trail. Someone was in a hurry. She slipped on her housecoat and joined her father on the porch as he peered into the dark. "Who's out there?"

"It's me, Mr. Levon —Sally. My sister Verda went into labor, and we need help real bad." Elizabeth's stomach constricted. Difficult births in the woods were often tragic for mother, baby, or both. Living twenty-five dirt road miles from a doctor often meant the difference between life and death.

Momma joined them. "Sally, I thought she was going into town until the baby came."

"She was, Mrs. Pearline. Planned on leaving in the morning, but went into labor early."

"Let me get the school bus cranked," Poppa said. Elizabeth grabbed her shoes and hurried to the bus with Momma, Peg, and Sally. Poppa was grinding on the starter to no avail. He turned to the women. "Everybody out. Give her a push down the hill, and she'll crank."

The women tromped through the mud and shoved until the bus slowly began rolling downhill. As Poppa let out on the clutch, it sputtered and bucked to life. He revved the engine as the women ran and jumped aboard. He flipped on the headlights. "It's a blackout night, but we ain't going far." The squeaky wipers swished back and forth as Poppa strained to see through the rain.

"I wish some M.P. would pull us over," Peg said. "Maybe he'd know how to deliver a baby."

"How bad is she, Sally?" Momma said.

"I ain't never seen so much blood in my life."

Elizabeth leaned her throbbing head against the window and whispered, "Lord, I don't believe I can do this." They arrived at the home of Verda Harper and her husband Gator where the women hurried into the house. Poppa kept the bus running in case they needed to transport Verda.

Elizabeth froze at the porch when she heard the terrible screaming and crying. A voice, which she recognized as Verda's mother Becky, was wailing, "Lord, don't let my daughter die. Please don't let them die." Pulled along against her will, Elizabeth turned the doorknob and entered the small lamp-lit cabin. Gator Harper, Verda's husband, stood forlornly in the corner. A group of local women were gathered around the bed. Peg pulled her aside, "This is way beyond us."

Elizabeth only shook her head. Peg waved a hand in her face. "Lizzie, are you here? We'll never get her to town in time."

"Moving her would kill her anyway. She's lost too much blood," Momma said.

Elizabeth felt faint. "If I was in Shreveport, I wouldn't be here."

"What'd you say?" Peg grabbed her arm.

Scanning the room, Elizabeth said, "I'm going to the medical camp."

"What medical tent?" Verda said.

"There's a medical camp across the creek. Someone from there can help." She turned and bounded out the house to the waiting bus.

Poppa opened the bus door. "What gives?"

"Drive to the medical tent. We need help." It was a muddy two-mile trip to the medical camp on White Onion Hill. Poppa began honking as soon as they got close to the darkened camp. A sentry, rifle in hand, trotted up. "What's wrong?"

"We need a doctor—a neighbor woman's dying in childbirth," Elizabeth said.

"The doctors and staff are all in the field."

"We've got to have some help."

"There's one nurse who's here, but she's bad sick with food poisoning." Elizabeth leaped off the bus, housecoat flying behind her. Seeing a lantern in a nearby tent, she ran in, nearly tripping over a cot on which a woman lay.

"Are you a nurse?"

"If I don't die from food poisoning, I am."

"You've got to help. A girl's in childbirth—"

"I don't know anything about delivering babies."

Elizabeth helped her out of bed. "You know more than any of the rest of us." She led the nurse as she wobbily boarded the bus. She leaned the sick nurse's head against her shoulder. "By the way, I'm Elizabeth Reed and this is my father."

The nurse weakly opened her eyes. "I'm Emily Larsen." She leaned into the aisle and vomited. When she finished, she said, "I'm sorry. It's the sickest I've ever been in my life."

The bus was dark, but Elizabeth recognized her. "I know you, Nurse Larsen. I met you at our church and house."

"I hope I looked better than I do now."

"You did—I mean, you looked mighty nice that day."

The crowd on the porch had grown at the Harper house. It parted as the two women rushed up. Elizabeth paused at the terrible wailing from inside. It sounded as if they were too late. She turned to Nurse Larsen, who had fallen to her knees with the dry heaves. Wiping her face on her sleeve, she staggered forward. "I'm ready. Let's go."

The room was filled with chaos. It was confusion where no one knew what to do, but everyone felt like they needed to be present. Elizabeth used her first-day-of-school-classroom-voice. "Nurse Larsen is here to help Verda. All of you can help by going out on the porch and praying." She turned to Verda's shrieking mother. "Mrs. Becky, you can help Verda more by going outside." Becky resisted, but Elizabeth didn't back down. "*Please*, Mrs. Becky. It's the best thing you can do for Verda." Finally, one of the ladies led her outside.

Peg eased up to Elizabeth. "Who died and put you in charge?"

"Verda's going to die if we don't all calm down."

Peg, who'd always been close friends with Verda, sat on the edge of the bed. "We got a nurse here who's going to help you. Lizzie's with me, and we ain't gonna leave you."

Nurse Larsen backed away, wiping her hands. "It's a breech." These were sobering words. Country people knew this: whether it was a calf or human, breech births were dangerous as well as dreaded.

"I can feel a foot but can't see—there's too much blood."

Peg grasped Verda's hand. "We've been friends since we started school together and we ain't leaving you."

"Peg, I don't wanna die."

"You ain't gonna die. You're going to hold this baby and be an old woman holding her children."

"How close is a hospital?" The fear in Nurse Larsen's eyes was not comforting.

Elizabeth touched the nurse's shoulder. "DeRidder—thirty miles in the rain on a muddy road. "Not enough time. You've got to do the best you can right here."

Emily Larsen went back to work. "She's got to push that breech down so I can help with the delivery."

"Have you done this before?" Peg whispered.

"Sister, I don't know nothin' bout birthing babies." She strained. "My training's in combat wounds."

"Peg, you and Momma may not recognize her now," Elizabeth said, "but Nurse Larsen was at our house several weeks ago." Both sisters continued talking with Verda and the Nurse, trying to calm them down. At three intervals, Nurse Larsen walked to the corner, and threw up before returning. Soon, she was just as bloody and sweat-soaked as her patient. The veins on her forehead bulged as she strained. "I've got to help without hurting the baby." Suddenly, she said, "I think we're making progress."

Thirty seconds later, she said, "Great. Now push, Sister. Push."

Peg joined in. "Come on, Verda. Your baby's ready to come."

Elizabeth leaned against the wall, her head pounding. "Lord, please be merciful and help this baby as well as spare Verda's life. If they live, it'll bring glory to you. Please help them."

The next sound answered at least one portion of her prayer. The room was filled with the sweet but loud crying of a newborn. The door flew open as the room filled up with family and neighbors.

"Sister, you've got a new baby girl." Peg said.

Verda looked near death but still managed a weak smile. "Is she . . . is she all right?"

"Looks perfectly healthy to me." Peg stood. "Her lungs sound strong." The nurse cleaned out the baby's mouth before swabbing her down. As she cut the umbilical cord, Elizabeth felt her knees weaken again. Her calling definitely wasn't in nursing.

Emily Larsen handed the baby to Peg before lunging toward Elizabeth. "I'm feeling kind of faint—need some fresh air." She collapsed at the door.

One of the women, who'd been on the porch, said, "She ain't got much of a strong stomach for a nurse."

Elizabeth, kneeling beside her, said, "This nurse is real strong—strong in every way that strength can be measured. If you'd been in here, you'd seen it."

The two sisters moved Emily out onto the porch and laid her on the rough floor. Peg said, "Lizzie, we've had plenty of excitement since these soldiers arrived. It'll be good when things return to normal."

"I'm not sure things will ever be normal again."

The nurse roused, trying to sit up. Peg leaned down. "Miz Scarlett, I don't know nothin' 'bout birthing babies."

Emily covered her eyes. "So . . . you've seen the movie?"

"Three times at the Realart in DeRidder." Peg said.

"I've seen it five."

Peg nodded toward Elizabeth. "But *Prissy* here has seen it seven times."

"I still say the book's better than the movie." Elizabeth said.

Peg, a born mimic, repeated, "Miz Scarlett, I don't know-nothin-bout-birthin-babies."

"But you know a lot more than you did two hours ago," Elizabeth said. "Emily, do you mind if I ask a question?"

"Sure."

"Were you throwing up because you were sick . . . or scared?"

"Both. Some of the former, a lot of the latter." She smiled. "My daddy always said that's what you do when facing a tough job: 'Stand at the door, throw up, then go in and do the job'."

"Well, that's what you did."

Gator Harper stood at the door, "Nurse, we need you inside."

Emily tried to stand. "Is she all right?"

"She's as weak as a March kitten, but wants a word with you."

The sisters helped the nurse up the steps, and Emily said, "What's a March kitten?"

"Who knows?" Elizabeth said. "Gator's family is renowned for mixing up those sayings."

"Is his name really *Gator*?"

Peg shrugged. "I've never heard him called anything else."

Elizabeth lowered her voice. "His real name is Sidney but he quit school when the teacher refused to call him Gator."

Sidney—or Gator—Harper stood by his wife Verda, who had a little more color and was trying to nurse the baby. Her voice was raspy. "Nurse, what's your name?"

"Larsen. Emily Larsen."

"Where you from?"

"Arizona. Yuma, Arizona."

"I like your name, Emily. That's what Gator and I are gonna name this baby girl: Emily. In honor of you. You saved our lives."

"I'm glad . . . I could help."

"We're much obliged for y'all helping us," Gator said, his voice breaking. "Lizzie, you and Peg . . . and your folks came through for us tonight. Thank you."

Peg hugged him. "You're welcome, *Sidney*."

His mouth gaped but he recovered with a smile as the three young women left the room. Elizabeth grabbed Peg. "You are so bad."

"I had him in a weak moment, didn't I?"

Nurse Larsen flopped down against a column. "Either one of you married or had children?"

"Heavens no." Peg said before turning toward Elizabeth.

"How about you?" The nurse asked Elizabeth.

"No, I'm not married." She deftly changed the subject. "I'm a schoolteacher. In your state—Arizona—do they allow school teachers to be married?"

"Of course they do. They don't here?"

"It's frowned on for elementary teachers. They don't believe you can do a good job if you have your own family to worry about."

"That's sad."

Elizabeth stared off into the dark. "It's sad, but it's true."

"Is that going to keep you from getting married?"

"Probably." She wiped the nurse's brow. "You've not thrown up since you collapsed."

She leaned wearily against Elizabeth. "I don't have anything left to throw up. I'm dry as a bone." Her eyes rolled back as she went limp. They gently eased her onto the porch, using a rolled-up feed sack for a pillow. The rhythmic rain on the tin roof was soon joined by the first brave light of dawn.

The twins sat quietly. The only sound was the Harper roosters crowing. Peg said, "What'd you mean when you said, 'If I was in Shreveport, I wouldn't be here'?"

"You don't miss a thing, do you?"

"I'm your twin—I'm not supposed to."

Elizabeth looked into her sister's eyes. Everything about them was different. The way they looked, definitely the way they talked, their goals and dreams. Sometimes Elizabeth felt as if the only thing they shared was the same womb and birthday. Yet there was a deep, unspoken love and respect between them that nothing could break. Not even a nosey question.

"If I'd taken that job in Shreveport, I wouldn't have been here tonight."

"Is that good or bad?"

"Verda and her baby are all right, so I guess it's good."

"It *was* good. Your idea to get help saved their lives." Peg leaned over where Elizabeth couldn't ignore her. "I got one more question: Are you going to tell Harry Miller about your baby?"

"Why would I?"

"I mean, if you marry him."

"Who said I was going to marry him?"

"I believe you are, so answer my question."

"What happened in my past has nothing to do with Harry Miller."

"What happened in your past has *everything* to do with Harry Miller." Peg's smirk always irritated her. Elizabeth lay back on the porch beside the sleeping nurse. "If I was in Shreveport, I wouldn't be here having to listen to you."

Chapter 34
Enemy of my Enemy

Saturday, Sept. 27

Company K moved at a leisurely pace as they advanced on the Blue Army objective of Shreveport. It was the third day of the battle, and they were somewhere east of Pleasant Hill, Louisiana—about sixty miles from Shreveport. They'd been advancing steadily for the last two days as Red resistance melted away.

Shorty stretched and yawned. "Where are we going to eat in Shreveport?" Suddenly, rifle and artillery fire exploded around them. They had lumbered into a trap. Sarge yelled. "It's an ambush. Drop back."

For most of the Blue soldiers on the company's left flank, the only thing to drop back to was a long line of advancing Red soldiers. On the right side, Harry saw Red infantrymen pouring from half-tracks and trucks. Their only chance of escape lay in the narrowing gap between the two flanks. He joined a group of soldiers running full tilt into a huge briar patch. A few minutes earlier, they'd skirted this towering thicket. Now, it was their best and only chance of escape. Like a rabbit chased by baying hounds, Harry waded into the chest-high briars. The thorns and vines tore at his face and arms, but he kept moving. Behind him, a soldier cussed. "I ain't going into that mess. I'd rather be a P.O.W."

He glanced back at a knot of Blue soldiers holding up their hands in surrender. Tearing deeper into the briar patch, he came face to face with Sergeant Kickland. "Follow me," Sarge said as he used his rifle as a battering ram to step over and through the briars. They were soon safely deep within the patch, where Sarge stopped, kneeling to catch his breath. Cohen, Shorty, Nickels, Shep, and Halverson—as well as three soldiers from another Blue Company—joined them. The noise of battle—vehicles, rifle fire, and shouting—echoed from three sides. "This briar patch is about a hundred yards long. They're just waiting for us to come out," Sarge said.

Scratched and bleeding, they huddled together. A rifle crackled from ahead. "You *blueberries* come on out. We got you surrounded." They each looked at Sarge. He wiped his brow and put his finger to his lips.

"Now don't make us come in there and smoke you out," A Red soldier taunted.

Shep pointed behind them. "We came from there." He nodded into the tall briars ahead. "And they're waiting at the end there. Listen." The sounds of vehicles and men to the left on the nearby road. "No reason to go that way." Shep stood, trying to look over the wall of briars to their right. "Looks like we ought to go thattaway."

One of the three soldiers who'd wandered up said, "This ain't nothing but a play war. I've been briar stuck enough for one day." He shouldered his rifle. "I'm giving up."

As his two other buddies stood to join him, Sarge spun the first one around. "Go ahead, but tell them you're the only ones in here."

"No problem there." He laughed as the three of them walked out the way they'd come.

"Anybody wanna join them?" Sarge said.

"I ain't having no Red soldier run his hands all over my junk, taking my candy bars and cigarettes." Shorty stood. "I'm for Shep's plan."

As the three soldiers disappeared into the thicket, something approached from ahead of Harry. Sarge took off his safety. "Sounds like we got company." The Company K men, rifles pointed toward the sound, waited. Suddenly, a hog, followed by a litter of piglets, charged through. Five or six more squealing hogs ran through, knocking Cohen to the ground. The terrified pigs charged out of the briar patch behind the retreating soldiers. Soon, a fine mixture of cursing, rifles firing, and pigs squealing erupted from the thicket.

Shorty stood. "I'd like to have seen it when they all charged out of the thicket at the same time."

"Somebody's going to have bacon tonight," Shep said.

"I dunno. It's hard to kill a hog with blanks." Shorty said as he turned to Cohen. "You all right?"

The New York soldier was ashen. "I thought I was a goner."

"No Passover for you this year." Shep helped Cohen brush off.

"I believe they were kosher pigs," Cohen said.

"What's *kosher*?" Shorty said.

"It's what those pigs were."

"I never heard of that breed—I thought they were just plain ol' piney woods rooters," Shorty said. "This area was once known as 'Hog Wallow Country.' That's what they had you doing—wallowing on the ground."

Harry joined the fun. "Cohen, those hogs were out to get you. They knew you were a Jew."

"I sure wasn't any danger to them," Cohen said. "You Gentiles are the ones to fear."

Kickland raised his hand. "Enough of this." He pointed toward the tallest of the briars. "Let's go." The seven Company K soldiers began taking turns tromping down the briars. Halverson was out front when they reached an opening created by a recent fire. He crawled on his belly to the edge, carefully surveying for any movement or soldiers. They hurried across the burnt patch and came to a fence. Tacked to a post was a sign: *Off Limits to Soldiers. Keep Out.*

Shorty walked to the fence, tore down the sign, and climbed through. "Right now we ain't soldiers. We're rabbits. Let's take our chances this way."

"It *is* the best direction to evade capture," Sarge said. They hurried across a hayfield toward a farmhouse. Watching carefully, they ran the hundred yards to a nearby barn. Once inside, Sarge spread his map and compass on the ground. "Miller, you watch the way we came for Reds."

But the attack didn't come from that end. The armed man appeared out of nowhere. A thin country man held a large pistol with both hands. As he loudly cocked it back, he swung it around. "Don't none of you boys move."

Halverson took aim with his rifle, but the old fellow grinned. "You boys are just shootin' blanks, but ol' Bessie here is loaded for bear."

Sarge motioned. "Hal, lower your rifle." He turned to the man. "We don't mean no harm."

"I'm tired of you soldiers tromping over my place."

"Give us a few minutes to get our bearings and we'll be out of here."

"You soldiers can't read? You had to climb my fence to git here. The signs said for soldiers to *keep out*."

Shorty raised his hand. "Sir, the sign we saw said, 'Off Limits to Red Soldiers.'" He tapped his armband. "We're Blue."

The man trained the pistol on Shorty, causing him to raise both hands. "I don't believe it said Red." Even when he put the pistol in his face, Shorty didn't flinch. Their Mexican standoff ended when a young freckle-faced girl, looking to be about eight or ten, came into the barn. "Daddy, they ain't hurting nothing. Let them go. Our trouble's been from the Reds."

He kept his pistol on Shorty as he backed away. He pointed at the girl. "Brit and I are going back to the house. We expect you fellows to be gone real soon."

"No problem. We'll be gone," Sarge said.

Within five minutes, Harry saw an approaching platoon of Red soldiers. Sarge led them up into the loft. Harry watched through a knothole as the farmer, pistol tucked in his belt, met the Red soldiers and gestured toward the barn. "What's going on?" Sarge said.

"They're coming toward the barn." The young girl walked out of the barn and Harry said, "That girl's stopped them."

"What's she doing?"

Harry studied the situation. "She's leading them away from us."

"Really?"

"Yeah, she's walking them past here." Harry went to the loft ladder. "I'm going down to find out what's going on." Using the barn wall to shield himself, he whispered, "Hey girl. Come over here."

She didn't move—her attention was focused on the Red soldiers.

"Psst, hey girl."

She motioned for him to come to the corner, nodding at the distant soldiers. "Watch them. They'll be walking over the yellow-jacket hole in about ten steps."

She counted. "Six, seven, eight, nine." On *ten* the platoon leaders passed between two oak trees. As the fifth man passed, the action began. He began swatting and dancing about and was soon joined by the others. She was enjoying their cussing and hollering. "Sweet revenge." She shrugged. "They wanted the fastest way, and I gave it to them."

"Why'd you protect us?" Harry said.

"Because I hate Red soldiers. They knocked over our beehives and stole my persimmons. Last week Daddy caught two Red cavalrymen stealing field corn out of our crib for their horses. Yep, and I just got even with the Reds."

"You led them toward the yellow-jackets?"

"Yes Sir. I told them to stay right between those two oak trees and they did."

Harry called up to the loft. "Come on down fellows, it's safe."

He stepped in front of the girl. "What's your name?"

"Brittany, but folks call me Brit."

"Well Brit, you got your revenge."

Motioning toward the two oak trees, she deadpanned, "Yep, they got in my bees, but in the end, my bees got in them."

As the men crowded around, Shep said, "What gives?"

Harry pointed at Brit. "The old military axiom: the enemy of my enemy is my friend."

Shorty walked up to her. "You sent them on a wild goose chase."

She beamed. "It was fine to see, weren't it?"

"They got *religion* when those yellow-jackets attacked them," Shorty said.

"No Sir, from what I heard them hollering, they *lost any religion* they had."

Brit's father, pistol still tucked in his front waistband, walked up, unfolding a faded red union suit. He lowered his voice conspiratorially. "Y'all can make armbands out of this."

Sarge took the cloth. "Thanks."

Shorty walked over to the farmer, who was about his same size and possessed the same swagger. Shep said, "Uh-oh. Two banty roosters in the same chicken yard."

The short soldier pointed at the tucked-in pistol. "Fellow, if that pistol went off, it'd make a gelding out of you."

The man jutted his chin. "Don't worry about me. You better worry about clearing out of here before more Reds get here."

Sarge stepped in. "What direction is the Blue Army?"

The farmer pointed west. "That direction." He turned to Brit. "Honey, go get your bike, and take these fellows as far as Robertson's Bridge."

The girl returned, pushing a rusty warped bicycle. Her father patted her shoulder. "Brit will scout ahead of you."

They each shook the farmer's hand, thanking him for his kindness. Shorty was last. "Where'd you get that hog leg gun?"

"My grandpappy brought it home from the war."

"When's the last time it was fired?"

"I'm not sure. I've never been brave enough to pop a cap on it."

They both laughed as Shorty slapped his shoulder. "From one Louisiana piney woods rooter to another, thanks a million."

The seven soldiers followed as Brit rode the wobbly bicycle down the road. They slipped along in the edge of the woods for cover. About every quarter mile, she'd circle back to report that the road was clear ahead. Just short of the bridge, she rode up. "I've got to turn back now."

They heard vehicles behind them, causing them to hurry ahead as they waved thanks.

Harry walked to her. "Thanks, Brit. We really appreciate it."

He pressed an object into her hand and closed her fingers around it. She stepped back and held up a medallion. "What's this?"

"It's a commemorative medal from our unit, the Red Arrow Division."

"Can I keep it?"

"It's yours."

She held up the medal. "I'll keep it till I die."

"I'm sure you will. Here, I got one more thing for you." He placed two twenty-dollar bills in her hand.

"What's that for?"

"Spy pay for a new bicycle." He hurried to join the other soldiers at the bridge.

She yelled, "I won't ever forget you!"

Harry turned and waved. "And I won't ever forget you either."

The enemy of my enemy is my friend, and Harry was glad it was so.

Chapter 35
P.O.W.s

Harry caught up with his six buddies at the bridge, where an umpire was explaining, "This bridge was bombed this morning." He nodded at the brackish creek. "You'll have to cross there."

"Are there Blue units in the direction we're heading?" Sarge said.

"Ahead of you it's all Blue." He waved in the direction they'd come from. "We're expecting a Red attack any time."

Shep said, "Sarge, I hope we have better luck on this crossing than the last one."

Looking back behind them, Sarge saw a huge cloud of dust boiling above the treetops. "The Reds are coming. Let's get across." As they reached the water's edge, the umpire yelled, "Watch it, there's a nest of cottonmouth moccasins by that log."

Sarge never paused as he waded into the chest deep water, holding his rifle above his head. "You guys follow me."

Shep stood at the water's edge. "I'm scared of those cottonmouths."

Shorty shoved him. "They can't bite underwater."

The seven of them hurried across the creek and emerged wet—but unbitten—on the west bank. Harry said, "Cottonmouths can't bite underwater?"

"Miller, they eat fish," Shorty said. "What do you think?"

"Why'd you tell Shep that?"

"To get him moving. It worked, didn't it?"

They came to the perimeter of the Blue advance line. Machine gun nests lined each side of the road and anti-tank weapons were hidden among the roadside trees. A young second Lieutenant stepped out of a bunker. "Where'd you boys come from?"

"We got mixed up in a fight back there," Sarge said. "Lots of Reds coming this way."

"We know that. We've got orders to advance on them at 1400. Y'all are welcome to join us."

"I believe we'll pass. We need to reconnect with our regiment."

"Then I have an assignment for you." The Lieutenant pointed to a group of soldiers sprawled under the pines. "There are about forty Red prisoners over there. We're holding them until an intelligence unit arrives for questioning. Sergeant, I'd like you and your men to guard them."

"We'll take care of them."

"Thanks. Now, if you'll excuse me." The officer stopped. "Don't be too nice to them. They did some pretty bad things to our men."

To Harry, guarding prisoners with blanks in your rifle was laughable. However, one look at the Red prisoners revealed that they weren't an escape threat. Most were sleeping in the shade, while others were smoking, visiting, and playing cards. All looked relieved to be out of the battle.

Sarge walked to a prisoner sprawled on a bed of pine straw. Kicking him to wake him, he said, "What unit are you from?"

The soldier put his hands behind his head and yawned. "I can't talk. I been dead for three days."

Harry walked up to a pudgy Blue guard who nodded. "I wish I had some real ammo. I'd at least make him think I'd shoot him."

"What'd they do that's so bad?"

The soldier lifted his shirt, revealing an ugly red welt on his belly. "One of them shot me."

"Shot you?"

The guard pointed at three prisoners sitting separate from the others. "It was one of those peckerwoods over there."

Another Blue soldier came over, holding up his left arm. "See that knot on my forearm? That's where they got me."

"What were they shooting?"

He reached in his back pocket, pulling out a slingshot. "This. We kept telling the Lieutenant they were shooting live ammo at us. He didn't believe us until he got a rock in the middle of the back. After we captured them, we found slingshots on those three."

The soldier with the stomach bruise said, "We were going to shoot them at sunrise, and not even give them a cigarette or a blindfold."

A whistle came from the bridge and the guard said, "Time to go. They're all yours."

He handed the slingshot to Harry. One of the Red marksmen said, "You're lucky Fatso. I could have shot you in the head if I'd wanted to. You were standing out in the open just asking to be shot."

The guard chunked a rock at him. "Think you're a good shot, eh?"

"Yep, I was aiming for your belly button and hit just above it."

The plump guard said to Harry. "Shoot that smart-mouthed one last. And shoot him right in the belly."

The seven Company K soldiers formed an outside perimeter around the P.O.W.s, most of whom slept through the change in guard. Harry walked over to the soldier who had admitted to shooting the pudgy guard and handed him the slingshot. "Show me."

The soldier pulled a pebble out of his sock. "See that small blackjack over there?" He pointed to a tree about thirty yards away. "I'm gonna hit it square just below that first limb." He shot from a sitting position, and the pop of the slingshot, whiz of the stone, and smack into the tree happened in an instant. He nailed it right where he'd aimed.

Harry rubbed his chin. "Where you from?"

"Ar-kan-saw."

Sarge coughed. "Miller, no fraternizing with the enemy. Back to your post." They stood guard over the prisoners for what seemed an eternity. Harry was jealous watching them sleep in the shade in their clean and dry uniforms. Finally, a staff car carrying an intelligence officer and his entourage arrived. As the prisoners were led away, the guys from Company K walked to their vacated shady spots and plopped down. Harry foggily tried to remember the last time he'd slept. He stretched out on a cushion of pine straw that was still warm from the Arkansas sniper who had lain there. As he drifted off to sleep, two thoughts came to mind.

I wonder what's next.

The second thought warmed him—the memory of Elizabeth Reed's lips against his. He fell asleep with a smile on his face.

Chapter 36

Twins

Sept. 24, 1941

Camp Leonard Wood, Missouri
Dear Momma and Poppa,
  I don't have long to write. They are really keeping us busy up here.
  I'm fine. They're pushing us hard, but I'm doing well. I haven't even seen an airplane, but I've seen this Missouri ground ten thousand times at the business end of a pushup.
  Tell the girls and Ben I said howdy. I hope the animals and farm are fine.
  I miss all of you.

Sincerely,

Jimmy Earl

Standing on the post office steps, Elizabeth read the letter and handed it to Peg. "He sounds homesick to me."

"Why wouldn't he be? He ain't been past Alexandria in his life."

"I imagine he'll be going a lot farther than there before this is all over."

Peg glanced up from the letter. "Is that what you believe?"

"I'm afraid so."

Finished, Peg folded the letter. "Let's go by the cutoff and check on Nurse Larsen." Elizabeth hated this shortcut since it meant walking a log across Bundick Creek. Arriving there, Peg pranced across. "All right, Sister. It's your turn."

Elizabeth tentatively stepped onto the slick log. "If I fall in…"

"You won't."

Elizabeth slipped on the mossy log, and only her grasp on a nearby limb kept her upright. She froze, not willing to move in either direction. Peg stepped back onto the log. "Come on, it's always easier going forward than backward."

Elizabeth said, "You stay right there. You'll make me fall in."

"The way you're slipping around, you don't need me to help you fall." Peg hopped toward her, extending her hand. "Let me help you."

"I don't need your help."

"That's your problem. You never let anyone help you." Peg winced as Elizabeth grasped her hand. "Woman, you got me in a death grip." She led her sideways on the log. "See, there's nothing to it."

Reaching the safety of the far bank, Elizabeth lunged for solid ground. "Terra Firma."

Peg brushed a leaf off her. "The only *terror* was yours." Getting no reply, she said, "Nothing to it. It's just like falling in love. Nothing hard about it at all."

Her sister's smug smirk always irritated Elizabeth. "Well, you ought to know about falling in love. I've seen you do it twice in one day."

"What's wrong with that?"

"Twice in one day with *two* different men?"

Peg shrugged. "What's wrong with that? Easy as falling off a log backwards."

Elizabeth walked up the trail, scanning for copperheads in the fallen leaves. "It's not the falling that hurts. It's when you hit the ground."

"Fall seven times. Get up eight," Peg said.

"Peg, speaking of seven *and* eight, how many soldiers are you writing?"

"Oh, I'm not sure. I'll have to check in my little black book." She counted on her fingers. "I believe it's six—seven if I count Emily Larsen."

They walked up the hill to the still-deserted medical headquarters. They found Emily still in bed. Peg sat beside her. "Girl, you still look peaked."

"What's *pee-kid*?"

"It's how you look: washed-out-sick."

The nurse placed her arm over her eyes. "I've never been so sick in my life!"

"Have you eaten anything?"

"No, and I don't care to." She propped herself up on her elbows. "How's our baby?"

"Better than you. Mother and child are both doing well."

Elizabeth brought the nurse a glass of water, which she gulped down. "It's been pretty lonely here. Just two guards and neither of them have an ounce of sympathy for a sick woman."

Peg rolled her eyes. "Men." She stood. "Elizabeth, you stay here with Emily. I'm going to the house and bring Momma. She's the world's best doctor for getting a person out of the sickbed."

Elizabeth sat in a chair beside the bed. "My sister's pretty impulsive."

"I can see that."

"Would you mind if I helped you clean up?"

"I know I must smell bad."

"You'll feel better when you're clean."

Elizabeth got a pan, found some soap, towels, and a washcloth and lit a small gas stove to boil water. The nurse climbed into the nearby chair as Elizabeth began washing her feet.

Emily sighed. "It sure has been lonely here." With Elizabeth's encouraging questions, she began telling of her journey from Arizona to how she ended up in Louisiana. She stopped. "What about your life, Elizabeth?"

"Pretty boring compared to yours."

The kettle on the stove began whistling, allowing Elizabeth to break off the conversation. She slowly mixed it with cold water until the temperature met her satisfaction. "A good hot spit bath will make anyone feel better."

She washed the nurse's face with a hot washcloth. "Emily, do you mind if I ask you a personal question?"

"I guess not."

"Have you ever fallen off a log into the creek?"

"What kind of question is that? There's not a wide enough creek in my part of Arizona that you can't jump."

Elizabeth squeezed out the washcloth. "I guess I mean *metaphorically*."

"How's that?"

"Have you ever fallen head-over-heels-stupid-slobbering-silly in love?"

"That's a fine description of love."

Elizabeth felt her face redden. "Do you understand my question?"

"Sure. I've fallen off *that* log more times than I can count. An Army nurse has plenty of chances: lonely soldiers, handsome medical officers, adoring civilians who like a woman in uniform." She winked. "I've fallen off that log plenty of times."

"Regrets?"

"Sure. Who doesn't have some? But overall, I'm fine." She shrugged. "Part of life is falling and getting back up."

Elizabeth laid out a fresh uniform. "I've got one more question."

"Go ahead."

"Would you marry . . . I mean . . . go with a man . . . a soldier . . . who wasn't on speaking terms with his own parents?"

"Girl, what are you getting at?"

"I won't go into the full story, but I *think* I've fallen in love with a soldier. He's from Wisconsin and for some reason is estranged from his parents."

Emily grabbed her arm. "What do you mean you *think* you're in love? Being in love is like joining the Army. You're either in or out. Which is it?"

Elizabeth wiped the nurse's face with the warm cloth. "I believe you're feeling better."

"Answer my question. Which is it?"

"Were you a lawyer before you became a nurse?"

"No, but my father was. Next witness, please. Now which is it?"

"I guess I'm in love." Elizabeth tried to hold back her tears, but felt one dribble down her cheek. "But I can't put my love . . . my trust . . . into the hands of a man who's not in touch with his own family."

"Then what are you going to do?"

She dug in her purse. "I'm not sure." She handed the photo to Emily. "That's him."

She studied the photo then glanced up. "I know him. Wasn't he at your church the Sunday I was there?"

"He was."

"He's cute. If you don't want him, I'd like to meet him."

Before Elizabeth could comment, her mother pulled back the tent flap, followed by Peg toting a large basket. "Nurse Pearline Reed is now on call," Momma said, eyeing Emily and Elizabeth. "Nurse Larsen, you look a hundred times better, but Lizzie looks as if she's caught what you had."

Peg set the basket down. "Hmm. My diagnosis is simple: My sister is sick. *Lovesick*."

Momma, rummaging through the basket, never looked up. "Lord, help us all."

Chapter 37
Pigeons and Horses

Sunday, September 28, 1941

Sarge studied the topographical map as Harry stood beside him. "Miller, it's nearly five o'clock. It'll be dark in about three hours." They listened to the faint sounds of artillery to the north. "I hate not to be in the middle of the action, but hate even worse wandering around blind."

Harry fought with a huge horsefly that had bitten him on the neck and arm, his hand poised for revenge. Shorty came up behind him. "It's bad luck to kill a horsefly on Sunday. *Extra* bad luck to kill a horsefly on the last Sunday of the month of a waning moon."

The horsefly made the last mistake of its life, landing on Harry's arm. *Whack*.

Shorty sadly shook his head. "You were warned."

"I'm not superstitious."

"Maybe you oughta be." Shorty rubbed his chin.

A vehicle's approach from the north caused the soldiers to melt into the bushes, even though they were in Blue territory. A truck loaded with a tall crate bounced along the road. Once he realized it was a Blue vehicle, Sarge flagged it down. As it squealed to a stop, Sarge said, "It's a Pigeon Patrol. I'll bet they'll know where we need to be."

The soldiers gathered around to inspect the truck and its cages. When a lieutenant climbed out of the cab, Shorty said, "How do those pigeons work?"

The officer stood erect. "We're the 132nd Signal Corps. We keep everyone in touch when all the other new-fangled stuff doesn't work."

"So you're Pigeoneers?"

The officer bristled. "We're the 132nd Signal Corps and are just as much soldiers as any of you."

"Sorry. I meant that you're 'Pigeoneers Soldiers'." Shorty winked at Harry.

"Soldier, I want some respect out of you."

Shorty put his hands up. "You don't have to be touchy about it, *Sir*."

The officer walked to the cage and removed a large white pigeon. "And this is Henry." He tapped the bird's leg band. "Also known as #634a-5789." He pointed to a tube on the bird's other leg. "This is the message tube." He removed a small note. "Messages can be sent back to headquarters or to this truck."

Shorty nudged Harry. "Kind of like your spent bullet and Elizabeth Reed."

The pigeon officer was passionate about his birds. "We've been working with a Blue tank unit. Tanks, with all of that metal, are bad for radio communications." He petted the pigeon. "The tankers sent Henry back yesterday with an important message about the Red armor's location. The bird flew back to our truck and we passed on the message to HQ."

"You're right proud of what you do," Shorty said.

"Rightfully so."

"I heard a story about you Pigeoneers . . . I mean pigeon units." Shorty was on a roll and even a cleared throat from Sarge didn't stop him. "It seems a *full bird* Colonel was giving orders to a regiment at Camp Beauregard. One of your carrier pigeons made a *bombing* raid overhead and dropped its 'calling card' right between his eyes."

The Lieutenant groaned, but Shorty continued, "The Colonel's aide ran to get him a Kleenex but a private stopped the aide. 'It ain't no use getting that, that bird's a mile away by now.'"

The pigeoneer officer bit his lip, trying not to smile, but the seven Company K soldiers laughed enough for him.

Sarge pushed Shorty out of the way. "We're looking for any 32nd Division boys. Have you seen any of them?"

"No."

"Do you know where we are?"

The pigeon officer grimaced. "To be honest, we're kind of turned around ourselves."

Shorty, peering around Sarge, said, "You mean your *pigeons* are lost?"

"Our pigeons aren't lost. It's us. . . ."

"Then why don't you just turn one loose, and—"

Sarge had had enough. "Johnson, shut your mouth."

The officer, still holding Henry, nodded behind him. "There's plenty of Blue strength back there. The scuttlebutt is that Patton's tanks are achieving a pincher action from the Texas border."

Sarge thanked him and they resumed their journey, not stopping until they came to a small creek where they filled their canteens. Harry stood. "I hear horses." They took cover before a blue cavalry company trotted up to the creek. As the seven soldiers came out of the bushes, a dust-encrusted sergeant rode over. "Well, it's over."

"What's over?" Harry said.

"The battle. They pulled the plug on it about an hour ago."

The sergeant watered his horse in the creek. When he removed his cap, Harry recognized him. "Hey, you're the guy that saved Sarge."

The cavalryman smiled. "And you're the drowned rat that saved him before me."

"Your name is Regan. Ed Regan." Harry looked for Sergeant Kickland. "Hey Sarge. Come over here. This is the trooper that saved you."

Sarge hurried over and began profusely thanking the cavalryman, quickly becoming quite emotional before changing the subject. "How did your unit do?"

Regan mounted his horse. "We did well. Covered lots of ground and even captured a convoy of fuel trucks." He adjusted his riding boots. "But the grapevine says we're through."

"What do you mean 'through'?" Sarge said.

The trooper tenderly stroked the mane of his strong brown horse. "Word is that this is the end of the horse cavalry. We've been told they plan to make mechanized forces out of our personnel."

"What about your horses?"

"They'll sell them to the glue factories, or shoot them back at Ft. Bliss."

"Really?"

"That's what they do with old cavalry horses." The trooper adjusted the saddle on his horse and patted the U.S. brand on his horse's flank. "But ol' Uncle Sam here, he ain't going to no glue factory." The trooper scanned the creek bottom. "I'm gonna turn him loose."

He whistled to his unit. "Load them up, men."

As they moved out, Harry caught up with the rider. "Will that get you in trouble?"

He shrugged. "Probably, but I don't care. Sam's been my partner for years. One way or the other, I'm going to take care of him." The rider's voice broke. "Like he's taken care of me."

He spurred the horse. "Let's get out of here." The riders blended into the dusk. Harry knew he was witnessing the passing of an era. He wondered what would happen to this horse named Uncle Sam and thousands more like it. What would happen to the sunburned cavalry sergeant whose entire way of life was also disappearing?

A convoy of honking trucks roared up to the creek, stopping only because the horses blocked the narrow trail. The quartermaster drivers were singing and shouting. A huge master sergeant climbed out of the nearest truck. "The battle's over." He nodded at the singers in the truck cab. "The battle's over, and we just happy." The men in the truck sang,

> *And when the battle's over,*
> *We shall wear a crown,*
> *In the New Jerusalem.*

Shorty walked up. "We sang that song back in our church."

Harry watched silently. He knew these men—he'd met them when he crossed the road and joined them for a night of music. But this was different. In the segregated army, he didn't risk even telling them hello. It made him sick, but that's the way it was.

"We're trying to get back to our assembly area at Mab Sawmill," Sarge said.

"Where's that?" The driver said.

"On Highway 10 between Oakdale and Elizabeth."

"It's a little out of the way, but we can drop you off there." He pointed to the back of the trucks. "Climb on."

So Harry Miller and his fellow Company K soldiers climbed in the back of the truck. He thought about the horses and their proud riders. The Army was modernizing and no longer had room for cavalry horses. The truck he was bumping along in was replacing the animals.

Additionally, telephone, radios, and modern communications equipment would eventually put the pigeons out to pasture. But he still couldn't ride in the same cab with these colored soldiers taking him back to his segregated camp. This Army—like the world around him—was sure *a strange* place.

Part IV

The Battle For A Heart

See the world,
Find an old fashioned girl.
And when all's been said and done
It's the things that are given, not won
Are the things that you want.

"See the World"
– Gomez

Chapter 38
Eavesdropping

Monday, September 29, 1941

There was an air of jubilation as Harry and his buddies climbed out of the truck at their assembly area. Happy soldiers lined the road, knowing their time in the field was over. The fact that the Blue Army had won both phases of the battle only added to the jubilation.

The grapevine buzzed with rumors of an October maneuver in the Carolinas. Shep, who always knew the latest info, said, "Word is that if we don't go to Carolina, we'll be shipped to a base closer to the Midwest. I've had enough of this Louisiana heat, and a long snowy winter sounds appealing."

The thought of being shipped out of Louisiana worried Harry. A month earlier, he'd have been thrilled, but that was before he'd fallen in love with Elizabeth Reed. Leaving Louisiana meant leaving her. It was a thought he refused to consider.

Something had happened during this month of September. He had become a soldier. He'd also decided to be a man who followed his heart, wherever it might *lead*. He wasn't sure if this change had been because of Elizabeth Reed, or if his becoming a real soldier had given him the boldness to pursue her at whatever cost. Most importantly, he'd decided to take responsibility for his life and actions. As Elizabeth's grandmother loved to say, "Every tub sits on its own bottom." He'd become accountable.

That afternoon Harry tried every trick in the book to get leave for the next afternoon, and it had worked. Of course, it didn't hurt that he had saved Sergeant Kickland's life.

Harry was cleared for leave at noon on Tuesday. With the high military traffic, it was easy to catch a ride to Bundick. In less than thirty minutes, Harry was walking up the dirt road to the Reed home place.

Elizabeth's mother was sweeping the front steps. She leaned on her broom. "Well, if it isn't Private Miller. What brings you here?"

"Where's Elizabeth?"

"Oh, she's down at the schoolhouse. You know, she's having an affair with Mr. Cole, the janitor."

She winked. "If we pick on you, it means we like you."

"So that means your family likes me?"

She swept the broom across the bottom step. "It means *at least* I like you."

Harry turned. "Well, I'd better get down there and whip Mr. Cole."

"I reckon you'd better." She shaded her eyes. "Supper or, as you people call it—'dinner'—will be about six. I hope you'll join us."

"Thanks." He hustled toward the school, remembering that time, not the Red Army, was now his enemy.

He eased up beside the window, and saw Elizabeth working at her desk. He hoped this surprise visit was welcome. Slipping in the side door, he crept to her classroom, tapping lightly on the door facing.

Papers shuffled from in the room. "Ben, what are you doing out there?"

He rapped with the six-tap "shave-and-a-haircut knock."

"Ben Reed. . . ." Her heels clicked across the hardwood floor, and she strode right into Harry. He wished he'd had a camera. In the space of five quick seconds, she showed surprise, anger, delight, aggravation, and embarrassment.

"Miss Reed, I've come to enroll in your class."

She shook back her long hair. "Well, you ought to make an appointment with the principal before you just show up out of the clear blue." There was a hint of exasperation in her voice, but Harry marched on. He placed his hand on the door facing and moved closer. He could smell her hair and placed his other hand on her shoulder. "I've come to dust your erasers."

"You're too late for that. Ben's beat you. He's out there pounding the erasers right now." The edges of her mouth curled, and Harry saw the hope of a smile in her eyes as she motioned him to a student desk. "Pull up a chair and let me finish." She rolled her teacher's chair around beside him. As she piddled with her roll book, Harry entertained her with stories of the latest battle—briar patches, P.O.W.s, carrier pigeons, and horse cavalry.

She flung the book aside. "I can't work with you talking. It'll wait."

"Tell me about life in Bundick."

She excitedly told about a neighbor's baby coming in the middle of the night, and how she, her family, and an Army nurse delivered the baby. "I'll never forget it as long as I live." He'd never seen her this animated, and he liked it, especially when she put her hand on his.

Harry tightly gripped her hand. "Elizabeth, you are a beautiful woman."

"Flattery won't get you anywhere in my class."

Ben Reed had been sitting under a shade tree watching a lizard show its money when Private Miller approached the school. Like any good soldier on patrol, Ben leaned behind the tree where he could see but not be seen. He petted Blue. "Quiet, boy." Stuffing the erasers in his overalls pocket, he eased to the window beside Elizabeth's room.

Bundick School was built on two-foot-high piers, so crawling under the building was easy. Scooting across the dirt, he tried to forget about how they'd killed a three-foot-long rattlesnake pilot under here last spring. He sat up when he reached a spot where he could hear the muffled conversation above him. He was directly underneath Elizabeth and Harry Miller.

He reached for a vertical pipe extending down from the floor. It came up right by the wall behind Elizabeth's desk. It was capped on the bottom but the end in the classroom was open. One day after school, he'd seen a boy stuffing crayons down it. Ben carefully unscrewed the cap off the bottom of the pipe. Pebbles, pennies, and crayons poured out. He peered up through the pipe, seeing dim light on the other end.

He couldn't understand what Private Miller had just said, but his sister's reply was sharp. "Flattery won't get you anywhere in my class." In the ensuing silence, Ben scooted to where he could best eavesdrop on the couple above. Blue crawled beside him and he petted him. "Stay quiet."

"Elizabeth, we've talked about everything. Let's talk about you and me." It was Private Miller. The open pipe was like a megaphone, amplifying everything in the room above.

"What do you *mean* about 'you and me'?" It was Elizabeth.

The soldier coughed. "I know you don't hardly know me, and I don't know you very well . . . yet."

Silence flowed down the pipe. *Sister, at least say something.*

"You know I'll be leaving soon. We're packing up for Camp Livingston and then who knows where. . . ." The poor soldier was toting the conversation alone.

Finally, Elizabeth said, "Go ahead."

"Well, you see. I'm not willing to leave here—to leave Louisiana—without knowing where we stand."

"Knowing where *we* stand? Harry, I barely know you."

"I know, but . . . but I'm determined to. The problem is time. It's short."

"Harry, time . . . time is always short." There was a catch in his sister's voice.

Private Miller cleared his throat. "I don't know how to say it, so I'll just come out: I'd like to ask you to marry me."

The teacher's chair wheels slid across the floor. "*Marry* you? I hardly know you." She lowered her voice. "Ben's out there. I don't want him to hear a word of this." She dropped another octave. "I don't know you well enough to marry you."

Ben put his hand over his mouth, before whispering, "Something's definitely rotten in . . . Dallas." Hiding under the building—listening to every word—this was maneuvering at its best.

"I'm serious about this," Harry said.

"I can see you are."

"I'm just asking you . . . to think about it."

"Okay, but there's one thing." Her voice was crisp. "Let me give *you* something to think about."

Ben recognized the familiar creak of a school desk. Evidently, Private Miller was sitting in a student desk and had scooted forward. "What is it?"

"I'd never marry a man not on speaking terms with his own mother."

"It's more complicated than you think."

"Probably, but I would *never* marry a man who's not on speaking terms. . . ."

"You're serious, aren't you?"

"As serious as I'll ever be."

"So if. . . ."

"I said I wouldn't even *consider* it. Family's too important to me."

Harry sighed. "So it's a deal breaker?"

"If that's what you want to call it."

"So, if I'm going to have any chance with you, I've got to patch that up?"

"Yes Sir."

"Well, it's just complicated. You see, I'm adopted." Ben could actually hear the clock ticking on the classroom wall during the long silence.

Finally, Elizabeth said, "When were you adopted?"

"As a baby. My parents were in their thirties and couldn't have children. So they adopted me from a Catholic orphanage." He chuckled. "Then my sister was born less than a year later. My two younger brothers followed within the next five years."

"I thought you said your parents. . . ."

"That's what they thought too, but somehow I opened the floodgates or something."

"So, you have three siblings and you're the only one adopted?"

"That's right, but there's just three of us now. My sister—the one my age—died in an accident three years ago."

I'm sorry."

Ben could barely hear Harry's reply. "So am I." His voice brightened. "Enough on that. So, to have any chance with you, I've got to try and patch things up?"

"Yes."

Frustration dripped from his voice. "I mean, I'll try. If it means getting you, I'm willing to try just about anything."

"Good, and I'll consider your, uh, request, uh, your invitation."

"It's a *proposal*, Elizabeth. A flat-out open marriage proposal."

Ben mouthed the words: Just say yes. *Say yes, sister.*

He heard both chairs move, as Elizabeth said, "Did you hear something?"

"I think I did."

"It sounded like someone said 'say yes.'"

"Maybe it was your heart," Harry said hopefully.

Elizabeth's heels echoed across the room. "It came from somewhere in this room. Someone said 'say yes'."

Ben slapped his forehead. He'd said it out loud. They'd heard him. Evidently the open pipe served as a megaphone on both ends.

Harry Miller said, "While we're being so bluntly honest, let me ask you something? Is there anything in *your* past I need to know before you'd marry me?"

"Why would you ask that?"

"Just a hunch."

"Who's talked to you?"

"No one, Elizabeth. It's just a hunch, but watching your reaction, I believe I've hit something."

"Listen, you're the one bringing up getting married. You take care of your business—getting right with your family—and we'll discuss it."

"Sounds like a deal to me."

The next sound was a school desk loudly bumping up and down. Ben heard Harry Miller's muffled voice. "Elizabeth, I'm stuck in this danged desk. I can't get out."

From under the building, Ben jammed the cap back on the pipe, pocketing the coins and crayons before scampering out on all fours. Something's definitely rotten in Deweyville—he had to see this for himself! Dusting off, he hurried down the hall, a clean eraser in each hand, innocently whistling as he stepped through the door. Elizabeth had Private Miller from behind, trying to get him loose. They were tangled up as the small desk bumped up and down.

An adult voice boomed. "*What's going on here?*" Ben and Elizabeth's father, his chin resting on the sill, stood at the outside window. "Are you two kids all right?"

Ben waved from the doorway. "Hey, Poppa."

"Howdy, Ben."

Elizabeth reddened. "How long have you two been standing there?"

Poppa shrugged. "I was coming from the sawmill and heard this thumping coming from the school house. I thought maybe a varmint was loose. . . ."

Elizabeth glared at Ben and he quickly shrugged. "Don't look at me. I just walked up." He nodded at the entwined couple. "What *are* y'all doing?"

"Private Miller is wedged in the desk, and can't get out."

Poppa pointed at the chair leg. "Until he gets his brogan out of that leg slat, he won't get loose." Ben knelt at the chair and twisted the toe of Harry's boot free as Poppa said, "You were kind of caught in the stirrup there, Private."

Harry squeezed out of the desk and stood beside Elizabeth, who was self-consciously smoothing her dress and hair. Poppa lifted his chin off the sill. "I just got *one* question, Lizzie: did Private Miller learn his lesson well today?"

She stabbed her hand. "Both of you. You—" She pointed at Poppa— "and you, Ben Franklin Reed. Out of my classroom!" As Ben turned on his heels, laughter burst forth from the desk where Harry Miller sat. He had a high-pitched cackle that Ma called "that Yankee way of laughing." He was trying to contain himself, but that only seemed to make him laugh harder. And his laughter was contagious, spreading to Poppa and then Ben. Only Elizabeth seemed inoculated against it. She turned on the soldier. "And you can go with them, Mister-Milwaukee-Wisconsin-Soldier."

He laughed himself out of the room. Ben backed away, covering their retreat, fully expecting an eraser or some object to be launched in the direction of their withdrawal. As he eased out the door, he saw the corners of her mouth twitching. She was either fixing to have a good laugh or a good cry.

Ben caught up with the men as they walked toward the house. Poppa said, "I hear her back in that classroom. Is she crying or laughing?"

"I'm not brave enough to look back," Harry said.

Ben glanced back. "She's leaning out of her schoolhouse window."

"What's she doing?"

"I'm not positive, but I believe she's laughing."

Poppa cut off a plug of tobacco, offering it to the soldier. "Son, you think you're strong enough to tame that woman?"

"I aim to find out."

"Well, good luck. I ain't made much headway in twenty years."

"I believe I smell fried chicken at the house," Ben said. "I'm gonna scout ahead and make sure there's no ambushes awaiting us."

His father draped an arm around Harry. "Son, I really did think a varmint was loose in that room—but the only wild thing there was Lizzie when she ran us out of there."

Ben, smelling the wonderful scent of hot grease and chicken, trotted away. As Blue loped along beside him, he said, "Boy, I hope she's got the good sense to say 'Yes.'"

Chapter 39

"Unbittered"

Two days later, Harry made his next visit to Bundick. The 32nd Division had left Mab Sawmill, returning to their prior camp at Fulton. They were busy policing up where they'd bivouacked, filling foxholes, cleaning latrines and burying trash. Shep and Harry were assigned the nasty job of filling in latrines. Shep, taking a break, leaned on his shovel. "What're your plans for the evening?"

"I'm going back to see Elizabeth Reed."

"You've really got it bad."

"No, I've got it good." That afternoon he left camp, hitchhiking east on US 190 and up the gravel road through Dry Creek to Bundick. Elizabeth was on the porch swing, cutting up cucumbers. Harry slid beside her, watching her slice off the cucumber ends, and rub the cut ends against the stalk. "Why do you do that?"

"It keeps the cucumber from tasting bitter."

"Really?"

She expertly peeled it. "Our cucumbers are never bitter."

"Have you ever tried eating one without doing your little rub?"

Elizabeth tossed the peeled cucumber in a pot by her feet. "Ma calls the rub 'unbittering'."

She cut off a slice, handing it to Harry. "Are you ready?"

"Ready for what?"

"Ready to get 'unbittered'—to call your folks."

He swatted at a fly. "Well. . . ."

"If you're going *on* with me, that's how it'll be. I'm not willing to be your woman *and* your momma."

"Okay. Let's get it over with."

Elizabeth sat her pan aside. "Right now?"

"Right now."

"Do you want me to dial it? Our party line system is complicated." He handed her the note with the number. She read it. "You came prepared."

Harry only nodded as she lifted the receiver. "Hey Jenny. This is Elizabeth. I need to make a long distance call to Milwaukee, Wisconsin. Person to Person. The number is 779 655 432."

She waited. "Yes. It's Private Harry Miller calling for Mary Miller." Elizabeth's face stiffened. "Aunt Maudie, I heard your click when you picked up. This is a private call. Now hang up and have a good day." She winked at Harry.

"It's ringing." She handed him the phone.

He swore it weighed two thousand pounds in his hand.

"Hello?" It was Viola.

The operator's voice was crisp. "I have a collect call from Mr. Harry Miller to Mary Miller."

"*Who's* calling Mrs. Mary?" Viola sounded confused.

"Viola, it's me, it's Harold."

Her voice cracked. "Harold Miller. I been praying every night for *two years* that you'd call. I'm going to fetch your mother." He heard the phone receiver clank against the table.

Harry motioned to Elizabeth. "Viola's our maid and she helped raise me." Elizabeth squeezed close to him, and he momentarily forgot about his distasteful chore. He liked how she felt and how she smelled and the sound of her breathing. He nearly forgot what he was doing until he heard footsteps in the receiver, and took a deep breath.

"Harold, are you all right?"

"I'm just fine, Mother."

"What's wrong?"

He nuzzled Elizabeth's ear. "Nothing. I've never been better."

"That's good."

"How are you?"

"I'm good. Harold, it's sure good to hear your voice."

"It's good to hear yours, too. How's Father?"

"Working hard." There was a catch in her voice.

"Mother, I've called because I want to begin picking up the pieces between you, me, and Father."

He glanced at Elizabeth, whose eyes were closed as if in prayer.

"Harold, I'd like that, but. . . ." His heart sank as she continued, "You'll have to take that up with your father first." She sighed. "My heart is still broken."

"So is mine." Tears streamed from Elizabeth's closed eyes.

"Is Father there?"

"No, he's in Chicago on business. He'll be back tomorrow night."

"Good. I'll be calling him at 8:00 p.m. sharp."

"I want to warn you—he's still bitter."

"I know, but I'm not." He visualized Elizabeth's hands rubbing the cucumber ends. "I'm learning about being 'un-bittered'."

"Harold, what kind of word is that?"

"Unbittered? It's a word that describes what's going on in my heart. I'm getting 'Unbittered'."

"Well, I hope it rubs off on your father. He's just as angry as the day of the . . . the day of the accident."

"Well, that's his decision, not mine." He drew in a breath. "I've wanted to ask you for something for a long time."

"What is it?"

"I've never said this before and it's hard. Will you forgive me for causing Beverly's death?"

He heard her crying on the other end.

"Mother, can you forgive me?"

"Of course I can, and I have. You're just as much my son as Beverly was my daughter. Yes, I've forgiven you."

His mother's silence on the other end signified that today's conversation had probably gone as far as it could. "Look, Mother, I'm going to let you go. I sure love you."

"Harold, I love you too."

"Mother, one more thing. I'm playing the violin again. I played 'Shenandoah' last week and thought of you."

"That's good to hear. It's always been my favorite."

"When I come home, I'll play it for you."

"That'll be wonderful."

Elizabeth gently took the phone. "Mrs. Miller?"

She motioned Harry toward a chair. "This is Elizabeth Reed. I'm the girl Harry's seeing."

Harry turned the chair around and straddled it. This was going to be interesting. He watched Elizabeth's face as a barometer of what the complete conversation was.

"Yes, Ma'am."

She nodded her head. "Yes, Ma'am. That's true."

"Yes, Ma'am. That's what he told me."

Her face softened as she winked at Harry. "Yes, Ma'am. We do say 'Yes Ma'am' often down here. It's how we talk."

She laughed. "I agree completely."

"I'm a schoolteacher."

Elizabeth was a study in concentration for the next minute or so, but Harry couldn't decipher the scratchy voice in the receiver. He eased nearer, but Elizabeth put her hand over the receiver. "This is girl talk. Trust me."

"Yes, Ma'am. He's sitting right here, trying to eavesdrop on every word." Elizabeth listened before replying, "Mrs. Miller, I'll tell him that." She lowered the receiver. "Your mother and I just had a committee meeting. We voted 2-0 for you to go outside."

He was too nervous to stay inside anyway, so he waved in fake disgust and gladly left for the porch steps, where he took a seat. Blue came out from under the porch and laid his muzzle on Harry's knee. He petted him. "Boy, I got two women in my heart. One I've loved all my life but could never get close to. Besides, there's one in there. . . ." He pointed to the house. "I've only known her for a month but. . . ."

The dog cocked its head as if trying to understand. "The bad thing is I suspect they're ganging up on me right now." He patted Blue's head. "What do you think about that?"

The dog turned, biting at some hidden flea on his flank.

"That's just about how much help I figured you'd be."

The screen door creaked open, and Elizabeth sat beside him. "She does love you."

Harry scratched on a loose floorboard.

"Why haven't you told me about the accident?"

"Did she tell you about it?"

"No, she just said that *you* needed to."

He grabbed at a dragonfly that had landed on the porch.

"Harry, that skeeter hawk isn't going to help you, but I can."

He looked into her eyes, knowing his revelation might kill their relationship, but also knowing he must come clean. "It's a night I'd take back if I could. I was eighteen and had starting drinking pretty heavily. One afternoon I went to pick my sister up . . . the one my age . . . after her tennis lessons. I was drunk and crashed the car going home. All I got was this scar here." He pointed to a scar on his forehead. "But my sister was ejected from the car and died at the scene."

He moved his hand over his heart. "And that's how I got this scar. It's one that won't ever heal."

"What was her name?"

"Beverly. My sister was Beverly Ann Miller." He dropped his head. "And she's gone and there's nothing I can do to bring her back."

"I'm so sorry, Harry."

"So am I."

Elizabeth moved toward him, embracing him and kissing him on top of the head. "I'm so sorry."

He looked up. "I was convicted of negligent homicide. In lieu of jail, I joined the National Guard . . . and that's how I ended up in Louisiana." He put his hand on her face. "I'd understand if you broke things off."

Elizabeth kissed him. "Why would I do that? I see the man you are *now* as well as the one you're becoming. You can't run me off that easy."

"I just feel like I'm a wounded man . . . a wounded soldier . . . and will never be whole."

"Harry, we all have deep wounds. It's the price of living."

"But not everyone has a wound like mine."

"Most of us do. Some folks just hide theirs better than others."

"You talk like you know."

"I do. It's self-inflicted just like yours."

"You can tell me."

She stood. "I will, but not today. There's one thing I've got to do before I tell you." He studied the tightness of her jaw as she said, "And I plan on doing it tomorrow."

Chapter 40

Up North

Elizabeth shivered as the whistle of the northbound train shattered the quiet morning at the DeRidder depot. She steeled herself. *I know I can do this. I must do this.*

The platform was a sea of military uniforms. Soldiers hefting duffel bags, all heading north, pushed forward as the train squealed to a stop. Elizabeth was traveling light with only her purse and a light jacket. But if one could weigh a heavy heart, she was carrying the heaviest load of anyone boarding the Shreveport train.

She'd brought her current book, *A Tale of Two Cities*. She was in the midst of her yearly reading of it. Also, by sticking her nose in a book, it might discourage the soldiers from bothering her. Today, she wanted only the company of Charles Dickens. She would measure the four-hour train ride in the chapters she read and the towns they stopped in.

More soldiers crowded on at each stop: Leesville. Many. Zwolle. Mansfield. At the Kansas City Southern Depot in Shreveport, she quickly found Dora Jo Cook, her college roommate. Dora hugged her. "Are you sure you want to do this?"

"I've got to."

"Are you sure it's a good idea?"

"No, but I can't move on unless I do."

Harry spent that entire day wondering where Elizabeth was and what she was doing.

He hadn't eaten much all day. The idea of sparring with his father had killed any appetite he had. He'd never been a match for the man's intellect or sharp tongue.

He'd made up his mind.

By 7:45, the lines of soldiers had petered out. Harry stood, trying to decide which phone to use. He'd set his watch earlier by the CBS radio tone. His father was expecting 8:00 and 8:00 it would be. Being punctual was a big deal to the man—one minute late would not do. Harry stood at the phone and inspected his watch. As the second hand swept over 7:59, he picked up the phone and placed the call. He nervously licked his lips at the sound of the familiar Milwaukee ring. He counted each ring. When it rang the seventh time, he glanced at his watch. Eight o'clock on the dot.

The operator said, "Sir, there doesn't seem to be an answer."

"Please let it ring a few more times."

He heard a click. "Hello."

"I have a collect call from Harold Miller in Ragley, Louisiana. Will you accept the charges?"

During the silence that ensued, Harry could hear his own heartbeat.

"Yes. I'll take the call."

"Father. It's Harold."

"This is sure a surprise."

"I'm sure it is. How are you?"

"Harold, did you call to check on me?"

"No Sir. I called to say I'm sorry."

Silence flowed out of the phone—a suffocating silence that seemed to grab Harry by the throat. It was time to take *charge* of his life, and he would begin by taking charge of this phone call.

"Harold, what's happened to you?"

"What do you mean?"

"You sound *different*."

"You mean my voice?"

"No, your attitude. I guess your . . . yes, your heart."

"You said not to contact you until I was ready to be a man. Being a man means taking responsibility for your actions. I've learned that every tub sits on its own bottom."

"Is that some Bible verse?"

"No sir. It's from 'Ma 18:69.'"

"Harold, have you got mixed up with some of those religious nuts down there?"

"Well, kind of. It's mainly that I've fallen in love."

"With whom?"

Harry laughed. "With a woman, of course. Her name is Elizabeth. Elizabeth Reed."

"Is she Southern?"

"As Southern as you can get."

"Do you *really* see any future in this?"

Harry wasn't falling into his father's cross-examination. "Yes, I do. I see a *wonderful* future with a *wonderful* woman."

"But—"

Harry cut him off. "Father, I'm not calling for permission to marry Elizabeth . . . I'm calling to say I'm sorry for the son I've been." He wiped away tears. "I'm calling to promise that I'm going to do better."

"You don't want my opinion?" His father's voice had its customary frostiness.

"Sir, I value your opinion, but this is *my* decision . . . not yours."

The Milwaukee end of the call was silent.

"Father, every tub sits on its own bottom."

"Where'd you hear that?"

"It's how they talk down here."

Silence. It was time to drop the bomb. "Father, I have a question: what do you know about the Kickland and Sons Boatbuilders out of Monitowoc?"

More silence. Harry waited.

"Why would you ask?" There was hesitation in his father's question.

"I'm just curious. My platoon sergeant is from that family and mentioned your name."

He heard the unmistakable click of the receiver on the other end. Even though it was fifteen hundred miles north, it echoed through the small grocery store in Ragley. He placed the receiver in its cradle and rubbed his temples. It had gone well. He'd expected his father to hang up. It was one of his ways of controlling the conversation. But this time it had ended with the question planted in his father's mind, not his.

He'd done his part. His father would come around. It was just a matter of time. For the past few weeks, time had been Harry's greatest enemy. In this relationship with his father, it was his strongest ally.

The shoe was now on the other foot, and Harry liked the way it fit.

Elizabeth's train ride back to DeRidder was much quieter. With few soldiers and only a few civilians, she was able to read undisturbed. But it was difficult concentrating on Dickens. From time to time, she flipped to the first page and re-read the greatest opening line in literature. *It was the best of times. It was the worst of times.*

Those two sentences aptly described September 1941 for her. It had been terribly wonderful as well as happily distressing. She wondered what the days ahead held.

Best and worst described her trip to Shreveport. She'd met Bradley's adoptive parents. They were shocked and coolly received her at their business. She explained that she had no desire to interfere in their lives but only wanted them to know who she was and of her great love for Bradley and appreciation for them.

They had offered to let her see him, but she declined. With their permission she'd be back in the future. Today her goal was simply to meet them.

The splitting headache she had lessened with each mile the train traveled toward home. She knew she'd done the right thing. The best thing for Bradley. She could live with that. Once more, with her book shut, she quoted the opening line

"It was the best of times. It was the worst of times."

A kindly conductor patted her shoulder. "You have a beautiful voice as well as a peaceful smile. You look happy. Happy and tired."

Elizabeth nodded. "I am. I am tired, but mostly I'm happy."

The train's whistle blew and the conductor moved down the aisle. "Next stop. DeRidder, Louisiana."

She was glad to be home.

Chapter 41

East from the West

Harry's Red Arrow division was due to return to Camp Livingston in two days. It was crunch time on winning Elizabeth Reed's heart, so the minute he received permission, he began the now familiar journey to Bundick Community. Arriving at the Reed home, he discovered that Elizabeth and Peg were in town grocery shopping. Mrs. Reed invited him in. "How about a cup of coffee?"

"Yes Ma'am."

She disappeared into the kitchen as Ben slid beside him on the sofa. From the kitchen, Mrs. Reed said, "Do you drink your coffee barefoot?"

"What?"

"How do you like your coffee?"

"I do … like it." Harry shrugged.

Ben elbowed him. "Momma means, 'Do you like your coffee black—or with sugar or cream?' *Barefoot* is black." He lowered his voice. "I'd advise a little cream. It's gonna be stout-sock-dripped-sawmill coffee."

She brought in a tray and Harry carefully doctored his cup with two spoons of sugar, while Ben had a cup of coffee milk. Mrs. Reed held her barefoot cup and sat across from them. "It sure is nice having you around, Private Miller."

"Thanks for your hospitality." He took a swig of the coffee and coughed and spewed coffee on his uniform. He finally caught his breath. "That sure is hot."

"Coffee's meant to be served hot."

"Well, it definitely is, and it's definitely strong." Harry's eyes were watering, and Ben handed him his handkerchief.

Ben winked at his mother. "You didn't put moonshine in it again, didya?"

Harry studied the cup. "No way, even moonshine isn't that strong."

Mrs. Reed laughed. "You're just used to coffee that someone's dragged a couple of coffee beans through real quick—the kind where you can see the bottom of the cup."

"I hope I'm man enough to get to the bottom of *this* cup."

Ben pointed toward the fireplace. "She puts fireplace scrapings in it for darkness."

"Private Miller, I been wondering." Mrs. Reed drained her cup. "What's most different here from your home town?"

"There's lots of things, but one we laugh about all the time. Down here, you have a church on every corner. In Milwaukee, we've got a saloon on every corner."

She shook her head. "That's 'cause we Baptists can't get along and are always splitting."

Ben stood. "I'm taking Private Miller on my chore run."

Mrs. Reed stood. "Private, do you want me to freshen your cup?"

"No Ma'am, my one cup was fine."

Harry liked being around Ben and found him to be a solid source of information on Elizabeth and the rest of her family. As they climbed the barn gate the boy said, "Private Miller, do you believe in keeping secrets?"

"Why don't you call me Harry?"

"All right, Harry, can you keep a secret?"

"If asked to, I do."

"I've got a secret I want to tell, but it'll cost you."

"How's that?"

"If I tell you mine, you've got to tell me one of yours."

Harry studied the boy. He wasn't sure he'd ever met anyone quite like Elizabeth's brother. "All right, it's a deal."

"I was under the school building when you proposed to Elizabeth."

"You were?"

Ben grinned. "*Just say yes*, Elizabeth."

Harry turned on him. "Why, you little rascal. You were listening at the school?"

Ben sang, "Slipping and a-sliding—peeking and a-hiding."

"Where were you?"

"I was under the building, listening through a pipe." He opened his palms in a what-me-I'm-innocent look. "I was just trying to help. *Just say yes*."

"You were eavesdropping?"

"Nope. I was floor-dropping."

"And you heard every word?"

"Yep."

"So, what do you think?"

"I think my sister oughta say yes."

Harry grinned. "So when Elizabeth heard a voice saying 'say yes,' it was you?"

Ben tapped his fingers on the barn wall. "I was hoping she thought it was the Lord."

"Ben, you're something!"

"Thank you, Harry."

"I didn't necessarily mean it as a compliment."

"Thank you anyway." Ben walked over by Harry. "Now, it's time for your secret."

Harry walked to the barn door and stared across the hayfield toward the woods. Reaching into his billfold, he unfolded a worn newspaper clipping, handing it to Ben.

The boy studied it before reading the headline aloud. "Milwaukee teen charged in fatal accident." Ben looked up. "With the death of an area teenage girl, criminal charges are pending against her brother on vehic—"

Harry helped him. "Vehicular homicide and intoxicated driving."

Ben stared at Harry for a long time. "Harold A. Miller, age 19, son of prom—"

"That's prominent businessman and attorney Rolling A. Miller."

The boy read on, "has been arrested—" Ben stopped, folded the clipping and pressed it into Harry's palm.

"So what do you think of *my* secret, Ben?"

"That it's safe with me."

"Do you still want me to marry your sister?"

"Why wouldn't I?" He didn't wait for a reply. "Do you regret what happened?"

"A day never goes by that I don't wish I could take it back."

"Have you gotten forgiveness from it?"

"Forgiveness from whom?"

"Well, God first of all."

Harry kicked at some dried manure with his boot. "I guess I've not wanted to bother Him about it."

Ben put his hand on Harry's arm. "God's forgiveness is a pretty amazing thing. The Bible says He removes our sin as far as the East is from the West, and that's as far apart as you can get."

But the boy wasn't through. "Have you asked your family to forgive you for killing your sister?"

His use of 'killing' chilled him, but Harry knew it was accurate.

"I did this week."

"How'd that feel?"

"Pretty doggone good."

Circling the stall like a good trial attorney, Ben stopped in mid-stride. "There's one more question I have: have you forgiven yourself?"

"I'm not sure I ever will."

Ben threw a clod of dirt at a lizard. "So you believe *God* can forgive you, but you can't forgive *yourself*?"

"You sound like you're going to be a preacher or something when you grow up."

He laughed. "Not unless the Lord calls me. My plan now is to buy out Mr. Kern in DeRidder."

"Who's Mr. Kern?"

"He owns Dixie Maid Ice Cream and the Coca-Cola plant." Ben shifted gears back to the deeper subject. "What do you think *regret* is?"

"For a young boy, you sure ask a lot of questions." Harry rubbed his neck. "For me, regret's wishing I hadn't done something. What about you? What do you regret?"

"I ain't but ten years old. I ain't lived long enough to regret much. In fact, I can't think of nothing I regret." He walked out to the fencerow. "Hey, come over here and see these spider lilies." He led Harry to a line of long-stalked red flowers with small legs growing out from the center. He touched the legs. "See why we call it a spider lily?" He broke off three stalks. "It's my momma's favorite flower. I'm taking her a bouquet. Do you know the story of the spider lilies?"

"I don't." He tousled Ben's hair. "But I have a feeling I'm going to."

"They only bloom in the fall. All of the rest of the year, they're unnoticed. Ma says there's an old legend that they once were a spring-blooming plant. When Jesus went to the cross, God changed them to blooming in the fall. As far away from Easter as you can get." He twirled the three flowers in his hand. "They'd had a yellow flower, but God changed it to bright red to remind us that the blood of Jesus washed away our sin. And he moved its blooming to the fall . . . away from Easter . . . to remind us that our sins—" He nodded at Harry. "Our sins are removed as far as the east is from the west."

"Are you making that up?"

"Ma told it to me."

"Do you think she made it up?"

"Nope."

Harry took one of the flowers. "So you believe it?"

"I believe it with all my heart. Do you?"

Harry handed the flower back to Ben. "I'm not sure, but I am thinking about it." He grinned at Ben. "You sure you're not going to be a preacher?"

"Maybe after I get my ice cream factory going."

The old school bus rattled along the country road, bouncing in the ruts left by the tanks. Peg and Elizabeth held the grocery bags tightly between their feet. They'd chosen the back seat to get away from the horrible fish odor in the front of the bus. Reas Weeks, an old bachelor who lived on the creek, had carried a large catfish to DeRidder on the bus's morning run. He now sat happily on the slimy bench seat with money in his pocket from selling the fish in the Colored Quarters.

Peg held her nose. "There's nothing worse than a dead fish." She fanned the air. "Ma says the only smell worse than dead fish is a lazy man."

Elizabeth put her head out the window. "I guess that comes from Ma 18:69."

"It's right there, sister." Peg shifted the groceries under her feet. "Last night Ma got started about regret. She said she only had two regrets after seventy-two years of living."

"What were they?"

"One was something she'd done—she regretted slapping her mother once when she was a girl. Said it still bothered her."

"What was the second one?"

Peg said, "Her second regret was something she *hadn't* done. Said she'd always wanted to visit Niagara Falls and was going to die without seeing it."

Elizabeth gritted her teeth as they bounced over a rough corduroy section of the road. "I guess two regrets in seventy years isn't bad."

"What's your biggest regret, Elizabeth?"

"Yours first—you were born first."

"By only ten minutes."

"That still makes you the oldest."

Peg stared out the bus window. "I regret that I haven't learned how to be a real lady like you. I don't talk right. I don't dress right. I wish . . . I just wish I could go to finishing school or something and be like you."

"You're fine just like you are."

"But I'm not like you."

"Thank God, you're not."

"All right. It's your turn," Peg said.

"It was about ten years ago in Alexandria. We were with Momma and I dared you to go inside the Hotel Bentley and run up the staircase, and slide down the banister.

"I regret I didn't run with you. You were pulling me, but I broke away. I'd always wanted to see the lobby of the Bentley."

Peg shrugged. "I never got to slide down. A bellhop collared me at the top of the stairs." She put her arm around her sister. "It's not too late for you to go run up those stairs."

"I'm afraid it is. I'm too old and serious."

"Speaking of being serious, that can't *really* be your biggest regret."

Elizabeth shuffled the bag on her lap. "It's what I wished I *had* done. It's kind of like Ma's Niagara Falls regret.

"Does it have to do with your baby?"

Elizabeth hardly ever cried, but her tears flowed freely. "He left me as soon as I told him I was pregnant."

Peg's grip tightened. "*My regret* is that I can't find him and kill him for you."

"He didn't do anything I didn't let him do. Loving him isn't even my regret. It's that I should've kept my baby."

Peg began crying, causing Mr. Reas Weeks to turn and stare. "Are you girls all right back there?"

Elizabeth waved. "It's fine, Mr. Reas. It's just that your catfish is a little strong."

He sniffed. "I don't smell a thing."

"It's good he can't smell himself," Elizabeth laughed, wiping at her eyes. "I'll live with that regret for the rest of my life. I should've kept him." She looked at Peg. "What do you think Momma and Poppa would have done if I'd kept him?"

"They'd been devastated at the news . . . at first, but would've circled the wagons and been the best grandparents in the world." She grasped Elizabeth's hand. "You can't continue to beat yourself up over that. It'll get you down. Is that why you went to Shreveport two days ago?"

"How'd you know I went?"

"I have my sources. You bought a ticket and came back the same day. What were you doing?"

"I just needed to do something."

"What was it?"

"I went to meet the family that adopted my baby, Bradley."

"Who named him *Bradley*—you or them?"

"It was the only stipulation in the adoption agreement. I got to name the baby, and I chose *Bradley*."

What if it'd been a girl?"

Elizabeth put her head down. "If it was a girl, I'd picked out *Peggy Sue*."

"That's sweet, but why did you go meet Bradley's parents?"

"I just wanted them to know who I was, and why I gave him up. When he gets old enough, I want him to know he was loved, not abandoned."

"That's good. What's next?"

"I've got to level with Harry Miller."

"When are you going to do that?"

"Today—if he comes."

"Whoa. Feed him a spoonful at a time. You don't want to mess up a good thing."

Elizabeth stared off dreamily. "I should've kept my baby and told the rest of the world to go to hell if they didn't like it."

"Sister, I think that's the first bad word I've ever heard you say."

"It's what I should've done, but I didn't. And now I've got a two-year old son in Shreveport I'll never know." She turned to Peg. "Do you think less of me for this?"

"Lizzie, you ain't just my twin sister, you're my hero. There ain't *nothing* you can do to make me love you less. Ain't nothing."

Elizabeth poked her. "You just said 'ain't' *twice* in *two* sentences."

Peg put her arm around her. "Don't lecture me. You just said 'hell.'"

Elizabeth leaned her head on her twin's shoulder. "I guess I did."

"That's all right. It's kind of like 'ain't.' Sometimes it's the best word that fits."

Elizabeth kissed Peg on the forehead. "Ain't it the truth?"

Ben balanced eight yard eggs in his cap as he led Harry toward the house. "Momma's gonna be some kind of excited about these eggs."

He saw her standing by the well. "Over here, Ben, I need your help." When he reached her, she said, "I hear chickens down in the well."

Ben walked to the well and peered down into its darkness. "Something's rotten in Detroit. A chicken's fallen in."

"Rotten in Detroit? What does that mean?" Harry said.

Ben winked. "Ain't that what ol' Shakespeare said?"

Harry leaned over the well wall. "I believe it sounds like more than one."

"I bet it's some of those new young pullets." Momma looked at Ben. "Baby, it's always been Jimmy Earl's job to go down into the well."

He shuffled his feet, glancing away. She put her arm around him. "He'd about outgrown it anyway. I guess it's your job now."

"How deep is it?" Harry peered into the hole.

"It's thirty-five feet to the water table," Momma said.

"What's a *pullet*?"

"A young hen."

Ben's head spun. There was nothing he hated more than the dark—unless it was being confined in a tight space. The well presented both in one big dose. He listened as the chickens clucked, their call echoing up the well. "I guess I'm the man to do it."

His mother hugged him. "You are my little man."

"But I'll do it only under one condition."

"What's that?"

"I'll go down in the well if Harry will hold the rope."

"I don't know about that." Harry backed away.

"Well, I do. I'd trust you with my life. I want you holding the rope." He walked to Harry, spat on his own palm before extending it. "Let's spit-shake on it."

"What?"

"A spit-shake. It seals a deal. It means I can trust you." Ben extended his slimy hand to the soldier, who hesitated before spitting on his own hand, grasping the boy's small hand. "It's a deal. I won't let go."

Ben placed a board across the well bucket as Momma instructed Harry on how to pay out the rope. Ben climbed into the well and straddled the board. As Momma handed him the carbide light, he nodded to Harry. "Easy does it now."

As he descended into the cool darkness, he prayed, *"The Lord is my shepherd. I shall not want."* It was sure hard acting all tough when you wanted to pee in your pants. He put his hand on the slimy cement walls. As the light above him faded, he looked up and saw the faces of his mother and Harry peering down.

Ben guessed that in a way this was like being put in a grave. Cool, quiet, and damp. Except in a grave there aren't chickens clucking . . . or water dripping. *He makes me lie down in green pastures. He leads me beside still waters.* He turned on his carbide light just before the bucket splashed into the water and hollered, "I'm on the bottom."

He saw a pullet to his right and snatched it up, stuffing it inside his shirt. The second one was more elusive, so he used the light to blind it and caught it. He scanned the bottom of the well, making sure there were no dead chickens or rats fouling the water. The spring-fed water gurgled out of the walls, and he splashed some on his face. It was cool down here and he warmed his hands on the metal of the lamp.

Ben turned off the light. In spite of his fear of being in the well, what he saw above made it worthwhile. The sky was the brightest blue he'd ever seen. He saw the silhouettes of Harry, his mother, and someone else watching from above. They seemed like angels looking down on him.

He remembered the next lines of the 23rd Psalm: *Even though I walk through the valley of the shadow of death, I fear no evil; for You are with me.*

He heard yelling from above. "It's Lizzie. How are you doing down there?"

The twins were back from town. "I'm fine. Where's Peg?"

"I'm up here. How many chickens are there?"

"Two pullets." He jerked on the rope. "All right, Private Miller, bring us up." He heard the windlass creaking as he slowly rose, trying to erase the troubling thought of the fall if the rope broke. As he neared the surface, fresh cool air rushed down. He was coming out of the grave. *Surely goodness and mercy shall follow me all the days of my life; and I shall dwell in the house of the Lord forever.*

When his head cleared the well, he tossed the two chickens onto the ground. Elizabeth grabbed him and helped lift him off the board.

He hugged her. "It was two of the young pullets we picked up at the depot. Elizabeth, I saw the bluest sky down there, and all of y'all looked like angels looking down at me." He looked at their faces, realizing that none of them really comprehended what he'd seen. They'd never been down in a well. He walked to Harry. "You believe me, don't you?"

"Ben, if you say it's so, I believe it." He knelt in front of him and took his hands. "Why'd you want me to hold the rope?"

"Because I trust you. I trust you with my life." He grabbed Harry's sleeve. "And because I'm trusting you with my sister."

He studied the soldier's expression. "Hey, I thought soldiers weren't supposed to cry?"

"Who told you something that stupid?" Harry Miller pulled Ben to him. "Thanks for trusting me. I won't let you down."

Chapter 42

Coming Clean

Harry helped Elizabeth carry in the groceries to where she plopped her bags on the counter. "Would you like to take a walk?"

"As long as it's with you," he said.

They held hands as they went down the path toward the creek. "Have I ever shown you the shallow water creek crossing?" She led him into the woods where every chance he got, Harry pulled her close for a long kiss. She didn't fight him off. It was good to be young and in love.

"Harry, that song you played at the singing, "Shenandoah." Do you know the words?"

"Some of them."

"Sing it for me."

He didn't consider himself a great soloist, but if Elizabeth Reed wanted *Shenandoah*, he'd deliver.

Oh Shenandoah,
I love your daughter
Away, you rolling river.

Before he could finish, she pulled him into an embrace and the singing stopped. It is difficult to sing when a woman's lips are pressed against yours, but Harry was not complaining.

When they finally reached the creek, she led him to a log. "Let's sit here. I want to tell you about my trip." She fiddled nervously with her collar.

Harry stroked her face. "Just relax."

"What I'm going to tell you is difficult, and I'm afraid things won't be the same after I do."

"It can't be any worse than what I told you two days ago."

She bit her lip. "Yesterday I caught the train to Shreveport, where I had some unfinished business."

"Did you finish it?"

"I hope so, but I'm not sure." She brushed back the dark hair from her face. "Harry, three years ago I went off to college in Natchitoches. It's where I got my teaching degree. During my first year there is when I met a man—a soldier like you. He literally swept me off my feet. He was an officer: dashing, and handsome. He was way out of my league. Anyway, we were in love, or at least I was. He told me how he loved me. Over time I gave him my heart, and it didn't stop there. We became intimate."

Elizabeth hung her head. "I was so naïve—I'd just turned eighteen. Anyway, early in 1939 I discovered I was pregnant. It wasn't the news I wanted to hear and neither did he: he dropped me like a hot potato, getting a quick transfer out of Louisiana and away from me. I had decisions to make: tough decisions. I had three choices. Keep the baby and face the talk of folks back home. Give the baby up for adoption. They told me about a place in Shreveport where girls like me could get it undone real easy."

Harry steeled himself to not show surprise no matter what came next.

"But that wasn't an option. If you make your bed, you have to sleep in it. I couldn't bear the thought of disappointing my parents, so I didn't tell them."

"Did they find out?"

"No. They still don't know. I moved to Shreveport to live with the parents of one of my college friends. When the baby was born in September 1939, I gave him up for adoption." She looked up. "Harry, if I had it to do over, I'd have kept him."

"The baby was a boy?"

"Yes. I named him Bradley. A fine family in Shreveport adopted him and he recently turned two. My college friend sees him at church and occasionally writes me about him. He's a lovely boy."

"Is that why you went to Shreveport yesterday?"

"I had to see him for myself. I wasn't there to interfere in his life or kidnap him. I just needed to see him."

Elizabeth looked up. "I don't know if you still want me after hearing all of this."

"Why wouldn't I?"

"I'm a woman who was used and discarded by another man. I had a baby and gave him up for adoption. That's not the track record you'd want for a wife."

"But I still want you."

"You do?"

"More than ever."

She glanced around. "It's getting dark. We'd best be going." They walked arm in arm back toward the house. As they got to the crossroads, she said, "I'm happy and sad."

"How's that?"

"I'm so happy I met you, and sad I didn't meet you years ago."

"Elizabeth, all that matters is now." They walked slowly, enjoying the end of a cool Louisiana evening. The first signs of fall had blown through in the last several days, lowering both the temperature and humidity. As the sun sank behind the trees, a nearby bird sang a beautiful solo. He said, "What kind of bird is that?"

"It's a Redbird—a Cardinal. Listen to its song: *Look out boys, look out.*"

Harry cocked his ear. "I don't hear—" Suddenly the sickening sound of shrieking brakes—followed by a truck horn—broke the peaceful quiet.

"That's near the crossroads." Elizabeth pulled on his arm. "We'd better go see." They hurried to the gravel road where three Army trucks were pulled to the shoulder. In the twilight, Harry made out several men kneeling between two of the vehicles.

Harry smelled burnt rubber and saw a sight that chilled him: Blue, Ben's hound, sniffing around the men. Wherever the dog was, Ben wasn't far. The soldiers were kneeling around a prone body. One of them flinched when he saw Harry. "He just came out of nowhere." He pointed at Blue. "He was chasing that dog."

Harry knew it was Ben. Pushing through the men, he knelt over Ben's unconscious body. A trickle of blood oozed from his ear. His chest was heaving up and down.

A Colored soldier, caressing Ben's shoulder, said, "I'm so sorry. I tried to dodge him."

Harry turned to see Elizabeth nearing, and he grabbed her around the shoulders. "It's Ben." She tried to pull away. "Elizabeth, it's bad."

"I've got to see him."

"I know, but look at me first—he's hurt bad." He slowly released his grip. "Let me walk with you."

She nodded. "I want you with me. I need you right now." The men parted and Elizabeth put her head on Ben's chest. Harry knelt and placed his arm around her. Soon, he heard feet crunching on the gravel. Mr. Reed gently pulled his daughter back where he could see. The pain of recognition etched on his face made Harry sick to his stomach. Elizabeth's mother collapsed at Ben's feet, crying horribly. Elizabeth moved beside her, joining in the weeping.

Suddenly Elizabeth stood and, in a voice he'd never heard, said, "We've got to get him to the hospital. Load him up."

The shocked soldiers didn't move.

"Load my brother up *now*. Do you understand?"

Mr. Reed lifted his son and carried him to the front truck, as Elizabeth helped her mom into the crowded cab. She leaned out the window. "Harry, go tell Ma." The truck roared down the road, leaving Harry standing in the dark with the two soldiers.

One soldier, evidently the one who'd hit Ben, was inconsolable. "I tried to miss him, Hezekiah. There was no time to brake."

His fellow driver patted his shoulder. "Ira Lee, there was nothin' you could do." Harry realized he knew these men—they were from the unit that he'd visited with on the blues music night.

Ben's dog, Blue, sniffed sadly at the spot where his master had lain. Whimpering, he lay down as if he realized the accident was his fault. Harry's mind went back to the night of *his* accident, remembering the awful weight of being responsible for the death of his own sister. At least Blue wouldn't have to carry that load. In some ways, dogs were more fortunate than humans.

Harry put his hand on the crying soldier, who shrank back as if he expected a blow. "Look, fellow, you. . . ."

"I tried to miss him."

"I know." Harry moved into the man's view. "I know you. I'm the soldier that slipped into your camp one night to listen to the blues."

The soldier glanced up, freezing at the sound of an approaching vehicle. The other driver pulled on his shirt. "Ira Lee, we in the middle of what may be Klan country, and you done run over a white child. Let's get out of here." Both men hurried to their trucks, leaving Harry alone in the dark.

A vehicle sped by, honking its horn as a pall of dust covered him. Harry whistled for Blue. "Let's go, boy." As the vehicles faded in the distance, the only sound was Blue trotting beside him. Harry felt more alone and helpless than he had in a long time.

He walked to the Reed house, wondering if Peg was home. Walking through the empty hall and rooms, he thought about how much music and laughter had been here. Now, there was only complete silence. Rubbing his hands across the rough logs, he pondered when there'd be joy again in this old house. He tried to take it all in: the smell of something cooking, the creak of the floor boards, the violin leaning by the pump organ. All spoke of family, stability, and roots.

He was no stranger to grief, and knew he was in its dark company again. It seemed as if grief always found him. Going to the porch, he sat in a rocker, listening to the night sounds: crickets, owls, and frogs. Lightning bugs flashed in the distance. He knew he needed to tell Ma, but first he needed to get his mind ready.

Harry was not much of a praying man, but he was becoming one. "Lord, I'm not much on talking to you, but here I am. You know what's happened here tonight. It's beyond me to know what to do, but you do. Help Ben. Lord, spare his life. Please let him live. Please."

He wondered if God had heard. If He even listened to a guy like him. He stood and headed out for Ma's house. He was unfamiliar with the path, but Blue trotted along beside him, quickly taking the lead down the dark path. A light from the old couple's home appeared through the woods. Ma, silhouetted by lantern light, was sitting by a window. She glanced up as the dogs began barking.

The door opened just as Harry stepped onto the porch. "Private Miller, what—is something wrong?"

Harry ducked his head and she grabbed his arm. "What's happened?"

"Ben's been hurt real bad. An Army truck hit him."

"Oh, my goodness." She went inside, closed her stroke-victim husband's door. "Where are they?"

"They took Ben to the hospital in DeRidder. Elizabeth and her parents."

"That's where I need to be. We don't have no car or phone. Will you go over to the neighbors and see if they'll take us to town?" She pointed through the woods. "See those distant lights? That's Earl and Minerva's house. Ask Earl if he'll take us, and see if his wife will come watch Spencer."

Harry stumbled through the underbrush, dodging low limbs as he neared the house. The neighbor's dogs began barking and at the porch, a growl came up behind him. A man cracked the door. "What you doin' coming up in the dark, soldier?" He was holding something behind him that appeared to be a gun.

"I was sent by the Reeds. Ben Reed's been hit by a truck and taken to the hospital. Ma needs you to take her to town and your wife to watch her husband."

"Let me get dressed and get the wife." A low guttural growl behind Harry caused him to turn and see a cur dog easing up the steps, tail tucked under, teeth bared. He eased inside the screen door.

Earl trotted out. "If we can get Sadie going, we'll be on our way." They went out to the small wooden garage, Harry keeping the man between him and the growling dog. "Oh, don't worry 'bout ol' Sue," Earl said, "she only bites soldiers on odd days of the week." Harry dove into the old truck before the dog could close ground.

After a coughing start, the truck cranked and sputtered out of the garage. Earl said, "Sadie's like me: kind of slow starting, but once she's warmed up she's as good as new."

His wife, clad in a housecoat, climbed in. "Is the child hurt bad?"

"I'm afraid so."

Ma hurried to the truck waiting in the yard. The woman climbed out. "Mrs. Doshie, you don't worry about Mr. Spencer. I'll watch him until you're back."

"Thanks Minerva. I appreciate it more than you'll ever know."

Harry climbed into the cab as the driver said, "Is he gonna make it?"

"I'm not sure." He saw Ma's forlorn look and looked away. The truck bounced along the road, and as they neared where the accident occurred, Harry said, "That's where it happened. They were blackout driving and didn't see him. . . . "

"That's right. Tonight's blackout driving." Earl geared down the truck, but Ma put her hand on his shoulder. "Getting to town quick is more important than any rules they got. You just follow those headlights."

"I just hope we don't meet a tank in this darkness," Earl said.

"Where are those trucks now?" Ma said.

"One took them to DeRidder. The other two drove off as I left. Those two drivers—they were Colored—were scared to death."

Ma craned her neck. "The driver who hit Ben—was he Colored?"

"He was." A brooding silence filled the vehicle, drawing every bit of the night's darkness into the car. Harry now understood more clearly why the two drivers hurried from the scene. Harry said, "He said that he tried. . . ." The words froze in his mouth as Ma and Earl stared blankly at him. A line from Shenandoah echoed in his mind. *Away, I'm bound away, 'cross the wide Missouri.*

There was a wide river between him and these woods people. He wondered if it could be bridged. Ma was studying him as if she were looking into his soul. Harry wasn't sure what she was looking for—at the moment, he wasn't even sure if he had a soul.

Chapter 43

Down The Road

No one spoke again until the truck reached the hospital. Rain started, adding to the sorrow already riding in the vehicle. Harry, used to the towering medical centers of Milwaukee, was surprised at how small the hospital was. Earl dropped them at the ER before wheeling the truck into a parking space.

Ma paused at the entrance. "Do you think we're ready for this?"

Harry held the door. "I'm not sure that's possible."

Elizabeth's parents were huddled in the corner, pain radiating from their faces as Ma strode to them. "How is he?"

"He's hurt real bad," Mr. Reed said. "Dr. Sartor's in there with him. He's got a head injury."

"Will he pull through?"

He looked down. "No way to know."

Elizabeth came out of a nearby room. Seeing Harry, she ran to him, and clasped her head to his chest. Her body shook with uncontrollable sobs. There was nothing he could say or do. He simply embraced her and patted her back. Elizabeth, her face still buried in his chest, said, "Maybe if I just stay right here, it'll all go away, and I'll wake up from this nightmare."

The emergency room doors swung open and a tired-looking doctor, hands jammed in his lab coat, walked toward Mr. and Mrs. Reed. He inhaled deeply, stopping well away from them, his eyes fixed on his shoes.

Elizabeth's mother stepped forward. "He's gone, ain't he?"

The doctor nodded.

"My baby's gone."

The doctor was crying as he walked to Mrs. Reed. "I'm sorry, Pearline." He draped an arm around Mr. Reed. "I'm so sorry, Levon."

Mr. Reed tenderly touched the doctor's arm. "Thanks, Doc. We know you did all you could."

"But it wasn't enough."

"You did your best, and we'll be grateful forever."

The doctor took off his glasses and wiped his eyes. "Would you like to see him . . . ?"

Elizabeth stepped forward. "Of course we would, Doctor Sartor." She kissed him lightly on the cheek before escorting her family toward the emergency room. Arm in arm, the four family members walked stiffly through the doors. It was as if Harry could see each of them withering right in front of him.

Earl had joined him. "Do Peg and Jimmy Earl know?"

"No, we'll have to find Peg. Jimmy's up at Camp Leonard Wood, Missouri, in basic training."

"They'll both take it hard." Earl pointed toward the door. "Why don't you go in there?"

"No, this is their time." The wailing that came from inside made him want to cover his ears. Sobs of pain and grief seemed to shake the very foundation of the hospital.

"I can't stand it," Earl said. "I'm going outside for a smoke."

The receptionist picked up a folder and hurried out. "I'll be back later."

That left Harry as the only witness to the cries of a family whose lives had just been changed forever. He fought the urge to join Earl outside, but didn't. It was his job to be here—he was on guard duty. The outside door burst open and Peg rushed in. "Where's Ben? Where's my family?" Harry stepped toward the emergency room door as she ran to his arms. "Tell me he's going to be all right."

"I can't."

Peg heard the wailing. "Oh, my God. Ben's gone, ain't he?" Harry couldn't understand one word she said from that point forward. Finally, she pulled loose and stumbled into the ER. The wailing intensified, before tapering off and being replaced by voices. Harry even heard the sound of laughter—then silence—followed by more crying. He didn't move from his duty spot. Elizabeth, when she finally came out, would find him waiting.

From behind the double doors, he heard an amazing sound. It was singing. He stepped to the doors. He heard Mr. Reed's deep voice:

> *"I will arise and go to Jesus,*
> *He will embrace me in his arms."*

Harry's heart was in his throat. What kind of folks are these people? At first, Mr. Reed was the only one singing, but gradually, other voices joined in:

> *"In the arms of my dear Savior,*
> *Oh there are ten thousand charms."*

He picked out the old woman's voice and Elizabeth's unmistakable tenor:

> *"Weak and wounded, sick and sore.*
> *Jesus ready stands to save you*
> *Full of pity, love, and power."*

Harry felt guilty for eavesdropping but couldn't pull himself away. These people really believed what they were singing, and he had to be a witness to it:

> *"I will arise and go to Jesus*
> *He will embrace me in his arms.*
> *In the arms of my dear Savior,*
> *Oh, there are ten thousand charms."*

The singing stopped and he heard Mr. Reed. He seemed to be praying, but it was impossible to sort out the words. What kind of people are these folks who can sing and pray when standing over the body of their son? It didn't seem real. *They* didn't seem real.

He just knew one thing: this family had something. They possessed something he wanted. He wasn't sure how you defined it. It wasn't religion. It was much more than that.

It was faith. A real faith.

It was hope. A hope that evidently could even withstand tragedy.

Harry wanted it, and he wanted it badly. When he heard "Amen," he backed away from the doors. Soon, Elizabeth's parents, leaning on each other, passed by. Mrs. Reed squeezed Harry's shoulder. In a few minutes, Ma, Peg, and Elizabeth came out. Ma hugged Harry and kissed him on the cheek. "Thank you."

Elizabeth collapsed in his arms. "Oh, Harry, he was the light of my life." She looked into his eyes. "What are we going to do?" Harry pulled her closer. He had the same question. What were *they* going to do? He was—for better or worse now—part of this family.

Ma and Peg left, leaving Elizabeth and him alone. She nodded toward the double doors. "Don't you want to tell him goodbye?"

"Do you think . . . I should?"

"If you'd like to."

"I want to." He moved toward the door. "Do you want to go with me?"

She shook her head. "No, I've already said my goodbye."

Harry pushed open the doors, walking in cement shoes into the emergency ward. A kind-eyed nurse met him. "Can I help you?"

"I'm here to say goodbye to Ben Reed."

"Are you family?"

"Yes Ma'am, in fact I am."

She led him into a small examining room, folding down the sheet that covered Ben. He lay there as if he might sit up at any minute and sing, whistle, or laugh. But he would never be doing any of those again, at least not on this old earth. Harry tenderly tousled his strawberry hair. "I believe you had way more than 800 freckles—way more."

It was difficult to believe that this was the boy whom he'd held a rope for just a few hours ago. A rope that descended down into the well. Harry stood a long time. He'd been unable to say goodbye to his sister Beverly. At least not like this. That was part of the reason he'd never gotten past her death. He had caused it—he had loved her—and he'd never gotten to say goodbye.

At least he would be able to do it with Ben, so he was in no hurry to leave. He had no idea of how long he stood there. Finally remembering that the others were outside waiting, he leaned down and kissed Ben's forehead. "I won't let go of the rope, Buddy. You've got my word on that. I'll take care of them all, especially Elizabeth."

Harry turned at the door, and gave a half-salute. "And I'll see you down the road." He hurried out of the hospital. It was raining harder. Mr. Reed was standing under the awning. "You and I are riding in the back." They climbed into the bed, sitting against the cab for protection from the rain while Earl and the Reed women were squeezed up front.

They rode through the wet darkened streets of DeRidder. Passing the depot, they turned south and bounced across the rough railroad crossing. "Sir, I'm so sorry for Ben's passing away," Harry said.

Mr. Reed put a calloused hand on Harry's arm. "Son, we're not gonna call a spade a hoe. Ben didn't pass away—he died—it's that simple. We might as well get used to saying it." He stared off into the rain, "My boy Ben's dead, and nothing can undo that."

Harry was embarrassed until he realized this wasn't a reprimand, but simply a statement of fact. Mr. Reed's next words proved this: "Thanks for being here for Elizabeth, and thanks for being here for all of us."

Twenty-five miles is a long trip in the depths of a blackout night. Through the cab window, Harry saw the women all silently staring ahead. The sputtering engine and rhythmic wipers were the only sounds. About halfway home, they rounded a large curve, and a vehicle with a red flashing light roared out of a side road. As the truck stopped, a jeep came alongside and an M.P. rushed to the cab. "What are you fools doing out on a blackout night?"

"We've been to the hospital." Earl nodded at the Reed women. "Their son was killed by an Army truck earlier in the night."

The M.P. softened. "I'm sorry. I heard about it on our radio." He stepped back. "I can't turn on my lights, but I'll lead you home." He turned toward his jeep, and then stopped. "You folks could've been killed by a tank driving in the black of night."

"We wouldn't be that lucky," Mr. Reed said, loud enough for only Harry to hear—and he shuddered at these words. They weren't spoken in bitterness or anger—it was a longing, even a wish. Harry understood it well: he'd felt it himself on his own black night.

A few miles down the road, Harry said, "Mr. Reed, I lost a sister in an accident."

"What happened?"

"I was driving. We had a wreck, and she was killed."

"How'd you get over it?"

"I haven't." Harry wanted to tell the entire story, but knew this wasn't the time. After another half hour of riding in the silence, they finally arrived home. The porch was full of neighbors and friends, and the news of Ben's death traveled through the yard like a shock wave. As these folks huddled around the Reeds, Harry melted into the dark. For the first time that night, he wondered what time it was. He glanced down at his wristwatch, but it was gone. He mentally retraced his steps of the night, but had no idea where he'd lost it. Easing to the porch, he asked an old man for the time. He struck a match, holding it to his watch face. "It's a little after four."

He was AWOL. Harry'd been in Louisiana for over nine months and never been late for anything. Yet, here he was AWOL. During the frantic hours after Ben's accident, he'd never considered the time. Being late to camp was the least of his worries, but now he was over four hours late.

Elizabeth waved to him from the porch. "Harry, come inside."

"I've got to be going. I'm late for getting back to camp."

She stepped into the yard and hugged him. "I don't want you to go."

"I was supposed to be—"

"Are you AWOL?"

"It'll be all right. I'll just explain when I get back."

She caressed his cheek and kissed him. "I'll never forget you being here for us."

"I'd better get on the road."

She pulled him close, kissing Harry like he'd never been kissed. His knees felt like ropes of sand from her passionate kiss that wasn't actually passionate. It was even deeper than that.

She finally pulled away. "I really love you."

"And I love you too."

"Promise me one thing."

"Yes?"

"That you won't leave me."

"Elizabeth, my feet may leave, but my heart's right here." He turned toward the crossroads and started walking. He kept looking back and saw her waving until the darkness separated them. In his mind, an eddy of swirling emotions spun. Love. Grief. Loss. Hope. But there was one emotion he didn't feel: *regret*. He'd decided to live without that word. It'd be hard, but not impossible.

At the crossroads, he turned left toward the bridge, so he could search the accident site for his watch. Dawn was creeping up as he came to the truck's skid marks in the gravel. At the spot where Ben had lain, Harry got on his hands and knees, feeling in the grass. His hand bumped against a metallic object, but it wasn't his watch. It was a harmonica. Ben's harmonica. He shook the dirt out of its keys, smiling at how Ben loved to irritate Elizabeth by playing "Battle Hymn of the Republic."

Harry placed it to his lips and blew softly, stopping as a noise drifted on the wind. He listened: nothing. Just as he put the harmonica to his lips, he heard it again. He wasn't scared; instead he sensed an unexplainable peace. Kneeling in the dim light, he heard it clearly.

Down the road.

He looked into the surrounding woods as well as up and down the road. No sign of anyone.

He stood and heard it again. *Down the road.*

Pocketing the harmonica, Harry blew out a breath. "I'll see you down the road too."

He turned south and began the long walk back to camp, running his finger over the cool metal of the harmonica. *I've always wanted to learn to play a harmonica. I wonder what key "Battle Hymn" is in?*

Chapter 44

AWOL

Harry walked south with daylight, but vehicle traffic was light. Two civilian vehicles passed but only left him eating dust. On each step toward camp, the reality of being AWOL seeped in. He had a valid excuse: he'd remained with Elizabeth and her family in their terrible hours after Ben's death. Leaving them had not been an option.

Still, the division had cracked down on AWOLs. This had led to the 32nd having the lowest number of absentee soldiers in the entire Third Army. Also, today was moving-out day, not the day you wanted to be absent without leave.

He heard the familiar whine of a jeep coming over the hill to the south. As it neared, the jeep veered around his outstretched thumb and screeched to a stop. The driver leaned out. "Hurry if you want a ride."

Harry trotted for the jeep and swung up into the passenger seat.

He and the driver said in unison. "Where're you heading?"

Laughing, the driver—a corporal—said, "I'm on my way to the 32nd HQ off Highway 190. How about you?"

"That's where I need to be." Harry glanced at his watch-less wrist. "It's where I needed to be six hours ago."

"That's not good." The corporal gunned the engine and the jeep fishtailed before roaring ahead. "Let's see if we can cut your AWOL time down a little."

Harry removed his cap. "Did you race cars before the army?"

"Nope, but I always wanted to."

"I can see that." Harry kept a death grip on the front windshield.

The corporal grinned and reached out his hand, eyes still focused on the bumpy road. "Name's Lawrence. Corporal Clyde Lawrence."

"I'm Harry Miller."

"Nice to meet you, Miller." He patted the steering wheel. "And this is my partner in crime, Jeep 1-9-3-1."

They roared into the village of Reeves at breathtaking speed. Harry said, "Our camp is about six miles west from here."

"We'll have you there in five minutes." The two left tires seemed to come off the ground as they careened around the corner and onto US 190. Harry leaned over toward the speedometer. It ended at 80 but the needle wasn't visible.

"Private, if you don't mind me asking, why are you AWOL?"

"I've got a girl near where you picked me up. Last night her brother was run over by a transport truck. He died at the hospital."

A cloud came over the driver's face. "What's your name again?"

"Harry Miller."

The driver winced. "What was the name of the boy?"

"Reed. Ben Reed. He was ten."

Lawrence jammed on the brakes of the jeep and veered to the shoulder. His face was ashen and his earlier cocky manner was replaced by a shaking voice. "Ben Reed? He's got a sister named Peg and another one . . ."

Harry finished, " . . . named Elizabeth."

Lawrence placed his forehead against the steering wheel. "That boy rode in this very jeep. I met them all. The daddy and momma." He looked up through tears. "Ben's dead?"

"I'm afraid so." Harry studied Lawrence. "How'd you know them?"

"I met them after a plane tore up their garden. I took an officer down to inspect it and later escorted Peg to Polk to complete the paperwork and get their money."

"Elizabeth told me all about that. So you're the Corporal Lawrence who drove Mr. Reed over that rickety bridge?"

"That's me."

"Didn't Ben go with you to Polk?"

Lawrence laughed. "Not because I invited him."

"He was a nosey little booger."

"I can't believe he's dead."

Harry sighed. "Neither can I, but he is." He pointed down the highway. "You better get me there to face the music."

Suddenly, Lawrence's driving was altogether different. It seemed the sad news had cured his heavy foot, replacing it with a heavy heart. As they entered the camp at Fulton, Harry said, "That's where I need to get off."

"You need me to put in a word for you?" Lawrence said.

"No, I'll be fine. It's not my habit of being late. Thanks a million."

"Glad to help. Good meeting you, Miller. I've become friends with Peg, so I'll see you down the road."

Down the road. Harry waved. "Sure hope so. Thanks for the ride."

Lawrence's jeep peeled out, heading toward the HQ tent. A soldier walked up beside Harry and said, "That's a tough little running machine. Ten thousand of them might help an army win a war."

Harry pointed to the dust cloud left by the jeep. "The way he's driving *that* jeep, it—or he—won't be around for any war that doesn't start in the next two months."

Normally, Sergeant Kickland would have been flexible about Harry's late arrival. Harry had a strong reason for today's tardiness and a clean record, but as soon as he saw Sarge, he knew something was different. "Miller, where in the hell have you been?"

He related the night's tragedy until Sarge stopped him. "It's out of my hands. A colonel was here during roll call, and there was no way to cover your absence." He shrugged. "We've got orders. All AWOLs to the MP office." He scribbled on a form, folded it and handed it to Harry. "Take this with you." His face softened. "Miller, I'm sorry. You just picked a bad time to be AWOL."

It was the longest walk of Harry's life to the tent. A jeep with a colonel's flag was outside the tent and that spelled bad news. Tucking in his shirt, Harry handed his papers to an orderly at the tent. The unsmiling junior officer read it before motioning for Harry to enter.

He walked right into a tall colonel. "Excuse me, Sir."

"Watch where you're going, Soldier."

A captain, his nameplate read 'Farrell,' sat at a desk. "What do you have, Soldier?"

"Papers, Sir."

"AWOL papers?"

"Yes Sir, but . . ."

The captain raised a hand. "Quiet. If I need anything from you, I'll ask." The older colonel came back in the tent and stood, cross-armed. Evidently the word "AWOL" had piqued his interest. The captain scanned the paper. "Anderson, get in here." The orderly hurried in. "Fill out AWOL charges on Private Miller." He glanced at his watch. "He's over seven hours late for duty."

"Sir, I can explain."

"Quiet. You'll get your chance later." Captain Farrell didn't even look at Harry. His eyes and actions were directed at the colonel.

"Anderson, go get a military policeman."

Harry couldn't believe it. He looked from Captain Farrell to the colonel, who seemed to be sizing him up for a brig cot. Finally, the colonel spoke, "Soldier, we don't take it lightly on derelict of duty. Just because the battle is over doesn't give you the right to be away."

"Yes Sir." This was not the time to argue.

An M.P. entered and unclasped his handcuffs. His entrance was followed by a voice from outside. "Permission to enter, Sir."

The Captain answered impatiently. "Permission granted." As an aside, he added, "But it'd better be good."

Shep strode into the tent. It didn't surprise Harry that the leader of the "Three Musketeers" was also in trouble.

"Private, what are you barging in like this for? What's your name and reason?"

Shep came to attention. "DeWayne J. Shepherd, Junior, Private. A matter of personal request."

The colonel's demeanor changed and he walked to Shep. "What you'd say you name was?"

"DeWayne J. Shepherd, Junior. Sir"

You're DeWayne Shepherd, *Junior*?"

"Yes Sir."

"Your old man was 'Bull' Shepherd with the Red Arrow in France?"

"That's my father."

The colonel walked around Shep in deep study. "What's old Bull's son doing as a private?"

"Well, uh, it's where he started, Sir," Shep said sheepishly.

"You're right." He calmly eyed Shep before stomping his foot. "But it's not where Bull stayed for very long." He stomped again. "And how long have you been a private?"

"Ouch." Shep snapped to attention. "Longer than I should have, Sir."

The colonel grinned. "What's Bull Shepherd's son bursting in here for?"

"For him." Shep nodded at Harry. "I'm here to put in a word for Private Miller."

Everyone in the tent seemed taken aback—no one more than Harry.

"May I speak, Sir?" Shep said.

"You may, but I'm listening only because of my respect for your old man."

"Good enough." He turned toward both officers. "Private Miller has revealed himself to be the best soldier in Company K during the maneuvers. He's earned the respect of every man in our unit." Shep winked at Harry. "And earning *my* respect wasn't easy, but he won it in spite of my misgivings. Word's spread in our platoon that Private Miller was helping out where a civilian boy was killed in a tragedy last night. That's why he was AWOL."

The colonel turned to Harry. "Are we talking about that boy being run over by one of our trucks north of Dry Creek?"

'Yes Sir. The boy, Ben Reed, is . . . was . . . the brother of my girl. I was at their house when the accident occurred."

"Continue on."

"I was with them most of the night at the DeRidder hospital. I traveled with them back to Bundick, before catching a ride back here."

Shep blurted out. "Sir, if Harry Miller *said* he was there, he was."

The colonel turned to the M.P. "Soldier, I don't believe we'll be needing your services. Dismissed." He turned to Captain Farrell, who was fumbling with the papers. "Destroy these papers and write a letter of clearance for Pvt. Miller."

Both officers wanted to know more about the accident and Ben's family. The colonel turned on Shep. "Private Shepherd, what gave you the gumption to think you could barge in here like this?"

"Sir, it's just what Red Arrow men do for each other. We stand shoulder to shoulder. It's how I was taught."

"Well said." He pointed a long finger in Shep's face and Harry's. "But next time I see either of you, you'd better have more than a buck private's stripe on your shoulder." He motioned toward the door. "And it'd better be because I'm pinning a medal on *you*."

Shep answered for them both: "Yes Sir."

As the two privates backed out of the tent, the colonel began reliving a rollicking tale about being in a Belgium bar with then-Captain DeWayne "Bull" Shepherd Senior.

Out in the freedom of the fresh air, Shep blew out a breath. "Let's double-time it before they change their mind."

"Shep, why'd you do that for me?"

"It's like I said. Red Arrow soldiers—"

"Get out of here!"

"Seriously, Harry, you've proven yourself. I owed you something for the way I treated you earlier. I had a chance to repay you today. Are we even?"

Harry put out his hand. "Even on my end."

"Good, and besides, it's my fault that you're mixed up with that schoolteacher and her family."

"I owe you, Buddy." Harry now had some insight on what made Shep tick. "Kind of tough walking in the shadow of your father?"

"I've dealt with it all of my life."

Harry shook his head. "So have I, Shep. So have I."

Chapter 45
Visitors

Two days later

As Elizabeth walked home from Ben's funeral, her left arm was numb. She hoped she wasn't having a heart attack or stroke. The two days since Ben's death had been a swirling fog of shock and grief. You never expect to lose your baby brother.

Still in spite of her great sorrow, she also had a strange sense of peace. Hundreds of folks had turned out for Ben's funeral and burial. This outpouring of love and kindness had surrounded and comforted her family. She'd left the Bundick graveyard alone, needing some space before getting to the house where piles of food and caring neighbors awaited. She wasn't sure she was ready for either.

Elizabeth saw Jimmy Earl was sitting beside Poppa on the porch. He'd arrived from basic training early that morning on a two-day emergency leave just in time for the funeral. In spite of only being gone a month, he'd seemingly changed into a man. It warmed her heart seeing her father and brother sitting together.

"It was a fine funeral, wasn't it?" Poppa quietly said. Elizabeth glanced at Jimmy Earl, not sure how to reply.

Her brother said, "He would've enjoyed it himself. Lots of good music and stories."

Poppa looked away. "Maybe he did enjoy it. We don't know about the other side of that curtain." He motioned for Elizabeth to sit beside him. "I want you two to listen. We're gonna get through this together. Families stick together in the storm. We're in one now, but we'll get through it."

The three of them sat silently for a few minutes until Jimmy Earl turned to Elizabeth, "Your man called a while ago—said he'd call back at seven on the dot."

"Did he sound okay?"

"He sounded worried about you, but other than that he sounded fine."

"She's worried," Poppa said, "about him being AWOL."

"That's something to be worried about," Jimmy Earl said.

Elizabeth paced back and forth as the clock chimed at seven. Ten minutes later it rang, and she rushed to the phone, wedging into the corner where a semi-private conversation might be possible. "Harry, are you okay?"

"Fine. I've been worried about you."

"We're all right—the funeral was today. What about your being AWOL?"

"It worked out."

"You're not in trouble?" she didn't wait for a reply. "When can you come?"

"We're moving back to Camp Livingston tomorrow. It may be the weekend before I can get there."

"I can't wait for you to get back here."

"Neither can I."

The phone clicked. Their connection had been broken.

As dusk approached, the neighbors began trickling home. As the last ones left, Poppa, Peg, and Elizabeth stood on the porch. Poppa pulled his twin daughters close to him. "My boys are gone. All it seems I got now is you two." A tear coursed down his wrinkled cheek. "You two stay close and safe, okay?"

"We will, Poppa," Peg said, but Elizabeth didn't reply, knowing she couldn't be honest. When the others went into the house, she sat in the rocker listening to the night sounds.

A few minutes later, Peg came around the house. "Elizabeth, come see something." She led her to the side of the house. "Watch up in that chinaberry tree."

It was so close to dark that Elizabeth couldn't make out a thing. "What is it?"

A large bird swooped down from the tree and clattered into a window. "It's a pigeon," Peg said. "Look, it's got a leg band. It's one of those Army carrier pigeons."

"Do you think it's got a message?"

"I've tried catching it, but I can't get close enough. It flutters off, but always comes back to that window." The bird continued to battle with the pane. "Do you think the lantern in that bedroom's attracting it?" Elizabeth said.

"Watch it," Peg nodded. "It's been doing it about every five minutes."

"I can't believe it. You think it's a *message*?"

Peg shrugged. "That's the window to Ben's room—what else could it be?"

The two sisters watched the pigeon. Peg spoke first, "I believe it's a messenger bird."

"What do you mean?"

"A message from the other side."

"You really think so?"

Peg pointed to the bird as it pecked on the thin plate glass. "Yes, I think so." The pigeon flew back to the tree limb, preening its feathers, then quickly returned to the window. Both sisters were startled when a face appeared from inside the window.

"It's Momma," Peg whispered. The two sisters watched as their mother peered through the glass at the bird. Their mother placed her hand against the glass and the pigeon stopped its steady rapping, cooing peacefully on the sill. Tears rolled down their mother's cheeks as her mouth moved. Suddenly the pigeon took flight. It bypassed its tree, heading across the open field before disappearing into the last light on the western horizon.

"It was a sign," Peg said.

"It had to be."

"I thought you didn't believe in signs and omens?"

Elizabeth brushed her hair back. "I don't, but this time, I do."

"What do you think Momma said to it?"

"I don't know, and I won't ask."

"Me neither." Peg brushed back her hair. "Did you see Momma's face?"

"She knew."

"She did. It's definitely a sign. Ben's okay."

"You're right. He's okay."

"But I'm sure not okay." Peg's body sagged like a punctured balloon. "I'm not sure I'll ever be okay."

Elizabeth put her arm around her. "Me neither. I feel like there's a hole in my heart that won't ever be filled in."

"There's a hole in our family, too."

The sisters walked around to the front porch. Their mother, illuminated by lantern light, had returned to washing dishes in the kitchen. Peg nodded. "It's got to be terrible to have a child and later have to bury it. It ain't the natural order of things. Mothers ain't supposed to lose babies."

Elizabeth kissed her sister on the forehead. "But sometimes they do."

"I'm sorry, Lizzie."

"No problem. No offense taken." She kissed her again and stopped. An approaching vehicle's lights bounced up and down the drive. "Someone's coming here."

Peg craned her ear. "Sounds like a jeep."

A dust-trailing jeep plowed through their front yard. Elizabeth said, "I believe it's Jeep 1931."

"It's Clyde Lawrence." Peg brushed her hair from her face.

"What number is he on your pen pal list?"

Peg playfully shoved her sister, before straightening her hair. "He's number one, and don't you forget it."

Lawrence, climbing out of his jeep, rushed over. "Peg, I'm sorry about Ben. This is my first chance to come by."

"How'd you find out?"

He hugged her. "I found out from Elizabeth's man, Miller."

"How?"

"I picked him up yesterday morning near here. He was hitchhiking back to his camp. I'm so sorry."

He turned to Elizabeth, "Did his AWOL thing work out?"

"I talked to him today, and he said it was fine."

Peg led Lawrence to the porch swing. Stopping before going inside, Elizabeth said, "I believe I'll leave you two alone. As they say, 'two's company, three's a crowd.'" As the screen door shut behind her, she murmured under her breath, "and Corporal Lawrence, you're number one on a list of six. Good luck on staying there."

Chapter 46
Lazy Susans

WEATHER REPORT
CAMP POLK, LOUISIANA
30 SEPTEMBER 1941

WELCOME COOLER WEATHER WILL COVER LOUISIANA AS A
PACIFIC FRONTAL SYSTEM BRINGS LOWER HUMIDITY AND
PLEASANT TEMPERATURES IN ALL MILITARY CAMP AREAS.
RAIN-WILL ACCOMPANY THE FRONT BUT SHOULD END BY NOON
WITH CLEARING SKIES TO FOLLOW.

As Harry and the rest of Company K loaded into their trucks, Cohen shared the latest rumor. "Word is they're taking us to Camp Polk."

"Why would they send us to Camp *Puke?*" Nickels said. "That doesn't make sense."

"Who said anything had to make sense in the Army?" The long column of trucks snaked toward Highway 190. Harry watched the lead truck turn east. "We're headed home to Livingston."

Cohen cleared his throat. "The other rumor was that we're going back to Camp Beauregard."

This brought groans from everyone, including Nickels. "If we're back at Camp *Disregard*, I'm deserting."

Shorty punched Cohen in the shoulder. "Why don't you quit raining on everyone's parade and just shut up."

"It's just a rumor. I thought you'd want to know."

Harry took one last look at the cutover field that'd been their home for the last six weeks. The tents were all gone, trash and munitions had been buried. As much as possible, tank ruts and foxholes had been filled in and communications wire rolled up.

As their convoy rumbled eastward, he thought about change—everything had changed in his life since coming to Louisiana. He wondered how the lives of the locals would continue to change. He knew that Elizabeth's family would be affected forever by this time. It'd been a time of gain and loss, profit and tragedy, and things would never be the same.

At the village of Reeves, they turned north. For some reason they weren't going by highway to Kinder. Instead they were going home by dirt road. "Here comes the dust," Cohen, their self-appointed tour guide, said. The red cloud enveloped them, obscuring the sights beyond the road. They ate dust for several miles until Cohen, peering over the cab announced, "Rain up ahead."

A light splatter of rain began and Cohen said, "Trading dust for rain. I guess that's a gain." They crossed a rickety bridge as they approached the village of Dry Creek. Harry stood up in the truck bed for a better look. The raindrops stung his face, but he didn't flinch. They passed in front of Pate's Store where a man was loading sacks of feed into the bed of a wagon. Ahead at the first crossroads, something quickened Harry's heart. A young overalled boy, dog by his side, stood waving at the passing trucks. The deep bass of the air horns answered the boy's waves.

He looked so much like Ben, but Harry didn't recognize the boy. He was just another country boy in overalls, barefooted, faithful dog by his side, waving at the soldiers. Harry reached in his shirt pocket, and as their truck passed, tossed a pack of gum at the boy's feet. The boy eagerly snatched up the gum and waved. "Thanks, Mister."

"Did you see that?" Cohen said. "That dog only had three legs."

Harry steeled himself as they passed the Bundick crossroad and neared the bridge where Ben's accident had occurred. He considered pointing the spot out to the others, but didn't. They could never understand. The trucks ahead of them slowly rumbled across the bridge. Harry rubbed his chin. Thousands of soldiers would pass by here today and none, except him, would realize that a family's life and future had changed in a moment at the foot of this bridge.

As they rolled by the spot, there was no visible sign where Ben had been killed. Elizabeth and her family would be forced to pass this spot daily on their way to church, school, the store, and town. Would they ever be able to pass here without thinking about it? He knew he wouldn't. The rain wet his face and he was glad. It hid his tears.

As the truck geared down on its climb out of Bundick Swamp, they were back in open cutover land and the rain slackened. The fields were crowned with yellow flowers as far as the eye could see. Harry sat down. "Hey Shorty, what do you call those yellow flowers?"

"Lazy Susans. They bloom yearly about now."

"They're everywhere!"

"They're just a weed. Ugly and good for nothing until late September when they cover the stump fields with color."

"They're pretty."

"Just goes to show you even an ugly old weed has a good side."

"Kind of like you, huh, Shorty?"

"Yep, just like me . . . and you too, Miller."

Harry tried to take it all in—the sights, smells, and sounds of rural Louisiana. He couldn't escape the irony: Six weeks ago, this field was just an unattractive cutover tract of land. Now it was actually beautiful. Had it changed or was it more in the eye of the beholder?

He'd had the same metamorphosis about the people of No Man's Land. Initially, he'd disdainfully viewed them as backwards and ignorant: useless as a field of tall weeds. It was different now. Elizabeth's family and the other folks in her community had gotten into his heart. He saw them differently—as beautiful flowers to behold and enjoy.

The clouds to the north were breaking up, as streams of sunlight seemed to melt them away. The first cooler wind of the cold front blew in his face. Just before the crossroads at Wye, they passed a freshly mown hayfield and the smell wafted over. One of the farm boys said, "Makes me kind of homesick." It was the first hint of changing seasons. The coolness reminded Harry of home and he wondered if this same breeze, much colder, had passed over Wisconsin.

As the convoy snaked northeast, they crossed the Calcasieu River and officially passed out of No Man's Land. Cohen called out. "It's good to be leaving No Man's Land for Clean Man's Land." Everyone laughed and Nickels said, "I'm glad to leave this God-forsaken place behind."

God-forsaken. That had been Harry's favorite term for western Louisiana, but that was not how he viewed it now. It was the place where he'd found God.

More accurately, it was the place where God had found him.

Chapter 47
The Visit

After Harry's fifth hitchhike ride, he reached the Bundick crossroads and hurried toward the Reed home. It was his first visit since Ben's death four days ago. The phones had been out, so he'd had no contact with Elizabeth. She ran to him at the gate. "I've been worried about you." Harry held her close as she relived the events of the past few days. She stepped away and looked into his eyes. "Momma is asking to see you. She's got a job for you."

"What is it?"

"You'll have to ask her." Elizabeth led him toward the porch. "She's been in bed the last two days." She stopped at the door. "It's really been tough." She led him into the darkened bedroom. "Momma, you asked for Harry and he's here."

He was shocked at Mrs. Reed's haggard appearance. She lay like a corpse with the bed as her coffin. Her husband sat next to her in a straight chair, a newspaper across his lap. Peg, head down, stood in the corner. Mrs. Reed rubbed her chin, while smiling tight-lipped. "I'm glad you've come, Private Miller. I've got a job for you."

She motioned to Elizabeth and Peg. "You girls go outside for a minute." Mr. Reed motioned Harry to his chair. Mrs. Reed said, "Come close where you can hear." Her fingernails dug into his arm as she spoke in a hoarse whisper. It took about a minute to give her assignment.

Harry dizzily sat back and turned to Mr. Reed. "Do the girls know?"

He shook his head. "Pearline's giving *you* this job, not them."

"You want me to take Elizabeth and Peg?" Mrs. Reed nodded.

"Yes. They'll represent our family, but you're in charge."

Harry turned back to Mr. Reed. "Is this what you want?"

He stared off. "Yep." He motioned to the door. "Why don't you wait outside while we explain it to the girls?" Elizabeth brushed up against him as she passed. Harry sat on the porch edge as Blue put his muzzle on his leg. "Blue, these people *ain't* real. I've never seen *nobody* like them." He stopped—"Blue, they're ruining me, too. Got me saying ain'ts and double negatives. If my mother heard me. . . ."

The dog cocked its head and Harry lifted its muzzle. "It wasn't your fault that Ben was run over. He was just trying to protect you." Blue whined and scratched at a flea as Harry laughed. "They even have me talking to dogs."

The Reed family briefing took about fifteen minutes, and as he expected, the girls came out crying. Elizabeth wiped her eyes. "I wouldn't do this for anyone but her."

Mr. Reed stood in the doorway, and Harry asked him, "Are you going with us?"

"No, the wife needs me here."

Harry walked to Mr. Reed. "Do you feel the same way as your wife?"

The man's long poker face twitched. "Now, it don't come as easy to me as it does to

Lizzie's momma." He nodded toward the house. "That woman in that bedroom—she's an angel." His jaw tightened. "But yes, it's got to be done."

Harry glanced at Elizabeth, Peg, and their father. Each had the same determined look, which he recognized as the dominant Reed trait.

Mr. Reed had borrowed a neighbor's car for the trip. The sisters walked with Harry to an old Model A, where he kicked one of the dry-rotted tires. "I hope we aren't going far."

"It'll get us there." Elizabeth said as she and Peg climbed in. Harry hadn't driven a vehicle in nearly a year. He cranked it and it backfired before spewing out a thick cloud of oily blue smoke. He let off the clutch too quickly, causing the car to buck, throwing both girls his way.

Peg said, "That's a soldier's trick if I've ever seen one." The car puttered in fits and starts down the driveway, turning onto the main gravel road toward the bridge.

As Harry neared the bridge, Elizabeth squeezed his arm. "Stop here." He pulled the car onto the shoulder, just shy of where Ben had been run over. Elizabeth put her head against the dash for a long time. "I guess the day'll come when it won't kill my soul to drive by here." She sighed. "I wonder how long that will be?"

Harry visualized the Milwaukee street where *his* accident had taken place. After that horrible day, he'd planned elaborate detours to avoid the spot. For Elizabeth and her family, that would be impossible. They'd pass this spot every day on the one road in and out.

Peg, staring out the window, said, "What's that glass on the ground?"

Harry said, "That's where the truck's headlight was shattered . . . when he . . . when he hit Ben."

Peg got out and scooped up a handful of glass. "That's just how my heart feels. Shattered in a million pieces."

When she climbed back in, Elizabeth motioned. "Okay. Let's go."

They drove a silent mile before Harry said, "Do you really think this is a good idea?"

Peg spoke first. "I guess we're gonna find out."

Harry shifted into third. "I'm not sure we'll even be able to find them."

"We'll try," Elizabeth said.

"They may already be gone."

"Then we'll go wherever they are."

"The guards may not even let us in."

Elizabeth stared straight ahead. "They'll let us in." Harry recalled her father's words: *So you think you can tame that woman? Good luck.*

The car lurched to the supply dump gate, where a guard with a limp walked to the car and stuck his head in. He stepped back, eyeing the old car as well as Harry. "Girls, you can't do any better than this?"

Elizabeth laughed. "Are you referring to this *borrowed* car?" She pointed at Harry, "Or him?"

The guard grinned. "Both." As Harry gave a thumbnail sketch of their mission, the guard's demeanor changed. "Private, if y'all are making this up—"

"Who'd make up a story like that?"

"I guess you're right." The guard looked around. "I'll give you thirty minutes."

"Good enough," Harry showered the guard with pea gravel as they spun out toward a row of tents near a dozen transport trucks. About a dozen colored soldiers were sitting outside the largest tent. Several stood as the old Ford wheeled up, and Harry climbed out. "We're looking for a driver from this unit, Private Ira Lee White."

The men stared sullenly. Finally, a beefy sergeant stepped forward. "I don't believe no Private White drives for this unit."

Harry saw the insignia on the trucks. "Look, I know I'm at the right place." He nodded at Elizabeth and Peg. "We're not here for trouble." He stepped to the Sergeant. "Besides, Reuben, we've met before."

"How you know my name?"

"I met you one night here during some blues music." Harry pointed to a nearby grove of trees. "Right over there."

A glint of recognition spread across the sergeant's face. "Yeah, I remember you." He turned to the others. "Hey, this is the guy I captured with a fiddlestick."

The soldiers laughed, but one seriously stepped toward Elizabeth. "You're from the family of the boy who got run over, ain't you?"

"I am."

"I'm Willie—Willie Jackson. I was one of the other drivers that night. Listen, it wasn't Ira Lee's fault. He's had a hard enough time without *you* people coming out here." A soldier came out of the tent. Harry recognized him as the driver who'd carried Ben to the hospital. The soldier walked straight to Elizabeth, wiping grease off his hands with a rag. "Can I help you, Miss Reed?"

"My sister and I have come to see Private White. Our mother sent us."

The soldier stuffed the rag in his back pocket. "White's had a mighty hard time." He hesitated. "I ain't trying to say his pain's the same as yours, but he's blaming himself—carrying a mighty heavy load."

"That's why we've come," Elizabeth said. "We've come to help with that load." She motioned toward the tent. "Go get him . . . please."

He shrugged at the others before returning to the tent. When he came out, a tall, balding soldier followed. He was much older than the others, probably in his thirties. He stopped in front of the sisters, twisting his cap in his hands. "I ain't never getting behind the wheel again." His voice trembled. "I want to tell you how sorry I am."

"Thank you, Private White," Elizabeth said.

He wiped his eyes with the cap. "I'm so sorry. I couldn't help it."

"We know that." Elizabeth moved toward him before hesitating. Harry realized she was toeing the invisible line in the sand that existed between Southern blacks and whites. "My momma—she's taken to bed over Ben's death—sent us to tell you it's all right."

"But it ain't all right—your brother's dead."

"But it wasn't your fault. My momma—and daddy too—sent us to say we don't blame you."

Elizabeth and Ira Lee stood inside a circle of the other soldiers, Peg, and Harry.

This circle of silence reminded Harry of being out in the Wisconsin woods after a fresh snow: A white quietness that hushed everything. Even the birds had stopped singing as if wanting to hear more. The only sound they could have heard was the soft crying of three grieving people: two twin sisters and an Army private named Ira Lee White.

Suddenly, Elizabeth strode to the soldier and embraced him, bringing gasps from the other men. He sobbed on her shoulder as she held him close. When she stepped back, she put her hands up on his shoulders. "My momma told me to give you that hug. Even if she hadn't, I'd have given it anyway. It's a reminder that it *ain't* your fault." She kissed him on his bald head. "Because of what happened at that bridge, our families are joined at the heart from now on." She wiped her eyes. "Do you have a mother?"

"Sure do—back in Monroeville, Alabama."

"My mother said to tell you this: 'That soldier's momma doesn't deserve to lose *her* son because of what happened that night. Losing one son's bad enough. Losing another *ain't* an option.' Momma said to tell you to go live a happy life. That's the best thing you can do for my baby brother Ben. Go live a good and happy life."

Elizabeth turned to Peg, "Anything you want to say, Sister?" Peg kicked at the dirt. Private White was crying too hard to speak, and his fellow soldiers were staring at their boots. They—like Harry—knew it was bad manners to speak in the presence of an angel. Far in the distance, Harry caught a faint whiff of a song on the wind. He cocked his ear, not sure if his mind was playing tricks. It sounded like one of the songs from the porch singing. Deciding it was his imagination, he turned away. Reuben, the sergeant who'd captured Harry, whispered, "You heard it too?"

Harry winced. "Heard what?"

"Sounded like 'Will the Circle' to me."

"You heard it?"

Reuben winked before humming a line. "Sure did."

Elizabeth walked slowly to the car, followed by Peg and Harry. As Harry shook Reuben's hand, the sergeant softly sang,

> *"Will the circle be unbroken?*
> *By and by, Lord, by and by.*
> *There's a better home awaiting*
> *In the sky, Lord, in the sky."*

"Do you believe that?" Harry said.

"I've got to." Reuben tightened his grip. "Do you?"

Harry looked into his dark eyes. "I'm beginning to." The soldier released his grip as Harry joined the sisters at the vehicle. The only sound was the hollow metallic slamming of the car doors. Dusk had come so he turned on the headlights. As Harry wheeled the car around, the car's high beams caught the soldiers standing as if frozen by that same sudden Wisconsin blizzard. At the gate, Harry glanced back to faintly see Ira Lee White following them down the drive, his right arm motionless in a wave. Harry knew he'd probably never see him again, but also knew he'd never forget the look on the soldier's face.

No one spoke until they'd driven through Reeves. Peg said, "Sister, I can't believe you said 'ain't,' not once, but twice . . . and you call yourself a schoolteacher!"

Elizabeth shrugged. "Sometimes breaking a grammar rule is needed to make a point."

"Give me a break," Peg huffed. "You been correcting my grammar for the last fifteen years."

"It's *you've* been; not *you* been."

"Harry, pull this car over so I can git out and whip your girlfriend's butt."

Harry deadpanned. "It's *get*, not git."

"Pull over right now. I'm gonna whip both of you."

A mile later, Peg began crying. "It's something, ain't it? People'll eat an egg that comes out of a chicken's behind, but won't let a man or woman with colored skin drink from their gourd dipper, or kiss a black man on his bald head."

Elizabeth stared ahead. "It was the appropriate thing to do."

"You think he'll be able to forgive?"

"Who?"

"Ira Lee White."

"No, I mean . . . forgive who?" Elizabeth said.

"Forgive himself."

Elizabeth looked in the rearview mirror. "That's always the hardest one to forgive."

"I agree." Peg said.

Harry, studying Elizabeth, added, "It sure is. I've been there too."

Elizabeth, fixated on the mirror, sighed. "I guess we all have."

Peg twisted the mirror away and wiped her eyes. "We can't live our lives looking back."

"We sure can't." Elizabeth was crying too.

Harry, looking ahead, drove down the gravel road in a beat up old car filled with a wonderfully terrible mixture of tears and laughter. He'd never encountered folks like this and was determined to find out what made them tick—or what made their hearts beat.

Right there as the old car rattled along the corduroy road, he made up his mind. They weren't going to be able to run him off, especially the dark-haired girl squeezed up against him. He was playing for keeps.

She had something. Something he wanted. He couldn't define it yet, but he wanted it.

He wanted *her*, but also he wanted *something* she had.

Chapter 48

An Empty Desk

It was the hardest thing Elizabeth had ever done. She dreaded it like doomsday—the idea of going into her empty classroom. It wasn't the classroom itself. It was the empty desk. Ben's empty desk. School would start in three more days, but she couldn't get the courage to go to the schoolhouse. In a way, it was ironic. Being in a classroom was where she was most at home, but now it repulsed her. She'd discussed it with Peg, who'd said, "Let me go and remove his desk."

"No, we're not going to just act like he never existed."

"How are you going to handle it with your students?"

"I don't know yet."

"Have you prayed about it?"

"So much that the Lord's tired of hearing about it from me."

"What about Harry?"

"We've talked about it, but I don't want him there when I first go to the school."

"Why don't you take Ma?"

"Why Ma?"

"Because she's got 'horse sense.'"

That's why later that day, Elizabeth and her grandmother walked hand-in-hand into the schoolhouse together. Harry had volunteered to sit with PawPaw Reed while they were gone.

Elizabeth ran her hand along the rough wooden wall as they peered into her classroom. The thirteen desks were arranged just as she'd left them.

"Your daddy said Harry Miller got caught in one of these desks," Ma said.

"It was something to see."

"Which one was it?"

Elizabeth patted the desktop. "This one."

"Your daddy said y'all were hung up together when he looked in the window."

Elizabeth burst out laughing. "Poppa said he thought a varmint was loose in here."

Ma snorted. "A varmint? That's what *my* daddy called *my* husband the first decade of our marriage."

"A varmint?"

"He called him 'the varmint' that stole my daughter."

"Really?"

"Honey, when I married your grandpa, nobody thought it'd work. Everyone and his brother tried to block it. My father didn't like your grandpa one bit, and sure didn't think he was up to my standards. It made my daddy mad enough to eat a june bug. He forbid me to marry Spencer Reed." Ma ran her hand along the slate board. "But we didn't listen—ran off and got married. My daddy claimed that I'd been stolen away, and swore never to forgive that 'varmint' who did it."

"PawPaw *stole* you away?"

"He did, and if my folks could've found us quick enough, they'd stolen me back."

"Ma, why haven't I ever heard this?"

"It's not exactly common knowledge here in Bundick. But back at Alco Sawmill, where I was raised, it was big talk." She stood proudly. "Your PawPaw and I proved them all wrong. After about ten years, my people fell in love with him as much as I had. And that's when my daddy quit calling him 'that varmint'."

Elizabeth studied her grandmother. Anything Ma said was spoken for a reason. "Ma, do you think marrying him is a good idea?"

"Marrying *who*?" There was a twinkle in her eye.

"You know who—Harry Miller."

Ma squared her shoulders. "I have no idea. You're the only one who can answer that. Besides, every tub sits on its own bottom." Elizabeth rolled her eyes as Ma walked down a row. "Baby, which desk was going to be Ben's?"

"That one on the third row." Elizabeth walked to it and rubbed its finish. "He would've sat right here." Removing the neatly lettered place note "Ben," she reached in the storage area and pulled out a box of pencils, handing one to Ma.

"Ben Reed," Ma said. "Who had pencils made with his name on it?"

"I did. It was going to be a surprise."

"He would've have liked it." Ma looked around the classroom. "It's sure gonna be quiet in here without him. It's gonna be quiet in lots of places, ain't it?" Her grandma leaned over and kissed the writing surface of the desk. "You don't realize how many places a person fills up until they're gone." She stepped around the desk and kissed Elizabeth. "See you later. You've got work to do and don't need some old woman in the way." Ma held up the pencil. "Mind if I keep it?" She tucked it into her jacket and pulled something out of another pocket. "I'll trade a pencil for this." The bright cartridge gleamed in her grandmother's age-spotted hands. She placed it in Elizabeth's palm. "I believe this belongs to you."

Unfolding the note stuffed in it, Elizabeth read, "Pvt. Harold A. Miller. . . ." She shook her head. "You and Ben were quite a pair."

Ma stopped at the door. "Ben and I were in 'cahoots' together."

"Ma, that's a good word for it." Elizabeth walked to her, brushing Ma's face with her hand. "Thanks for coming with me."

"You're mighty welcome." Her grandmother slowly made her way out of the classroom. Elizabeth listened to her steady steps echoing in the hallway. She placed Ben's name tag back where it had been, staring at the brown spot on the desk—it was Ma's 'snuff lipstick' on the desktop. Elizabeth could have wiped it off, but didn't. It was the same thing with the snuff kiss lingering on her cheek. There would come a day when she'd give a king's ransom to be kissed by her grandmother.

Some things are meant as a reminder. She put a handful of the pencils in her dress pocket, right beside the spent bullet.

Harry had been assigned guard duty with Elizabeth's grandfather while the two women were gone. He'd pulled a chair up by the old man. It was eerie sitting with someone who couldn't speak but never took his eyes off you. Harry felt that he was being studied—sized up. He held up an old copy of the DeRidder paper to get the man's eyes off him, but still felt them, burning two searing holes through the newsprint. The old man coughed and rattled, causing Harry to lower the paper. Spittle dripped down his chin and Harry used his handkerchief to wipe it off.

The old man was trying to talk. "Liz…"

Harry was startled. He was under the impression that he couldn't say a word. "Liz . . . zi"

"Pa, are you trying to say 'Lizzie?'"

He nodded.

Harry said, "Can I call you 'Pa'?"

Another nod.

"What are you trying to tell me about Elizabeth?"

Pa struggled for breath and Harry worried that something was wrong. Finally, he relaxed. "Lizzi . . . best."

"Lizzie . . . Elizabeth's the best?" The old man's eyes sparkled. Harry moved to the bed edge. "Pa, I believe she's the best. If she'll have me, I'm going to take good care of her."

Pa grabbed him by the forearm, and his vise-like grip in his good arm surprised Harry. In a few minutes, Pa dropped off to sleep but didn't lessen his grip. Harry could have pulled away, but didn't. Even when he heard the screen door slam, he sat stock-still. The sun was setting outside and it silhouetted Elizabeth's grandmother as she stood, arms crossed. "It looks like you two boys have taken a liking to each other." Nodding at her husband's grip on Harry's arm, she said, "I believe he's fallen in love with you, too."

He slowly pulled out of the old man's grip, as Ma said, "He's still got a strong grip, don't he?"

"I believe he's a strong man in every way." He rubbed his hand and watched the couple as Ma stroked her husband's hair. He liked these people. He liked them a lot.

Chapter 49

The Fair

Tuesday, October 7, 1941

ATTENTION:

SPECIFIED REGIMENTS OF THE 32ND ID WILL BE ASSIGNED AS A 'SURPRISE FORCE' TO BE INSERTED INTO THE CAROLINA MANEUVERS. TENTATIVE DEPARTURE IS SCHEDULED FOR FRIDAY 10 OCTOBER. MORE INSTRUCTIONS AND BATTLE ORDER WILL BE DETAILED ON ARRIVAL IN CAMDEN, SC.

Word spread like an M-1 shot around Camp Claiborne: part of the 32nd was being shipped to the Carolina Maneuvers. Harry's Regiment would leave in four days and would be gone through all of November. This was terrible news for Harry. The only salvation was they would receive three days off before leaving. It was all Harry needed: one more chance to be with Elizabeth. He was ready to put a full-court press on her to marry him. This upcoming two-month absence would either make or break their relationship. He was determined it would be the former.

The phones were working again and he got through. She was excited to hear from him. School had started the day before and Elizabeth was full of stories.

He broke the news about the Carolina Maneuvers, and added, "But I've got three days off before we leave. I'm coming down."

"Can you make it here by 5:00? We're going to the parish fair."

"To the *what*?"

"You've never been to a parish fair?"

"We don't have parishes."

"A county fair?"

"Not in Milwaukee. I'll be at your house by five."

Several soldiers in their regiment had gone together and bought a used Studebaker, renting it out for $10 per day. Being a weeknight, it was available and Harry happily paid thirty dollars to have it for the next three days. He motored down Highway 165, hustling to make it before five. He slowed down in Woodworth and near the entrance to Camp Claiborne; both were infamous for giving speeding tickets to soldiers.

When he skidded up at Elizabeth's house, she met him at the gate. "Poppa's taking his school bus so local folks can go to the fair. I promised I'd ride with Ma." She looked at the car. "Where'd you get this?"

"I rented it from some soldiers." He tried to hide his disappointment at not getting her alone in the car.

"Let's hurry, the bus is leaving in ten minutes. Poppa will pick us up at the crossroads. Tonight is the Parish Fiddling Contest and Ma's the reigning champion." They boarded the crowded bus. He and Elizabeth sat behind her grandmother, whose seat was filled with a large box and several jars of preserves.

Harry leaned up. "Do you have your violin?"

"No, but I've got my fiddle." She tapped her case. "I've got my big gun and it's loaded."

"How many years have you been champion?"

"Four or five years hand-running."

"Ma, it's seven years," Elizabeth said.

The old woman shrugged. "So, it's seven years-hand-running." She lifted her case. "Lots of folks thought I wouldn't play this year because of Ben." She peered wistfully out the window. "He'd want me to play."

"What are you playing?" Harry said.

"'Eighth of January.' It's the song she wins with every year," Elizabeth said.

"But that's not what I'm playing."

Elizabeth arched her eyes. "You've *always* played it."

"But not tonight."

"What are you playing?"

Ma grinned. "Keep your hat on. You'll just have to wait and see."

The bus pulled into the fairgrounds and they unloaded, joining the long line of excited fairgoers at the admission gate. "I've never seen the crowd this big. People have cash in their pockets," Elizabeth said.

"Is it because of the Maneuvers?" Harry said.

"I'm sure it is. They're here to blow that money." In addition to civilians, soldiers were everywhere—from nearby Camp Polk and the DeRidder Air Base—many escorting local girls on their arm, or looking to find one.

Elizabeth stopped at the crowded midway. "No one enjoyed the fair more than Ben."

Harry took her hand. "I bet he did—he enjoyed all of life."

She pulled him toward the rides. "But the fair was his favorite." Elizabeth pointed at the spinning Ferris wheel. "Harry, let's ride it. It looks romantic."

Harry cringed at the squeaking wheel and screaming riders. "Why don't you ride it with Peg?"

She looked hurt. "You don't want to ride it with me?"

Harry fumbled in his pockets. "I'm scared of heights."

"Really?"

He watched the spinning ride. "I'd rather wrestle a bear than get up there."

"Oh, come on."

Mercifully, the loudspeaker blared, "In fifteen minutes, the Parish Fiddle Contest will begin at the main pavilion."

Elizabeth said, "Let's go and get a good seat. We'll come back later." Harry gulped as he left the looming shadow of the spinning wheel. *Lord, please make it break down before we get back.* The pavilion was crowded with several hundred people. They spotted

Ma and the others on the front row, but Elizabeth led him to a seat in the back. "I'm too nervous to sit up front."

A quartet, featuring several guitars, was vying with the fiddle players tuning near the stage. After four more songs, the emcee quieted the crowd. "First, we'll have the novice division." One by one, the young fiddlers took their turns, playing with passion, if not great skill. In spite of their squeaks and sour notes, Harry enjoyed each piece, a fine blend of hymns, Irish jigs, and mountain tunes. There were none of the classical songs Harry'd learned at that age. This was a different world.

Next, the emcee announced the six contestants for the main contest. Each of the first four played peppy fiddle tunes and played quite well. As the fifth contestant came to the rostrum, Elizabeth whispered, "That's Aubrey Cole. Ma says he's the one who'll eventually unseat her as the champion."

"Wasn't he at the front porch singing?" Harry said.

"He was."

The fiddler tapped the microphone with his bow. "I'm going to play 'Rubber Dolly.'" He launched into a stirring rendition that had the crowd clapping and whistling. When he finished, Elizabeth said, "He gets better every year."

The emcee announced, "It's always our tradition to allow the defending champion to play last. Not only is Doshie Reed the parish champion, but she's won it seven years in a row." He coughed before continuing. "We've been praying for the Reed family in the loss of their loved one, Ben." He turned to Ma. "Mrs. Doshie, we weren't sure you'd be here tonight, but we're delighted you are. It wouldn't be the parish fair contest without 'Eighth of January.'" He assisted Ma up onto the riser, and she smiled shyly and drew the bow across the fiddle. The microphone carried the first searing note across the open-air pavilion.

She played the first lines painfully slow and mournful. It was so different from the previous five contestant's peppy tunes. A woman behind Harry said, "That's not 'Eighth of January.'" Clapping and stomping had accompanied the earlier songs, but the only accompaniment now was Ma's steady tapping foot on the hollow riser.

Elizabeth, with no irony, whispered, "It's deathly quiet in here." Harry suddenly connected the haunting melody. It was the same song Elizabeth's family had sung over Ben's body at the hospital. Elizabeth confirmed this. "She's playing 'I Will Arise'."

A woman behind them began softly singing,

"I will arise and go to Jesus,
He will embrace me in his arms.
In the arms of my dear Savior,
Oh there are ten thousand charms."

Ma swayed, her eyes closed, seemingly unaware of the audience or where she was. Behind them, the singing woman said, "My Lord, she's not playing—she's grieving." Elizabeth, crying softly, laid her head on Harry's shoulder. On the fourth verse, Ma changed keys and quickened the pace, moving the song from a dirge to a song of hope.

Harry closed his eyes, determined to suck in every note and ragged emotion floating from her strings.

Elizabeth's gasp caused him to look up. Levon Reed had joined his mother on the stage where he took one of the quartet's guitars and began chording softly. They swayed in unison on two more verses as the powerful song slowed back down and came to a dramatic conclusion.

As Ma removed her bow from the fiddle, the crowd sat in stunned silence. It was so quiet that Harry heard the faraway noise of the merry-go-round. Suddenly, one man stood and clapped and was joined by the entire pavilion, which broke out in sustained clapping and cheering. A loud whistler next to Harry put two fingers in his mouth and gave a shrill call that caused everyone around them to cover their ears.

Ma and her son stood arms entwined. They took a bow together before returning to their seats. Elizabeth shook her head. "I can't believe Poppa did that."

Harry put his arm around her. "It was beautiful."

The smiling emcee stood at the mike as the crowd quieted. "That wasn't 'Eighth of January,' but it was wonderful." He motioned for Ma to stand. "Mrs. Doshie, that was just the song we needed to hear. Thank you. Thank you. Thank you." He turned to the crowd. "It'll take our judges a few minutes to compile their scores. Let's welcome back to the stage The Spikes Quartet from Bancroft."

As the quartet launched into a fast gospel number, Harry turned to Elizabeth. "Did you know she was going to do that song?"

"I had *no* idea." She was distracted due to a commotion at the judges' table. "There must be a problem." A judge motioned the emcee over and a long animated conversation ensued. "I wonder what's going on. Something must be rotten in Denmark."

"Ben loved that saying."

"He did but he never used the right location." She grasped his hand. "He was something, wasn't he?"

After two more gospel songs, the emcee returned to the microphone and cleared his throat. "Thank you folks for your patience. We're ready to announce our winners." A player from Merryville was awarded third place followed by a woman from DeRidder winning second.

Elizabeth gripped his hand. "Something's wrong."

The emcee nervously announced, "We're ready to announce our winner of the 1941 Beauregard Parish Fiddler's Contest." He hesitated. "Our judges have had a difficult decision due to a disqualification." A murmur rippled through the crowd and Harry felt Elizabeth stiffen. The emcee waved for quiet. "The contest rules specify that no fiddler may have accompaniment. Due to this, we've been forced to disqualify contestant number six, Mrs. Doshie Reed."

A smattering of boos rippled across the pavilion as the emcee held up his hand. "However, the judges have declared Mrs. Reed—due to her seven years as champion and tonight's unforgettable performance—be named 'champion emeritus.'" Ma stood and bowed, before quickly sitting down. Mr. Reed put one arm around his mother and the other around his wife. The announcer tapped the microphone. "I'm happy to announce this year's champion as one of our younger players, Aubrey Cole of Cole Central Community."

The crowd clapped politely, but Harry's attention was riveted on Elizabeth's heated reaction: "They *stole it* from my grandma." He chuckled until he realized he saw her balled fists. "I'm going to give those judges a piece of my mind." Harry caught her before she got loose. The crowd around them stared in disbelief and Harry smiled. "Just ignore her. She's a little emotional right now."

Elizabeth bit off her words. "I'm not emotional. I'm *mad*. They *stole* the championship from my grandma." As the program ended with the quartet singing "Amazing Grace," Harry led Elizabeth away from the pavilion, toward where Ma and the rest of the family stood in the grass. Elizabeth ran to her father. "Poppa, they cheated Ma out of her title."

"No they didn't, Honey. When I went up there, I knew it'd disqualify her."

Elizabeth's jaw dropped. "Did you two plan this?"

"No, Baby," Ma said. "No one knew I was going to play 'I Will Arise.' Not even your Poppa."

Elizabeth turned on her father. "Then it's *your* fault she lost her title."

He smiled evenly. "Well, I guess it is."

Ma put her hand on Elizabeth's shoulder. "Your father coming up to play with me was something I'll cherish 'til the day I die." She kissed her granddaughter's cheek. "Tonight I wasn't playing for a title, I was playing for your brother Ben."

Elizabeth's face reddened and she burst out crying on Ma's shoulder. Mr. Reed led Harry a few steps away. "Private Reed, now that's the high-strung catty-wampus you're trying to tame. You still think you're game?"

"I'm not sure, but I'm going to give it my best."

"Well, good luck, Son."

Elizabeth stepped away from Ma. "I'm the one who is wrong." She kissed her. "If you're happy with things, so am I."

"Baby, I'm happy. Besides," Ma said. "Every tub sits on its own bottom."

Elizabeth wiped her eyes, smiled, and grabbed Harry's arm. "We're going to ride the Ferris wheel." She waited until they were out of earshot. "I'm so sorry I showed myself."

Harry nodded, not being brave enough to set off another eruption.

"It's just that I'm like an old momma bear if someone's messing with my family."

He laughed. "I'll be sure not to bother your family." As they walked hand in hand to the midway, a soft rain started. Harry hoped the rain would help cool down her anger, but he knew it couldn't dampen the love he felt for her.

Chapter 50
Bird's Eye View

Elizabeth pulled Harry toward the Ferris wheel. As they passed a group of soldiers, one was cussing. "I can't believe that happened in the World Series."

Harry stopped. "Let me hear this."

She tugged on his arm. "You're not getting out of riding!"

He walked over to the soldiers. "What happened in the Series?"

An Air Corpsman said, "The Dodgers had it won. The last Yankee batter struck out to end the game, but the catcher missed the ball and the runner got on. Damn Yankees came back and won." He spat. "Instead of being tied two games apiece, the Yankees are up 3-1. It's over."

"Let's go." Elizabeth pulled him toward the ride. It was empty and the carnie, cigarette dangling from his mouth, said, "I'll give you two a ride you won't forget." They climbed into the seat, the clicking of the lap bar signaling they'd passed the point of no return. The carnie, true to his word, kept the ride going.

Elizabeth looked over at Harry and saw his death grip on the lap bar. "Having fun?" They made three more fast revolutions before she had the heart to even look at him again. "Why are you so green around the gills?"

"I'm getting sick." Beads of sweat had formed on his forehead.

"You're not kidding, are you?"

"I told you I was afraid of heights and spinning around always nauseates me."

"I'm sorry, Harry." She regretted not taking his fear seriously just as a terrible gnashing sound shook the entire ride. The Ferris wheel sickeningly sped up before coming to a jarring stop. Their car was at the top of the wheel and it rocked violently. She grabbed hold of Harry as the car swung like a pendulum. Gradually, the car slowed, and Elizabeth regained her sense of equilibrium. Harry was still frozen with both hands on the safety bar. He looked toward the ground. "I smell something burning."

Elizabeth looked down and saw blue smoke billowing from the base of the ride. A hot metallic electrical smell turned her stomach to mush. All of her life, she'd feared burning to death, and now it was coming true. Harry pointed to a group of men gathered around the Ferris wheel motor. "The motor's on fire."

It was now her turn with the death grip. She clung to Harry, eyes closed. "I don't want to burn up."

Harry laughed. "You're not going to burn up. This thing's metal and . . ." A man sprinted up with a fire extinguisher and sprayed the fire. He poked her. "Fire's out." Elizabeth sat trembling as Harry said, "Yep, everybody's got something they're scared of."

Not liking the sarcasm in his voice, Elizabeth rocked the car, causing him to wince. "Look, I'm serious about not liking heights. . . ."

She answered, "And I'm serious about being burnt alive."

He waved one hand, the other firmly welded to the bar. "Let's call a truce." They both peered down at the gathering circle around the motor. Harry cupped his hands. "Hey, down there. What's going on?"

A worker looked up. "The motor froze up when it burned." Onlookers split their time examining the smoking motor and gawking at the couple atop the wheel. A voice yelled. "How's the view up there?" It was Poppa. Behind him stood the rest of family—Momma, Peg, and Ma—none even attempting to hide their delight at the situation.

Poppa called up. "Looks like you love birds are stuck up there." He walked to the clump of workers and returned. "Y'all may be up there a while. Motor's burnt up and they'll have to find another one."

"How long?" Harry said.

Poppa put his palms up and shrugged his shoulders. "Who knows?"

Elizabeth leaned forward. "If it wasn't unladylike, I'd spit on Peg."

Harry gingerly moved closer. "That wouldn't be very lady-like."

She said, "My second cousin, T-Bone, got whipped one year at the fair. He was riding the Ferris wheel, spitting down on people on each spin. A fellow looked up just as T-Bone spat. He was waiting for him when he climbed off the ride. The man was a pulpwood hauler from Singer, and he trimmed T-Bone's tree down to size. It cured him of spitting from the Ferris wheel."

"You sounded just like Ben when you told that story." He pulled her closer.

"It *was* the kind of story he liked." She felt emotion rising in her voice. "Plus it was the kind of thing he was prone to do himself."

Harry slipped his hand into hers. "Does it bother you when I mention him?"

"No. I want him remembered. We're not going to act like he didn't live."

"You really miss him, don't you?"

"Like the dawn misses the day." She sighed. "I walk through the house waiting to hear him whistling, then realize I'll never hear him again. There's a hole in my heart."

He put his arm around her. She liked the way it felt, especially knowing how difficult it must have been letting go of the lap bar. She laid her head on his shoulder. "I shouldn't have made fun of your fear of heights."

Suddenly, the entire Ferris wheel shuddered. The men below were using a pry bar to try to force the wheel to turn. Harry shouted down, "Hey, cut that out."

From down in the crowd, a distinctly local voice rang out. "Don't worry, Yankee, we'll have you down by sunrise."

"I wonder how he knew I was from up North?" Harry said.

"When you opened your mouth." Elizabeth glanced down at the upturned faces on the ground. "They ought to sell tickets and popcorn. How long have we been up here?"

Harry glanced at his watch. "Oh, about an hour and fifteen minutes. Look, I've got a new watch." He slid closer. "I've been wanting to get you off alone."

"Is this what you had in mind?"

"Well, not exactly."

She shook the car, causing Harry to stiffen. "Hey, that's not fair."

"Well, they say all's fair in love and war."

He grinned. "So, is *this* love or war?"

"I'm not sure, maybe a little of both. You tell me, you're the *soldier.*"

"I think I know a lot more about war than love." He looked into her eyes. "And then again, when I look at you, I'm not sure." She could tell he wanted to say more. Time ticked on and the gawkers dispersed, leaving only three men working on the motor. The only others were her mother and Ma sitting on the edge of a ride, where Ma was playing solitaire on the decking.

"Elizabeth, there's something I've wanted to talk to you about, and this looks like a good time."

Her stomach rebelled and she remembered that there were fears worse than burning.

He glanced down. "Why don't we jump?"

"What?"

He leaned forward. "Let's jump. If we don't jump now, we'll never do it." Harry tried to stand. "Probably our only chance."

"Harry Miller, are you crazy?"

He eased back into his seat. "I'm talking about us getting married."

"What?"

"Let's get married now."

She fumbled for words, suddenly feeling dizzy. "I don't see how it'd work."

"What do you mean?"

"How long have you and I known each other?"

"Thirty-eight days." He glanced at his watch. "And eight hours."

"And you expect me to just jump up and marry you?"

"Don't folks down here call it 'jumping the broom'?" Harry said.

She stared down toward her mother and grandmother. Harry put his hand on her face. "You told me last week that I needed to get things right with my parents, and I did that. Didn't that show you?"

"It showed me a lot, but this is moving along a little fast for me."

"This ride or my offer?"

"Your offer. It's sure not this stuck ride."

He kissed her. "It wasn't an offer. It's a proposal. A serious proposal."

She started to name one of the forty-one reasons why they couldn't, or shouldn't, get married, but he kissed her again. "Elizabeth, how long has it been?"

"You're the one with the watch."

"How long has it been since you trusted *yourself* to trust a man?"

"What do you mean?"

"How long has it been?"

She wasn't going to answer his question. "Harry Miller, my life was a lot simpler before the Army came to Louisiana."

"But was your life . . . better?"

She looked away. "Is this some kind of interview or something?"

"No, but I've got a beautiful woman captive, and I'm trying to make the most of it." He tapped his watch. "By the way, it's been nearly two hours."

"Time flies when you're having fun." She regretted saying it—being alone with Harry was *exactly* where she wanted to be. *Why couldn't she just say it?*

He lightly rocked the car. "You know I'm deathly afraid of heights, but I'm not afraid of commitment."

"Well, neither am I." She tried to keep the irritation out of her voice.

"I've learned one thing hanging around here in Louisiana: every tub sits on its own bottom. It's up to you and me." Harry patted the seat of the car. "I didn't want to sit my bottom on this ride, but if that's what it took to be with you, I was glad to do it." Harry rocked the car again. "See, it's worth being scared and unsure if you're *with* the right person."

She looked into his eyes. "Do you *really* think I'm the right person?"

"Absolutely." She looked off into the night sky and he nudged her. "Go on, Elizabeth."

"It's just not simple."

"Who said life was simple?"

"How do I know I'm not just a passing fancy?" She felt the same old fear creeping up her throat.

"Because I promise you're not."

"You expect me to marry you on a simple promise—your word?"

He smiled. "I've always kind of thought that's how it worked." He shrugged. "Look, I've got plenty of faults but breaking promises isn't one of them. When I make up my mind, it's made up. My mother always said it's the Irish in us."

Harry held out his palm and spit on it. "I'll even spit-shake on it."

"You're gross." She put her hands on her hips. "Who taught you that?"

"Your brother Ben."

"I should've known."

Harry pointed at a searchlight to the southwest. "That's the DeRidder Airbase. Which way is Bundick?"

Elizabeth squinted. "Probably in the direction of the exhibit building."

Harry twisted around to look north. "There's the Big Dipper and North Star." He spread his forefinger and thumb like a compass. "Milwaukee's probably about in that direction." He turned east and pointed over the football stadium. "And if I'm right, Europe's that direction." His face brushed against hers as he whispered, "I don't know which direction I'm going, but I know this: I want you for my wife, and will do whatever it takes to get you to say yes." Elizabeth felt paralyzed. He leaned forward in the car, tilting it slightly. "You'll never know you can fly until you're ready to leap."

When he rocked the car again, she said, "I thought you were scared of heights."

"I am. But I'm willing to do whatever it takes to get your attention and get you to say yes."

A voice called from below. "Hey up there." They looked down and saw Momma and Ma waving. Elizabeth said, "They wouldn't be waving if they knew what you're trying to get me to do."

Momma cupped her hands. "Hey kids. We're catching the bus home. Uncle Rob's leaving his car for you. The key's under the seat. Be careful coming home."

As usual, Ma got the last word in. "Keep 'er in low gear and between the ditches—and don't forget you've got school in the morning."

The two women walked out of sight as Elizabeth sighed, "They're quite a pair, aren't they?"

"How long has it been?" Harry said.

"Since *what*?"

He put his lips against hers. "Since a man kissed you on the Ferris wheel?" She never had a chance to answer. That kiss was long, sweet and just what she'd needed. Once again, she was dizzy, but this was a *good* dizziness. "You're not fighting fair when you kiss me like that."

He kissed her again. "All's fair in love and war."

Chapter 51

Shot in the Dark

Harry checked his watch. It was well after midnight when the new motor arrived and he and Elizabeth were finally delivered from their Ferris-wheel perch. The midway was darkened and only a handful of carnival workers and a lone deputy were present to welcome them back to solid ground. The deputy winked. "Looks like you two had a good time up there."

Harry waved him off as they made their way to the dimly lit parking lot, stumbling around trying to locate Rob Lindsey's old car. This didn't bother Harry or Elizabeth as they embraced for passionate kisses about every ten steps. He remembered his classic statement, *The last thing I'd ever want is a Louisiana woman.* He had hold of one now and wouldn't—or couldn't—let go. When they finally found the car, he said, "Woman, you're some kind of good kisser."

Elizabeth nibbled his neck. "I thought I'd forgotten how."

"We'll get you back in practice." It was a long bumpy ride home maneuvering around the ruts and potholes. Each time Harry geared down, Elizabeth began kissing him, and he soon began looking for obstacles to slow down for. When they finally neared Bundick, he said, "Wonder what time it is?"

She unstrapped his watch and tossed it on the floorboard. "Who cares?" It was getting steamy when she finally pushed him away. "I believe that's enough for tonight." She rested her head on his shoulder as they wound up the driveway of the darkened Reed home. He walked her to the porch and held her for another long kiss. From inside the house, someone coughed and she drew away. Harry pulled her back. "You haven't given me an answer."

"An answer to what?"

"Marry me."

She stomped his foot. "Can't you whisper?"

"Well, what about it?"

"I don't ever make a decision without sleeping on it." She kissed his cheek. "Good night. You remember how to get to Ma's house? I'll see you after school tomorrow." Harry hopped off the porch, walking toward his rental Studebaker. Something brushed against his leg and he jumped back. Hearing a whimper, Harry knelt. "Come here, Blue." He petted the dog, pointing toward Elizabeth's lamp-lit bedroom. "Hey boy, this is all your master's fault." Blue whined. "You miss Ben too, don't you?" He looked up at the canopy of twinkling stars. "I guess he's an angel now. Heck, he was *already* an angel when he picked up that bullet."

Blue pulled his ears back and seemed to grin as Harry stroked his back. "But he could also be a little devil at times." Feeling silly for talking with a dog, he got in the Studebaker. The old car wouldn't start, so he finally got out and walked to Ma's in the darkness, whistling loudly. It didn't worry him a bit. Tonight, he believed he could fly.

245

Harry slept in the next morning. After wolfing down the breakfast Ma made for him, he spent the day helping her with chores. That afternoon, he hurried toward Elizabeth's house. Peg was raking leaves when he walked up. She leaned on her rake as Harry said, "Did your sister mention last night?"

"No, but I could see something in her eyes."

"I asked her to marry me."

"She'll say yes." Peg turned toward the drive. "Look, there she comes now." She cupped her hands. "Lizzie, your Ferris wheel partner's here."

Elizabeth smiled. "It was a short night, wasn't it?" She and Harry sat in the porch swing and talked about their day, until Harry said, "Have you thought about what I asked you?"

"Sure, but it's not like we have to get married. It's not a shotgun wedding or anything."

"But it could be a *rifle* wedding. There's a rifle in my hand that's not going away. I probably won't be back from Carolina until the end of November. Beyond that, it's anyone's guess." He squeezed her hand. "This is our chance to take a leap. If we pass it up now, we might not have another chance."

She took a deep breath and after a painful, pregnant pause, Harry said, "Elizabeth, did you hear me?"

"I'm thinking."

"Thinking about what?"

"You'll need to talk to my father."

"I'm not asking your *father* to marry me. I'm asking *you*."

"I know, but that's how we do it here."

He tried to hide his frustration. "All right, I'll talk with him when he gets home from the sawmill."

He spent the rest of the day helping Elizabeth at school as she prepared for tomorrow's opening. About four o'clock, her father stuck his head in the classroom window. Seeing Harry, he said, "You haven't got stuck in a desk again, have you? Or a Ferris wheel?"

When he left, Elizabeth said, "See, he likes you. He picked on you." She grabbed her purse and belongings. "Let's go home so you can talk with him."

Reaching the front gate, she stopped. "All right, soldier, you're on your own."

"Where are you going?"

"I'm walking over to Ma's." She kissed him and nibbled on his ear. "Go on. He doesn't bite." Harry stood at the front door and drew a deep breath, looking back. She nodded her head, motioning for him to knock. He clenched his fist to knock, hesitated, and rapped four times.

"Come in." The door creaked open and Harry stuck his head inside. Levon Reed was sitting in a rocker, drinking coffee, a .22 rifle across his lap.

At the sight of the gun, Harry stepped back, "Excuse me?"

Mr. Reed put his finger to his mouth, motioning Harry to a chair beside him. "A chicken snake's been sticking its head out of the chimney. Next time he does, I'm going to get him." Never taking his eyes off the hearth, Mr. Reed sipped his coffee, engaged in the age-old struggle between hunter and prey. The only sound was the ticking of the mantel clock. Harry sat stiffly for about fifteen minutes, when he heard Elizabeth outside. He whispered to Mr. Reed. "Elizabeth's waiting on me. Good luck."

She was waiting in the front yard. "Well, what'd he say?"

"Nothing."

"*Nothing?* You didn't ask him?"

"No." He craned toward the house. "Your daddy's in there with a gun across his lap. I'm not talking to any armed man about marrying his daughter."

"Poppa's got his gun?"

"He's waiting to shoot a snake that's in the chimney." Harry felt the color returning to his face. "I was just afraid the snake he might shoot was *me*."

"Oh, that's just Daddy being Daddy."

A sudden rifle crack rattled the windows. Elizabeth, followed by Harry, ran inside. There sat Mr. Reed, still sipping his coffee, gun across his knees, as a sheen of cement dust wafting across the room. Lying on the floor among shards of mortar was a writhing four-foot-long snake with a bullet hole in its head.

"That's a fine shot." Harry whistled.

Mr. Reed took a sip. "That chicken snake won't bother us again."

Harry laughed. "I guess I'd better behave around here too."

Mr. Reed's face twitched. "I guess you'd better."

Harry turned to the door, nearly walking over Elizabeth. He hurried outside, with her a step behind. She grabbed his shoulder, spinning him around. "Harry Miller, if you're not man enough to talk to my daddy, I'm not. . . . "

He put his hand up. "I don't understand why I even need to talk to him. You and I are grown people. We don't need anyone's permission to get married."

Her anger softened to tears. "I know that, but you've got to trust me that this is the right way." They walked through the pasture, but she wouldn't hold his hand and looked away when he tried to explain. Silently, they circled back to the porch swing where they swung for several minutes.

Crack. What sounded like another rifle shot echoed off the roof above them, causing Harry to duck and cover his head. An object rolling down the roof and plopping onto the yard followed this. Elizabeth burst out laughing. "That was just a pecan on the tin roof." She put her hand over her mouth and began laughing all the way down to her shoes. "Kind of jumpy, huh?"

"You'd be too if your girl's father was carrying a rifle." Harry put his arm around her. "You said he's a crack shot and I'm afraid he might shoot another nut—me."

The pecan shot had broken the impasse and Elizabeth couldn't stop laughing. The swing creaked as Elizabeth kissed him, placing her hand on his. He couldn't remember when something so simple had felt so good. The cool wind's soothing song blew through front yard cedars as katydids and insects sang in the edge of the swamp.

Harry Miller had one thought as he eased closer to Elizabeth: I believe I could get to like this place. I really could. But he still had one thing to prove: convincing Elizabeth's family that marrying him was a sure thing, not just some shot in the dark.

About thirty minutes later, Harry heard the back door slam. Elizabeth hurried to the porch edge. "Poppa's going toward the field. It'll be the perfect time."

"Does he have his rifle?"

"Sure, but he always carries it."

Harry sprung from the porch swing. "I'm going to get it over with."

Elizabeth grabbed the swing chains to quieten them. "Come back either with your shield or on it."

Harry furrowed his brow. "Gee, thanks for the encouragement." He tromped across the yard toward the field, as if back on patrol in Red Army territory. He caught up with Mr. Reed in the back corner of a field, where he was rolling up telephone wire.

"Son, your army sure does waste a lot of stuff." He held up the large roll of wire. "This is good telephone wire they left behind."

"How will you use it?"

He shrugged. "Not sure yet, but it'll come in handy sooner or later." He threw the wire over by three other rolls and removed his gloves. "I'm sure you didn't walk all this way to watch me roll wire. What's on your mind?"

Harry squinted toward the .22 rifle leaning against a nearby tree. "Sir, Elizabeth and I are planning on getting married."

Levon Reed picked up a loose end of wire and began wrapping it around his hand and elbow. "Kinda quick, ain't it?"

"Yes sir, but *unusual* times call for *prompt* decisions."

Mr. Reed's mouth turned down. "*Prompt*." He looked up and studied Harry for nearly a minute. "And what if I tell you no?"

"I'll still marry her."

Her father's jaw tightened. "So you're not asking for permission to marry my daughter. You're jes' telling me."

"No Sir, I *am* asking for permission, and I'm trying to do it respectfully."

"But if I say no . . . "

"I guess I'm . . . " Harry stepped forward. "Sir, we're asking for your *blessing*, not permission."

"So y'all are going to get married or bust wide open?"

The fear had ebbed from Harry's heart. "Yes Sir. We are."

Mr. Reed kicked at an anthill before looking up. "You know you're catching her at a weak moment—what with Ben's death and everything." Harry bit his tongue, knowing he needed to listen. Mr. Reed's eyes glistened. "Son, people make poor decisions at weak moments."

Once again, an uneasy silence filled the pasture, broken only by the nearby cawing of two crows. Mr. Reed dug in his overalls pocket, drawing out his pocketknife. From his bib, he pulled out a twist of tobacco. With one hand, he unfolded the knife and pointed it toward Harry, "Want a plug of Cotton Boll?"

"No Sir."

"Well, I'll take your plug *and* mine. For some reason, I need a strong chew." He deftly sliced off a huge chunk and tossed it in his mouth. As he worked it around in his mouth, he never took his gaze off Harry. He spat a rich stream of amber liquid.

"Mind if I tell you a story? One time I'd got kind of dissatisfied with my life and even my wife. We were having lots of money trouble and arguing. I'd even thought about leaving. One day I came home from the sawmill just after dark and stopped at the gate. Warm light came from inside the house and I smelled chimney smoke and bread baking. I thought, 'This sure looks like it'd be a nice place to live—big porch, plenty of firewood, I can smell supper cooking. And look at that pretty woman working in the kitchen. She'd probably be nice to live with. She's good-looking and evidently not afraid of work. I like this place. I think I'll go inside and see if I can stay."

He folded the knife, dropping it in his pocket. "You see, son, what kills good marriages is when folks *forget* what they have. They let it get stale and quit counting their blessings. Then they *forget how to forgive*. It's a marriage breaker. Right now, you love Lizzie-Beth enough to eat her with a spoon. I wanna know that you'll love her that much when the bloom's off the rose."

"Mr. Reed, all I can do is promise you, man to man, that I'll take care of your daughter. I love her and I know she loves me."

Her father rubbed his calloused hands. "She got hurt, evidently by some soldier. I'm just protecting her. I've done lost one son to the Army." He gestured toward the east. "And I've just buried another one over there. I'm not quite ready to lose another child. I feel like my world's crumbling all around me and there ain't one thing I can do." Harry bit his tongue. *Just listen.*

Mr. Reed pointed toward his house. "I can't ever predict what Peg will do. She may run off tomorrow with one of those two dozen soldiers she's playing patty-cake with." His voice shook and tears filled his eyes. "Son, Lizzie is about all I have that I can depend on. If I lost her, it might just break my mind."

Harry drew in a breath. "Mr. Reed, I've been hurt too. I know how it feels to be abandoned. Stood up. Left out to dry. All I can do is promise Elizabeth—and you and her mother—that I won't do that to her."

Mr. Reed's face softened and the hint of a smile appeared. "I feel like they're going to have to send me to Pineville."

"Pineville?"

"Pineville—it's where the crazy house is. You know: 'the nut house.' That's how we say it around here: they're going to send me to Pineville."

Harry laughed. "I'll take you there—it's on the way to Camp Livingston."

Mr. Reed put his strong hand on Harry's shoulder. "If you marry that stubborn girl of mine, you may be going to Pineville with me."

He nodded toward the field. "Have you noticed all of the stumps around here? Earlier in this century, timber companies from up north came in, bought up cheap land, cut all of the timber, and cleared out—leaving behind hardly nothing but sawdust." Mr. Reed sat on one of the stumps. "I worry that soldiers—like you—are akin to those timber people. Get in, get what they want, and clear out."

"That's not how I work," Harry said.

"I guess we'll find out, won't we?" Mr. Reed picked up a strand of wire. "Now get the other end of this wire. If you're going to be in my family, I'm going to work you to death." He spat a stream of tobacco. "Besides, the problem ain't gonna be with me. It's the women folk you've got to pass muster with." He scratched his two-day growth of beard. "The idea of you taking her off is gonna go over like a pianer at a Church-a-Christ convention."

"What?"

"Son, if you're gonna be in our family, you'll need to get cultured. Them Church-a-Christ folks don't believe in musical instruments in their services."

Harry winked. "Kind of like you deep-water Baptists don't believe in dancing?"

Levon Reed spat again. "Boy, you might fit in with this family after all." He tossed a loose end of wire at Harry. "Now start making yourself useful."

Harry Miller had never been so happy to be using his hands. They worked for another half hour with hardly a word. The only sound was Levon Reed's whistling and singing of the same song over and over. Harry recognized it as the tune Ma'd played at the fiddle contest. "I Will Arise and Go to Jesus." As the last of the wire was rolled up, Mr. Reed stopped. "Son, I know we seem like backwards folk to a city boy like you, but we're just different."

He pointed toward a nearby lone pine. "Our tap root's pretty deep too."

"Mr. Reed, your tap root is way deeper than mine will ever be." Harry picked up a coil of wire. "I got a question that's been bugging me: what do folks mean when you talk about being 'born again'?"

Levon Reed hefted three rolls of wire on his shoulder. "It's something that happens in a fellow's heart." He seemed deep in thought as they walked toward the house.

"Let me give you an example: my boy, Jimmy Earl, joined the Air Corps. He and I both love aeroplanes, but there's a distinct difference. He's flying in them now. I've never flown in one and probably will die without getting off the ground. We both *believe* planes can fly, but there's a difference in our beliefs. Jimmy Earl believes *in* planes."

He scanned the horizon as if he expected a plane to fly over at any moment. "He's willing to put his butt in a seat and let someone fly him up into the wild blue yonder. Me? I just believe *about* planes. I believe they can fly, but I'm not willing to commit."

Mr. Reed pointed to his head and then his heart. "There's a heap of difference between head knowledge and heart knowledge. It's commitment. It's a willingness to strap yourself in and trust something else or someone. I believe a fellow's 'born again' when he goes from standing on the ground admiring the plane to crawling in and trusting. It's letting Jesus be the pilot of your life."

"Do you trust Jesus like that?" Harry said.

"Sure I do."

"Even . . . uh, even after what happened to Ben?" Harry shuddered at his own question, but had to hear the answer.

Tears filled Mr. Reed's eyes and he sighed. "That's a good question and also a hard one." He removed his hat, wiping his forehead. "I've been trusting Jesus all of my life. I've trusted him with all I've got, including my family. I can't get my arms around why God let Ben die. Been talking to the Lord about it—haven't got a good answer yet."

"Do you think God caused the accident?" Harry said.

"Heck, no. A boy chasing a dog ran out in front of a moving truck. That's what caused it. I don't believe God caused it, but I do believe he allowed it. And I trust him *in spite* of my son dying."

"How do I get that kind of faith, Mr. Reed?"

"I believe you're getting it."

"But I haven't . . . I haven't felt any fireworks go off."

"Fireworks ain't a sign of being born again. I've seen folks jump high for Jesus and two weeks later be back living like the devil. My experience has been that being born again happens in an instant, but becoming a true follower of Jesus—growing to be like him—is a lifetime process."

Harry kicked at a clod of dirt. "I can feel some changes, but there's a lot more needed."

"It's a process. It doesn't happen at once. Let me see. . . ." Pulling his pliers out, Mr. Reed clipped off the wire. "Son, let me think about how to best describe the Christian growth process." They walked in silence for about a minute.

"I was in the Great War. When my unit went across the Atlantic—The Big Pond—I studied that big ocean liner, and watched how they adjusted course. It wasn't all at once. It was more a matter of the captain bumping—or nudging—that rudder a wee bit at a time. Crossing the ocean on a liner isn't made with 180-degree turns, but steady bumps on the wheel. Same thing's true in life-change. Often it's a series of gradual and overlooked changes that determine a man's course and direction."

They walked on, nearing the house. "You really love this land, don't you?" Harry said.

Mr. Reed took a few steps and knelt, scooping up a handful of soil. "Son, when you look at this, all you see is dust . . . or if it rains, Louisiana mud . . . but to me, it's life. This is sacred ground, homesteaded last century by my forebears. My people have lived on this land, tried to farm it, and been buried on it for five generations." He threw the dirt into the air, watching as the wind carried it away. "This dust blows and irritates your eyes. But it also gets into your heart and makes it sing, and this dirt will make things grow in a heart too. You probably look at this dirt a lot differently than I do."

His eyes brightened. "The same thing's true with Elizabeth. You look at her and see a beautiful woman that you say you love."

Harry interrupted. "I do love her."

Mr. Reed put up a hand. "Hear me out. You're a young man—so was I one time—I know how a fellow your age looks at a pretty girl. But Lizzie's way more than a pretty girl to me. She's the light of my heart. Me and her momma have lost a lot lately. We're just concerned—this is all so quick."

"Mr. Reed, what can I say that'll settle this?"

He got nose to nose with Harry. "I want you to give me a promise—from one man to another—that you'll take care of her for the rest of your life."

"I swear to God . . . ."

He poked Harry in the chest. "I know that you'll promise her and God at the wedding. I want a promise from *you* to *me* and I want it *now*."

"Just like that?"

"Yes."

Harry put out his hand. "I promise. . . ."

Mr. Reed's grip pulled Harry closer where the strong smell of tobacco nearly overwhelmed Harry. "Before you promise, what about *war*?"

"What about it?"

"When war comes, will you keep your promise?"

"If war comes, I'll keep my word."

Mr. Reed's grip tightened. "Go ahead, Son."

Harry felt something soft and warm between their hands. "I promise that I'll love and take care of your daughter Elizabeth as long as I'm alive."

"That's good enough for me." Mr. Reed relaxed his grip.

Harry looked at the clump of dirt in his hand. The sweat from their hands had changed the edges of it into mud.

"All right." Mr. Reed stepped back. "Here's your answer."

"To what?" Harry was trying to squeeze life back into his hand.

"I thought you were asking if I'd let my daughter marry you?"

"Yes sir. I was."

"I'm willing to give you that blessing. But you and Elizabeth need to talk to her mother, too. The real resistance will come from her. She's agin it. If you go and break Elizabeth's heart, I'm not sure her mother will ever get over it."

"I'm not going to break her heart."

"Well, you'll need to convince her of that." They reached the barn where they loaded the rolls of wire onto a wagon. Mr. Reed sat on the wagon's tongue. "I don't know nothing about *your* family. You've never spoken of them."

"My family's not real proud of me."

"Why not?"

"I haven't turned out the way they wanted."

"Why not?"

"Being a soldier wasn't my parents' idea of success."

"Tell me about them."

"My parents? They're wealthy." Harry looked into Mr. Reed's tanned face. "But, I'm not sure that's how you judge another man."

"There's lots of ways of judging a man."

"I've learned that."

"What will your folks think about you getting married?"

Harry winked. "They're *agin* it."

Mr. Reed slapped his back. "We're gonna make a redneck out of you yet. I got one more question: Does your family own lots of land?"

"My father owns apartments and office buildings, but not land in the way you look at it." Harry lifted his chin toward the field. "By the way, how much of this land do you own?"

"I'm not sure I own any of it. It's more of a matter of *it* owning *me*."

As they took their boots off on the back porch, Mr. Reed knocked the mud off his. "I do like walking my property and thinking that the mud on my boots is mine—and the Lord's." He put an arm around Harry. "Now if you marry into my family, you gotta promise me one more thing."

"You've got me over a barrel, so go ahead."

"Promise that you won't ever sell our family land to no dang timber company."

"Agreed!" Harry stood beside Mr. Reed as he watched through the door window where the four women—Mrs. Reed, Ma, Peg, and Elizabeth—were drinking coffee. They were in the midst of a lively discussion and hadn't noticed the eavesdropping men at the window.

Ma was worked up. "Pearline, do you remember when you and Levon fell in love?"

"I faintly remember it."

"Your momma came to see me. First thing out of her mouth was, 'That boy of yours ain't got sense enough to pour water out of a boot with the instructions writ' on the heel.' I started to get my double-bit ax after her. Our families hadn't never had much use for one another."

"My own momma said that?" Mrs. Reed shifted uncomfortably.

"Yep, and I told *your* mother that you probably couldn't boil water without her holding your hand." Ma wasn't through. "At least we two mothers agreed on one thing: you two kids didn't have a pot to pee in, or a window to throw it out. The idea of you children getting married . . . ha!"

Harry glanced at Mr. Reed, who shook his head and whispered, "That's my momma."

Ma continued, "You know something about me and your momma, Pearline? We wuz both wrong. Look at you and Levon."

Elizabeth's mother said, "But Ma, it's different when it's one of your own."

"Sure it is, but it's called *life*. L-I-F-E. Life. It's meant to be lived. It's meant to be grabbed ahold of."

Pearline Reed sniffed and pointed at Ma. "It's your fault they're even together."

Ma put her hands on her hips. "You mean that bullet?"

"No, that fake letter."

"You think it's me that got them together?"

"You and Ben Franklin Reed."

"I think the Lord put them together. It was meant to be."

Elizabeth and Peg were giggling, so Ma turned on them. "And you listen here Elizabeth Jane Reed. If you marry this man, you're going to make it work. None of this running home to Momma. And Peggy Sue Reed—I haven't got time nor patience to try to straighten out your life. *That's* for *another* day." Ma walked to the door and jerked it open, exposing the two male eavesdroppers. She pointed her skinny arm at Harry. "And listen here, melon head, you better take good care of our girl. If you don't, I'll hunt you down with Ma's double-bit ax and chop your fingers off one at a time."

She turned as if finished before turning on Harry. "And one more thing—if I ever find out about you fooling around on her, I'm gonna use that double bit ax somewhere else." She stepped toward him. "Even if it means coming back from the grave to do it!"

She walked across the room. "I got one more thing to say and I'm through: It's a family tradition of marrying oddballs." She pointed at Harry. "By that I mean folks you wouldn't normally put in the same yoke or even in the same stall."

Harry hoped she was finished but she wasn't. "Now, *one more thing*."

Mr. Reed picked up a dishtowel, waving it in surrender. "Momma, quit saying that. We know you don't mean that."

"And one more thing. It's also a tradition in this family of making it work. Lizzie, you and ol' melon head here are going to *make it work*. Make a good life together."

"Momma, if you were a preacher, we'd let you marry them right now," Mr. Reed said.

"And if I was a preacher, I'd do it." She turned and marched out the door.

Harry looked at Elizabeth. "Was she serious?"

"I don't know. You tell me."

"Is she going to call me 'melon head' all of the time?"

"When she gives you a nickname, it means you've been accepted as family."

"Well, I guess I have been."

Elizabeth's mother walked by. "Yes you have, melon head. I guess you have."

Chapter 52

In Class

Thursday, October 9, 1941

The next morning Harry was up early. He had to be back at Camp Livingston before 5:00 p.m. He walked Elizabeth to school, where he received a rousing welcome from her students. All of the girls stepped back, giggling as he stood close by their teacher. Several of the boys shyly touched his uniform. Elizabeth introduced each student by name to Harry.

After this round of show and tell, Elizabeth directed him to a seat in the corner from where he observed the glow in her eyes as she taught reading. She worked hurriedly with the fourth graders—all five of them—leaving them with desk work as she scooted across the room to teach the third graders. There were eight third-grade students and every desk was full. Harry looked for where Ben's desk had been but couldn't locate it.

Elizabeth came by his corner. "What do you think?"

"It looks like a three-ring circus!"

She laughed. "It's at least a two-ring circus."

"You look like you love it."

"I do."

Harry jumped at the opportunity. "When I get back from Carolina, I want you to say that."

"Say what?"

"I do."

"I will."

Harry smiled and caressed her hand. "I'd better be going."

She pulled him toward the second row. "First, I want you to say hello to Darrell." A shy, redheaded boy shuffled nervously in the third desk. "Darrell, this is Private Harry Miller."

She turned to Harry. "Darrell has just moved here. His father's in the Army in the Philippines. He and his mother are staying with family here."

Harry saluted. "Good meeting you, Darrell."

The boy scribbled on his paper, a big smile crowding out his timidity.

"You take care of my girl for me, will you?" The boy nodded as Harry ran his hand across the desktop. "That's a special desk you're sitting in. It belonged to a fine boy named Ben."

Then much to the amusement of Darrell and the rest of the students, he kissed Elizabeth and backed out the door.

The next day Harry's unit was on their way to North Carolina Maneuvers. All of the veterans of the Louisiana Maneuvers mocked the complaints of soldiers who had not spent August and September in the Deep South. The cooler weather, smaller numbers, and their prior experience caused them to call the Carolina Maneuvers a "cakewalk."

During his nearly two months in North Carolina, Harry worked hard at staying in touch with Elizabeth by both telephone and letter. Harry achieved lasting fame among the men of Company K. He went from the soldier who never received mail to the one who received the most. Not only did Elizabeth write daily, but her students practiced their penmanship on letters and packages to Private Harry Miller, APO, Camden, North Carolina.

The Carolina Maneuvers ended in late November and within three days, Harry was back in Louisiana at Camp Livingston.

During their frenetic letter writing and phone calls, Harry and Elizabeth had decided to marry on the first weekend of December. She didn't want a fancy wedding and insisted on wearing a regular Sunday dress much to the surprise of everyone in Bundick. And much to the surprise and shock of the local womenfolk, she didn't want a church wedding. It would be at the Reed home with just family present.

It didn't matter to Harry. He would have agreed to marry her whenever, wherever, and however.

Chapter 53

Cold Water

Six weeks later: Sunday, November 30, 1941

"Are you sure you want to go through with this?" Elizabeth held Harry's hand and shivered.

"I'm committed to do it."

"You could wait until spring when it's warmer."

"Nope, I want to do it now." Harry waded into the creek, gritting his teeth as the cold water worked its way up his body. He glanced back at the congregation of Bundick Baptist Church huddled on the upper bank. They were clad in overcoats and winter hats. Several men were gathered around a smoking pine-knot fire.

The pastor followed him into the creek, clad in a pair of chest waders he'd borrowed for the occasion. In spite of the waders, he cringed when the water reached his waist. Teeth chattering, he said, "This is going to be the shortest baptism in church history." He motioned for Harry. "Private Miller insisted on being baptized now. We offered to do it at First Baptist DeRidder's indoor baptizing pool, but he insisted it be here . . . and now." He raised his right hand, "Harry Miller, do you believe that Jesus is the Son of God, died for your sins, and is now alive?"

"Absolutely."

"Are you willing to trust Him with your life and soul?"

Harry felt the well's rough rope in his hands and recalled Ben's words as he climbed out: *I trust you with my life.* He'd taught Harry what trust really meant that day. He turned to the waiting pastor. "I am."

"Have you, as best as you know how, seriously turned from your sin and given your life to Him?"

"That's why I'm here."

A man in the crowd called out, "If he's getting creek-baptized in winter, he's *serious.*" The crowd's response was a mixture of 'amens,' clapping, and lots of laughing. The preacher put one hand behind Harry's head and held a handkerchief over his nose. "In the name of the Father, the Son, and the—" Harry went under before he'd finished and came up sputtering in the cold water. This brought more applause as the two men hurried from the water.

Elizabeth met him with a towel. "I'm proud of you." She pulled him close, getting her dress wet as she kissed him. "I'm proud of the man you are."

They walked over to the fire. One of the men said, "I guess being from Wisconsin that water wasn't cold to you."

"Fellow, that creek would have made an Eskimo shiver. It was *cold.*"

"Why'd you insist on doing it this way?" the man said.

"I guess it was about commitment." He looked into Elizabeth's eyes. "I'm the kind of man that when he makes up his mind, he sticks with it. Commitment."

She repeated softly, "Commitment."

Ma walked up. "You're serious about this, ain't you?"

"Yes Ma'am. It was my decision." He winked at the old woman. "Every tub sits on its own bottom."

"Son, I believe we might make a Southern man out of you yet."

Later that afternoon, after he'd dried out, and thawed out by pouring down eight cups of strong Louisiana coffee, Harry walked with Elizabeth through Bundick swamp. The leaves were falling and everything about this area had changed since his last visit. Even their love had changed. The time apart had solidified the strong feeling each had in their heart. They talked of their wedding, set for the next Sunday, as Elizabeth led him by the hand toward the creek to a grove of large trees. "See those beech trees? They're special."

"How so?"

She led him around to the back side of the largest beech. About head high was carved, "LR & PM."

Harry smiled. "Let me guess. Levon Reed and Pearline—"

"Melder. Pearline Melder. That was momma's maiden name. They carved their names back when they were courting."

She led Harry to an older beech. "This one's dying, but look—" She ran her fingers over the faded initials: SR DR LR 10/8/03. "That's my grandparents, Spencer Reed and Doshie Reed. L.R.— that's Poppa. They carved that when he was a baby."

Harry pulled out his pocketknife. "Where do you want me to put ours?"

She pointed at a young beech. "That one. It looks strong and should be here for a while." As Harry put the point of the knife to the bark, she placed her hand on his. "You know it's for keeps."

He pushed the blade deep into the rough bark. "It's called commitment: playing for keeps." In large block letters, he carefully carved: E R & H M. He hesitated. "Can I put our wedding date instead of today's date?"

She kissed him. "I think that'd be nice."

Harry scratched his head and winked. "Now what date will that be?"

"12/7/41."

He pushed the sharp knife into the bark. "December 7, 1941. Sounds like a good date to remember."

"At least for us it will be."

Finished, he rubbed the fresh initials and date cut into the beech. "Playing for keeps."

She hugged him. "Commitment. Playing for keeps."

Harry Miller folded the knife and dropped it into his pocket. "Commitment. Every tub sits on its own bottom."

Coming Soon

Uncle Sam:
A Horse's Tale

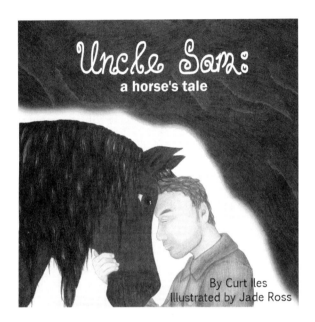

The first children's book from Curt Iles
Illustrated by Jade Ross

Uncle Sam: A Horse's Tale, a companion book to *A Spent Bullet*, relates the story of Uncle Sam, a cavalry horse taking part in the Louisiana Army Maneuvers. Learn about the origin of the wild horse herd that still roams Fort Polk.

Readers of all ages will enjoy meeting Uncle Sam, Sergeant Ed, and their friends.

Learn more at www.creekbank.net.

Author Notes

A long-forgotten World War II movie, "A Walk in the Sun," contains a memorable line. As a squad of American G.I.s prepares to storm an Italian farmhouse brimming with German machine guns, a grizzled veteran takes a drag on a cigarette and assures the others, "Aw, come on. It can't be worse than the Louisiana Maneuvers!"

Such was the impression the Louisiana Maneuvers made on both soldiers and civilians. My dad, who turned seven during the 1941 Maneuvers, vividly described the soldiers and their effect on our community. Whether it was a cable strung in a tree, a rutted tank track in the swamp, or an old foxhole, he'd say, "That's from when the soldiers were here."

A Spent Bullet is simply my attempt to recreate this time and place in the minds and hearts of readers. If this novel reminds you of a simpler time seventy years ago when the entire world was shaking beneath the feet of oncoming war, it will gratify this author.

Curt Iles
Dry Creek, Louisiana
June 2011

One of the challenges of writing *A Spent Bullet* was dealing with the reality that soldiers curse as bad as ... well, sailors. I pride myself on writing books that all ages of young people, in addition to adults, can enjoy. Therefore I straddled the horns of a dilemma. The goal of historical fiction is to be realistic as well as reliable. Yet I wanted to write a book that a father could read, chapter by chapter, each night to his children.

The solution came from a writer way out of my league, Herman Wouk. In the preface to his masterpiece, *The Caine Mutiny*, Wouk, himself a naval veteran of the Second World War, states, "One comment on style: the general obscenity and blasphemy of shipboard talk have gone almost wholly unrecorded. This . . . is largely monotonous and not significant, mere verbal punctuation of a sort, and its appearance in print annoys some readers. The traces that remain are necessary where occurring."

I hope readers will benefit from my attempt in following Wouk's wise advice.

Song List

I'd like to thank the English indie band Gomez for use of their song, "See the World." Learn more about them at www.gomeztheband.com.

Other songs quoted in *A Spent Bullet* are public domain titles loved and sang by generations in the Deep South.

"Lindbergh: Eagle of the USA"	Howard Johnson and Al Sherman
"Angels in Harlem"	Peter Joe "Doctor" Clayton
"Walking Blues"	Robert Johnson
"The Wayfaring Stranger"	Traditional
"Uncle Sam's Planes"	Josh White
"Battle Hymn of the Republic"	Julia Ward Howe
"The Burning of the School"	with apologies to Julia Ward Howe
"Blue Yodel No. 5 (T for Texas)"	Jimmy Rodgers
"Leaning on the Everlasting Arms"	Elisha Hoffman
"The Ninety and Nine"	Elizabeth Clephane and Ira Sankey
"On Jordan's Stormy Banks"	Samuel Stennett
"Angel Band"	William B. Bradbury
"Shenandoah"	Traditional American Folk Song
"I Will Arise and Go to Jesus"	Joseph Hart
"When the Battle's Over"	Isaac Watts
"Will the Circle Be Unbroken"	Ada Habershon
"Eighth of January"	Traditional Southern Fiddle Tune

Further Reading and Bibliography

Lindbergh vs. Roosevelt: The Rivalry That Divided America James F. Duffy
1941: The Greatest Year in Sports Mike Vaccaro
32d Infantry Division: World War II Major General H.W. Blakeley
The U.S. Army GHQ Maneuvers of 1941 Christopher Gabel
Louisiana During World War II Jerry Sanson
History of the U.S. Cavalry Swafford Johnson
When the Fiddle Was King Ron Yule

Acknowledgements

There are several true experts on the Louisiana Army Maneuvers. I am indebted for their time, patience, and input. Rickey Robertson has spent his entire life gathering stories and memorabilia of this event. His help and encouragement was invaluable. Velmer Smith of DeRidder, Capt. Richard Moran of Camp Beauregard's Louisiana Maneuvers Museum, as well as Gordon Rottman and Nick Pollacia each contributed stories and facts from their lifetimes of research.

Because music is an integral part of this novel, I'm indebted to those who directed me on the music of this era. Thanks go to Ron Yule, Kevin and Donna Johnson, June Reeves, Sue Blackmon, and Nelda Ballard.

My friend, Dr. David Jones, was a great help on medical accuracy within the manuscript.

The best part of writing *A Spent Bullet* has been learning the stories of those who participated in or were observers of the maneuvers. Among those are Martha Palmer, June Calhoun, Imogene Garst, Franklin Miller, Riley Martin, Erbon Wise, Harold Iles, Thomas Joseph Slover, and Virgil Orr.

Two of my heroes, my father-in-law Sgt. Herbert Terry and my father Clayton Iles, each planted seeds that led to this project. I believe my father would have really enjoyed this book.

I am blessed with excellent editors who proof and teach me. Thanks to Don Brewer, Julie Johnson, Melinda Shirley, Melanie Rigney, Diann Mills, Frank and Weeda McConnell, Joy Reeves Pitre, Paul Conant, Coleen Roberts Ritter, Connie Richard, Mike Chapman, Mark and Kari Miller, Joan Friend, Dempsey Parden, and Debra Tyler.

I appreciate the young people who work hard in keeping me as a 'high-tech redneck.' Thanks to Will and Kyle Johnston, Caleb Willis, Ashley Miller, Haley Laird, Jade Perkins, Julian Quebedeaux, and Chad Smith.

The addition of Judi Reeves as my personal assistant has been a great asset. Thanks for all you do, Judi.

My mother, Mary Iles, and my sister, Colleen Iles Glaser, provided early draft consultation and encouraged me when I doubted this project.

I'm able to research, write, and speak due to the love, patience, and dedication of my sweet wife DeDe. During the three years of putting together *A Spent Bullet*, she graciously put up with me "living in 1941." I couldn't dream of a better wife or friend than DeDe.

Other Books by Curt Iles
Historical Fiction:

The Wayfaring Stranger
ISBN: 978-0-9705236-9-6

THE WESTPORT SERIES

A Good Place
A Novel

Curt Iles
Author of The Wayfaring Stranger

A Good Place
ISBN: 978-0-9826492-1-3

Short Story Collections:

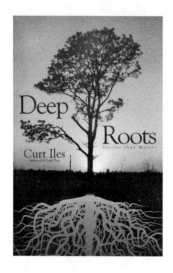

Deep Roots
ISBN: 978-0-9826492-0-6

The Mockingbird's Song
ISBN: 0-9705236-4-5
Hearts across the Water
ISBN: 0-9705236-3-7
Wind in the Pines
ISBN: 0-97505236-1-0
The Old House
ISBN: 1-4033-5227-5
Stories from the Creekbank
ISBN: 0-759-69895-3

Curt Iles writes from his hometown of Dry Creek, Louisiana. He is the author of nine books celebrating the history and culture of Piney Woods, Louisiana. To learn more about his writing and speaking, visit www.creekbank.net or Facebook/Twitter.